FUSE

BOLT SAGA: VOLUME FOUR
PARTS 10 - 11 - 12

ANGEL PAYNE

T0273691

FUSE

BOLT SAGA: VOLUME FOUR
PARTS 10 - 11 - 12

ANGEL PAYNE

WATERHOUSE PRESS

TABLE OF CONTENTS

For Thomas.

You are the fusion of my soul and the source of my fire, forever and always.

And for Jess.

The source of my ultimate superpower— which is loving you each and every day.

FUSE

PART 10

CHAPTER ONE

As daybreak arrives, I send my brother into his final night.

It's only the last week of June, but all the summer renters down in Malibu are eager to get started on their Independence Day celebrations. Though the coast is a few miles away, the clear morning air allows me to see a few small fireworks over the ocean, likely hand-launched by some reveler on the brink of passing out from last night's fun.

I want to envy that asshole.

I almost do.

But I still remember what it's like to wake up with vodka-soaked cells and sand-filled teeth. Alone.

So much time wasted. So many nights I don't remember over the years. So much hating myself for them. I've changed into my leathers just in case my rage fries my composure. Nothing like the possibility of turning into a walking lightning storm to guarantee a guy stays in touch with his feelings.

But opting out of feelings isn't an option today. No place is far enough away to hide from this truth.

I have to face it, no matter how brutal the sunlight that crests over the hills behind me. Those harsh rays sear the back of my neck. Rivers of sweat trickle between my hair and the collar of my thick black jacket. *Sauna of agony, party of one...*

Nothing less than what I deserve.

Because this sure as hell isn't what Tyce deserved.

What's left of him is in an urn.

That urn is in a vault four feet underground.

That vault—marked by a granite stone—is embedded with a plaque engraved with his name and a couple of dates.

Cold stone. Colder metal. Colder still, the numbers that do nothing to represent what his life was really all about. What *he* was all about.

And what his death meant.

His hero's death.

I shake my head, struggling even a month after it all happened, to wrap my mind around the goddamned irony he's dumped on me. That the twists of our lives, thanks to the Consortium's torture factory, allowed us to see each other again—to become true brothers again. Except our glimpse at each other's truth was just that. A teasing taste, ripped away by those fuckers when Tyce jumped on their freak electric grenade.

The memory of that moment slams the center of my gut.

And drops me.

I crumble to one knee in the dirt in front of the marker though manage to keep one hand around the edge of the huge rock. The other I scrabble into the dirt, watching jolts of blue energy spider out from my fingertips before fizzling out a few feet away. Fucking perfect. As if I need a reminder of how far fate's letting me get with defiance today.

About the same progress it's been allowing me all month. On every fucking level.

But no matter how many desperate bargains and promises I offer to God or fate or karma or *whatever*, the lightning in my blood still can't be amped enough for the power of reanimation—if the results of a hundred serious attempts can be believed. And yeah, there's always the option behind door number two, but digging a trench and then sealing myself in next to my brother isn't the simple emo-rock-ballad solution that it seems. Death isn't the issue—I faced worse every day for six months, thanks to my standing reservation in the Consortium's hive of horrors—but my eradication would be the beginning of the end for Emmalina. The woman who's changed everything. The first creature who's truly seen my heart and believed in it. Believed that I'm the man who can live up to every ounce of that expectation.

So much light she's brought to my world. So much light she's still destined to give the *entire* world.

But not if the Consortium knows she's fair game.

The cocksuckers will *not* go quietly into the night after their humiliation in Paris last month. Not after their global exposure at our hands, even though they took Team Bolt down by two lives. I struck back with brutal force, airing their laundry in all its vile glory and promising the world we'd find them and destroy them. But in doing so, I've willingly stepped into the one category I can't stand more than *party player, bad boy, heir with the hair,* and *billionaire with the bulge* put together.

Superhero.

"Damn it." I growl it into a wind as scorching as it is uncaring, at a ghost who's probably perched atop this marker right now, snickering his pretty-boy ass off at me. "You're a dick, Tyce Frederick. You know that?"

Heat pricks the backs of my eyes as his chuckles turn to snorts, despite my purposeful lob of the middle name he hates so much. *Used* to hate.

"You like that, dickhead? Now I can say it as much as I want. *Frederick, Frederick, Frederick.* And if you think that felt good for me, it fucking didn't."

He's not laughing anymore. I hate the stillness he leaves instead. I peer harder at the air over the boulder, begging him to come back. Begging him to just be here again. Maybe if I focus harder...plead longer...

"Just come back, you asshole." But my thick grate is lost in the stiffening wind as I knock my forehead against the marker. "Just...come back." I envision every syllable plummeting down through the soil and into the ears of his soul. "I'll never say it again, all right? You can change your middle name to Epic Dong, for all I care. We could be Dong and Bolt, teaming up to defeat those bastards." I slide my hand down, tracing a finger over the engraved epitaph. "You can even have first billing. You'd like that, wouldn't you, dickface?"

He still isn't listening.

The only entity that is? My heart, beating with shallow grief.

The lonely cadence quickens a little as I rise. I glare at the solitary shadow that moves with me. The image of my hunched shoulders, balled fists, and dropped head reminds me of the truth kicking at my tormented brain.

The truth, darker and shittier than ever.

The silhouette of a superhero who doesn't deserve the designation.

Who grunts in furious acknowledgment of that fact.

Who the hell am I kidding?

Those aren't grunts on my lips. They're sobs.

I knock my head back, ordering the fuckers back the direction they came. Yes, past the twisted fist of my throat.

Past the brick lodged in my chest. Then deeper, into the chasm somewhere south of my ribs, where I've managed, until now, to keep this pain stored at the perfect temperature between denial and confusion.

But the second I finally regain control, there's a noticeable shift in the air—bringing the scent of honeysuckle and rain, even here in the summer heat, soothing and sizzling my blood at the same time. A tangible energy shoots an undeniable thrill up my spine.

She's here. The one person on the planet who'll make this a day I can get through but understands it won't be pretty or clean. Who knows that while I need this day, I already want to torpedo it. Who's not going to leave, no matter what. I see it in the steady oceans of her eyes, with their fathoms of compassion. I feel it in the wisdom of her touch as she traces the crest of my cheek and then delves a hand into my hair. And I definitely know it in the strength of her grip as she tugs on me, guiding my head down to the graceful curve of her shoulder.

Thank fuck for her.

Thank every deity I can think of and even the ones I can't.

As my jaw slides against the cotton of her sundress, I fill my nostrils once more with the sweetness of her scent and the softness of her comfort. I look out toward the sparkling sea in the distance as the sun extends its reach over the world. But the line where the water meets the sky is still blurred by morning mist, fate's all-too-obvious reminder of the mental marsh in which I'm still trapped. Have *been* trapped for the last month.

And have hated every second of the experience.

Another truth Emma just seems to know, no matter how hard it's been to cope with. Maybe that's the explanation for the lights in her gaze as we tug apart, gleaming brighter as she searches my features in fierce swoops. "You ready for this, Zeus?"

I shoot back a narrowed gaze and an arid huff. "You're enjoying the hell out of that one, aren't you?"

"As long as the shoe fits..." While her face maintains its reverence, she taps a playful beat against my left boot with her toe. "And it sure as hell fits again this morning, oh insane god of my heart and soul."

"*Pfffft.*" I lift her hand. Press a fervent kiss into her palm and breathe her in again. It's true what they say about smells having the power to transform a person's mindset. For a few perfect seconds, I'm no longer here on the ridge, getting ready to memorialize my brother. It's twelve hours ago, and I'm watching the sunset from the lawn next to the pool with her stretched out next to me, naked and satiated. For a few flawless moments, I really feel like Zeus, without the hundreds of lovers. This woman is *all* those women. Everything I could ever want or need in a lover, a partner, a soul mate, a best friend.

"*Psssshhh.*"

Even when I know exactly where she's going with sounds like that. "Em..."

"*Three hours*, Reece." She uses the palm I've just kissed to grab the side of my head again. "You slept three hours last night. And the night before that. And the night before *that.*"

"And I'm fine." As I push to my feet, I hook the backs of her elbows to bring her up with me. "Look. See? *Fine.*" I'm lying but hide that too. I fire up the booster rockets in my blood to counterbalance the fact that a gust across the hilltop nearly knocks me to my ass.

"You know, your eyes are turning brown, Mr. Richards."

I grimace. "I liked Zeus better."

"Well, I like it better when you fling the truth instead of bullshit."

A deeper scowl. "Emma. For fuck's—" And then a tight rumble as she shoves the sleeve of my jacket to expose several fresh needle punctures in my arm. Though they haven't been caused by what a stranger might assume, Emma's glower makes me wonder if she'd be happier with a lie about me shooting smack instead.

"How much did you give the guys today already?" she demands.

"Christ."

"Fine. I'll just go and ask Wade and Fersh myself."

"*Christ*. Emma!" I grab one of her hands. "I promised them some time to work in peace."

"You mean without you hovering, pacing, and hovering some more?"

A lower grumble. "Yeah. Something like that."

"And what happens if they run a hundred more tests and they still come back negative or inconclusive?" Into the weight of my silence, she throws a harrowed huff. "What happens when you let them take more of your blood? Then more? And what happens when you've gotten out of bed in the middle of the night for the hundredth time to reread their reports, only to find nothing? And then the thousandth?"

I wrench from her. Then whip away to cover the five feet between Tyce's marker and the next boulder over. The second monument is embedded with another steel plate, filled with words and numbers that are just as meaningless in representing the life and personality of Mitch Mora, who also died that disgusting night in Paris.

But unlike Tyce's memorial, there's no vault of ashes

beneath this surface. After the mission became a nightmare and we retrieved Mitch's body, Kane Alighieri swooped in and grabbed his husband with a bawl of such primal anguish, nobody dared to cross his claim on the fallen man. Right after, he disappeared from the Hotel Virage, the newest Richards Resort to be funded by the dirtiest money on earth, and we tracked him to the point when he left France for Tibet.

Since then, Kane's turned himself into as much of a ghost as his husband—a truth that won't change until he decides he's ready to rejoin the living. None of us is stupid enough to waste a word of challenge on it.

Instead, I'm focusing where it makes the most sense—even if it means answering my fiancée in a surly growl. "If this takes a thousand tries, then that's what we'll do." Inventors played with electricity for decades before Ben Franklin flew his kite. Tesla was labeled a lunatic for his crazy inventions before innovating electrical delivery. Edison's teachers called him too stupid to live. Yeah, a guy accumulates weird trivia when he has lightning for blood—and a lot of midnight disappointment to slog through.

But I'm damn sure Emma isn't thinking of Franklin, Tesla, or Edison right now. "A thousand—or two or *three*... You know I'll support you in each and every one of them, okay? Just not all in the same day." As she pushes out another frustrated sigh, more sunlight takes over the ridge. The turquoise sheen in her eyes turns intense. "*Please*, Reece."

I grit my teeth again. If she'd keep the castigation to just those tiny tears, this whole moment would be different. But the hitch in her voice and the wobble of her chin create barbed wire twists in my gut. "I'm doing this for us, damn it."

"There's not going to *be* an us if you kill yourself doing this!"

"There's also not going to be an us if the Consortium is allowed to exist!"

I let my drilling glare convey the rest of it—words I'm neither sane nor strong enough to elucidate right now. She already knows that. Since my declaration of Team Bolt's war on those fuckers, they've gone even deeper underground but at the same time have taken public bites out of our collective backside. On three occasions, Foley's motorcycle has been tampered with. Freakish accidents have plagued the Hotel Brocade, all due to electrical issues. But worst of all, four prominent public figures have disappeared as if they were sucked into cosmic holes. One leading investment specialist, one Irish soccer champion, and two chart-topping pop divas have vanished seemingly without explanation. Each time, the Scorpio cartel has shown up claiming a distant connection to someone on their management team or family circle.

Thinking of those four now, along with the nameless prisoners those bastards have likely snatched in the last four weeks, brings a new seethe to my lips and a fresh coil to my fists. "They're going to get bolder and bolder," I utter. "Which means—"

"That they'll eventually mess up," she cuts in. "That they'll get cocky and careless. And when they do, we'll be watching and waiting."

"And then what?" I counter. "What are we 'watching and waiting' for? The chance to march in and storm their little shop of laboratory fun? And you really think they're going to let their location just slip out? Who's going to step forward from *our* team to torture the information out of them?" As I pace my way through the diatribe—the first time I've really voiced all of this out loud—I look up to see her gaze doesn't once leave me.

I'm just not sure if that's a good or bad thing yet, so I simply keep going. "We've tried staying two steps ahead, Velvet, but they've already gained four." I scuff to a stop, covering my feet in dust. "And that's why we're here right now...doing this."

I'm seriously tempted to hurl in the bushes now, but she's honored me with exposing her truth, and I owe her the same in return. She sees and accepts all of my conflict. I feel that even though I turn from her—and still when she steps over and presses her cheek against my back. I'm uncertain whether she'll lift me or break me because of it, but pushing her away would be like thrusting my lungs out of my body.

"I know," she murmurs into the taut muscles between my shoulder blades. "I *know*." She slides her arms beneath mine and flattens her hands against my stomach. "I also know that you feel this is necessary. That tearing apart every electron in your blood is a key step for the cause—"

"*For* the cause?" I'm sure she hears every note of the low thunder pushing at the confines of my torso. "This isn't *for* the cause, Emmalina. This *is* the cause."

She keeps her arms around me while slowly pacing around until we're again facing each other. She lifts her head high, her face imprinted with graceful strength and purposeful clarity. Those qualities were such huge parts of why I fell in love with her to begin with and why she can still peel my composure back by several meaningful layers. Just by standing here. Just by being *her*.

And why I'm not sure whether to damn her or adore her for it.

Especially when she frees her next words. The statement for which she's obviously taken up this position.

"Okay, it's the cause now." She jogs up her chin by another

fraction, making sure I see her unequivocal support. "Both Tyce and Mitch died for that cause. But at this rate, Mr. Richards, you'll be soon joining them in martyrdom."

CHAPTER TWO

EMMA

I'm right.

He knows it.

Though he peers up, still all hunched and brooding gargoyle about it, and bites out enough profanity to prove that he knows.

And isn't happy about it.

Which could have to do with that sausage grinder of a few other emotions too. Yeah, the ones I feel as clearly and painfully as my own. Frustration, rage...grief.

But that's the thing about meat grinders. In the end, the pile is still just a carcass.

"Reece—"

"Don't."

"Damn it—"

"I said *don't*, Emmalina."

He slashes his arm out, which propels his fresh escape from me. The distance is more than physical. I pull in a deep breath, telling myself it's temporary. Everything's simply going to be hard today, and I've only made it harder by serving him a huge platter of tough love. But damn it, if the man wants to find the golden ticket to being mortal again, he has to start *acting* mortal again. He has to realize he's not really from another planet and that the electricity in his veins doesn't preclude him from being a *homo sapiens* who needs shit like food and sleep and mental health breaks to survive. Commodities he's been *skipping* more often than *accepting.*

A conclusion that's going to make my next words sound like I'm the one who needs several hours of sleep and an hour of punching bag time. Or, damn it, the Plan B option—aptly named, considering the power of a certain B-word around here...

"Maybe...you need to do a patrol in town tonight." Oh, yes. That *did* taste as bad as I thought it would. Though, like a vegan pizza, I know it's good for us both. "I mean, you're already dressed for it—and maybe blowing off some steam will help you clear out the cobwebs." In more ways than one. Or five or six. Or twelve. But damn it, my quip clearly goes over like two-day-old soda alongside the pizza. "You could take Sawyer."

He snorts. "What? So he can keep me in line?"

"So someone can say when you've had enough."

He barks out a laugh, bracing hands on his hips. I try not to fixate on how that stretches the black leather across his taut backside in all the right ways. It has to be the most inappropriate thought at the absolute worst time—especially because my priority here is keeping that ass, and everything attached to it, alive.

"When I've had *enough*?"

I fold my arms. If I don't, I seriously might summon my inner Ant Girl, swing the stubborn ox over my head, and haul him for a lengthy lockdown in the walk-in freezer. "Of driving yourself, as well as everyone around here, to the brink of exhaustion." I first go for the voice of—*gasp*—reason. "It's the truth and you know it, baby," I level as gently as I can. "Wade,

Fersh, Alex...they're all barely thinking straight. *You* hit that point at least a week ago."

"I'm fine."

"Sure," I retort. "And that's why you're looking ready to fight enemy orcs from the hills at any second?"

"I'm *fine*, damn it."

"You're not fine."

"God*damn*it, Emma."

"Sure. I'm fine with God joining us too." I push my feet into a ready stance, undeterred by his battering-ram glare. "He'll tell you I'm right too. That you're still seeing all the damage your dad caused as some kind of punishment from him to you—and that by fixing the issues, you'll somehow redeem yourself." I symbolize that with a sweep of one hand and then the other. "You're on a mission to make things right, which is why you refuse to stop. Why all the tests, experiments, analyses, and theories still don't feel like enough."

He huffs in a bullish rhythm. "*Look*, baby. We *have* to keep clawing our way to results on this shit. We're not playing subterfuge softball with those bastards anymore."

"I'm aware of that, Reece."

"Then you also remember that this is the Big Show, with cowhide balls and ace batters in the box ready to crack line drives into our gonads. We don't have time to binge a bunch of CGI cinema with guys in tights and call it corporate training videos."

"I'm not talking Netflix and beer for three days." I return my hands to my sides. "This is simply about actually sleeping a full eight hours, or—oh, my *God*—sitting down at the table, with silverware and place settings, for a whole meal. And perhaps— *gasp*—actually talking to your friends about something other than platelet count, DNA variables, and—"

"I stopped for a full meal with you last night."

I return his adamant finger by jabbing up one of my own. "That was a last-minute picnic on the backyard lawn, with cold chicken on plastic plates," I parry. "Besides, you barely ate anything."

"I snacked on...other things." The smoke in his voice filters into the heat in his stare as he pivots all the way back to me. I'm sorely tempted to sock him in the shoulder, except the only bearable hour in his week—and mine—was our escape by the pool last night.

But I'm not up here to be his meal-replacement option again. The darker cast in his gaze confirms he knows that too. With heavy steps, he returns to my side, latches his hand into mine, and keeps trudging until we've stopped on the sundrenched curve of hill between the two memorial markers.

Golden sun. Gray granite. Summer heat across the land.

A winter of grief sucking at my man.

And despite all of the brutal honesty I've just force-fed into his psyche, including every accusation about ducking his feelings short of the ostrich-in-the-sand cliché, all I long to do this moment is yank him hard, hold him close, and croon that everything will be all right. That he doesn't have to face any of this right now.

But that would be a lie.

We *all* have to face this.

I'm reminded of that as soon as a stiff breeze picks up, bearing the familiar sounds of our families' voices, the air itself changing as their energies impact the atmosphere. Their arrival is still a few minutes away; the path is steep, and the day is already heating up.

So I get to Reece's side and pull him close.

Letting him know that while I don't get his nonstop work obsession of the last few weeks, I *do* get the sadness and weight on his spirit right now. But the process has to go on. *Life* has to go on. Life can't move back into brightness unless there's a tunnel to compare it to. The brightest dawns can't come from anything but the darkest nights—even if they take place on a blazing Southern California summer morning.

I attempt to say as much to Reece with the pressure of my grip and the compassion of my eyes. The gaze with which he answers is a silver slice of acknowledgment, gleaming brighter as I crush him closer, my voice fervent in his ear for a few precious seconds.

Not to tell him it'll be okay—because today it might not be.

Not to tell him I'm here for him—because he already knows that.

Only to tell him what he needs to hear for this moment alone.

"We'll get through this, baby," I whisper. "In some ways, we always have. We'll do it by crawling inch by inch if we have to."

I've rarely meant words more. And I can feel, through all of the heightened electricity in his system, that he's rarely been more open to them. He affirms it deeper by finding my lips with his and melding our breaths with tender, almost reverent care. It's only a moment. I know it as surely as the voices from the wind become the conversation that's about to change the air— but it's a moment I make count, letting him know the openness of my senses and the offering of my heart.

"Dear God, Emmalina. How I love you."

And smiling as every note of his impassioned grate fills me.

The approaching voices become more prominent. We look up in tandem to see the heads and shoulders of our families and friends on approach.

At the front of the small group are Wade, Fershan, and Alex, making their way with confidence—not surprising, since the three of them come up here for a lot of brainstorming sessions. Behind the Team Bolt guys are Trixie and an attractive petite brunette. The women are dressed in nearly identical black pantsuits, which is no surprise. Joany Richards, Chase's wife, is a lot like Trixie in overall grace and underlying humor, unless the subject is protecting her loved ones. I barely knew the woman until four weeks ago, when the family pulled together after the catastrophe in Paris. "Demure" Joany handled everything from beating off the press to booking flights back home to whipping up batches of Totino's rolls once we got here. As much as I love Anya's cauliflower popcorn and kale chips, sometimes a girl just needs a premade pizza roll.

And the best part about all that? Chase seems to have woken up and smelled the Totino's where his wife is concerned too. Correction: Chase has opened his eyes about *a lot* of things since the events in Paris. Even as he comes into view now, there's no Bluetooth in his ear or cell phone in his hand. The anomaly would've dropped everyone's jaw six weeks ago, and it likely should now as well, considering how much Chase is juggling as the head of the Richards Family empire in a post-Lawson Richards world.

Lawson Richards.

The name nobody will speak today but the ghost sitting solidly on all our shoulders. Who doesn't even deserve the designation of "ghost," considering he tried to sell his three sons to the mad scientists of the Consortium. That was after he pissed on nearly thirty-five years of adoration from his wife by sleeping with one of the head bitches of the Scorpio crime cartel—on top of betraying his company's shareholders by letting his ambition override his better sense.

He is dead because of it.

A death he deserved—though he took down two lives with him.

Which circles everything right back to here and now—and the necessary suck-all of moving on, since we're all still having trouble grasping the awful truth. But it's been a month, and now it's time.

It's time.

The pain is eased, at least a little, by the appearance of a face that warms so many corners of my heart. At the end of the procession, my sister Lydia is walking arm-in-arm with Reece's key wingman, Sawyer Foley. Honestly, they look like the cutest couple on campus who've decided to "go public," bringing half a smile to my lips despite the solemnity of the occasion. *It's about damn time.*

That theme is destined for repetition today. We've waited a *month* to do this. Even by abnormal standards, the occasion is long overdue. But abnormal has been my *new* normal for a year now, since that night when the man at my side became a force in every breath I took and every move I made. Since that night in the penthouse at the Brocade, I have not regretted the choice to heed our connection and listen to our destiny—especially now. Imagining Reece facing this day by himself, let alone all the bullshit that led up to this day, makes me shiver in awful, visceral ways. My heart cracks at the vistas of solitude in his eyes and the giant weight of responsibility he's scooped up and taken on his shoulders. Even now, he clearly still thinks he can change the course of time, of fate, and of his father's selfishness with the singular force of his will.

Even now—with reality literally etched in stone in front of us.

His mother and brother detach from everyone else and approach him. He releases my hand in order to become the third part of their grieving huddle, but he's jarringly stiff and noticeably quiet. Even his energy field is like a muted version of itself. Part of that is due, no doubt, to the thicker leathers he's wearing along with his half-fingered gloves. But based on the intensity of everyone's emotions pulsing the air, at least his fingertips should look phosphorescent blue by now.

He's holding back. I'm not sure whether to be curious or alarmed as I confirm the signs. His refusal to bend, even when Trixie clutches him harder. The tension that turns his arms into I-beams and his hands into staunch fists. The way he breaks from the embrace as soon as the other two relent their holds even an inch—

And with his Frankenstein steps, showing me the full spectrum of the monster he's fighting from the inside out.

Not a creature who doesn't want their love.

A man who blatantly thinks he doesn't deserve it.

Oddly, I'm not surprised when Trixie lets him go, despite how Chase tries to pull him back. After a few seconds, even Chase sees the grief that crashes over Reece as he hikes back up to the slope between Mitch's and Tyce's markers.

Chase grabs Trixie's hand while sending his mother a look of gratitude and then helps her climb the rise too. I link elbows with Joany, and we follow them. In a flash, I remember the last time I did this to bond with a girlfriend: Angelique and I had Rachel-and-Monica'ed along the Quai de Conti in Paris on our way back to the apartment she'd lent to Reece and me. It had been the hideaway rendezvous she'd shared with her lover, Dario, before the Consortium killed him—only that morning, we'd learned that they hadn't, and that a very alive Dario was none other than a very alive Tyce Richards.

Only now, Tyce really is dead. And with him, so is the man Angelique's had to mourn a second time—a double hit of karmic payback for her role in helping the Consortium abduct Reece to begin with. But my conclusion about that is colored by my ferocious love for the man she sent to hell that night, which often prevents me from remembering that she too was tortured by those monsters, even before they took the life of the man she loved. She's more than paid her price to fate. She's racking up points in her divine good column by refusing to wallow in her grief. After the fiasco of Paris, she returned at once to the Consortium, where her deep cover with the bastards continues to be one of our strongholds in the fight to take them down forever.

The weirdness of it all isn't lost on me, even now.

We've taken the war public but are still fighting the battles in secret.

We've called the Consortium out by name but know less about their real identities than before, especially with Tyce and Lawson dead.

Worst of all, we know we're likely sitting on a ticking time bomb—but because there's been no contact from Angie in ten days, we're blind to the length of the fuse.

It's all been pricking at Reece extra hard, though he's not spoken a word to that effect. I see it in the tension stiffening his movements and the sharp slashes defining his jawline. He's concerned but hiding that torment well from everyone—and probably thinks *I* don't notice either.

But right now, I think "stress" is *everyone's* middle name.

In a pre-Paris world, a ten-day lag from Angelique wouldn't have made any of us blink twice. But since that incident, as well as Reece's ballsy action of publicly calling out the Consortium afterward, Angie's been pinging every few days—sometimes, if there's a lot going on, even a number of times *every* day. According to her, the Consortium has been frantic about running deeper underground to hide from a world that now knows who they are and how deep into the scientific cookie jar they've been reaching.

That doesn't match what the bastards have been doing on a public level—actions that have been, in a word, brazen. Since they've accelerated their abductions in the aftermath of Paris, we can only assume they are boldly flaunting how easily they can get to all of *us*. And while that possibility might be true, a frightening enough consideration on its own, it's also led us to question how thoroughly their right hands are talking to their left hands these days.

So they're fragmented; maybe worse. This is possibly some of the best news for us but the worst for Angie. With her going totally dark, we have no way of really knowing—and that might continue to be the case until it's too damn late.

Right now, all we can do is force one foot in front of the other. Get through every day. Trudge up each hill as it comes.

Even this one.

Especially this one.

Wade, Fershan, and Alex join us on the top of the ridge and we form a haphazard semicircle behind Reece. He steps forward, sagging his head between shoulders that look as if the weight on them has tripled. The shitty thing is, it probably has. The even shittier thing is, I have to simply watch and let him be in that space. It damn near kills me, but I do. He has to endure this journey. There's no shortcut for the canyon of grief.

He descends to one knee. Then the other. His shoulders rise and fall like massive tectonic plates trying to lift miles of the earth at once. I'm helpless to do little but drop down next to him, pressing against one side of him. Trixie mirrors the hold against his other side.

There are words inside him. I don't know what they are, but I feel them as potently as my own heartbeats as he struggles to translate the sludge of his emotions into sounds on his lips. I try to help him by stroking a hand along his back and forming my forehead to the side of his neck. I don't utter a word myself. I just need him to know I'm here. And again, like a surety in my soul, I recognize that he needs that too.

At last, after a massive inhalation, he says on a sparse rasp, "They were...my thunder." Another searching pause, followed by another unsure breath. "Both of them. My brother...Tyce. My friend...Mitch. They helped me harness impossibility..."

"So you could do impossible things." The conclusion, uttered with the care of a poet, belongs to Chase. He paces forward until he's right in front of Reece, but at the moment I predict he'll kneel and join his little brother, he instead grips Reece's shoulders and yanks him. "So you could be every bolt of lightning you were destined to be, brother," he grates as they stare eye-to-eye. "And take those fucking moonbats down for good."

My heartbeat surges with an inspired thrill. I trade a tearful glance with Joany, seeing that she agrees, and I wonder if Reece does too. I'm only able to see his profile, but there's a lot of information even in that. His jaw hardens again. The dark slashes of his eyebrows emphasize his curious gaze. He's peering at Chase like the guy's just landed in a spaceship with a talking raccoon as a copilot and then told him ELO's the greatest band to ever live. Funny thing is, until everything went down in Paris, that scenario was higher on the probability scale than this open compassion and support from Chase.

As if still in a daze, Reece stammers, "Wh-What are you saying, man?"

Chase wraps his fingers against Reece's nape. "I'm saying you have our support." He encourages Trixie and Joany over with a determined nod. "*All* of us, Reece. We've talked about it, and we're in agreement. You're not alone in this anymore. You'll not be alone *ever* again."

Trixie steps closer. At least I think she does. It's hard to clearly discern anything through the tears bashing my composure—especially as I hear the words Trixie adds to Chase's.

"Your father wasn't always a horrific person, boys. But the choices he made, in the name of bringing glory to our family, led him into dark quicksand." She sniffs while turning toward Tyce's boulder and flattens both hands to the monument, her fingertips trembling against the stone. "You saw that," she raggedly whispers. "You saw that, my amazing boy, and you tried to stop the slide. And in the end, in your incredible way, you did."

My vision blurs as I watch Chase and Reece surge over, securing their mother in their combined embrace. With their silent permission to let her grief tumble out, she does. It takes over her body in racking sobs and aching mewls.

A needed step...a necessary moment.

A shared love.

But as soundly as my head embraces the knowledge, my spirit rebels. I glare out at the ocean and then up into the olive and sycamore trees, attempting to gain the connection I have always found in nature, but the effort is useless. *Hasn't she endured enough? Can't she have some comfort now and recognize her son as the hero he was...he always will be?*

There's no answer for me except Trixie's continuing cries, stolen by a hot wind that moans through the trees with cold castigation. Frustration and sadness fill me—and for the first time, I start to understand the frenetic force that's turned Reece into damn near a madman for the last three weeks.

Will we ever be able to get the upper hand on the Consortium? And if so, at what price?

Not more lives.

A hard swallow is my only way of holding back an anguished gasp.

Not Reece's *life.*

We have to push harder for answers.

Try harder.

Be better.

Somehow. *Somehow...*

I'm on the verge of congratulating myself for the private pep talk when the wind shifts direction, bringing the odd sense that someone else is climbing the hill to join us.

Inside a heartbeat, I see that Reece notices too—and reacts by shoving Trixie and me behind him. Before I can stutter out a solid protest, Joany's hissing something similar to Chase, who does the same thing with her. Sawyer moves to shield Lydia, but she fumes and fights him off.

"What the hell is with you guys?" she charges. "It's just—
holy shit."

I don't blame her for the gasping reaction to the sight
before us on the hill.

Though we've both seen Angelique in the fullness of her
post-Consortium-fuckery mode before, with her thick blond
hair replaced by a burned black dome and her green gaze
turned the eerie shade of an approaching hurricane, this is the
first time she's borne the new look with her old imperiousness.
To be honest, it works. To be *really* honest, it's kind of badass.
To be brutally clear, it might even be what we all need in this
moment...

Until the woman turns the hurricane gaze into a green
steel stare and wields every inch of that blade directly at Reece.

And follows up the stab with equally gut-dicing words.

"We need to talk."

I swallow against a surge of reactions. *Not* exactly the
words a girl wants to hear from her fiancé's sultry siren of an
ex, despite the melted bowling ball skull and crazy emotional
history. But Angelique wouldn't have found a way to get out of
the Source and then all the way to California for simple surface
facts. She's arrived in person for a reason.

One that's turning my guts into barbed wire and my
stomach into a lake of acid.

Reece pivots and braces in a stiff stance that matches hers.
"Then let's talk," he charges. "What the hell is it?"

I swap gazes with Sawyer, the unspoken communication
a fast note of needed comfort for me. The guy has heard the
same subtext in Reece's tone as me: the hundred questions
that didn't get asked on top of that. *Where have you been for
ten days? What the hell is going on? Do we need to be worried?*

Has the Consortium found us? Has your cover been blown?

But worse than all the unasked queries is the feeling I get by looking back at Angelique.

And the sense that she's about to answer them all anyway.

Just not exactly with the answers we're going to like.

Angie shores up her posture with a measured, heavy breath. "They are ready," she finally declares. "And they are bringing the storm this time."

Reece marches at her by a couple more steps. Small clouds of dust kick up around his boots. Small blue sparks crackle from between his fisted fingers. "When? How?"

Angelique dips her head as proxy for fully shaking it. "I do not know exactly when—but soon."

"And the 'how?'" Reece demands.

She lifts her head back up. This time, there are no hurricanes or cutlasses in her gaze. It's permeated with only one defined energy.

Fear.

"A weapon they have been working diligently on. I do not know what they are calling it right now, but..."

"But what?" Sawyer gives the order now, stomping up to stand next to Reece—until Angie pins him in place with a gaze distorted by even more apprehension.

At last, she whispers, "But we used to call him Kane."

CHAPTER THREE

REECE

Every single sense in my body—yeah, the sixth one too, whatever the hell that means right now—is on high alert, crackling with awareness every time Angie's face changes by the slightest nuance. Anyone who's ever written off the theory that humans aren't creatures capable of raw electric energy simply hasn't been plugged in to someone bristling with intense emotion.

I'm really plugged into Angelique La Salle now. Whether either of us likes it or not. Though at the moment, I'm not certain she's given herself permission to feel *anything*, bad or good, about the bomb of information she's just dropped on us. I'm also considering that might be the hugest chunk of wisdom the woman's ever had. *I'm* sure as hell struggling for the same neutrality, though failing miserably, while processing the announcement that's just tumbled out of her.

We used to call him Kane.

"Holy. Fucking. Hell." I say it with soft volume but harsh emphasis.

Angelique looks ready to roll her eyes. The haunted darkness in them serves as the instant *off* button for the notion. "I am not certain there is anything 'holy' about any of this," she mutters.

"About *what*?" Sawyer interjects. "The last time we saw Kane, he'd signed for Mitch's body and then left for Charles de Gaulle."

"Tibet." I blurt it as if everyone needs to be filled in. They all *know* where Kane has been for the last month. They all know, because each of us at some point has voiced that we wished we were in the same place. Even yours truly, the head taskmaster of the Team Bolt research crew, has had at least a couple of moments a day of yearning for the peace and pulchritude of the Himalayas.

Angelique eyes me with anything *but* peace and pulchritude. "He did not go to Tibet."

"What the *hell*?" Wade, who's been dutifully quiet along with Fershan and Alex, finally fires it.

It's oddly comforting to watch Angelique respond by thrusting out a hip and folding her arms. For an awesome moment, the woman who arrived up here beneath a cloud of her own trepidation is back to being the *bitch de fantastique*, complete with a pouty scowl. "He did *not* go to Tibet."

I draw in a deep breath, surprised when I don't inhale the stench of shit. Though Angie's simply *relaying* the mess Kane got himself into, the news itself is disgusting enough for a tangible reek. "He went to Spain," I finally state, grimacing from the equally fetid burn of the words. But just wiping them away and moving along isn't anywhere near an option anymore—a truth getting a solid underline in the distinct tension of Angelique's posture and the way she sweeps the toe of one elegant boot back and forth through the dirt.

"Fucking. Hell." The echo gets extra punctuation in the form of my heavy stomps—backward. If I don't get some distance from everyone, I'm liable to clock *someone* in Kane's place. And yeah, probably in my own place too—because if it had been me having to sign for Emma's body in Paris, I'd have done the same thing he did. Screw peace and pulchritude; the only obsession on my mind would have been vengeance on everyone in the Source I could get my hands on.

No matter how high the shitpile I created because of it.

The massive mound poor Angie has had to haul all the way here from Spain.

The least I can do is relieve her of it now.

During another labored inhalation, I concentrate on flexing my fingers in place of fisting them up. Only when I'm sure all ten will stay spread and at my sides do I go on.

"Okay, so let me take a spin at the rest of this now," I growl. "He never got on the plane to Lhasa. He had Mitch cremated in Paris, which is why the ashes got back to us so fast." Not observing a speck of denial in Angie's gaze, I barely pause before going on. "He flew straight to Barcelona instead—but passed up the castles, the churches, the aqueduct, and Ibiza and instantly went for the gutter. Started scratching all the right underbellies in all the right places. And surprise, surprise, the Scorpios scratched right back."

Angelique's posture remains steady; her stare continues as clear as a windless sea—but she's changing too. Subtly. Enough to tell me that whatever I've assumed as the facts in all this, it gets even worse.

"But the Scorpios didn't stop at just scratching, did they?" I get out with deceptive calm. "*Goddamnit.*" And maybe calm is fucking overrated. "They got him, didn't they?" I stomp back over the dried twigs and pebbles beneath us while struggling to dig my mind into the sickening truth I have to vocalize. "Those monsters got their claws into him. And...changed him."

From the second Angelique dives her gaze to the ground, I already know I've banged that gong of fact. But the ominous gulp she lets me see as a follow-up? I'm clueless about interpreting that and not sure I want to. My relief hits in a rush as the woman pulls in a noticeable breath and then starts to pace in a careful circle herself. She's not going to make me guess at the next part—though my heart rams my ribs harder as she contemplates how to express it.

"He was very upset," she mutters. "And bitter. And determined. He wanted vengeance for Mitch."

I jerk my way through another nod. "I know. His death haunts me every day too." Another step, a louder crunch underfoot. "It's a hell I wouldn't wish on anyone I care for."

She nods, but not as if my consolation has changed anything. Knowing Kane, even if I stood here and professed it to his face, it wouldn't. "He refused to listen to me, even after they brought him in and locked him up," she declares, swiping a hand back across her mottled skull. She curls her fingers at her nape, as though she's forgotten she's not wearing her wig, and there's no real hair left to grab. For a telling instant, a wince takes over her face, though I sense the expression has nothing to do with her missing hair. Clearly she's just figured out what the two boulders on the ridge stand for.

"He told me that getting caught was part of his plan. He also insisted he did not want my help, that he had plenty of training." She goes on in a somber murmur. "He said he knew what he was doing and was only there to get the intel he needed before he escaped and brought it to you. I believe his exact words were that it was not his first time 'being in the shackles of terrorists.'"

"Why doesn't that part surprise me?" Foley mutters.

"Why doesn't *any* of this surprise me?" I retort.

"What the *fuck* was he thinking?"

"You assume he was *thinking*?"

During our parrying, a defined frisson of confusion crosses Angelique's eyes. As soon as she blinks those kohl-lined greens again, the woman is back to embodying refined French poise from head to toe.

"They took him straight to the hive," she explains, referring to the slang term for the Source's lab facilities with their hexagon-shaped experiment rooms. "But I was on duty in another area and did not realize it until they had him on the lab table for several days." Her veneer finally cracks a little, but not enough that she surrenders her crisp composure. "Everyone seemed to realize his connection to you, as well as his Special Operations history. The security watches were tight."

"Tighter than what?" I challenge. "Their system already scrambles GPS, cellular, Wi-Fi, stereo analytics, and even old-fashioned tracking technology." Of course, I'm preaching to the proverbial choir. The woman knows this because we've tried tracing her using all the above plus a few others. Whatever cloaking device the Consortium has makes their compound a candidate for a damn sci-fi movie.

Angie offers a small shrug. "I only know he was raising eyebrows—and that was before he started yelling."

A gruff snort from Foley. "Why doesn't that surprise me either?"

I don't afford him more than one jumped eyebrow, choosing to concentrate on Angelique. The tiny tells in her behavior are finally starting to register with me. She's toeing the dirt too much. Pumping air in and out with noticeable force. Kneading her lips together like a junkie needing a fix, only nothing else tells me she's strung out. Her skin is flawless and her eyes are clear—if anything, a little *too* clear.

"So what happened next?" I finally question, only to stop and stomp forward again. "Wait. Hold the phone." I lift a hand with my sizzling fingers curled in, as if actually holding such a device. "Before we go on, you need to tell me, *right now*, if that asshole has exposed the ridge in any way." I lean in, making damn sure I have Angelique's very full, very undivided focus. "If he's responsible for bringing Consortium bullshit to my front door, then let me take care of clearing everyone else out and—"

"No!" It's actually Emma's strident wail, along with the sounds of her struggling against someone. I don't look but hope 'Dia's stepped in as the tether. When my woman's fully determined, there are few who can rein her in. "Reece! Damn it!"

I push a hand of authority in her direction. "Let it, Emmalina."

"I will *not*—"

"I said let it!"

My bellow stops the ground squirrels and launches a dozen birds into flight. The animals aren't finished resettling before Angie pulls in air through flaring nostrils and folds her arms, still attempting *le nonchalance* with her overall demeanor. Does the woman really think she's fooling anyone, especially after the fortieth time she casts a yearning stare toward Tyce's memorial? And yeah, there's nothing I want more than to let her have the solitude to grieve there too, but I'm not clearing anyone off this hill until I know it's completely safe—and in order to know that, I have to collect every damn detail from her first.

"Nobody is in danger," Angie asserts into the new stillness. "I swear it," she states, swinging up her head in order to drill her direct gaze into me. Despite the skittishness in all her other behaviors, the stare is steady and smooth as green glass. She's giving it to me straight.

So why don't I feel better?

I answer my own question the very next second. "So...that means they still have him?"

Before Angie answers, the query visibly affects the air, as well as everyone in it. Mom, Joany, and Lydia rub their hands against opposite shoulders, shivering against nonexistent chills. Chase noticeably stiffens, and Foley's already poised like a gunslinger, arms stiff at his sides. The wind gusts up, wanes, and then blows back the other direction, providing damn appropriate symbolism for how many places my thoughts have whipped in the last hour alone. From loss and grief and fury to shock and bewilderment and—well, fury—especially if Angie's answer is what I'm expecting...

"*Je suis désolée, Reece*. He is still there."

Shit.

Yep. Just what I supposed it'd be.

Which leads to my next recognition. Which is worse than the last.

"He's...still there." I enunciate every syllable with defined comprehension. That's usually what happens when I grasp a clarifying fact...that's leading to a staggering revelation. "But *you're* here."

Her stare flickers back to me for a second. In that flash alone, I'm able to spot so much anxious meaning, but once again, the woman flips to stoicism to cover her smooth sidestep of a reply. "Well, when the *branleur* began yelling about sizes of needles compensating for other things, I knew I *must* get out of there as fast as I could."

In spite of this entire insane turn to the day, her quip sparks a small smile from me. "Oh, shit," I mutter, shaking my head. "Did I use that one on the bouncer from Le Chat Rouge or the maître d' at Arpège?"

Angie's answering smirk is nice to see, despite it not having a prayer of reaching her eyes. "It was our *driver* back to the hotel," she reprimands. "You were very drunk and started asking if his stick shift was sized in proportion to other things."

"Ah, yes." I chuckle. "He wasn't very happy with me."

"No, he was not."

I'm thankful she leaves the explanation at that, though there's enough implied meaning in what we've both said that anyone with half a brain can deduce what happened that night. Not that Emma's brain has *ever* been satisfied with running at just fifty percent capacity. Her silent fume brings me back to the edge of uncomfortable with Angelique—though it's not like either of us can bail out from the subject this time.

"Okay. Full stop," I reprimand Angelique—wanting to go easier on the tone but keeping it edged. If I don't, she'll go for some other evasion tactic, and physically guiding her back to the subject is out of the question. "You're here because you had no other choice, aren't you? Because you tried to help Kane escape..."

"*Merde.*" She dashes her gaze down anyway and purposely retracts her stance a little. "Reece, do not ask if you do not want to hear—"

"Wanting has nothing to do with this anymore." And damn it, before I realize it, I'm grabbing her by the shoulders. Silently, I plead that she doesn't make it necessary to grab her by the chin too. This information is fucking necessary to get out of her, but I'm really fond of keeping my balls in the process. I can *feel* Emma's stare, fixated on every move we make—thank God. That means she also sees the painful grit of my jaw, joined with the steeled lock of my stare. "I *need* to know this, Angelique." I twist my grip tighter. This really is all business, and damn it, the woman in my hold has to be informed of that more than anyone. "Did you blow your cover for just the *chance* to save Kane's ass from those bastards?"

The woman's responding nod is sleek and gracious—even before she utters words that are astoundingly tenuous. "If I did...is it so, so horrible?"

"Christ." I can't clutch her any tighter, so I take the chance of pushing in toward her by another inch—hoping the determination of my stare fully conveys the intense meaning in my heart. "Of course it isn't. *Angie*"—I'm failing to get through, so I risk one adamant squeeze of her nape—"you're not *there* anymore. You're *here*. This is *us*. And you blew your cover, and probably risked your whole neck too, in trying to save one of us."

"But I failed." Her voice is wobbly.

"But you *tried*."

At last, thank fuck, she looks up. I'm able to return my hand to her shoulder, despite how a dozen tears are tracking down her flushed cheeks. "I...I at least can relay some information. It is not much, but—"

"Not much is better than nothing at all." As Foley scoots around, he whips his phone from his back pocket and scrolls to a blank page on his notepad. "Give it to us, Alain." And then adds a fast wink, lightening the mood at least a little by using Angie's pretentious radio call sign.

Angelique laughs a little, dipping an equally miniscule nod. "There is much—how do you say?—absence of minds in the Source," she tells us, though quickly shakes her head as if the words aren't adding up.

"Absence of minds," Foley repeats. "You mean absent-minded? Distracted?"

"*Oui.*" Her face lights up, and she taps her nose with a rapid-fire finger. "They are *distracted.*"

"Why?" I speak up.

"There is a sense of pressure," she answers. "As if filtering down from the top—"

"Wherever or whoever *that* is," Foley comments.

"It is feeling so much like a ticking bomb, no?" she finishes, though adds a validating nod to Foley's point. "As if everyone is racing the clock, preparing for a deadline, though nobody knows exactly when it is coming."

I let a chuff escape. "I know the feeling."

"And have made damn sure the rest of us do too."

Though Foley finishes it with a kidding-not-kidding bump to my shoulder, Angie nods as if sarcasm was in fashion four seasons ago. "*Bien,*" she murmurs, nodding with matching solemnity. "Yes. That is *very* good."

I refrain from gloating. "Why?" I press, just a few notches shy of flaunting my victory with neon fingers in his face. Instead, I refocus back to Angelique, who's observing our testosterone war with bemusement.

"The *connards* have been skittish of their own shadows since you took this fight public," she finally responds. "But something has changed within the last week." She adds a thoughtful shake of her head. "Something big."

"Big...how?" Foley interjects.

"I do not know, exactly." She grimaces. "*Désolée*. I am sorry. Things have been very different lately at the Source. We have all been more monitored."

Foley narrows his eyes. "You just said everyone is distracted."

"And they are," she explains. "In many ways. But in others..."

I hold up a hand, the motion as much to dim Foley as it is to acknowledge Angie. "To get from one room to the next, someone likely has to punch in three passwords and have their retina and fingerprint scanned. But once they're through, they can strip naked, smear themselves with Dijon mustard, and do the *Hamilton* opening rap without anyone caring."

Foley cocks a brow at Angie. "Is that what you had to do to try to spring Kane?"

"Almost." More mirth flicks through her eyes, but it only lasts a second. "Though I might have gladly preferred that."

"Why?" When Angie answers with nothing but a tighter scowl, I repeat it from tight teeth. "*Why?*"

She answers my seethe by shuffling her balance and rolling her eyes. The woman looks as insouciant as an exotic house cat again—which pricks at every nerve ending in my body, and *not* in the great do-that-to-me-again-baby way. "*Mon dieu*," she huffs, waving a hand as if brandishing a handkerchief. "*Votre femme est correcte. Tu es un bœuf têtu.*"

"Yep. A stubborn fucking ox," I snarl. "And for the record, I proudly own every damn syllable."

I relish the few seconds in which she fumbles for an adequate reply. If the woman thinks a spitting throwdown is going to make me back off, she really *has* forgotten how stubborn I *can* be.

"Fine," she finally concedes, getting in another eye roll. "The apartment in Paris was burned down last night."

Emma's gasp beats even my gritted profanity. She paces over, her attention locked on Angie. "Dear God. That beautiful place..." She stops to frantically chew her lower lip. "The entire building?"

"No." Angie's shoulders rise as she pulls in a hard breath. "But enough that the intent was clear. It was not an accident."

The wind, with ideal timing, beats through our four-way silence. Hell; through the *nine*-way silence. Even Wade, Fershan, Joany, Lydia, and Mom realize this isn't just another of Angelique's progress reports from behind the Consortium lines. All of this information is game-changing—and not in favor of the right team, goddamnit.

"So they've probably learned about your relationship with Tyce too," I finally grate.

She stares back up the hill, at my brother's grave marker. Her eyes go dark as midnight forests. "*Oui.*"

"And they went fire fetish on the apartment, just to make sure you were filled in on the scoop," Foley adds.

"*Oui.*"

"Which means they probably know you were the one who tried to free Kane," Emma utters.

"*Oui.*" This time, she only whispers it.

"So you really are blown." I hate how it loads more tension onto Angie's shoulders, despite how my intuition has been pounding with the conclusion since the woman appeared in the flesh fifteen minutes ago, following the eerie lapse in her updates.

"*Désolée.*" Her whisper is barely audible.

"Why?" I damn near growl in return. "At least *you* got

out alive, Angie—and we at least know that Kane's alive too." I insist on tucking her close, resting my chin atop her head as I grate, "Nothing sucks worse than being in that place and assuming nobody even knows you're there." I mean it from the fucking follicles of my toe hairs.

"That's exactly right." Emma curls against my other side, though there's tangible tension in her form even as I stretch a hand down to her waist and tug in, keeping her close. She relaxes only when Wade and Fersh amble over and yank Angie away into short but meaningful hugs.

"We're glad as hell you made it out too," Wade confesses.

"Bet your bottom cellar!" Fershan beams a blinding smile.

"You mean bottom *dollar*?" Wade jerks up a brow.

"Sure. If she needs one."

Wade shakes his head, clearly mulling over whether Fersh's gaffe is worth a full explanation, before Angelique gives him a hand by changing the subject—so to speak. They're both consumed by smitten silence from the second she mushes red-lipped kisses on both their cheeks.

"You truly believe that, *oui*?" she rasps. As they nod again, she bursts with a teary gasp. "*Merci, mon amis. Merci, merci, du fond de mon cœur.*" Then a long rip of a sniff. "I did try, so hard...when I finally realized that Alpha Three-Twenty-Three was actually our Kane..."

She trails off, with actual sobs taking over her memories now.

Though I sure as fuck don't blame her.

Now that her sadness overlays my shock.

My shock, which doubles upon itself.

Then quadruples.

From the ultra-firestorm her confession has swept over

the landscape of my psyche and flattened every section of my soul.

The explosion that blasts me free from all of them, tilting away and stumbling back over to Tyce's memorial marker. But though I brace myself over the plaque, hands flat and locked against the stone, none of the engraved words make any sense.

Nothing makes sense.

I'm ripped open as if by a *harakiri* sword. I'm standing with my guts in my hand...

And my heart swollen in my throat.

"Alpha Three-Twenty-Three." I really do want to believe my intestines have been split open more than accepting this reality. "Three. Twenty. Three."

Somehow I manage to lift the bowl of rocks once known as my head, though I realize they aren't rocks at all. The weight in my senses is the burden of despair—a heavier load than any I endured during those days when nothing lay ahead but hours of pain and fear atop a steel lab table.

Unbelievably, this mess is worse.

Way worse.

The feeling of knowing that over two hundred other alpha subjects have been processed by the Consortium between myself and Kane. If they've captured and experimented on half as many omegas, the other designation the bastards gave their prisoners, then that makes nearly three hundred and twenty-five innocents those monsters have captured and tortured in their giant hive of a cage.

A cage we still can't fucking find.

People we still can't save.

Horrors we'll never reverse.

More markers we'll have to engrave.

A force churns through me. Hot then cold, pain then nausea, grief then rage, thunder then lightning. Through foggy vision, I watch the storm of it move down my arms, surging through my muscles and burning through my blood, until it slams its bright-blue force into my fingers. I hiss through my teeth but let the tempest strike again, erupting in electric arcs as I raise my hands off the stone only to bring them back down in fisted fury.

Somewhere behind me, Mom's stunned cry is backed by tearful gasps and gritted oaths. I don't say a damn word. I'm not sorry for beating on my brother's grave so hard that the boulder looks like a fallen comet from some exotic cobalt planet. Tyce would be the first one to laugh at that, asking if a bevy of blue babes arrived with the order too.

"Damn it." I get that much out, though barely. My lungs are beaten to shit, and my throat is a tight tunnel of grief. "God*damn*it!"

Upside to the outburst: a moment of clearer vision, though that does me no damn good. As I take in the stony letters that are all I have left of Tyce, my hearing is sharpened as well—to the point that I swear I can hear the cocky bastard chuckling in amusement at all this goddamned pathos.

Which makes me pummel at his stone again.

And again.

And again.

No way, fucker. You don't get to do this, Tyce Frederick. *You do* not *get to laugh in my face after pulling all this bullshit. After showing me what you were really made of and then stealing every chance I ever had to know you. To honor you. To love you. Goddamn you!*

"Love of Christ." Something about the stringent command

punctures through my pain, making me stop, blink, and dip my head to the side. Vaguely, I acknowledge Chase's presence in that spot—but only for the few seconds before Foley appears, attempting to haul him back like a bystander at a car crash.

"Dude." Foley tugs harder at my big brother. "It's so *not* the time to go Good Damon on Bad Stefan right now, okay?"

"Please, Chase." Joany sprints forward, grabbing Chase's elbow with an impressive grip. "Listen to the man. If Reece needs space..."

I shove down a calming breath, nodding to appreciate her consideration—though right now, I need a hell of a lot more than space, damn it.

I need answers. Vital ones.

If cockroaches can't hide forever, why can't we find the Consortium's nest?

If good is supposed to win over bad, why have they captured and tortured hundreds of others since I escaped—including my brother?

If love is supposed to trump evil, why was Tyce the one who died and Faline the bitch who got away?

And why am I standing here, moaning about the fact that I have none of those answers instead of being back down the hill in the lab, trying to discover them?

Why haven't I made a single dent in the hides of these cocksuckers?

Why haven't I made a difference at all?

Why?

My psyche has no answer but helpless rage, merciless frustration, and more of the blue inferno that blazes through my bloodstream. Before I can generate a thought to control it, that same fire is carving apart the boulder in front of me, and

Mom's shrieks are slicing the air around me, joined by Chase's countering shouts. Then Foley's bellowing again too, and Wade is putting in his two cents, followed by Fershan's strident shouts and Joany's gentle chides...

But I don't hear her. The one voice I need. The logic in my chaos. The hope in my heartbreak.

Fuck.

My heart *is* breaking.

And though I fight the rift, it widens. Beckoning with a blackness she'll never understand—nor do I ever want her to—though I need her to help heal it. To help close it back up so I can turn away and move on...

But when a slender hand squeezes my shoulder, it's not hers. The scent is way off. Though other elements sometimes get mixed in, that clean core of my Emma, rain and wind and sea, stays the same.

I tilt my head, recognizing the blended colors of a bare and mottled head, before meeting the direct attention of a clear green gaze.

Angelique says nothing.

And because of that, says everything.

I am your friend now. And I understand now. Perhaps more than ever.

"Three-Twenty-Three." I let the syllables rivet themselves to the air like the profanity they should be. "Alpha Three-Twenty-Three, damn it. *Damn it.*"

"I know." She releases my shoulder. Extends her arm to rub my upper back instead.

"How can there be that many?" I turn all the way toward her, needing to get the ugliness of it out, even if just through the virulence in my posture and the agony in my stare. "How can there be that goddamned many without the world knowing about it? Without us doing *more* to stop it?"

"I do not know. I am sorry. So sorry. I hurt for them too. I hurt for all of us."

I'm comforted, at least a little, to hear the desperation in her voice. Then to see the defeat and horror in her eyes as I hug her close. When I release her, I feel a little better. Somehow we've managed to slog through the murk of our souls and past the ugliness of our history to lend commiseration to each other.

But commiseration is far from completion, and no matter what peace we can make with each other, Angelique will always be part of the biggest mistake of my past, not the light of my future. There's only one woman on earth good enough for that designation, and I pivot as I seek her with a gaze starved too long of her strength, her hope, her beauty.

The search doesn't take long. If she were a flower, I'd find her in the middle of a giant meadow from a hundred miles away.

At once, despite every shit factor of this situation, I smile.

Only to see that in reaching for the flower, I've also grabbed a bee.

Except instead of fuzzy bee legs, this ball of nectar has smooth, curvy, creamy limbs that consume my desire, haunt my fantasies, and turn moments like this into acute lessons in torture.

Definitely torture.

As she flicks that figurative stinger with one exquisite spin, embedding the fucker deep with the awkward dip of her shoulders and the nervous jab she takes at her hair with one hand. Then the other.

Shit.

Then the way she heads straight for the path back down to the house without looking back, even once.

Hell.

Then as I recognize, courtesy of the censuring stare emanating from my own mother, that letting my ex-girlfriend "comfort" me, even during this bizarre fiasco of a memorial service, was a choice as wise as greasing Randall Getty's skateboard ramp.

And that's not even the most slippery part of the equation.

All Mom's been told about Angie is that she's an agent for the Consortium who went rogue after the bastards supposedly killed Tyce—and that's the way it's going to stay. Especially now. No need to muddle this situation by lobbing a wad of TMI in the form of Angelique's "extended" involvement in my past.

Because right now, the situation's muddled enough as it is.

CHAPTER FOUR

EMMA

Will any of this ever stop being such a mess?

The question bashes the inside of my brain like an NBA team training for the championship—weirdly appropriate, since I'm pounding out a great acoustic support track by jerking doors, slamming drawers, and stomping around our arena of a kitchen.

The din is easy to get away with, since everyone has filtered out to the backyard, where Anya's setting out plates of snacks and Chase is opening wine. I volunteered to stay in here and set up the buffet-style brunch foods—a collection of salads, sandwiches, finger foods, and desserts easily capable of feeding that basketball team five times over—in hopes of dealing with all my weirdness about this morning in a more constructive way than a classic Emma retreat-and-hide. So far, so good.

Sure as hell doesn't mean I'm not still tempted.

Especially as I swing around, a bowl of Greek salad in one hand and a tray of stuffed peppers in the other, to confront a pair of insightful golden eyes ensconced in a petite, perceptive face. Especially as my I'm-so-busy act is shot to hell before I can fake five seconds of it. And *especially* as Joany pops up to park herself on one of the high barstools along the other side of the granite island.

"Hey." I force out the breezy tone while peeling back the plastic wrap from the peppers.

"Hey yourself." Her tone is light but meaningful, doubling my shock that she's a savvy stock analyst instead of a high-end psychotherapist. But now that I think about it, the professions are scarily similar.

"Everything going okay out there?" I nod toward the patio. To any outsider, the scene is simply a group of family and friends enjoying an early summer day, not the survivors of a memorial service that was turned into a crazy installment of a superhero summer blockbuster, minus anyone flying or dissolving. But as the cliché goes, the day isn't over yet...

And I find clichés fascinating...why?

"Oh, just peaches and roses." Joany's smile is a combination of both, with her high cheekbones evoking the fruit and her stunning skin tone borrowing from the flower. With her silk blouse and tailored palazzo pants completing the scenario of Southern belle chic, I'm forced to remember that she's probably readying to drop a zinger of a follow-up to that. "But it's definitely not the case in here, is it?"

Like that one.

Swoosh. Two points.

I puff out my cheeks and then release the air on a big whoosh. "You don't beat around the bush, do you?"

"Why waste time?" She rests her elbows on the bar and then turns her hands upside down, cupping one inside the other. It's like a finger steeple, only slightly less intimidating. "Especially when someone I care deeply about has a crap day thrown at them."

I almost think of taking a lap around that proverbial

bush myself and pretend she's talking about Chase instead of me, but as the woman has perfectly said, why waste time. "Thanks," I murmur. "I think you're pretty awesome too." And I mean every syllable. As future sisters-in-law go, I've hit the jackpot, but that still doesn't mean I want to spill to her about Angelique's true impact on Reece's life. "But honestly, the tale is long and messy and—"

"Isn't *this* a fun conversation to walk in on." The comment comes from the last person, besides maybe Angie, that I want to see strolling in right now. But as Lydia parks herself on a chair next to Joany, I'm almost tempted to laugh. The pair of them are like Buffy and Willow rebooted, ready to kick ass and take names—only with cheerleading uniforms that would have to be emblazoned with *Spill it all now, bitch.*

Crap, crap, crap.

"What?" I volley, circling back for the next load out of the fridge. I palm the bottom of the pan with the Southwestern chili pie I made last night while adding, "You have anything long and messy you'd like to discuss, sister of mine?"

"Ew." 'Dia's retort already conveys her grimace, so I don't look away while punching in the preheat number for the pie.

"Well, this is getting interesting," Joany chimes. "Good thing I refilled my glass before coming in."

"Nothing interesting here," Lydia slings back. "Move along, kids. Nothing interesting at all."

I pivot back around, ending with arms spread, hands planted, and both brows raised. "Except for the fact that our favorite golden-haired commitment-phobe has all but moved you into his place?"

My sister winces again. Then turns nearly as magenta as her wine while waving her free hand around like a twerking butterfly. "Temporarily," she stresses. "*Very* temporarily. And only because of everything that went down in Paris. He's still freaked about it all and just wants—"

I cut her off with a yap as soon as her words really sink in. Though I cushion the blow with an apologetic wince, I ask, "Freaked out? Sawyer? Still?"

Legitimate queries. Sawyer can't talk about a lot of his past because he'd actually have to kill us if he did, which has always made me assume that his Team Bolt duties are softballs and popcorn by comparison—but the pensive look on my sister's face is far from a Saturday ballgame face.

"I know," 'Dia finally mutters. "I don't understand it either."

"Nor are you comfortable with it."

Joany's observation turns Lydia into a block of discernible stillness. Me too. For the last six weeks, ever since she first confessed as much during the big formal party at the Griffith Observatory, there have been *several* conversations—'Dia moaning into my shoulder or a glass of wine or both—about Sawyer's missing commitment chip and all the places he might have misplaced it in his psyche. But since he seems to have found it, even temporarily...

"She's right." I ignore the oven's temp-ready ding in order to blurt it, not ripping my stare from my sister. "You really *aren't* comfortable with it. What the hell, Princess Purple Pants?"

'Dia takes a hefty gulp of her wine. Uses the move to swing a deft toss-toss of her strawberry-blond mane, which she's chosen to wear down on a day that's already eighty-five degrees Fahrenheit and counting. So maybe heatstroke's the reason for her derangement.

"So *who's* the one we're here to grill again?" she flings, gaze narrowed.

Maybe Sawyer has actually called *her* bluff on the commit-or-get-off-the-pot issue and she's feeling that damn testy about it.

Joany chuckles while casually tossing up both hands. "I save the grillwork for my job, ladies. I do, however, like to be concerned about friends."

"Amen." Lydia raises her glass, taking advantage of the juicy chance to point at me with the same motion. "And she's concerned about *you*, missy." Her mien turns solemn. "We both are. Honestly." A tiny V appears between her eyebrows. "You okay?"

I snort softly and get ready to slough that off, but something happens between shutting the oven and jabbing ten minutes into the timer. Something slips inside...something I don't have the mental power to pull back again. Not right now. Emotional shields are hell to keep fortified, especially when confusion corrodes them from every edge. And yeah, I grudgingly acknowledge the advantage of getting to show Lydia how this emotional exposure stuff can be beneficial—though right now, with all the self-doubt added to my vexation, I'm not throwing all my eggs into that motivational basket. Not that I know where I *am* tossing the things. I just pray I'm making an omelet instead of a new mess here.

On that encouraging—*choke choke*—sentiment, I let out a sigh. Take a pause to eyeball Buffy and Willow via the reflection from the glass door of the microwave. Finding it easier to gather my thoughts by beholding them this way, I finally mutter, "All right, fine. So I wasn't as smooth with... things...at the memorial as I should've been."

"'Things.'" 'Dia's snort is oddly satisfying to hear. "You mean like your fiancé's ex turning herself into his human sympathy wreath?"

"Well, he and Angie share things." I'm battling for the kick-ass, CEO-in-the-corner-office vibe—but I'm pretty sure I've only gotten as far as second assistant in the mailroom so far. "Specific things and unique experiences that none of us can even begin to comprehend."

Yep. Mailroom. And with the admission, I understand—with crystal freaking clarity—how ridiculous it is to feel so insecure about a woman still clearly grieving for the man she desperately loves and who deserves to do that with *his* brother. To be able to talk to him and hug him and even be consoled by him...

"Okay." Now Lydia's the one raising her hands. "Great. Awesome. So does that mean that if some CIA operative from Sawyer's past suddenly pops up and starts talking about their 'good old days' in shithole war zones, I'm supposed to give her carte blanche to his cock again?"

I spin all the way around to face her again. "Is *that* what's going on with you two?"

"What?" Lydia scowls and gives a violent shake of her head. "No! *Sheez.*"

"But it *has* happened," I prompt.

"This isn't about Sawyer and me, damn it."

My turn for the lifted hands. I do so with my oven mitts still on, acquiescing. "You're right. And I've got to be honest about that if I'm ever going to accept it."

Joany's gaze instantly bugs wide. "*Accept it?*"

"What she said." Lydia fist bumps the woman. "You're not 'accepting' anything about this, sister. I don't care how much that woman plays the Camp Consortium sympathy card with that marble on top of her shoulders; she's *not* going to play the sympathy card here. *Or* the 'for old time's sake' card. Or even the 'no one understands the torture I've endured' card."

"But what if that's exactly the case?" I don't flinch a millimeter, even when 'Dia snaps her stare back to me.

"Excuse me?" she snaps.

"You heard me. What if that's the case? It's possible, damn it," I rush out, stomping on whatever she was preparing to say with her flashing gaze and deep-drawn breath. "There's no support group he can go to for this. No therapist who's going to give him a list of deep-breathing techniques and an order to take me away for a long weekend somewhere. To Reece, a night of 'taking it easy' means he's not setting half the city on fire just because his bloodstream is ordering him to get naughty with me. Then when he *can* relax enough to slip into a deep sleep, it's almost not worth it for him."

Joany frowns. "What do you mean?"

I tilt my head and copy her expression. "What if your alarm clock wired itself to your whole body, and it woke you by sticking your finger into an electrical outlet?"

Lydia, getting ready to sip some more wine, stops the glass halfway. "Well, shit."

"If you think it sucks hearing about it, try *watching* it." And that gets me nowhere in the sharing-is-a-*good*-thing department. A morose cloud seems to flow in—even from the blazing-hot day—and blankets itself over my shoulders and through my senses. "And every time I do, I feel like crap for not being able to understand or feel any of it along with him." I shake my head, giving up the fight against the rest of the confession in my heart. "I love him." Forget trying to hide the tears that swell along with it. "But I don't know *how* to love him. Or even if I'm the best person to do that."

"Oh, for the love of..." 'Dia slams down her glass, sloshing dark-fuchsia droplets across the discarded plastic wrap next to the stuffed peppers. "And you're expecting us to buy that *how*? Or *why*?"

"What she said." Joany initiates the fist bump this time, though the action's faster in light of their dual irritation with me. "And I'll be kind about this and not bring up the obvious..."

"You mean like—hmmm, let's see—the freaking *hillside* the man's bought and built a mansion on for her? And the numerous bad guys he's put down for her? And—oh, yeah—the whole putting up with our *mother* thing for her?"

I fling a determined glower. "So much for not bringing up the obvious, lovely sibling."

'Dia nods toward Joany. "*She* promised it, not me."

Joany swivels off her stool and glides gracefully back to her feet. Her golden eyes are practically dancing, though I somehow know she's invigorated, not gloating. "And I felt confident in doing so," she affirms, "because now I get to tell you about the *non*-obvious stuff."

I cock my head. "About what?"

"Not what." She smiles gently. "*Who*. The thousand things that maybe you *haven't* yet seen about Reece yet. All the things, beyond his superhero blazes, his press conference declarations, and even this incredible castle on the hill, that *I* see in that guy for the very first time since I've known him. Every stare he rivets into you, as if it's his last. Every touch he reaches toward you, he looks as if he's trying not to break glass. But most of all, in how you've changed everything that nobody can see on the outside." She takes a determined breath before going on. "You've transformed that man, Emma. *Wait*." She interrupts herself with a broader smile and an upheld finger. "You've transformed that *boy*, Emma. He's determined to not just become a man but a *better* man than we all imagined. Than we all ever thought possible."

For a long moment, I simply let my heart sit—and be jubilant in—that precious knowledge. I'm relieved to see Lydia seemingly doing the same, until she breaks the pause by reiterating, "Since you've known him." Then asking Joany, "So how long has that been?"

"Since I started dating Chase in college," Joany elucidates. "Nearly ten years."

Lydia gives in to a long, low whistle. I swiftly spin away, presumably to check on the pie. It's a great excuse for hiding the intensity of my reaction. *Ten years*. That's a long damn time.

On the other hand...

"But wasn't Reece estranged from most of you during all that time?" I have to ask, no matter how much I hate myself for it. "I only mean that there's a possibility you don't know all about him either. He was a person with a lot of complexities, even before becoming Bolt. Discovering *that* man would take—"

"A woman like *you*." Joany, uncorking a bottle of Cabernet, motions my way with the corkscrew. "You really don't see it, do you?" She glances at 'Dia. "Does she really not see it?"

Lydia drains her glass and ponies up to Joany for more Beringer. "Not one damn bit. I can tell you *that* with certainty."

"See *what*?" I throw my mitt-covered hands out to demonstrate my frustration with their cahoots.

Lydia pings her stare between Joany and her glass. "Put

a lot of gas in that can, baby. I think we'll have to spell all this out for her."

"Not. Necessary."

The new voice in the room makes Joany miss 'Dia's glass on the pour. I don't blame her. Every distinct note of that familiar growl invades every heated, heightened nerve in my body. With arms still splayed, I whip toward the right—though the room could be plunged in total blackness and I'd find him. Feel him. Know him like the hairs on my own head and every blood cell pumping through my body. Blood that percolates and electrifies because of him. Always, *always*, all too aware of him...

She doesn't see it...

I chomp the inside of my bottom lip. So maybe they're right. Maybe I don't *see* it—but I sure as hell *feel* it, and right now, that's all I freaking need. And I mean *need*—as in, I'm going to revel in every possible moment of the man's electric enchantment. That means openly, hungrily raking my stare all the way from his bare feet, over every powerful inch of the long legs still sheathed in his leathers, eye-licking all the defined edges of his torso beneath the cobalt T-shirt for which he's switched out his jacket, and finally lusting over the cords of his taut, burnished neck...

In which several veins are thudding pretty damn hard.

Matching every rapid tick in his jaw.

Firing in time to every turbulent lightning flash in his stare.

Giving away the fact that he's likely been hovering there for more than a few seconds.

Shit.

I swallow hard. He starts his approach.

Double shit.

"Enjoy your wine, ladies." His unwavering stare clarifies I'm the exemption to the statement—the order?—as he yanks the mitts off my hands and then tosses them to the counter with the same commanding motion. "The 'spelling it out' will be handled from here."

My mouth falls open. There are words ready to come out, I swear it, but all I manage is an incensed growl. "Handled?" I snap. "You're going to 'handle' the fact that all I want is for you to be understood and happy?" Because now, it's damn obvious he's been lurking there long enough to hear all the key parts of this exchange. "That my heart is in the right place here?"

He doesn't back off. Keeps looming and coiling, thoroughly in stubborn ox mode. And being too brawny and beautiful about it. "Not your heart I'm here for," he charges softly. "Your head, on the other hand..."

"Is also screwed on fine. Not that any of you are *listening.*" But the second I retort it, I recognize the mistake. It might be a valid message, but even the truth is wasted if falling on deaf ears.

It might also be a mistake because of how I'm hefted right off my feet, despite my outraged shriek, and then flung over the ox's shoulder right out of the room—as my sister and Joany replace their fist bumps for applause and their huffs for approving laughter.

"Spell it *all* out for her," Lydia yells as Reece heads for the stairs leading to the master bedroom. "And be sure to start with *A!*"

CHAPTER FIVE

Oh, I'll start with *A*, all right.

Why even wait until we get to the bedroom?

I've never wasted a chance to pay special attention to this woman's fine ass, and this moment is no exception. Despite my irritation with her—perhaps because of it—a small thrill jacks my blood as I bring my free hand down across the perfect globes that are lodged so ideally against the side of my face.

Hard.

All right, I'm a little more than jacked.

Damn, how the woman can squirm when she wants to.

Smack.

"Ahhhh!" Her second yelp is more perfect than the first. "Damn it! What the—"

"Hush," I admonish.

Smack.

"Seriously? Reece!"

"I said *hush.*"

I emphasize with one more spank, because I *did* send that promising nod to Lydia about covering the whole alphabet. And *B* stands for *beautiful butt.* And on to *C*, because her *crazy curves* are perhaps only matched by her *crazy* mind, seeming to pour out of her skull via her throaty screams as I clear the landing and kick our bedroom door shut.

"Are you kidding me?" she yells as I deposit her on the bed. She props herself up on her elbows to gash a fresh glare into me. Her irises are a vibrant, sexy cobalt through the tousled mess of her hair. "The grunting caveman treatment? *Today? Now?*"

"Yeah." Good thing we're at *D*, because all that fight and fire in her face has absolutely spoken to the swelling *dick* between my thighs. "What can I say? Your timing sucks ass, Bunny."

"*My* timing?" She pushes out a bitter laugh. "Excuse the hell out of me? For *what?*"

"For trying to toss aside Joany's valid point."

"About *what?*"

"About what you've done to me, woman."

I brace my stance, letting her drop her jaw as far as she damn well wants to. Doesn't change a thing. She may still be considering my sister-in-law's point as some trivial comment made during girl talk, but that's what I'm here for. That's *exactly* what I've brought her up here for. So she'll see—with every fucking letter of the alphabet to help me out, if need be.

"You think she was just being nice, Bunny? Making girl talk? Spinning up compliments to make you feel better?" I fold my arms across my chest and tighten my jaw until I feel it tick. "Let me tell you something about our little Joany. She's a tigress in the guise of a kitten, okay? She doesn't say anything she doesn't mean, and what she *always* means is the truth."

"Fine." Emma's lips twist. She shores up her balance on her elbows, her chest undulating in mesmerizing ways against her cotton dress. Thank fuck her tone adds a brat factor to balance the heat in my libido. "But she was meaning the truth in a *private* conversation that—"

"Had everything to do with *me*?" I cock my brows. "So who was the one really sneaking around, Emmalina Paisley?"

Using her full name gets me two places at once. I've hurdled the *E* requirement and jumped into the next level of her comprehension. Though she's still fuming, I can see she's at least taking me seriously. She recognizes that I've hauled her up here because I mean business about addressing this. About addressing her blind spot to this goddamned *important* point. Making her *see* exactly how much light she's really brought to me—especially on a day that's been as dark and unbearable as this.

But with her here, I've been able to do it. To bear it.

With the promise of her light in my tomorrow, I know I'll be able to get up and grow again. To *live* again.

Even if it means she'll be this obstinate and pouty about something else. Hell, even if she's continuing on about this.

Damn, I almost hope for it.

Because *fuck*, she's adorable when she's obstinate and pouty.

Yeah, even when she's pushing upright and then demanding through her teeth, "So what's your point?" And then surging off the bed, only to try a huff—ineffectual at best— at the arm I clamp around her middle. "Reece, we have guests."

"Not guests." I already have the comeback prepared. "Family and friends—who also understand that when you've got your logic scrambled, it's up to me to unscramble you."

She doesn't fight my hold. She *does* twist in it, lifting a searching stare up at me. At last, starting to get that I'm serious about making her see *my* side of this. About exactly how I intend to do that.

"Going to 'spell it all out,' are you?" While there's still plenty—too much—defiance in her challenge, there's a new element too. A roughened edge. And now, lusty glitter strewn through her gaze...seeking out the lightning in mine... "So what letter are we at now?"

For a moment, without even our heartbeats marring the energy between us, I let her wait...and wonder...

Before I finally, softly answer.

"*F.*"

No sight has ever stolen my breath more than her instant blush. No sound has ever captivated me more than her halting inhalation. No action has ever galvanized me more than the sigh that follows right after...

Making me reach for her.

Making me claim her mouth beneath mine.

Making me lunge my tongue inside, rolling through her perfect wetness, tasting her incredible essence. I savor the wine she's been sipping, the cheese she's been nibbling, and yes, the spice of the sass she's still doling. I'm even a greedy bastard about sucking down the smoke of her anger, battling deliciously with the sugar of her arousal.

But most of all, I drink in every precious, pulsing drop of her heady, perfect arousal.

And in that feasting, am completely connected to her again.

Together, we banish the world once more. We exist only for each other. Only *through* each other...

At once, I'm fire and fury and pressure and pain, balancing on a ledge between intellect and insanity, though I hardly know which extreme belongs where. Maybe the world beyond this room, beyond the sweet soft arms around my neck, is the illusion. This has to be the reality instead. The only place where my life, including all my power, really makes the most sense.

"So what *does* the *F* stand for?"

Especially when this creature whispers questions like *that*.

With my lips half a breath above hers, I reply, "You'll find out once you've gotten naked for me. And after I've watched you get that way."

My blood throbs as she moves back from me. She doesn't go far but affords enough distance to work her elegant fingers at the buttoned bodice of her cotton dress. My stare descends as her hands do. She opens the navy fabric to reveal the matching lace cups of her bra. My breath might as well be fire as she slips free of the dress, letting it puddle at her feet before shimmying her matching lace boy shorts to the middle of her creamy thighs.

"*Fuck.*" I help her with things by scooping a finger into the center of that delectable underwear and pushing them farther south. On my way back up, I keep that digit curled—and slide the tip between the slick lips beneath her trimmed curls.

She gasps.

I growl. "*Gorgeous.*"

And there go *F* and *G*, though I'm not worried. With the way I want to take her now, *humping* is going to be a damn fine stand-in for *fucking*. And yeah, there's also *hard*. And *hot*. And *horny* as a goddamned *horse* ready to rut.

"Oh, *hell* yeah." Another *H*, tumbling from me in a ruthless whisper as she unclasps her bra, freeing her breathtaking breasts for my ravenous view. Yeah, to the point that I lick my damn lips because of it. To the point that I yank her over with one hand while grazing one of her nipples with the flat of my thumb, hissing when that succulent tip gets even tighter for me.

"Damn," I utter. "God*damn*." And then smash her mouth beneath mine again, matching her harsh whimper with my primal moan, making her tongue take my stabbing, passionate force as I slide my hand to her other breast—and twist that sweet berry between my hot, seeking fingers. Her mewl hikes with arousal just as she twines her hands into my hair and yanks with hard, lusty strength. I accept the scalding punishment and celebrate the burn across my scalp as we kiss deeper and harder, warring with groans that blaze each other's bloodstream with raw, raging, aching need. My lungs burn to get in a full breath, but I'll be damned if I'm going to give in. If this is what it takes to show the stubborn woman what she means to me—what she alone will *always* mean to me—then I'll readily pass out a thousand times from the potency of my own lust.

And Jesus God, what lust.

I'm floored from the might of it. The crashing, awestriking glory of it. The way I can't ever get enough of her pure need, her bold strength, her honest courage, and her unabashed love. *Every time* we're together, this is what she brings me. *Every time* I kiss her, she's this responsive and open and hot for me. *Every time* I touch her, she shivers as if I've just cut her open with a diamond and poured all the shine right into her wound.

Because of her, the wounds of my soul are healed too.

Through loving her, that soul now longs to do good things.

In fucking her, my body's going to give that mission a damn good start.

"Get on the bed, Velvet," I instruct, savoring every erotic

syllable. "And make yourself very comfortable. This is going to be a hell of a ride."

I watch as her breathing noticeably snags and her nipples pucker even harder. All the exquisite ways she honors me—as she turns and obeys me without hesitation—lend new inspiration for the letters of the new law I'm determined to detail for her right now.

I peel off my shirt, flip the bedspread up, and root beneath the mattress for a couple of seconds. *There*. Right where I've stowed them, ensuring they're ready for the most perfect of special occasions.

Or maybe I just knew, even back then, that the woman was going to need exactly this lesson taught to her. In exactly this way. At exactly this time.

Or maybe I realized that *I'd* need this.

Yeah, right here. Especially right now.

To have this respite of something *good*. Something *right*. Something to latch me back to her again. To remind us both of the connection that keeps us bound in the face of insanity and solid in the center of loss. Of course, I had no idea that Angelique would show up in the middle of the memorial and inadvertently add another strange twist to the day.

Which makes this, right now, even more important.

The *most* important.

Screw everything we had to do this morning. Screw our full house of guests. Screw the lunatics who are still lurking somewhere out there and everything they did to fuck up my head before this—and likely after this.

Screw it all.

Just for this bubble of perfect passion—*her* perfect passion—screw it all.

"Both hands up to the headboard," I instruct before opening my hand to expose the special contents that fit so well against my palm. "Grab the rail and don't let go."

Not that I intend to let her have a choice.

"What the—" Her croak of astonishment slices into the air as I secure the first clasp of the handcuffs around her left wrist and the rail. "Reece?" But she's quickly spitting and snarling as I do the same thing to her right. "Wh-What the hell is this?"

I'm not ashamed about the arrogance in my smile or the kiss it turns into just before I respond, "Isn't it obvious? This is *H.*"

"Oh, dear God." She jerks at the bonds, a reaction to be expected, though as she realigns her gaze with mine, it's with an openly perplexed frown. "These are made of...steel." And with the clarification fires the full question in her eyes as well. Why did I pick steel and not simply a rope of electrons or a lasso of light? I have to admit, I haven't been sure of the answer myself—until this very moment. Yes, in this place. Yes, in this time. Perhaps *because* of everything that's already gone down today. Gazing at my woman, naked and bound to our bed by them, the answer's as smooth and bright as her bared beauty.

I need this. *I need this.*

Sometimes, I'm a fucking genius and don't even know it.

And sometimes, especially in moments when this goddess is waiting and panting like this beneath me, I *completely* know it.

"Because they're real." I enforce the point by sliding my thighs between hers and then spreading her out with my knees, relentlessly sliding and rolling my hips while roaming my hands over her fingers, her wrists, her knuckles, her palms.

At once, she bucks and lunges beneath me. *Fuck, yes.* A

desperate growl rips from my throat in response. The contrasts strike my senses with visceral clarity. Flesh and steel. Leather and skin. Hard and soft. Tangible textures and raw sensations, not invisible pulses and lightning flashes. "They're *real*, Emma," I repeat, rocking harder against her. "Like us." I need her to hear that. Hell, *I* need to hear it. To be *sure* of it. "They can't be zapped away or erased with a keystroke."

Without ceasing my undulations, I kiss her again. This time, it's not a demand or a thrust. I draw out the contact, lingering and tasting and treasuring. Needing to cherish her with every part of me that's still *me*. A man who has good days and bad days, dreams and desires, hopes and visions and aspirations. A *man*, not a machine.

"You're not just the electricity in my blood," I rasp, punctuating it with another gentle caress of a kiss. "You're the light in my psyche, Emma." I lift enough that she sees all the truth in my eyes and every shred of meaning in my spirit. "You're the match to my soul. *You*, damn it. *Only* you."

Her lips fall apart. They're the color of strawberries from our kisses, but damn it, that only makes me crave her more. "And only you. Always and only for me." She rolls her head and jerks up her chin, all but begging for more contact of our mouths. But I hold back, purposely denying her so I can linger here and remember her...

exactly...

like...

this.

Finally, I dip back down—but only for a second. "You're inside me now," I confess. "So deep inside. You'll never leave me even if you want to."

And now, certain I've chucked my sensibility over the cliff

of emotional extremes, I yank back a little further. And get ready to see her silent safe word climb all over her features. And then prepare a couple of my fingers to zap into the locks on the cuffs, setting her free to deal with my extreme ramblings—which I'll refuse to take back even if she really does decide all of this, and all of me, are too much to handle.

But I won't—I can't—take back a fucking syllable. Because it's all the truth.

Which is why I'm blown away when a dazzling smile inches over the elegant hills of her lips instead. And then just goddamned jubilant when listening to the sweet, sensual words she forms with them too.

"Inside. That's a damn good one for *I*, isn't it?"

I start my answer with a slow, sultry smile. Add my touch in the form of adoring strokes to the edges of her forehead before curling my fingers in to smooth the hair back from her face. Nothing can get in the way of getting a long, lingering view of her incredible turquoise eyes. "Well, *now* my bunny's hopping with the program."

As she giggles at my tease, I kiss my way down the center of the face that truly is embedded everywhere inside me. The gentle sweep of her nose, with its perfect flare at the end. The high, proud cheeks that always flush when I say something too filthy. The tiny valleys of her dimples, which turn into entrancing indentations when I make her laugh aloud. All of her, so soft and silken and smelling so damn good, to the point that my head is spinning all over again by the time I'm suckling my way down the graceful slope of her neck.

The muscles beneath my questing lips go tight for a second, constricting with a deep swallow before vibrating with the words she rasps to me. "S-So...wh-what's *J*?"

I lift my lips just before getting to the hollow of her neck and freeing a shuddering breath against her skin. If the gang at Schoolhouse Rock ever heard the letter *J* get her husky treatment, *K* would've never gotten his day in the sun.

But right now, it's *my* turn in the sun—translation, in the embrace of this woman's legs—as she wraps her softness and warmth and life and passion around me. Making me understand all the reasons the ancients bowed in worship of the sky's most fiery star. She's my bright, blazing obsession, her heat drenching and slicking me as I stroke a couple of fingers through her throbbing pussy—and then torturing my cock with a harder, hotter rush of my blood.

The arousal turns my reply into words of throaty reverence. "*J* and *K* have their turns together."

"Oh?" Her new laugh is softer, but her new body rolls are urgent and damn near demanding, causing the cuffs to clink against the headboard. Holy God, that has to be the most erotic sound I've ever heard in my life—followed by the hottest sight, as I watch the perception broadside Emma at the same time. The artery in her neck thumps harder. Her nipples turn the texture of hard red candies. Her chest pumps as she struggles for steady breaths, let alone the words she tries to form with undulations of her kiss-stung lips.

Finally, she gets it out in a serrated murmur, "*J* and *K*... why're *they* so special?"

I slide my head back up, tracing the gorgeous curves of her creamy features, until our noses are less than an inch apart. "Isn't that obvious?" But before she can insert the full force of her puzzled scowl, I crash in, accepting nothing less than a sucking, savoring, saliva-drenched kiss that has her helplessly moaning, writhing—and yes, clinking—for me. I finally drag myself away long enough to justify, *"Juicy kisses,"* before plunging back for another of these hot, deep, perfect mind-benders—which, for all the emphasis on mush and wetness and tongue, impacts my cock like a sword sent into the forge. I'm hard as steel but trapped in heat, my leathers doing a damn good job of keeping the lightning in my erection contained. Trouble is, the arousal has nowhere to go except back where it came. I'm swollen to the point of agony, tempered to the edge of samurai readiness—which I prove with another crush of a kiss, sucking her tongue hard against mine, ensuring her senses are sliced open with the surety of what I plan on doing to her next.

"Oh, God." Her high sigh bursts up from her throat the second we break apart. Our breaths are thick and labored and nearly synched, an outward sign of how linked our minds and hearts and libidos are too. "I love you so much, Reece."

I take her lips again but purposely keep my tongue where it belongs this time. "And I'm damn glad, my little Bunny." Then sweep my lips across the silken plane of her forehead. "Because I love you too—so much that it fucking scares me. All the damn time."

Little furrows form beneath my mouth. "Really?"

A short chuckle. "Yeah, really."

"But—"

"But what? You don't think I see the hundred reasons why you wouldn't want me anymore? That I don't mentally count them down to myself every damn day?"

She jacks her head back. Impales me with an aqua glower. "Well, stop that!"

A fuller laugh now. Has that order really just come from the woman handcuffed to our bed and pinned beneath my body? "I can't stop all those thoughts any more than you can control what you see between Angelique and me, okay?"

And yeah, I just went there. Because yeah, in so many ways, it's a damn elephant in the room. It has been since up on the ridge, a fact I recognized from the moment we all returned to the house—and likely should've addressed with Emma then and there. But like an idiot, I pussied out to her "I need space" vibe instead—and wound up as the enabler for her bruise instead of being the hero who soothed it.

Not. Anymore.

That motivation spurring me, I brush my fingers through her hair with gentle determination. Thankfully, the motion helps my erection stand down its revolt against my pants. Well, a little. "In some ways, what you're torturing yourself with is even worse, woman," I finally go on, sticking to the unflinching message. "I'm not bound to Angie by anything more than our mutual grief over Tyce—"

"And the fact that she's been to Camp Consortium as well?"

"*Not* something we're reminiscing over with s'mores and Fireball, okay? But the rest of it is fiction in your head, Emma. I guarantee it. And one day, I promise you'll see that for yourself as well. But I, on the other hand, will never stop waking up most mornings like a freak pop-up toy, or turning raindrops into atmospheric pinballs, or making you feel like my personal Lite-Brite board every time I come at you with stars in my eyes..."

"I *love* the stars in your eyes." She lifts her head, blatantly begging for a new kiss despite the rebellion I've sparked in her gaze. "And I love being your Lite-Brite."

Though I deny her the kiss, I lap at her with the tip of

my tongue. She opens her mouth wider after I slide along the seam of her lips, gasping softly as I take soft, wet jabs into her delicious, dark depths.

"That so?" I take adamant note of every tiny tremor I induce along the length of her body. When she gives back a couple of fervent nods, I prod, "Even now? Like this?"

She kicks up the corners of her mouth. Purposely rattles the cuffs again, as if to confirm she's on exactly the same page as my sensual subtext. "Uh-huh."

Well...damn.

Just a couple of unintelligible grunts, and the woman's worked a whole Hogwarts house worth of magic on me again. I'm helpless to resist, letting my libido take over more of my control as I somehow manage words in return. "You want to glow for me, little bunny? Even when you're helpless in my trap? Even knowing you can't fight back?"

"Ohhhh..."

I add a couple of commanding bites to my lascivious laves along the lush pads of her lips. "*Tell me*, Emmalina."

"Uh...huh," she finally stammers.

Magic.

"Ohhhh!"

And then pure enchantment as I finally unsnap my fly, tear down my zipper, and pull out the heat that's been my torture master since we stepped foot in here.

"Yes. Oh *yes*, Reece. Light me up. *Please*."

I take myself in hand, having to lock my teeth while distributing my precome up and down the shaft to avoid dripping it directly onto her. My juices will instantly make *hers* explode, and that's *not* going to happen yet. No immediate orgasms for *either* of us today.

I underline the directive with a tight smirk, as well as the slow, deliberate caresses I give my swollen, gleaming length. "Say it again," I order in a tone of gathering thunder. "Say it *again*, Bunny."

At first, she can do nothing but gulp hard and then cry out, sweat glistening across every inch of her naked beauty. "Anything," she rasps. "Wh-What part? Wh-What do you need?"

"All of it." I rock back to my haunches to make sure she sees every inch of what I'm doing. The throbbing balls I'm rolling in my fingers. The cobalt veins I'm massaging, priming the electric essence her pussy craves from me... "All of it," I echo on a husk. "Tell me you love me." I start with what I need the most. What I'll never *stop* needing the most.

"I do," she sighs out at once. "I do love you. I love you, I love you, I love you."

"Tell me I light you up."

"All of me. Always. You do."

"Tell me you lust for me."

"In more ways than you know."

I don't miss the meaning behind her vow, and it impacts me as if she's turned back into the sun and then dived into the middle of my chest. The heat waterfalls against my ribs, suffuses my stomach and hips, and then—

Fuck.

With a barely suppressed growl, I guide my tip to her entrance. Did I really have to ask her about the lust part with this glistening flower spread open for me like this? But god*damn*, what hearing the words has done to me. What she always does for me. I'm pulled apart from the inside out, a fucking bloom of something in my own right, all my leaves blown away until only the pistil of my need is left, stiff and ready for her. *So ready...*

"Tell me one more thing." I feed just my bulging tip into her, gritting back the urge to embed myself with one thrust. Purely selfish move. What she's surrendered to me right now, in her control and in her words, has been like watching the dawn over the ocean. I never want it to end. Fuck, how I need it to end. "Tell me you need me, Velvet."

Strangely, she seems to double-take at me. "Need?" she murmurs.

I move over her, bracing myself on both elbows. "There a problem with that, Miss Crist?"

That same wash of intangible emotion drenches her face. "*Love. Light. Lust.*" She releases each like a sundrenched prayer. "But then...*need?*"

"Aha." I punctuate it with a purposeful roll of my hips. "You want your missing *M*. Is that it?"

"Uh..." She swallows again, arching a little as I swivel and then dip, which pushes my length just a little farther in. Enough for her deeper muscles to engage and constrict. Enough that everything south of her navel shudders. Enough that she finally stutters, "C-Could you r-repeat the question, please?"

"Hmmm." I vibrate it into her neck between hot licks and soft scrapes of my teeth, until my mouth is fitted against her ear and I'm bearing down on the sensitive place near its base. As she moans in mindless desire, I murmur, "*Please?* Well, *now* who's skipped ahead?"

"Ohhhh!" It's more a collection of gasps and groans than a cohesive exclamation, but I'm feeling a hundred kinds of opportunistic bastard right now—and prove as much with my long, dominant, decadent surge all the way inside her. If that drawn-out vowel isn't the only way she can respond, then I'm not firing enough electrons right.

But I guess the circuits are connecting fine, because her second iteration is more fragmented than the first. Could have something to do with my *really* bastard move of sliding my grip to her ass and parting the cheeks far enough to gently finger her back there.

"Oh, baby. Now you're really mixed up. *O* is after *M* too."

"Damn it!" She all but snarls it while pounding my spine with her heels and thrusting her berry-hard nipples into my chest. "Who cares? For the love of *fuck*, who cares?"

Damn great point. Not that I'm weighing her logic, once her filthy word choice rockets all the way up my cock. But hell, how I love ramping her to the point that F-bombs flow from her, meaning more of the perfect honey from her pussy will soon follow.

And it does.

Yesssss, how it does, until the slicks between our crotches are as loud as the harsh, hard pants from our lips and the rhythmic, erotic *chings* of the handcuffs.

"So you're serving me alphabet soup instead, Miss Crist?"

She opens her eyes enough to show me the thick lust in her gorgeous turquoise depths. The rest of her face is sheened in sweat and passion, with the exception of her kiss-stained lips. "Soup is good food, Mr. Richards."

I lift a smile that darkens her stare and hardens her nipples. Both beckon me to twist a bruising kiss on her succulent mouth before I push myself all the way back up and in, using my hold on her ass to turn her body into my grinding, pounding plaything, her pussy lips ignited by my juices as they suck me inside over and over again.

"You're just...good," I grit out. "Dear *Christ*, Emmalina, you're so good to me." And perfect for me. And spellbinding to me. She's got me damn near hypnotized now, filled with demented victory as the electricity from my thrusts grows and spreads along the plump tissues continuing to let me invade and incinerate and excite and ignite. I never just fuck this woman. I fuse with her. Unite with her. Lose myself in her. And never, ever want to be found. I'm going to wander in her wilderness for the rest of my days. Roam in the electric abyss of her blissful heat and offer every drop of my energy in worship to her magnificent matrix...

"Reece. *Reece!*"

"I know, baby. *I know.*"

"Then set me free. I need to touch you. I need to show you..."

"You already are, Velvet." I stretch a forefinger in, circling her asshole with insistence—and delighting in what my glowing digit does to the hot torque of her cunt. "*Fuck*, in so many ways."

"But—"

"Just take me, Emma."

"But it's so—"

"*Take me*, Emma!" I bellow it because I don't have any choice now either. Because the heat and pressure and need in my dick are at the complete command of my senses, ordering me to push and pound and stretch toward a conclusion as inevitable as lightning erupting from clouds and the earth it'll scorch in the end.

I need to scorch her.

Gash her.

Mark her.

As she's already branded me. Emblazoned herself onto me. *Forever.*

"*God!*" She thrashes her head from side to side as her skin breaks out in a million points of bejeweled light. Damn, the woman turns even sweat into a work of art. I'm in awe as I continue to plunge in, ramming her deep every time, watching her carefully. Waiting for just...the right...moment...

As her womb seizes.

As her channel constricts.

As her breathing stops.

And becomes a scream.

I fall forward again, landing back on my elbows but gripping her face between my hands. "Watch me," I dictate, digging fingertips into her hairline. "Watch me as you come."

And then I rejoice. She doesn't hesitate to obey, the flushed curves of her face fixed in a mixture of agony and ecstasy, of climax and completion, of orgasm and ovation. Just as that intensity wanes, her eyes pop wide from the force of her second climax—as my balls squeeze in and then punch a load of liquid light through my shaft, exploding deep inside her with rope after rope of blinding, blaring, bursting fulfillment.

"Oh. *Fuck!*"

I go completely still. Okay, not true. Every inch of my dick is still shooting off inside her, throbbing like no other orgasm I've ever felt, but I fight my way past the brainless heaven to rediscover my gray matter and grate, "Is soup still good food?"

She ekes out a smile, though giant tears thread out from the corners of her eyes. "Just...just hot." A shiver consumes her, and her tunnel thrums around me. "Really, really hot."

I roam my stare urgently over her. "But still good?"

"Yeah." She nods but then hums as if trying to stave off

pain. "*Fuck* yeah." But even the profanity does nothing to help me believe her—until she turns her legs into a pair of boa constrictors, squeezing the air from my lungs as she rocks her head back and screams—at the same moment her sex grips me with twice the force as before.

And just like that, I'm coming all over again. With her. Into her. Because of her.

My balls thunder in protest as a roar rips up my throat and liquid fire gushes from my cock. Emma rides the tsunami with me, clearly lost in as much dazzled disbelief as me. Amazement illuminates her face as wave after wave of carnal force flows through us, pushing us toward a shore where we're finally collapsing, spent and sweaty and sated, tangled in each other's arms.

"Holy shit." Her sentiment is so perfect, especially completed by her cute little laugh, that I just bury my face in her neck and grunt out an approval. "I...I can't move."

"No kidding." I don't fight the post-tsunami lethargy, because even that's perfect. I even ponder the possibility of getting in a nap. Yeah, right here. Yeah, just like this. My leathers can't exactly be shucked off from where they are, halfway to my knees, but everything's just fine where it is anyway.

Everything couldn't be more fucking perfect...

"No. Reece. I mean I *can't move.*"

"Damn." I rustle out of my post-coital coma to send small zaps from a forefinger into the keyholes of the cuffs, clicking them open at once. As soon as Emma pulls her arms free, I pull them between our chests and carefully rub her fingers, palms, and wrists. "You okay?" I murmur. Though everything appears that way, this isn't my first spin on the yay-yay-kinky thrill ride. Endorphins and adrenaline make people blurt all kinds of things for the sake of keeping the feelings going. "You'll probably have a few minor marks"—I capture her gaze with mine while kissing the inside of one wrist and then the other, communicating how thoroughly that turns me on again already—"but nothing's in a lot of pain otherwise?"

"Only all the parts that matter." The humor in her voice flows across every beautiful inch of her face, especially the smiling ribbons of her lips, which I can't resist claiming in an adoring kiss.

"Thank you," I whisper several minutes later, after I've explored her mouth with all my senses along for the ride instead of my lust being the bull in front of the cart. "Holy hell, woman. That was like my birthday, Christmas, and National Soup Day wrapped up in one."

She bursts into a full laugh, which contracts her muscles hard enough to push me out, even with the half-wood I've still got going on. Sometimes, it really is a good-thing-bad-thing situation to be a walking libido factory—though it's tough as hell to summon even half a grimace about that, as the music of her mirth fills the air.

"National Soup Day is *that* special to you?" she quips with a wry smirk.

"It is now," I growl. "Which reminds me..." I fix my expression with new determination while rolling off the bed, hitching my leathers back up, and retrieving my phone from the top of the dresser. Without ripping my gaze from the nude goddess still lounging across the bed, I tap the device's self-messaging button. "Tell Chase to add a soup company to the Richards portfolio."

And what's better than a lounging nude goddess? That deity turned into a giggling nymph instead. "For the love of cheddar potato, Reece Richards."

"That your favorite flavor?" I toss my finest rogue's smirk. "I'm ordering six cases now."

"Oh, my God!"

She springs to her feet as well, snatching my phone out of my grip and tossing it to the built-in loveseat under the window. As the device lands, the screen lights up with an incoming call, but I'm too far away to read it and too taken away by this woman to care. Neeta's handling everything at the Brocade and the other properties in the region today, and if something's up with the Richards empire as a whole, Chase knows he can yell up the stairs at me.

Everyone and everything else do not matter. Not today.

"Come here."

And especially not right now, as Emma turns the tables to become *my* conqueror. At once, she traps me with her sweet whisper, cuffs me with her gentle grasp, and tosses away the key of my resistance with the captivity of her soft, lingering kiss.

At once, it's not enough.

Will it ever be with her?

I move in, yanking her close with digging grips to her hips, delving my tongue inside her mouth and sending my moan deep into her throat. And still—yes, already—I need more. Always more...

"Ohhhh, man." But instead, she's dragging away with a cute little whine, giving back as good as I'm giving in the disgruntled glare department. "You really would've done it, wouldn't you?" she charges. "Told Chase to look into buying that company. Had six cases of prepackaged soup delivered up here." She adds a little grin. "And dealt with Anya chucking every single can at your head..."

"Worth it." I've rarely been more sure of a statement—and guarantee she knows it, as I change my hold into a tight circle around her graceful curves. "I'd face a thousand soup can firing squads for you, woman."

She doesn't hide the massive chomp on her lower lip, minimizing her laughter by a little. She's not so successful with the glints in her eyes, like sunshine on the Caribbean, as she rewards the metaphor with a solid kiss. "You know what kind a visual I just got on that, right? Especially with you standing here like this?"

"Depends." I nudge her crotch with mine. "Are you in the visual too? Like *this*?"

"Hmmm." She lets me lean her back a little, going at her neck again with my mouth as I glide a hand in for an eager cop at her breast before softly venturing, "That...errrm...depends."

I still my ravishment. Even stop my fingers from fully yanking at her nipple as I was originally planning. "On what?"

"On whether Angelique's there with us too."

I drop my hand all the way. Rear back to explore her face in full. "You're serious."

It's definitely not a question. She nods anyway. Bites at her lip even harder.

Hell.

She's not just serious. She's nervous.

"I think we need to talk about some boundaries, Reece."

Perplexed grimace. *Really* perplexed. "About Angie?"

"About *Angelique*. Your ex-lover. And the fact that with her cover now made, she's a recognizable fugitive from the Consortium too. And the fact that a member of our team, still in their captivity, is responsible for that—which makes *us* responsible for that. But with responsibility, there are rules. And with *this* responsibility, they're *my* rules."

She straightens, possessing the pride of an Amazonian even with pink handcuff marks on her wrists and dampened curls between her thighs, reminders of the multiple orgasms I've just ordered her to have.

Dear fuck.

I've never been in more awe of the woman.

Of *any* woman.

CHAPTER SIX

EMMA

Why does the expression on the man's face make me yearn to forget this fungus of a subject and just haul him back into bed with me? Only this time, he'll be the one on the bottom. Maybe even wearing the handcuffs...

But fate, with its sick sense of humor, lets a distinct group of sounds break into our sanctuary. They're coming from the dining room and kitchen. Laughter. First Lydia and Joany together—but then joined by Angelique.

Right. The subject. And the fact that it can't be put on hold.

But even before the glaring reminder, Reece turns our embrace into a handclasp. He maintains the hold while pulling me into the small sitting area adjacent to the bedroom. "While your rule-making *la reine* mode makes me want to lay my 'scepter' into your palm in a dozen ways, maybe it's best that we get away from the bed." As we pass the closet, he scoops my satin bathrobe off the hook just inside and then thrusts it at me. "And that you get into this as well."

"Yes, sir."

My comeback is automatic, perhaps even natural, given the growl beneath his words. At once, he casts back a look that's almost censuring, upending the energy between us once again. "Ohhhh, no you don't." Then emphasizes the flip by laying me down onto the Craftsman-style couch—before sinking to his knees on the floor next to me. The muscles of his shoulders visibly bunch as he folds my hands between his. When he lifts his gaze again, its steady, steel-colored strength wraps around me. "You are my queen, Emma Crist. Your rules are my commands. Let's hear every single one of them."

Well, damn it.

I open my mouth because I owe him that much, not because any words will follow. I'll get there, just not at the moment. Not as I work my mind around the sight of my strapping superhero of a man kneeling before me in his kick-ass leather pants and nothing else, the beautiful physical embodiment of the words he's already given me without hesitation or constraint.

Holy shit.

I love him so.

"*Damn it.*" The oath falls out of me just as the soft tears do, seeping even as Reece ducks his head over and under, leaning in like everything else in his world has fallen away. So of course, my tears get heavier and harder.

"Okay." He extends the word a little, vocalizing obvious confusion. "Is that a good 'damn it,' or..."

"Both." I sniff.

"Both?"

I fill my cheeks with air and then shove it all out. "You're treating me like a queen, literally, but I may as well be stamping my foot like an ingrate. I'm a regular Christine freaking Daaé."

"Only you have the sense to love the man in the shadows instead of all the fops in the opera house."

I let out a watery giggle as he lifts one hand to shield a side of his face, ala the iconic Phantom.

"Plus, I sing like a goose."

He lowers the hand to reveal *he's* actually doing the lip-chewing thing. "Well, you're not awful..."

I whack his shoulder. "You're pushing your credibility now, mister."

He shrugs. Not a bad thing, considering this man's flexing muscles really do belong in some high-end graphic novel, no artist embellishment needed. After my overt ogling, I tilt a grateful glance his way. He's letting the subject drop so I can recollect my thoughts—meaning he's probably already figured out a bunch of them but is willing to let me sort them out for myself too.

God. I really *do* love him so.

Doesn't stop me from yanking my hands away and tucking them between my thighs. Or from grumbling, "I'll bet Angelique sings like a nightingale."

"Wouldn't know." Reece all but spits the reply. "And don't care."

"That was *really* the right answer."

"It's the truth."

"And the truth also is, I'm still being an ingrate."

He leans back over. Pushes a thumb beneath my chin, compelling my face back up—and my stare directly into the burn line of his. "You're being *human*, baby. There's nothing wrong with admitting that."

I scrape my thumb across the rugged fullness of his lower lip. "Yeah, well...your very human fiancée is admitting to being very conflicted right now."

He dips his head just enough to suckle the pad of my thumb. "I know."

A weighted breath leaves me. His credibility is in fine

shape, because I believe him a hundred and fifty percent. He *does* know—and more than that, he understands. But I can also see the flickers of conflict in his gaze, tiny silver knives beneath his gorgeous grays. He's beginning to comprehend the rest of our situation too. Angelique has put everything on the line, perhaps even her life, for our team—including the failed attempt to get Kane safely out of the hive, as well as everything she risked to deliver the intel to us in person. And there's the not-so-little factor that she's also his brother's grieving girlfriend.

So no way can we just turn the woman away now. But if she stays, then what's *that* situation going to look and feel like? Her history with the Richards men isn't a normal one by any stretch of the imagination—even using the king-sized rubber band's worth of stretching that's required here.

So where's the line we draw between comping her room but restricting the amenities?

I've never been happier to see harsher angles take over Reece's face. *Whew.* He's being racked by the same weird dilemmas, a conclusion backed by the fresher alloy in his eyes and the determined set of his jaw. I just hope he's got a better plan than I do wavering at the crossroads of conscience and possessiveness.

Until he's suddenly jerking me back to my feet and stripping the robe off my shoulders. Yes, in one incredibly slick move. Yes, even for him. Yes, with an unmistakable quirk across his lips—even as I gasp out, "Mr. Richards? What the hell?"

A new shrug. A fiercer wolf beneath his smirk. "I like you better in naked Amazon mode."

"Huh?"

"Go with it." He presses close enough to rub the beautiful slabs of his pecs against my pebbled breasts. "You think clearer this way."

I jolt my eyebrows up. Attempt a haughty inhalation but wind up with jerky little gasps that add to the friction between our chests. Holy God, what he does to me...all the static and magic and turbulence he brings to me. But if this is what he calls clarity, I'm turning in my sanity card this very second.

Maybe I'll be doing that regardless—as I jump at least a foot, even with Reece steadying me, when there's a booming knock at the bedroom door.

"What the hell?" he growls, though most of it is stifled by another round of the noise, sounding more and more like someone's gotten hold of a full battering ram and is using it on the portal.

"Reece!"

I jerk again when Sawyer's bellow all but blasts down the wall. What's going on? He's using Reece's first name. Not *Richards* or *Boss-alicious* or *Assjerk* or *Bolt Burger*. The guy has only gone first-name basis with Reece on occasions I can count with one hand. But the times he's done that *and* gone to this level of thunder and lightning about it?

Zero.

Reece, clearly putting all that together a few seconds faster, yanks me against his chest with a fierce grip. "Foley!" he roars over my head. "What the *fuck*?"

"Sawyer! Stop!" It's Lydia now, though she interrupts herself with a bunch of grunts, conveying her valiant fight to hold him back. "You can't just—"

But Sawyer cuts her off by opening the door. Correction. Opening it and slamming it to the wall so hard, I'm shocked the thing is still on its hinges. Or maybe it's not—not that I'm given a chance to double-check, being yanked in by Reece so my naked form is flat against him.

"For the love of *fuck*, Foley!" He rips a pashmina from a hook in the closet to cover my important bits in the nick of time. "The house better be burning down—"

"It isn't," Sawyer snaps.

"Then what the hell—"

"It's worse."

"What is?"

"The city."

"The city...where?"

"It's burning down."

"What are you talking about?" I blurt it the second Lydia helps me scramble back into my robe, my movements sharp but shaky. My blood is running on alternating taps of scalding and freezing, the trepidation only enforced by the glance I get from my sister. She already knows why Sawyer looks like he's just seen the start of a zombie apocalypse and the implosion of the sun at the same time. She knows—because her red-rimmed gaze tells me she's seen the same damn thing. "*Shit*, you two." I cinch my robe so hard, the pressure bites into my waist. "Do we have to play charades here?"

Sawyer answers that with a fierce shake of his head, which breaks him out of his strange catatonia. He wheels around, snatches the TV remote, and clicks the green button.

As soon as the screen fills with an image, Reece clutches my hand. Grips it with brutal force. I barely register the pain because I'm doing the same to him.

"Dear fuck," he finally utters. Then steps slowly forward, taking me with him...

As we gape at a live feed of downtown LA...

That really does look like a zombie apocalypse has hit it.

The cone at the top of City Hall is no longer there. Same with the corrugated crown that defines the top of the US Bank building. There are burn marks all over Disney Hall, as if a titan with matches has indulged some parkour fun all over the distinctive metallic wings. The Wilshire Grand's iconic spire has been toppled over and teeters at the top of the skyscraper, looking like a giant needle about to tumble off the edge of a table.

A giant *threaded* needle.

But what's forming the "thread" that's blowing in the wind at the end of the thing?

As if Reece has sheared the thought from my brain, he pushes even closer to the screen, aligning shoulder to shoulder with Sawyer. "What the hell am I looking at?" he demands. "What *is* that shit?"

"Strands of electricity." Surprisingly, Lydia supplies the answer. It gives me an excuse to really look at her, though the shock of doing so makes me gulp on a throat gone utterly arid. Even the night we spent in Faline's captivity didn't turn my girl gladiator of a sister this glaringly scared.

"Oh, my God." I mumble it so fast, it's nearly one word of rushed horror. "The Brocade. Neeta...and the team..."

"No casualties at the hotel," Sawyer supplies—sending a look to Reece that's as transparent with its bad news as the man was with the good.

Sure enough, Reece follows up with a low growl. "No *human* casualties."

Sawyer, already watching Reece track a glare to the area where the distinct golden glass of the Brocade's spire should be, doesn't bother sugarcoating the rest. "Neeta was smart. She evacuated it from the top down. Thankfully, the hotel was only half occupied. They got everyone out before—"

"How much is gone?" Reece's interjection is like a vocalized dagger.

Still no needless sugar from Sawyer. "Top fifteen floors. And all of the rooftop garden, of course."

As I gasp, Reece grabs my hand and squeezes. The garden has been a project of both our hearts and employed twenty of RRO's most promising candidates for careers in sustainable design.

But other than that silent show of commiseration, Reece maintains his outward mien of clipped efficiency. "What the actual fuck has happened?" he finally challenges in a vicious snarl.

Foley pumps out an equally rough breath. "Not what," he counters. "*Who.*"

At once, the leap of Reece's fury explodes the impact of his aura on the air—a *whomp* of energy so powerful, even my stare pops for a second. With discernible effort, he ramps it back, only to let it go once more as he snarls, "Faline."

Sawyer's exhalation is heavier now. "She'd probably be our preference...compared to this," he mutters.

"Excuse the fuck out of me?"

Reece has barely spit it before being handed his answer—and his figurative heart, still beating on a symbolic platter—via the new image consuming the screen. It's taken from a TV camera at street level, where a horrifically familiar figure stomps toward the lens with sweat-drenched hair, wild eyes, and lips pulled back to reveal a full seethe of locked teeth...

And a hand, closing into a downward fist, so the tattoos

emblazoned across the grimy knuckles are pushed together to form a complete image.

A scorpion.

"Holy...shit." Reece grates it out in two disbelieving bursts. I'm not sure my mind has caught up to even that level of shock yet. Am I really watching this? Is this really happening?

As the questions explode through my senses, the creature on the screen finally lowers his hand. Replaces it with the bulk of his face.

A face I can't believe I'm staring at right now. Not against the backdrop of the city he's just torn apart. Not with all that vicious purpose in his stare and that smile quivering at the edges of his lips. Not like this. *Nothing* like this.

Because just four weeks ago in Paris, he looked very different. *Totally* different.

I was watching all those features dissolve in grief as he signed the release forms for the body of his fallen husband.

"Christ." Reece walks forward while stabbing a hand through his dark waves. That doesn't prevent a shock of them from falling forward again at once, blocking the silver flashes in his glare as he grits, "Jesus *Christ*..."

"Wrong dude wanting to change the world," Sawyer mutters. "Or in this case, a major metropolis." He exhales as if the entire top of the US Bank tower has fallen on *him*. "Though I definitely prefer my friend Jesus over Kane fucking Alighieri."

Reece doesn't get a chance to respond to that—because on the screen, Kane has pulled in a breath and starts to speak.

"Well, hello, LA. How are you all enjoying this afternoon's entertainment?" The second he proclaims it, I'm sure my jaw collides with the floor along with Lydia's. Reece and Sawyer grit theirs so tightly, their teeth could be buzz saws. Either way, the shock is tangible. The creature on the monitor looks like Kane and moves like Kane, but nothing about his talk show host pleasantry is anything close to the strong, sedate warrior we've all come to know and like.

We *came* to know and like.

What the *hell* did those bastards do to him?

I'm about to ask it aloud, but the pseudo-Kane on the screen sweeps his other hand up, instructing the cameraman to pan toward the Wilshire Grand's teetering spire. When the lens dips back down to him, he goes on. "As you can likely tell, this program is *not* brought to you by your friendly neighborhood Bolt Man—though the Scorpio cartel is thrilled to invite him on our show as a special guest star, should he be in the neighborhood and wish to drop in."

"*Mon dieu.*"

None of us looks away from the screen, seeing as how the new arrival to the room—my damn *bedroom*—has invited herself in, despite how we can hear everyone else watching the same broadcast down in the living room. But right now, the only boundary I'm going to stress is keeping my hand firmly fixed to Reece's. Keeping him strong for this. Keeping him grounded for this.

Probably because I sense exactly what's about to happen with this.

Starting with the blaring ring of Sawyer's phone.

He picks up and answers tersely but instantly clicks the device into speaker mode. "He's right here, Mr. Mayor."

For a second, the connection is dominated by the static from a violent huff. Reece slices into it by barking, "Troy. I guess 'good afternoons' are out for now."

"Where the hell have you been?" the mayor bellows. "I've been trying you for the last hour, damn it!"

Reece's lips flatten. He flashes a lightning-flared look at me, but in that split second, his message resonates to the bottom of my heart. *No regrets. Ever. Not when it comes to one damn moment of being with you.*

"Who—*what*—the hell is this thing?" the voice from the phone charges. "And why does it want to tear apart my fucking city?"

Sawyer leans in a little. "We're not certain yet, but I've already got a team working on it." He makes a gesture to Reece, indicating he's already sent Wade, Fershan, and Alex to the command center for that exact purpose. "Trouble is, this guy is formerly one of ours." He leaves out that it was literally as recently as a month ago and that Kane is fully capable of leading a lot of bad guys past the ridge's security perimeter and straight to the gates of our home as well. "Though we've got a strong hunch the Scorpios are now controlling him via some sophisticated Consortium technology."

I don't miss Reece's side-eye toward his lieutenant or the look Sawyer flicks in return. Obviously, sending the tech team down for research has already gleaned vital information. As the same conclusion wallops Reece, he jabs at the mute button on the phone.

"They're *controlling* him?" he spits out. "In what fucking ways? With *what* sophisticated technology?"

"We're working on it." Sawyer's riposte is all teeth and complete business.

The second Reece unmutes the line, it's taken over by another enraged grunt. "That doesn't help me, gentlemen," the mayor barks.

Reece steps in again. "All right. What *can* we do?"

"You can get your Team Bolt asses to City Hall!"

"*Finally.*" Sawyer whips his head to the side and mutters it under his breath. "Was thinking he'd never ask."

Reece isn't so cavalier and immediately explains why. "Troy, I'm an hour out."

"The hell you are," the mayor rebuts. "I'll patch you through to the Chief of Police, and she'll get your coordinates. We'll have a chopper up in three minutes."

"We'll be ready." Reece nods at Sawyer, who mirrors the action.

"I'm going with you."

And why am I not stunned when my insistence is matched, word for word, by the woman who steps in with her supermodel legs, blond wig newly reaffixed, and huge green gaze brimming with intense "concern" to "help"?

And don't I give in to the fire in my belly now, ordering me to go ahead and rip out with a scream of fury, frustration, and exasperation?

Answers all too easily given.

As soon as Reece dips his stare back down to me again.

And drenches me in the bright love, edged all around the dark regret, in his eyes.

"Velvet." He turns his back on everyone else, cupping my face and pushing in until he consumes every fraction of my vision...until his desperate energy consumes every electron of my nervous system. "You need to understand..."

"No." I wrench against his grip. He holds tight. *Really* fucking tight. "*You* need to understand!" I try to twist again. He's even more unrelenting. "You say we're partners?" I use the only weapon I have now, my gritted seethe, to fight him.

"You say we're in this together? You say you want me by your side forev—"

He halts me with a steel hammer of a kiss that radiates raw shockwaves through my system. I sway in place, probably looking like the Valhalla maiden just tamed into place by the conqueror Viking, and I long to clock him for it. And, damn it, jump him for it. Holy shit, even now. *Bastard.*

"Goddamnit," he growls. "I want you *alive* more."

And now, *bastard* doesn't even cut it. I can't even call him on not playing fair, because he isn't playing. As a minute stretches by—at least I think it does, because Sawyer has finished giving the coordinates of the clearing behind the house to the police chief and starts nervously pacing—Reece doesn't move. The edges of his gaze thicken with emotion. The whites of his eyes are bright cobalt tumults, begging me to understand but telling me it's not going to matter if I don't. In less than fifteen minutes, he's going to take off for a war zone. Without me. Without a clue of what he could be facing.

But with the best team he can possibly gather around him.

With the intention of not becoming a casualty of that war.

Yes. I see that in every tormented flash in his eyes too. More than that, I *know* it in all the throbs of my heart and all the fibers of my soul. And the rest of me may hate the crap out of that certainty, but right now, none of that matters. I have to slam my rubber against this awful road, give up both my hands on the steering wheel of this speeding car, and surrender them to an unknown neither Reece nor I can know or predict.

And worst of all, I'll have to do nothing but watch. And pray.

And keep hoping he feels the force of the words I give him now, as I yank on the back of his head so he's bent low for my lips to be at his ear.

"Come back to me, you big ox." My voice cracks before I kiss his neck hard. "Do you fucking understand me?"

"Yeah, baby. I do." He rolls his head, finding my forehead with his. And I hate him all over again because he knows how much I melt when he does this. How much I wish *we'd* just melt together like this and be fused until the end of time.

But that's not what I get here. Not what I signed up for when accepting his presence in my life, his engagement ring on my finger, his place in my soul.

I fell in love with a superhero. So that means pulling myself back, no matter how fast the sweet fusion turns back into bitter tears, and forcing even harder words to my lips. "*Go,* damn it. Save the city, Reece Richards."

He pulls away a little. There's a faint but beautiful smile across his lips. Some of his hair falls into his electric eyes, and my breath is punched from my lungs. *Hell.* He has to go and be *this* beautiful, in *this* outrageously dire moment? I'm tempted to hate him for real now.

Until he pushes back in, palming my nape and yanking my head up. "Only if I know you'll be waiting when I'm done."

I part my lips, knowing he'll cover them with tender possession—and he does. Then set my chin, knowing he needs to hear my determined pledge.

And he does.

"I'll be waiting, my love."

He inhales as if he was waiting to do so. After his equally heavy exhale, he states, "And you get Mom and the rest into the bunker under the command center. Make sure you're all secure. If Kane's really in cahoots with those bastards and he's told them—"

I take my turn to slam the interrupting kiss, because if I even hear the whole thing out loud, it'll make the horror all too real. "I'll make sure everyone is safe. And we're going to be fine. And *you're* going to be fine." Because I refuse to say anything else. To believe anything else. To accept or live with any other reality right now.

Knowing that if I really want it to *stay* a reality, I have to let him go. I have to watch him go and get the bad guys and trust that the team by his side will help lift him to another victory.

And concede that once more, I won't be one of them.

No matter how much that truth rips me the hell up inside.

FUSE

PART 11

CHAPTER ONE

EMMA

"What the hell do you want, Kane?"

As my superhero fiancé bellows from the roof of a Los Angeles skyscraper, my mind plunges into a war of reactions. Two huge monitors on the concrete bunker wall in front of me perfectly embody my mental adversaries. The first screen carries multiple images from Reece's body cams that are embedded in his sturdiest battle leathers. The feeds are a little shaky, giving away the force of the wind, the eye-popping height of that rooftop, and the crackling energy of every breath Reece takes. I don't fight my instinctual pull to that feed, stepping closer to the monitor with every excruciating second, mentally tethering myself so I don't reach up and try to touch him. To soothe his rage, his confusion, and yes, even his fear.

But I can't control my longing looks, either—along with the urge to lick along with the touching. And yes, I'm a little ashamed of that, especially now, but—

No. I'm not one bit ashamed. And am thoroughly blaming the local news, whose coverage is consuming the second monitor, their camera angle even including the lightning-shaped "summoning beam" that rakes back and forth across the smoke-darkened sky. The media is all about extolling the glory of Bolt, the superhero savior of LA—with every sexy-as-hell connotation the label implies. Their lenses capture every dramatic, sinewy, alpha-male inch of him, from his wide-legged stance to his glowing, splayed fingers, to his hair blowing so perfectly, a computer could have generated the effect instead.

I know differently. So much differently.

Over the last year, my fingers have been immersed in those dark, breathtaking waves. I've held them through heartbreak, twisted them with frustration, and clutched them at the peak of my passion—and his. I've learned every expression of the face framed by those mesmerizing strands and discovered the man behind every one of those nuances.

I've learned that the drool-worthy hero captured by those media lenses is only a fraction of the real man—and lover—beneath.

So yeah, I gawk along with everyone else.

But keep the gloating to a private roar.

Not that my stress is giving me a lot of time for that. Thankfully, I don't have to keep that so private—not when I feel it on every molecule of air around me, courtesy of the two other women in this security bunker with me.

At my side with one hand entwined in mine is my sister Lydia, her gaze glued as hard to the screens as mine. Her brutal grip gives up the truth she's been denying to my face for so long—things between her and Sawyer Foley are intensifying, and though her lover is nowhere to be seen, she's terrified he's not too far from Reece's side. In the small kitchen behind us, Trixie Richards makes a halfhearted attempt to make coffee. Her other son, Chase, isn't "on scene" with his little brother but is arguably in just as much danger, having chosen to stay upstairs with his wife, Joany, to lend much-needed extra eyes to survey the dizzying data flooding into the Team Bolt command center overhead. If there's anyone down here with tension levels close to mine, it has to be my future mother-in-law, who shovels grounds into the coffee maker with war-room intensity.

In short, Trixie's in the same mood as her son—minus the spark-wrapped fingertips, lightning-laced eyes, and dragon-inspired voice.

"I'll only repeat it once, man." The monitor on the right, labeled *BBC, Minus the Tea*—Wade's cheeky way of saying *Bolt Body Cams*—quivers from the force of Reece's shout. "What the *hell* do you want?"

The feed shudders even harder, but not from any boosted effort on Reece's part. This time, the lumbering steps of an approaching creature are the clear cause: a verifiable hulk. Not a mutant in torn clothes, painted thirteen shades of green—but the stranger we used to know as Kane Alighieri, a warrior who, despite being built like a tank, was always the Hodor to Mitch's Bran. The guy who openly cried at every mushy Super Bowl commercial. The one among us who really did stop to smell the flowers. But now, he's so transformed from that sweet hero, I expect to see his former clothes in tatters, as more pain fills his glare, more rage pumps into his bulwark shoulders, and more tension notches the virulence of his war-ready stance.

And he funnels every drop of his rage toward the man I desperately love.

If the torque of Lydia's grip means what I think it does, she's hopped into the same camp. Kane's far beyond what any of us expected, even after the warning Angelique brought us earlier today during the memorial service for Tyce and Mitch. Yes, she told us that Kane had voluntarily fallen in with the Scorpios and the Consortium, thinking he could obtain the intel that would take them down from the inside out. And yes, her own cover had been blown once his plan failed and she'd tried—and failed—to help him get back out. So yes, that meant we had to conclude that the shitwads had done their worst to him.

But this is beyond "worst."

And Kane's beyond derailed.

He's on a track of his own, custom-built for him by the Consortium, carrying him into a wilderness of insanity, vengeance, and violence.

"Oh, I think we both already know the answer to that, Bolt Man."

He seethes it while filling more of the camera's view, the wind flapping fiercely in his hair and fatigues.

"How's the expression go?" he charges. "Oh, come on, Reece. I'm sure you know it. A pound of flesh? An eye for an eye? A superhero for a *real* hero?"

Trixie abandons the coffee machine to rush back up next to us, jabbing a thumb between her teeth as a deep V appears atop her angular nose. Lydia shifts her hold on me, clamping an arm around my shoulders. She holds me up while we watch that gleaming-gazed warrior stomp straight for Reece.

The giant who's already maimed half the downtown Los Angeles skyline. The hulk who openly bares his teeth at Reece, his gaze flashing in malevolent spurts.

The guy who's clearly not playing for Team Bolt anymore.

The animal who's obeying another master.

But has that allegiance been wrought by Kane's choice—or has he been forced to accept the fusion of the Consortium's puppet strings? Is he Faline Garand's new boy toy because of audition or subjugation?

And at this point, does the answer even matter?

My heart cracks from the admission that it doesn't. However the change has happened, Team Bolt's gruff but gentle giant is gone. He's a wraith with flexing muscles. A leather-clad mammoth on a disturbingly clear mission.

Which he puts back into motion the next second—channeling the purpose of a charging bull.

Obviously the man won't stop unless he's forced to, but does Reece see that yet? Or is my man still so blinded by his guilt over all the fatal hits the team has taken from the Consortium that he can't see every change in Kane now? The guy's gothic storm gaze. The surreal speed in his sudden sprint across the rooftop. Every indent he's putting into the surface of that rooftop with every stomp of that attacking gait.

"Holy shit on a shingle," 'Dia exclaims. At the same time, Trixie and I cry out from the mutual awareness that Kane's barreling way too fast and Reece is holding way too stubbornly for any other result than what happens. "What the hell is he think—"

The collision sounds and looks like a nuclear explosion. An otherworldly silence, followed by both monitors flooding with terrifying white light.

I ram my face against Lydia's shoulder, unsure what else to do about fate's vicious slam of anger and horror. It's compounded by remorse when Trixie lets out a sharp wail and crumples onto the couch, burying her face in her hands.

"*Damn it*," I sob, turning to join Trixie. I have to be stronger than this! I need to tell this giant wad of wuss to go suck it so I can be there for the woman who gave birth to him. And if this is the moment Trixie has to look on as her *second* son dies...

No. *No!*

This isn't the off switch for him, damn it. Even from fifty miles away, I'm as certain of his heartbeat as I am of mine. The sensation's not as clear as when Reece is in the same building or room, when my entire body sizzles to life from the impact of his presence, but our connection isn't about the powers the Consortium gave him. It's about the essence the *angels* gave him. A life force that resounds in my soul, breathes in my psyche, lives in my heart.

Several seconds drag by like knives through congealing blood. But finally, at Lydia's burst of laughter, I tug my head back up in time to watch her nod at the monitors. "Look who knows how to make double layer cake out of shit and a shingle."

Under any other circumstances, I'd fist-bump the woman and her metaphor, but there's not a second to waste as I swing my sights back to the monitors. Well, *one* of them. Though the feed from Reece's body cams is still a garbled mess, the local news crews have recovered as fast as they can, scrambling into the building and up the elevators before the cops and security guards notice them. Not a surprise, since every available person in a uniform and badge not dealing with their own shell shock is helping to corral the screaming throngs in the streets.

So by the time the cops have recovered and are onto the crew, the news team is already on their way to the roof. Nothing's going to stop them from getting their scoop, though I don't know if that's a good or bad thing this second. The crew on the ground is trying to get the best beat on what's happening, but that structure is at least ten floors higher than the Brocade. Eighty floors up is a long damn distance, especially when the end point contains a pair of supercharged humans in an electronic pissing match.

An assessment I seriously hope I'm wrong about.

But swiftly learn, as soon as Reece's body cams reboot after their jolt, that I couldn't be more right.

Once more, the monitor is filled with a view of Kane coming at Reece in a livid charge. And once more, I wonder when we'll see bovine horns popping from the guy's stringy hair. But he flashes a wickedly human snarl as the flares in his unblinking eyes get sharper. And while his black battle fatigues are ripped and scuffed in a bunch of places, he keeps approaching Reece in volatile stomps, more undeterred than before.

"Christ." Reece's guttural expulsion is only for his and our ears, followed by a huge inhalation. He boosts his volume to address Kane again. "Damn it, man. Do we *have* to fucking do it like this?"

Kane doesn't stop. While his approach is just shy of a full stampede, he maintains that smooth, eerie smile—matching the voice that hasn't stopped chilling my blood since we first watched him on the TV monitor upstairs, when he challenged Reece from the midst of the chaos.

"Oh Reecey, Reecey, Reecey." He shakes his head, adding a trio of *tsks*. I share a gape with Lydia. Kane Alighieri *tsk*ing is like John Cena in a Tinkerbell costume. "There is *no other* way to do this." He swings an arm, deflecting a pulse Reece has thrown out as if swatting at a fly. "You, of all people, know that better than anyone, darling."

"*Darling?*" 'Dia beats me to the blurt by a second.

"That's a Faline word." I despise giving her name the honor of volume, but the reality of what I'm witnessing—of what my gut told me half an hour ago when Sawyer clicked on the news feed and Kane appeared with the Scorpio cartel tattoos across his knuckles—is getting horribly clearer by the second. "Seems as though they've been hanging out. And clearly, not to grab some milk tea and have glitter stars painted on their toenails."

Lydia huffs. "So what the hell? Has the bitch somehow figured out how to...what...*possess* him?"

"I don't think so." I stare harder at the screen as Kane deflects another pulse from Reece, looking ready to attack again. "Tyce could change his face, but we always knew it was still him underneath. There wasn't ever anyone else inside there with him."

"Then why are those words *hers* and not Kane's?" Lydia challenges. "As if...she's controlling everything he's saying..."

"And doing," Trixie adds—at the same moment Reece growls a low profanity. It sounds like he's patched the same details together and arrived at the same conclusion but is likely taking it further. He's the one facing off against this creature, which also means confronting one central, harrowing question.

If Faline has access to Kane's body and speech patterns, can she also see inside his brain? All the battle practices he's been to with Reece? All the strategies he's honed? His strongest and weakest powers? His favored attack plans?

Does she know all of Team Bolt's deepest secrets?

Does she know how to get *here*?

I feel every one of these questions punching into Reece, just by the wobble of his body cam feed. But I also see him breathing composure back in, shoving away the terror in order to focus on his bizarre battle foe.

"So that's really how you want to take your coffee today, huh?" His voice is consumed by a dreaded ferocity I haven't heard from him for a month—not since that night in the tunnels beneath Paris, when his father was about to turn Chase,

Tyce, and him over to the Consortium via their heartless henchwoman. The same bitch who's worked her electronic fuckery on *Kane*. Zapped him into her personal Frankenstein, only with better moves, faster reflexes, and a lot more anger issues.

Certified in full as he casts off two more of Reece's strongest electric punches.

As he spreads a smile as eerie as Faline's most gloating mien.

As he says, with her same purring inflection, "There's never enough cream in the tea, darling."

Right before he reaches in, aiming his huge hand toward the direction of Reece's neck...

"Noooooo!" Trixie leaps up as she shrieks it—though not loud enough. I hear every awful octave of Reece's strained chokes. I feel, even across the fifty miles between us, the ribbons of electrons stretching around his throat and then up around his ears, behind his eyes, across his frontal lobe.

I share his torment as everything on the feed looks like it's shot from the back of a flipped apple cart, followed by his pained grunt as his knees hit the roof. As I crumple too, my legs the texture of dry twigs as I slump all the way off the couch, my terrified moan takes over my chest, my throat, my heart, and this whole bunker.

But I can't look away.

I refuse to.

The video feed turns to snow again, leaving us only with the audio of a long growl that, while resonant with Kane's bass, is all Faline in its gloating ferocity. The sound taunts every corner of my psyche, making me curl into myself, preparing to deal with the agony of a world without Reece Richards in it.

Who the hell am I kidding?

I can't.

I'm already lost and destroyed and desolate and empty—and hunching over to rasp a plea that mixes with the splash of my tears on the floor.

"Please. Out there. *Anywhere*. Dear God. Dear anyone or anything who'll listen. *Please*. I can't. I...can't..."

But the fuzz on the monitor continues, a perfect depiction of the air in my lungs. An electric freeze, endless and unforgiving. I only attempt to breathe because I have to.

A chore I'm suddenly thankful for as soon as the news station feed blips for a second, switching to another view.

Their intrepid camera crew has actually gotten to the roof.

And yes, Reece is still on his knees.

Only now, he's straddling Kane's broad chest, his hands on the guy's thick neck.

"What...on...earth?" I stammer.

"How the hell..." Trixie inserts.

"*Triple* layer cake," Lydia declares before hauling me back to my feet with dizzying speed. Thank God she maintains her steady clutch, because my emotions are whirling with equal velocity. And as epic as it feels to burst the piñata of destiny and learn the light of my existence isn't about to be snuffed, there's nothing joyous about watching him in a position to take someone else's life—yes, even if the tables were turned the other direction just a few seconds ago. Kane is someone I know. A person I value.

Someone I *knew*?

And as for value...

I wince as my gut wrenches—and my mind whirls. In

the last year, I've been able to accept that the man I love was kidnapped by crazy scientists, kept hidden from the world for six months, and then transformed into an electric super being, while a global crime cartel funded the effort. But this is somehow harder to grasp, despite knowing that Kane took up with the Scorpios with the full understanding that he might end up in the hive, locked in the Faline Fun House of Horrors.

But did Kane expect it all to go this far? Would he have launched his plan to avenge Mitch if he'd known he'd be Faline's instrument of biblical destruction over Los Angeles? Responsible for a swath of civilian deaths and turned into the bait to draw Reece into this treacherous showdown? Or did he sign up for this gig with full consent, offering himself to the bitch as her ready and willing mutant for hire?

Holy shit.

Could that really be possible?

Did Faline talk Kane into *liking* his Consortium-style lightning jolt so he could have this chance to kick Reece's ass—or worse? Does Kane hold Reece responsible for Mitch's death?

He did let us all think he'd gone off to Tibet, when he was actually launching a solo campaign to take down the Consortium. His heart and mind could have really been so twisted and vulnerable, they might have truly become the putty of Faline's psycho treachery. In fully turning Kane against us, she'll have delivered a double blow to Reece...to the entire team. The physical defeat that Kane looks more than ready to mete. The emotional crush of his angry retribution.

Of knowing our former teammate has been driven to this.

Of realizing that in so many ways, we won't even be able to blame him.

How is this happening? How is this *right*?

I'm unable to answer that except with the words that do tumble out, riding the waves of my disbelief, anguish, and confusion.

"Shit, shit, *shit.*"

CHAPTER TWO

REECE

"Fuck, fuck, *fuck*."

I grit it out while whipping my hands away from Kane's neck, though I already know the image will be branded on my memory for a long time to come. My fingers locked beneath his ears. My thumbs aligned atop his windpipe.

My instinct, raw and raging and unthinking, telling me to crush it.

To kill a guy who helped me save the love of my life. Who watched the love of *his* life die in the name of our cause.

Who, because of that, may or may not turn around and try the same goddamned move on me.

Thoughts best left for another time. As in, perhaps, the next second.

"Fuck!" I'm on my ass now, dragging a quaking hand through my hair as I stare out over the city that's come to call me its own, with streets and stores and windows that should be bustling and sundrenched, now dismal with smoke, screams, sirens, and destruction.

But I freeze as terror yanks me down like sand in a riptide. As I fully comprehend just how deep Kane's brain has been fucked over by Faline—and what all the implications of that could be. As clearly as if it's happening in front of me...

I see the top of our ridge, drenched in darker smoke than all of the shit surrounding me. Then I see the pile of rubble into which Faline has turned our home. Then I see the harpy herself, accompanied by her goons, discovering the bunker under the command center. I watch them blasting back the door and then dragging out Joany, Mom, and—

"Fuck."

With hardly a shout of warning, I lurch off my ass and launch myself like a Mack truck shot out of a hurricane at Kane. Somewhere during the strike, I'm conscious of raucous whoops off to my right, too damn close for comfort. Already knowing it's a mistake, I look up and over and try not to be even more incensed at whatever dumbshit let that news crew up here.

"Yeeeaaah!" One of them pumps a fist as I smack Kane back down. "Get him, Bolt Man!"

The guy next to him, with the camera on his shoulder, cheers, "Way to go, big guy!"

"Feed that fucker his own dick!" And there's the real kicker. Not many days—as in none—can I claim hearing that line from the mouth of a pink-haired pixie in full Lolita regalia. Next to her, the pseudo-preppy anchorwoman simply adds an eager nod, her face betraying the thousand-and-one questions she's already got pulled up on her tablet.

Kane doesn't give me another second to be concerned about them. He connects a punch to my jaw that I feel in every hair follicle. Christ on a cracker. Either the fucker's been holding back on me in sparring practice or part of his stay at the Consortium Spa included some finesse on his close-quarters battle work.

Which, despite the Tweety Bird light show still circling in

my senses, hones my thoughts back in on the curiosities that *do* matter here.

What the hell *is* going on with Alighieri? Has Kane been "inspired" to do all this—or compelled?

Is he following Faline's orders—or acting beneath her control?

Needing those answers isn't an opt-out clause. So yeah, pancaking the big guy back down to prone position doesn't just serve my wrath—though that's a damn good start, especially when my imagination feeds me the rest of my nightmare on a custom platter.

And in my mind, I'm right back at the ridge again. Witnessing it all, helpless and motionless, again.

With the house still burning, Faline makes Mom and Emma watch while her guys cart the others away, bound for their journey to Spain and the Source's torture chambers. Or maybe they won't bother with the effort and simply execute everyone. But the two most important women in my life will be spared, at least for a little while. Faline will want to play with her food first.

And I know firsthand what that bitch considers "playtime."

My roar doesn't stay confined to my chest. I punctuate the burst with intentional snarls as the frustration and fury become an electric fever, burning my nerves and empowering my muscles. With a satisfied grunt, I lodge my knees into the crooks of Kane's elbows. With an equal economy of motion, I lodge one hand at the center of his throat. At the same time, I part my lips to expose the full snarl of my determination. The extra intensity will be needed if the guy opens his eyes back up...

And looks exactly like this.

"Christ," I mutter, despite expecting it. Despite being

prepared to face him like this, all but wired to detonate on impact, with his locked and seething teeth, wide and pumping nostrils, and eyes...

Shit.

His eyes have gone fluorescent white, glowing like a pair of nuclear reactors. The irises pulse neon purple and blue. His lashes have turned into iridescent LED strands.

"My friend." I need to say it, to confirm that I still *see* it. Even just faintly. I have to know he's still in there somewhere. To know that in a different time and place, all of this might even be comical. I'd tease him about how pretty he is. Goddamnit, Mitch would even be jealous that he was the one to get all the good bling.

In a different time and place.

Much different.

But in this one, all I can do is grate it out again. "My friend." And then utter, barely pushing breath beneath it, "What the hell has she done to you?"

And yeah, I realize that, because he's the robot being worked by Faline's joystick, she may even have just heard me ask that. Weirdly, there's a part of me that hopes she has. If the bitch really is playing with her fun Kane-bot, maybe she's not focusing on destroying everything out at the ridge.

With that damn fine motivation, I fight her even harder.

By fighting *him* even harder.

I shove my knees down harder and twist my hand tighter. There's a gurgle of breath in the windpipe I compress, but I'm not stopping. *Goddamnit. You have to stop.* But as a long, savoring laugh makes its way around my hold, Kane's proud bass raped by Faline's salient purr, I'm filled with nothing but the drive to shut it off. To shut *her* down.

No. You're better than this. You're better than her.

On a vicious bellow, I ease back on the choke but fortify the lock of my knees, expecting Kane to cough from the infusion of air. When he barely gets out a wheeze, I'm surprised for all of two seconds. If the bitch really is controlling him somehow, this is exactly what I expect from her. What I should never *stop* expecting—especially as Kane's eyes glow brighter and his rough gasp gives way to a gloating laugh.

"What's she done to *me*?" he finally drawls, sounding like his throat is lined with two inches of nicotine. "Not half of what she still wants to do to you, man. What she's damned and determined to do *with* you, Alpha Two."

Straw. Camel's back. My conscience. My control.

My hand, which I willfully close back in while savoring the vengeance I've dreamed about for so long. The chance to break those bastards' bonds. To squeeze the lifeblood out of them the same way they drained it from me and replaced it with a mutant monster. *Alpha Two.*

No, damn it!

Better. Than. This.

Better. Than. Her.

But there's nothing left of the better me to listen. Nothing inside but an animal that's grabbed the keys to the cage, breaking out and breaking down, seething and snarling. "How do you like your Alpha goddamned Two now, you bitch?"

Beneath my hand, Kane's veins pulse brighter shades of purple and blue. Airways work to swallow and breathe, but I don't let them, cutting my clutch deeper into them. And holy fuck, does it feel good. Better and better with every passing second.

Yes. *Yes.* I'm really going to do it.

Until suddenly, an epiphany blares.

No. It's the fucking fireworks show of epiphanies.

I'm not Alpha Two anymore.

I am Bolt.

I have a city to protect. A code to follow. A whole damn backup team.

A team.

Including the man I've nearly strangled.

The man who, even with waning air and a weakening body, blinks hard up at me—with eyelashes that have returned to their normal texture. In his purposeful gaze, the pupils are back to being nearly black, just like always.

With a stunned grunt, I slacken my clutch—only to have Kane hiss so loud in protest that I freeze. "God*damn*it, Richards," he rasps. "D-Don't l-let up!"

I bug out my glare. Or funnel it in. I'm not sure of anything, especially the order I've just been given. "You've... You've been deprived of air, man. You don't know—"

"I know damn f-fucking well what I'm asking!"

I stare harder. Yeah, definitely going for bugged-out. "But I'm killing you."

"N-N-No. You've brought me...b-back."

Riding a surge of comprehension, I squeeze my hand back in. "Shit." Sure enough, the luster of his eyes strengthens as the air in his throat thins. "You're right."

He smirks. Only a little. A look completely worthy of the real Kane Alighieri. "Usually...am."

I want to laugh. I can tell he wants to as well. He's as freaked about this conundrum as I am. Letting him physically live will keep him bound by Faline's shackles. But setting him free means—

"Damn it."

Appropriate. I really am damned if I do and damned if I don't.

"Richards!" Even as he croak-bellows it, I know I've vacillated too long. Like a superhero suit in reverse, the shell of the bitch's control snaps back over his huge body and his formidable face. His stare is back to silver; his smirk is back to a prurient preen.

Fuck.

Faline's back in.

"Are we having fun yet?" She's enjoying every second of the thrill, even pulsing the glow of Kane's eyelashes in time to the strains of some frothy pop song that's burst out along the streets below. The voice of the artist, a throaty alto who's crooning about dancing all night long in her killer shoes, is distorted into a ghostly moan that mixes in with the nonstop siren wails along the empty city streets. "You know that girls just want to have fun, Richards. Why can't boys do the same?"

I drop my head. "Fuck me."

"Hmmm. I'd rather not. Though I wouldn't rule it out at this point. Our darling does enjoy embracing her inner voyeur, doesn't she?" While he weaves a relishing chuckle atop my exploding grimace that's a confusing mix of his Kane husk with a Faline lilt, he wastes no more than two seconds on it. At once, his gaze is determined atomic light aimed directly at me. "Though at the moment, she's more interested in penetration of a *different* sort..."

And what the living fuck does *that* mean?

Though I'm hardly finished processing the words in my mind, let alone worried about churning them out to my lips, Kane's already acting on cues that have clearly come somehow from Faline. With one eye-popping sweep, he's got a hand buried in my hair and my head jerked around to the side. And though my hands are still fitted around his neck, he's the one who may as well have my goddamned balls in his palm.

The next moment, I wish that were the case.

He wrenches my head back harder so my jaw and ear are facing the sky.

Clearly preparing to invade some part of me with the item in his *other* hand.

It's sure as hell not my balls.

"Holy. *Fuck*."

"Hold still for me, sweet Reecey. It doesn't hurt. Much."

"Wh-What..."

As if I'm even going to finish that. As if he'd answer me if I did. All I can do is watch the squirming thing, which looks like a bright-red electric Mexican jumping bean with the worm half-escaped, as Kane lifts it closer to my ear. Then brighter and brighter, the little tongue squirming faster and faster, as that fucking thing nears my canal.

"Kane! *No!* Goddamnit!"

"Almost..."

"Alighieri! You don't have to do this! Break free, man. Break—"

But then, I'm only capable of a scream. Hot, hostile, horrified.

My own.

The fucker is pouring magma from the fucking River Styx into my head. Which, upon further thought—using the three cells that are still functioning in my brain—might just actually be the gift from fate that I need.

At once, the agony ignites every circuit of strength in my

blood. I twist my head free from Kane's grip in time to watch the electric worm in its death throes next to my right knee—as I pin the guy down by both elbows again.

As I rewrap my hands around his throat.

Squeezing tighter. *Tighter.*

But as the authentic Kane breaks out and shows himself again, I'm unsure whether to roar in relief or sob in remorse.

One look at the guy's face and I already see which option he'd urge me to. "Hey," he gurgles and even attempts a wan smile.

I flash a tortured grimace. "Hey."

"Th-That's good, Richards. K-K-Keep going. Come on. *Keep going.* It's— It's all right."

I flash a new glower. "It's *all right*?" Out of every puddle of surreal bullshit I've had to slog through over the last two years, this has to be one of the deepest. "There isn't *one thing* 'all right' about this situation, you fucking cretin."

He laughs. Yeah, *laughs.* But at once, that has him wheezing for more air—though this time, I don't let up on my hold. Karma *has* to be cackling over a cauldron of her most evil brew at this very moment.

Still, he manages to sputter, "*Richards.* It's *all right.*"

"And what part of 'that's bullshit' aren't you getting?" The part before or after Faline fun-botted him into destroying every building around us like a child tearing apart a Lego set? Or the part where he came at *me* like I was just a bigger version of those plastic toys? Or the part where she compelled him into switching out the Legos for a goddamned Glo-Worm and feeding the fucking thing into my brain? As it is, the whole shell of my ear and part of the canal are still doused in the neurotic napalm of whatever that creature was dragging. But, thank fuck, my mind is completely still my own. I still abhor Faline Garand with every fiber of my being.

Especially right now.

Especially facing this.

My friend, struggling for air beneath *my* brutal grip. The sound of his breaths scraping the air mix with that ridiculous dance song, the yowls of more sirens, and the steady *whops* of helicopters in the smoky murk above. His forehead crumples as he wobbles another entreaty. "Reece...man...it—it *is* going to be okay..."

"Says the asshole *not* asphyxiating his friend?"

"F-F-Fuck you."

"Fuck *you*!"

The snarl doesn't help. Frustration and rage boil through my blood. Fear and grief engulf my senses. This is all leading to one immutable outcome. I recognize it in my soul. I watch Kane doing the same but confronting it with a lot more courage than me.

He tries to swallow, but I'm holding on too hard now. Crushing his air too deep. He changes tack, jutting his chin up, indicating he needs to say something and *I* need to listen the hell up. "Th-The tatts. Th-That scorpion. You n-n-need to know, man...I d-d-didn't—"

"I know." My voice shreds, but I suck my shit together, summoning the fortitude to add, "I *know*, man." And I really do. He never would have consented to be inked with the symbol of the cocksuckers partly responsible for Mitch's death.

With a crazy burst of force, the guy clutches me by one knee. "And I— I d-d-didn't tell them anything, Reece. A-About the ridge." He sucks in shallow spurts of air through his gritted teeth. "I d-d-didn't betray you...or th-the team. Everyone is safe."

I'm suddenly fucking glad he's made me look. That despite his agony—the suffering *I'm* inflicting—my gaze is soldered on him and my soul is able to confirm his absolute truth. Only after my tsunami of relief fades can I plug into enough brain cells to form new words. "But...how?" I blurt at last.

"Tr-Trick I l-l-learned...in spec ops," he explains. "Forced m-myself to remember the location d-d-differently. If the bitch d-did yank it out of me, sh-she'll be ch-chasing you s-s-somewhere out n-n-near Ojai and Lake Casitas."

I shake my head, fighting another flood of astonishment and guilt. *Fuck*, the *guilt*. "And you're still really asking me to repay you like *this*?"

Unbelievably, he digs his hand harder into my knee. "I'm asking you t-t-to h-h-help me with what I've d-d-dreamed of since Paris."

I drop my head all the way down. I've never felt more like a privileged punk who got away with everything short of murder growing up, only to *be* grown-up but still prancing around like a fool, taking out bad guys with the same disconnected ease with which I spiked the principal's thermos with laxatives or charmed cheerleaders out of their panties. And I've been doing it while readily thinking the superhero antics have been my grand installment pay-off plan to karma.

But everything's changed, damn it. The stakes have climbed terrifyingly high. Friends. Family. The cause I realize I've been called to. The woman I've been destined for. The choices I've had to make with every one of those weights on my soul. Dealing with the consequences. *Living* with the consequences.

So goddamned unsure about whether I can live with this one.

"Kane. *Fuck.* Don't put this on me." Air slices in and out of my lungs, harsh and heavy, as if making up for every one I'm taking from him. "I'm begging you..."

"I-I'm begging h-harder."

Shit. We sound like a couple of teenagers messing around with each other in the schoolyard, comparing our piss streams, except there's nothing juvenile about what he's asking of me. "We'll...we'll find another way to get you away from her, okay? If you and I learned about this trick by accident, there have to be some more loopholes around her shit. We can block the signals somehow. Wade and Fersh can make you a helmet or ear plugs. Maybe there are liquid firewalls we can formulate. We can inject you... *Fuck. Listen* to me. Kane."

"No."

"The guys—Wade, Fersh, Alex—have amassed a lot of data about those fuckers." Not the exact information *I've* been looking for but a lot we never knew all the same. "Just listen to what they have to—"

"*No.*"

I shove up, resulting in my hand plunging harder on his windpipe. "Just like that? No?"

"Not j-j-just like that." His gaze alters, darkening to the texture of twin onyx chunks. Glittering. Impenetrable. "*Not* just like that, and you kn-know it."

I lock my teeth. Another roar brews in my gut, as dark as the smoke turning the sun into a ball of burnt oil, but it lodges in my throat like a rag in that oil, soaked in the awful awareness of what he's implying. But I have to hear it for myself, perhaps because I still don't believe it for myself.

"How many times, Kane?" I lean over him, hyper-alert to how he frantically glances to the side. I twist my free hand into the collar of his fatigues. "How many times have you already tried to kill yourself, damn it?"

His breathing gets shallower. His eyes tighten at the corners. "F-F-Five."

I release his collar. "*Five?*"

"T-Twice in Paris," he rasps. "Three more times in Sp-Spain before those f-f-fuckers f-f-finally came for me."

He finishes by scrabbling his grip up to my waist, causing his jacket sleeve to hitch back.

Revealing the scabbed-over gashes in his wrist.

Fucking. Shit.

I lock my teeth and curl my lips, readying to spit the same words, but the bastard blurts out, "You...you see now? I...I d-d-don't want firewalls or magic helmets or f-f-fixes." As he rummages his hand back to my wrist, I once again have to confront the black ink along his knuckles. Brandings he never asked for. A fate he never deserved. "I...I just want to be with Mitch again."

A love he knows only I will understand.

Because I do.

Because if it were me having to live with the memory of Emma falling to her death, could I stand to confront another sunrise or sunset?

If my plan to avenge her death wound up in becoming Faline Garand's remote-controlled hit man, would I want to take one more step? Even one more mortal breath?

The answer is an instant, unstoppable swell from the center of my being. It crashes me into a glass window of a destiny I do *not* fucking want—but now, in a moment in which all the chaos around us seems to stop, I can't ignore.

I slide my hands up, bracing them on either side of Kane's

neck. My fingers are wet and wobbly. My friend's proud features are blurry.

I inhale hard, steeling myself. Psyching myself.

"I'm sorry," I whisper.

"So am I," Kane rasps back.

"You?" Scowling puzzlement. "Why?"

With my padlock of a hold on him, his head shake is implied more than implemented. "Doesn't m-m-matter anymore. I'm done taking her orders. Th-thank fuck. It's...done. All...done..."

He drifts his eyes closed.

"*Now*, Bolt Man. Send me back to him now."

And then he smiles.

And I pray.

For his soul and for mine.

CHAPTER THREE

EMMA

Trixie, Chase, and I watch the LAPD helicopter carrying Reece approach the wide field behind the ridge.

The rotor wash slaps the wild grasses against our shins and knees, whipping the air into chaos that matches my mind. We lift our elbows to shield our faces from the swirling dust and pebbles, ideal stand-ins for the thousand-plus questions comprising a lot of that turmoil.

Funny how those questions build up when a girl has a few hours to do nothing but wait after her fiancé has survived a trip to a burning war zone and a confrontation with the soldier responsible for all of it.

Soldier. I still can't believe I'm aligning the word with Kane Alighieri. Though I first met him under violent circumstances—the night so many months ago when he helped Reece save me from the trap Faline had set with 'Dia and me as bait—I've since discovered the real person: the nerd who spent hours at the public library, knew every line of *Cats*, and deliberately held back when working out at Muscle Beach so he wouldn't make the other guys feel bad. But that *was* the guy I knew. As soon as Mitch took that fall and left this realm behind, part of Kane departed with him.

Clearly, a more significant part than any of us understood.

More than I could force my mind to admit to itself—even when I kissed Reece goodbye and sent him off to battle the man.

Not when I knew—*I knew*—there could be only one explanation for Kane, or whatever the hell he's become, to be preening like a talk show queen just minutes after destroying the city like an avenging king. Only one way he could have gone from being Team Bolt's Gentle Ben to LA's vengeful dragon.

Sawyer and Angie provided some theories of explanation as soon as they arrived back at the ridge three hours ago, having borrowed a truck from the city's Parks and Rec department. Wade, Alex, and Fershan confirmed Sawyer's original postulate could be possible. Kane's actions likely had been joysticked by higher forces inside the Consortium. But Angelique stood firm in her stance that Kane had been infected or bitten by something, noting his near-zombie glare and oblivion to all the chaos he'd caused.

The explanations were better than anything I'd come up with but were still far from the answers I needed. The only comparison I had to what the guy did to downtown was the state in which we'd found the Brocade's Presidential Suite after a speed metal band's Grammy celebration party. But like then, shuffling through the aftermath only means a lot of theories and not a lot of answers—with which Sawyer and Angie haven't exactly been helpful, aside from their insights, since returning *without* Reece.

Damn it, both of them stood and watched as I begged him not to leave me behind again. Both of them already *know* how agonizing it is for me to be waiting like a damn prairie wife on the homestead, watching the horizon for the light of her man. And God, how that last part is true. Reece Andrew Richards *is* my light—which makes it doubly unfair that I can't share that horizon with him. That I can't do anything but play the watching-and-waiting game...

Until I finally get to have moments like this.

Knowing he's near again.

Knowing he's *alive.*

However strangely that definition may play itself out.

However far I need to stretch the word *strangely.*

As the pilot sets the chopper down, Reece shoves open the door and jumps out. He trudges a few steps but stops, seeming to wonder where he is and what he's doing. His hands are ridged claws. His stance is braced as if his battle has only begun. His forehead, nearly the only part of his face I can fully see, is a topographical map of anguish.

Making me nearly dread the moment he exposes his full gaze again.

But never solidifying the purpose of my prairie porch more.

Past the whipping mane of his hair, even across the fifty feet still separating us, his grief pierces my heart like flying glass. I gasp from the impact right before a similar sound erupts from Trixie. I automatically reach for her, as much to rein her as comfort her. She longs to go to him. I get the maternal instinct and even understand it because of my own aching protectiveness for him—but there's a deeper instinct ordering me to stand back. A dictate twined with the spiritual strands of my bond to him. That intangible energy that blares a signal in my head as loud as it is clear.

"He needs space."

"Space?" she snaps at me. "Are you *looking* at him?"

I nod sorrowfully—as I comprehend exactly why he's

returned three hours after Sawyer and Angie. Grasping why the two of them held back on telling me everything that happened on the rooftop with Kane. If they had, I'd be heading into the third hour of my own agony instead of throwing sandbags on my shock to keep the flood from swallowing me whole.

"Yes," I tell Trixie. "I'm looking." *And I'm seeing.*

"But—"

I'm not the one who yanks her back this time. Quickly, I follow the hand that's encased her elbow, up a lean-muscled arm to Chase's determined face. "I'm hurting for him too, Mom. But we need to trust Emma." He dips his head toward me with the weight of respect. "She has the full window to Reece now."

No sooner has he said that then the chopper lifts up and away, leaving Reece standing in the field by himself. At once, he reels back by a few steps. He lifts his hands higher but then spins around as if needing to run from them—and does. As he breaks into a full sprint, his aching bellow shudders the air and echoes through the entire canyon. As energy explodes off his fingers, he disappears into the hills that are washed into the mix of late afternoon gold and early evening black. They welcome him with restless winds that crackle from the force of his speed.

He moves so fast, Trixie and Chase hardly realize the deafening *whomp* is Reece and not the departing helicopter.

"R-Reece?" Trixie stammers. "*Reece?* What on *earth*?"

She rushes forward, bending the tall grass back the other way, easily able to escape Chase, who's slowed by his own version of incredulity as he joins her in eyeballing the new dust cloud that billows close to the hills in the distance. A cloud that's laced by lightning in all-too-familiar shades of blue.

Trixie's gaze bulges. "Oh, dear heavens. What should we... *shouldn't* we..."

I wrap one of her hands with both of mine. As obvious as the action seems, I do it with torn feelings. I'll never be a mother in the biological sense, but it doesn't take emotional rocket science to relate to why Trixie's close to a basket case after everything that's happened in the last twelve hours. In the last twelve *months*. She's had to accept that one of her children was permanently mutated by mad scientists before another died in battle against those same psychopaths—all because of her husband of nearly thirty-five years. It hasn't felt right to ask if Lawson's death worsened or bettered her ordeal, but the way she's immersed herself in caring for Reece, Chase, Joany, and me, constantly flying between New York and here to do so, has struck us all as a viable therapy regime. Since we're all so grateful she hasn't chosen alcohol, sex, or boy toys as her therapy of choice, the four of us have formed a tacit agreement not to challenge her decisions.

Which makes me feel like a sizable shit right now.

Still, I state with quiet firmness, "He knows you're here for him." I include Chase in my regard too. "That *everyone* is. But he can't deal with bad days by just coming home and grabbing a hot shower and a cold beer."

Chase moans softly. "Which sounds like a damn good plan."

"Which you need to go *do*." I clarify it as encouragement and not commandment, with a tight but sincere smile. "Please." My addendum isn't so tactful, because my senses start to crackle again. Yanked from their moorings by Reece's furious, flaring beacon again. He's alone and adrift, grieving and angry—and right now, all that matters is just getting to him. "I'm...I'm sure he just needs to clear the mental cache and cookies," I add, squeezing Trixie's hand once more. I look down at our twined fingers, noting that Reece definitely got his long fingers from his maternal side.

"And she's his tech support." Chase is equally resolute about his message, calmly extricating his mother's hand from mine, seeming to sense my compulsion about hurrying to his brother's side. "So let her go and *be* that, Mom. Come on. I'm sure Joany's rustling something up for dinner."

For a second, Trixie still vacillates as if deciding between one muddy slope and another, her face crunched with conflict. "Tell him I'll make chocolate chip cookies for dessert," she finally urges to me. "His favorite. With the walnuts."

The breath she hitches between the sentences sends a little hook into my heart. All too clearly, I can imagine Reece as a boy, running into a huge kitchen in which Trixie is pulling out a tray filled with those cookies. That kitchen is inside a place called Richards Hall, where the woman probably had a staff numbering in double digits who could've baked those cookies—but she knew that the most valuable ingredient in fresh-baked cookies was, and always will be, a mother's love. It's a perfect reminder that no matter what state I'm about to find Reece in, he's a man beneath it all. The man I love, part of a family I'm growing to adore just as equally.

"Of course I'll tell him." It comes from the center of my soul, which flares again from the inescapable call of its mate. Reece's need is so intense, I have to fight the rage at my human limitations as I run-walk across the distance to him. Already knowing, despite no other guidance system but the ache in my chest, that I'm going the right way.

The pain worsens, meaning I'm either about to have heart

failure or I'm closing in on him. I don't dismiss the possibility of the former, since the journey into the depths of the canyon covers some seriously rocky terrain. But just when I'm getting ready to curse the unsteady ground, the prickly coastal shrubs, and the strengthening nighttime gusts, I let out a cry of gratitude.

And then awe.

And then alarm.

Gratitude because that wind now carries brilliant blue sparks, as if a cosmic torch welder is doing repair work just around the corner.

Awe because all those lights look dipped in a puddle of blue magma. I've never seen the blue so rich and vibrant and concentrated before.

And alarm—because I realize that where there's magma, there has to be a volcano.

A volcano with a god in its core.

Never have I truly been tempted to apply the label to him—and wonder, in every clamoring, chaotic corner of my being, if it might really be true. That all the ancient mythmakers and storytellers might have been on to something the modern world has dismissed as a cute story. An adventurous tale for fireside fantasies.

But no.

Zeus is real. And I'm engaged to him.

If he survives long enough to marry me.

At this moment, I'm not sure he remembers who I am. Who *he* is.

Though I've been summoned here by the call of his soul, I barely recognize the force of the fury he's spewing from his mind and heart—which spins around him like a gyroscopic firestorm, his bare-torsoed body serving as the hub for hundreds of electric lassos that snap and spark and hiss, lighting up the twilight as if it's high noon again. If sunlight were actually blue. And if everyone actually walked around in vortexes of their own anguish all the time.

Maybe that's why the gods chose to stay on Olympus.

Because speaking as the mortal in this equation, I don't know how much longer I can watch him do this. His face, contorted with self-loathing. His body, flinching from the searing self-floggings. But that's not even the worst of it.

What the hell is he doing to his hands?

What he *continues* to do, over and over again, driving them at full intensity into the canyon wall—a rock face that was probably striated with amber, brown, and bronze as little as an hour ago. Now, the stone drips with metallic red and brilliant blue, the same pigments covering Reece's knuckles, wrists, and forearms. He barely stops to stretch out his fists, but when he does, he glares at them like winter tree limbs weighted beneath a ruthless storm.

Only...the storm is *him*, and ruthlessness is just the start of his self-inflicted bloodletting.

As swiftly as he stops, he's back at boxing with the cliff. He snarls from the pain and slips in the dark-red puddle around his feet, letting the falling rocks cut into his naked back but refusing to let up by one degree. Denying himself even a shred of mercy. As if I need to have that thesis confirmed, he joins a savage grunt to every blow, adding a visceral version of his pain to the surreal glow on the air.

And the girl who just moaned about getting off the porch and taking action?

She does nothing but stare.

Damn it!

The last time I felt this helpless, Reece had just fried nearly every electron in his blood to rescue me from Faline and was crouched inside a New York apartment shower stall that had turned into a plasma storm. But this canyon isn't a shower stall, and he's doing a lot more than crouching and shivering. Yet, like then, he's aware that I'm here. And that his every pound impacts me too. Though it's not *my* blood pooling on the ground, it may as well be.

And that despite how he may be ordering himself to ignore me, his soul has called mine here for a reason.

A certainty that couldn't be better timed. Because as his next punch reverberates hard and deep into the rock, I fortify my resolve to stay.

Even as his blows cause a twelve-foot-high chunk of cliff to shear off.

I fall to my knees and shield my head as pebbles and dirt pelt around me. A stunned gasp gets me two lungs full of the same grit, and I cough in a fight to survive the blast.

And in that crazy dust fog, I recognize *another* significant change.

In New York, Kane had been there with one last atta-girl before I'd dared to step into the storm.

But one look up at Reece's profile, every virulent angle defined by grit and dust and stubble, and I now know the truth behind what my gut's only suspected to this point.

There won't be any more encouragements from Kane again.

We've really lost him.

The whole world has.

The reality gouges me as deeply as the next punch Reece

takes to the cliff. Then the next. The next. *The next.* More sickening fist cracks. More of his primal growls, escalating into brutal, mournful barks. I force myself to watch despite the stinging tears and wet soot clouding my eyes and new spike every one of his blows hurls into my stomach. But I don't know how much more I can take. This is more than grief. A further cry than just *avoiding* his tears.

"Shit." I gain my feet like rockets have fired beneath me— and if dread can also be rocket fuel, maybe they have. "Reece!" But my voice is the opposite, scratchy and shaky. A girl can't be blamed after jog-hiking the distance of a few football fields and then finding her fiancé picking a fight with the side of a cliff while wrapped in a scary-as-hell electric vortex.

"Reece!" I edge as close as I can to the outskirts of the sizzling wheels of light, fighting fear as their velocity blows my hair back and yanks on the fine hairs of my arms. "Please!" I yell out. "Baby, it's me. You know it is. If you can hear me"— *holy crap, please hear me*—"you've got to stop!"

The gyroscope falters.

His sweat-slickened chest rises and falls on a hesitant breath.

"Oh, thank God." I allow myself a full breath too.

He pulls his next punch.

Yes. Yes!

But lands the next one twice as hard.

"Gaaaahhh!" It's the expression I usually save for snark or shock, neither of which apply right now, but typical profanity isn't enough for the fear and frustration as he knocks new rocks loose. They're the size of bowling balls, splashing into the puddles of his charged blood and detonating like geological mortar bombs.

I dive back down, dropping my head against my knees and clutching my hands around my neck, but not before desperately screaming his name again. Not that it makes a damn difference. Not against the lightning of his electric armor, the thunder of the cascading rocks, and the gale of his fury, swirling and growing on the air like a living creature.

Until suddenly dying into silence.

But not exactly silence.

Now, I can just hear other things better. The ringing in my ears, like Notre-Dame's belfry on Christmas. The disorientation of my mind, like bats cavorting around that belfry. The thrum of my heartbeat as I slowly inch my head up and my sightlines are filled with something besides the sky and the trees and the hills.

Something a thousand times more beautiful.

My Reece, the most perfect creation God has put on this planet for me, still standing there.

But only for one moment longer, until he lets his arms drop again.

Their weight becomes his burden, pulling him all the way to his hands and knees, making the mud slurp and sizzle around him at the same time.

The vortex wavers again.

Then completely fizzles out.

He's motionless. So am I. And feeling a thousand kinds of awful about my paralysis, because it has nothing to do with dread anymore but everything to do with a slam of pure awe.

"Ohhhh, God." The sound spills out of me with a strange mix of reverence and remorse. How can I be this transfixed by his terrible, dirty glory? By the otherworldly blue veins glowing across the clenched muscles of his arms? By the mesmerizing disappearance of them beneath the mounds of mud covering his hands, only to reemerge and fan along the ground as his electrons find the tributaries of blood in the sludge.

Never has his power stunned me more.

Never has his desolation joined it—and sucked all the air from me.

But never have I felt more abysmally ill-prepared to help him.

Crawling to him means I'll have to navigate through all those skeins of electrical thread. But staying right here means he'll keep glowering as if I'm a complete stranger. That he'll keep rolling his head and adding his stare to the lightning tracks in the mud, as if he's become a stranger to *himself*.

I hold my breath. And start to slog forward.

And whisper, with every filament of patience and passion in my heart, "Reece. It's *me*."

Still realizing he could choose to supercharge this muck any second—immobilizing if not killing me—but praying he won't.

And somehow, in that deep part of my soul where truths like "the sky is blue" and "nobody buys less than fifteen things at Target" live, *knowing* he won't.

Even though the man still glowers as if he doesn't know me or *want* to know me, I inch closer to him. Not letting my gaze leave him. Showing him, every time I shift nearer, I've refused to give up on him. Not now. Not ever.

Even when his face twists as if I've brought a knife and suddenly used it on him.

Even when he snarls as if tempted to yank the blade out, figuratively or not, and use it on *me*.

I stop—but only to raise a hand, palm out. "Stop," I rasp.

"Just *stop it,* mister. You're not in your damn tower at the Brocade anymore."

I lower my hand, cupping it atop one of his knees, affirming that I used the noun on purpose. It's a throwback to the first days of our intense mutual attraction—and the special language of our souls, fusing us just as strongly now. Back then, he was just my hotter-than-sin boss who saw every reason we connected and I was the anxious new girl looking for every excuse we couldn't. But in the end, he bashed down every wall of my resistance. He showed me that the guy in the tower didn't want to live in the clouds by himself anymore. I succumbed to his love, expecting to be dragged back to the tower, only he did something much better. Built a new one. For me. For *us.*

Which is exactly what *I'll* do for him right now, if that's what it'll take to get through to him. To penetrate the agony racking his body and claiming every inch of his beautiful, noble face...

"It's just me, Reece. It's just us, okay? You and me, baby. Remember that? Remember *this*?" I fight to keep the tears from my throat, but they undermine me anyway. "Baby, listen to me. I'm here. You're *not* alone."

I'm cut off by a growl so deep and dark, it takes a long moment to register it's really emerged from him.

"Maybe I should be."

He casts a shadowed glare around at the dirt and destruction.

"Yeah." His volume is just a rasp, but his tone is defined. "Maybe that's exactly what needs to be happening here." With a grunt, he slides backward. "Maybe alone is just fucking perfect."

"Guess what?" I dip my head to emphasize my direct

seethe. "Life doesn't always give you perfect, buddy."

Spokes of lightning ignite in his eyes just before he snarls, almost as if in warning, "Emma..."

"I'm not leaving." I push up to a high kneel, flicking my fingertips to rid them of bloody mud despite how the stuff still sends mini jolts through my skin. "And you'd better not even try to make me, Mr. Richards."

"*Emma.*"

"I'm. Not. Leaving."

"God*damn*it, woman." He copies my pose but goes full-scale Bolt with his posture. As he stretches his fingers toward the ground, blue lights dazzle and dance out from the elegant tips. As he straightens his torso, at least an inch of new breadth coils across his shoulders.

"You really trying intimidation now?" I counter his muscly Rasputin with my personal Maleficent, baring my teeth but smiling my challenge. "What, because you think it'll *work* on me? Well, here's another piece of news, mister. If you want a little bunny to frighten, I can show you a whole canyon of them."

"Fuck." His stance doesn't change, and his voice plunges into a dark grate. But his glare keeps intensifying toward the opposite, his eyes turning into brilliant silver storms. Twilight settles deeper into the hills around us, enriching the pigments of the shadows until they're lush shades of purple and green and gray, providing a starker contrast for this man's pulsating fingertips and electric irises. He exposes both without shame, obviously clinging to a last hope of daunting me with his mutant light show.

Until he finally seems to remember what that glow really does to me.

Or perhaps...as he realizes what I do to him in return.

What we do to each other now, surging toward each other through the mud on our knees. How the force of our attraction magnetizes us together, the spark of our passion turning to full flames as we collide, discovering each other all over again with heated fingers, meshing kisses, guttural groans...empowered passion.

He slides his hands along my sides, down my hips, around the curves of my ass. I run my fingertips from the center of his sternum to the top of his waistband. Then lower. *Lower.*

Yes.

Oh.

Him.

His glory and girth and pulsation. His size and heat and sensation.

His mesmerizing, hypnotizing force as he gulps deeply. "Holy God."

My shivering delight as I smile softly. "You rang?"

A moan erupts from someplace low and sinful in his throat. His flesh swells and throbs beneath my fingers. He's huge and hot, even beneath the tight black leather. I sigh in throaty triumph, but it becomes a yelp as soon as he grabs my wrist, yanking me away. Shame—or maybe not—that the guy mistakes my surprise as surrender. The second he slackens the hold, I move in even closer, cupping him with twice the determination.

He amps the groan into a full grunt. Ends it by kissing me again, briefly but brutally, before spitting out, "Ignorant, stubborn woman."

At once, I retaliate. "Ridiculous, senseless man." And barely refrain from grinning again as his balls vibrate under my fingertips. If he wants to play adjectives-only Scrabble, I'm so in. I have a list ready to go. *Obstinate. Audacious. Courageous. Luminous. Brave. Beautiful. Prideful.*

Yes, even with every single one of those words. With every damn moment of his chaos. With every crazy, complicated piece of baggage he brings to this life of ours—bringing me back to the sole term that fits it all the very best.

Perfect.

Yes, even now.

Even with my knees sunk in the mud and my senses filled with his despair—and my head being yanked back as he twists a hand into my hair and then smashes his face against my neck, unfurling a moan of such dark torment, it takes over every inch of my skin like a cloud of black smoke from a *Call of Duty* plot.

Like a doomed warrior from one of those battlefields, he snarls into my nape, "Not a man. *Not a man*, damn it. *A killer.*"

A new wind gusts through the night, still threaded with the warmth of the day, though I'm chilled to the bone. "Oh, God," I whisper as compassion rushes in and jerks my hands around his head instead. I haul him harder to me, gulping against tears despite how I thought I was ready for this. How I braced myself from those moments I watched, along with the rest of the world, as Reece hunched over Kane's prone form on that skyscraper roof. While everyone else, including his family, saw a man confronting the nemesis he'd once called friend, I saw different things. The defined tension along the ridge of his back. The way he cradled yet subdued Kane at the same time. But most of all, how he finally threw his head back with such sorrow and fury and loss—but more. With pain so virulent, it was like he poured salt into his own wound.

And now I know exactly why.

I know, without him having to say more. But I clutch him tighter, letting him know it's all right if he needs to get those words out. Ensuring him that I'm agonizing right along with him, grieving the loss. Remembering a friend who was always as calm as the moon on the outside but burned like Mars on the inside; a soul as deep as the galaxies but as strong as the sun; a gladiator who's become the latest victim of the Consortium's evil. No matter how it went down or what he did before it happened, I know that. I *believe* it. Kane would never have wrought all that destruction and hurt all those people for his own jollies.

Which was why he couldn't bear existing in this realm anymore.

A fact the man in my arms still can't seem to comprehend.

"No." Though my tone is gentle, I demand his attention by twisting at his hair. With his damp, thick strands filling my grip, I dictate, "Damn it, *no*, Reece. You're not a killer." Then burrow my lips against the strained cords of his neck, kissing him fervently between my rasped rebukes. "He wanted to leave...didn't he? And you just helped him do it. If he'd stayed, he would have been Faline's trick pony. He would've been deeper under her control. Probably forced to do even worse things than—"

His rough groan cuts me short as he hunches in lower. Then seizes me tighter. Then makes the muck around us slurp as his chest pumps viciously against mine and his throat convulses around taut, animalistic sounds of suffering. "I hate her," he finally croaks. "I hate her for what she did to him. What she made him." The virulence of his words is matched by the barely reined savagery through his body. He's a huge, heaving oak tree next to me—and more and more, around me.

"For what she's made *me*."

"I know." I spurt it past the moisture of *my* tears, unstoppable now, while sliding my hands down to the center of his chest. It's a symbol of where I yearn to touch him the deepest, aiming for the core of pain under his rage and desolation. "But you did what you did because of *love*. Because you knew he was suffering. You needed to help him. You wouldn't have given yourself any other choice."

He responds with a low, terrible moan, fully communicating the harsh clash in his soul. I don't move my hold, needing him to know I understand. How I feel him longing to believe me yet struggling to accept what's happened. That he used the strength of his existence to cut short another's. A *friend's*. That he needs to figure out how to go on from here...

I feel it all. I accept it all.

As an aching sigh takes over, I blink against heavier tears—blending with the dark but dry eruptions erupting from deep inside him, as if whole cliffs of his soul have been sheared away by blowtorch.

"It's all right, my love," I desperately whisper. "It's all right. *You're* all right."

Okay, maybe not *right*. Not yet.

And he'll sure as hell never be the same.

Today will change him forever. And, in some ways, will change us too.

Changed—but not destroyed.

Different—but not decimated.

I refuse to accept any other truth. And I refuse to let him, either.

"*Reece*. My beautiful man." I twist my head while pulling his down, wetting down his forehead as I attempt to press the adoration right into his brain. "My beautiful, incredible man. My astounding, amazing hero."

For a long moment, he's motionless—until he starts rolling his head in a grieving perversion of a full denial. "Not a hero," he growls, working his hands up until he grabs me by my upper arms as if to push me away before coming to a trembling stop. And yet tangible energy still crackles through him, like embers burning beneath the bark of a campfire log. "I'm *nobody's* goddamned hero."

I slide a hand up to the side of his face. Roll my thumb to the edge of his gaze, which is the color of the ash from that smoldering log. And surrender to another long sigh as I pour as much comfort and tenderness and devotion as I can into him. It's not difficult. I have loved this man beyond any reason or limit since the night we met, and he's taken my breath away through every exhilarating, kick-ass moment of the last year, but he's never been more unspeakably beautiful to me than now.

In his defeat.

In his conflict.

In his need.

In the choice he's making to show them all to me.

In choosing to expose all mine as well.

I keep my head lifted, letting him see my fresh tears—the ones I truly shed in hope instead of heartache. I frame the tense, rugged edges of his face with my pressing, marveling touch...

Before pulling him down and kissing him with the full, tender force of my adoration.

"Okay," I whisper when we pull apart after an all-too-short minute. "That's okay, baby. No more heroes tonight." I trace the words along the line of his jaw. I stop my lips in the indent between his face and ear and rasp, "I don't need my hero right now. But I do need my man. My lover."

It's no ploy. It's my complete truth. Even as he responds with a vehement snarl, my necessity is sealed and confirmed—and I'm ready to do whatever it takes to bring out the man who owns every fiber of my heart, consumes every corner of my soul...and calls to every awakened pore in my body.

Because of that, I welcome every note of his ferocious sound, even as he repeats it. I treasure his sizzling, mesmerizing sparks. Crave even more of his searing, penetrating fire.

The flames I need to stoke higher.

And do now, with steady but silken coaxing.

"Just be my lover, Mr. Richards." I purposely emphasize the formal address, letting my body soften and surrender as he intensifies his hold around me. I focus on offering everything to him, just as I did the last time I saw this much intense conflict in him. It's been nearly a year since then. The night we first met. In the scant hours before we fully acknowledged our inescapable, electric desire, he was exactly like this: filled with hesitation, trepidation, and fear. Of course, he'd also been certain he was about to kill me—a factor I didn't learn about until weeks later—but that doesn't make me blind to how he longs to deny everything he's come to feel. He's overwhelmed by it. Terrified by it.

No.

Not terrified.

Worse.

Every minute, every hour, and every day of the last year, the two of us have fallen into richer, deeper love with each other.

But after what love has cost him today...

"No heroes." Though I've figured out exactly why he doesn't want to hear the "h" word ever again, I repeat the banishment because I need it too. At the same time, I wrap my hands into his dark, lustrous hair—needing that too. With the beautiful strands in my grip, I reassure him in a throaty husk, "It's just us, Reece. Just this."

At once, a gruff sound emerges from the base of his throat. "Just this?" he retorts. "Fuck." As if the word is his personal Burst button, he grabs me even harder, one hand around my ass and the other against my spine, locking all of our body parts from thighs to necks. There's not a single breath between us now—and I can't think of anything more complete or right. "You'll never be just this for me, Emmalina. You'll never be just anything for me. You're always, always my everything. My reason. My more."

All right, nothing more complete except for words like that.

"You know what it felt like up on that roof today, knowing that in so many ways, Faline had won? Knowing that I could have ripped that victory out of her hands by throwing myself to the street below?" His stare intensifies, turning the color of braided steel cables. "You want to know how fucking tempted I was to just do it—and then why I eventually didn't? Why every cell of my body felt like a lead brick as I got back on the police chopper but still ordered myself to do it anyway?" His lips part, revealing his gritted teeth. His nostrils flare, underlining his fierce torment. "Because you're not just this."

In one breathtaking sweep, I realize I'm even more wrong than before.

Because he's never been more right.

Or made me want to lunge at him with more passion, losing myself to the dizzying fall of loving him more than I ever thought I would. Then kissing him with the open urgency to prove it. Then letting him pour his long, furious moan into me in return. And tangling my high, hurting sigh with the sound. And gripping him with all the frantic fever as he does me, until our passion is nearly a wild war of wills, except that we've both already gotten the ultimate prize.

The reward of each other.

The treasure of us.

The magic of this.

Oh...this.

Oh...him.

The vigor of his lunging, sweeping mouth. The power of his towering, straining body. The strokes of his huge, possessive hands and the rolls of his muscled, mesmerizing hips. In record time, my blood is singing, my sex is throbbing, and my senses are screaming. I'm beyond the point of need, past caring what the hell he's calling himself or me or anything else tonight. Hero? Savior? Man? Lover? It's all true and yet none of it is, because right now he's only my desire, my heat, my hunger.

Only?

No.

He's more. He always will be.

"Don't stop." I rush out the plea while seizing his scalp harder, hating even the shallow heaves of breath between us. "Don't stop." I slide his forehead down against mine. "Kiss me. Touch me. Everywhere."

His face contorts once more, but this time, I feel every drop of the desire that motivates the expression searing away the remaining condensation of his conflict. He emphasizes the point with a pure caveman rumble, resettling his hands around the spheres of my ass. I match his sound with a primeval purr, spreading my legs to mold tighter against him, exulting in how he splays his sinfully long fingers around every inch of my clenching backside.

It's all so incredible.

Because it's all filled with him.

Every touch, every breath, every moment, every sense. Joined with him. Getting through this with him. Helping him through it too.

Surviving the storm. Facing the fallout. Healing the damage.

Together.

As it's meant to be.

As it always will be.

"Yesssss." I press the hiss up from the depths of my throat, which he's started to attack with husky tugs of his teeth and savoring suckles of his lips. Between both, there's the magic that has his bunny turning into a writhing, lusty snake. He intensifies my serpent side with the twirling, tantalizing treatment of his wicked tongue...and then the sublime command of his hands as he starts rocking my aching core up and down his hot, beautiful bulge...

"Oh, yes! Oh, Reece!"

He snarls as his erection pulses. As if his penis knows how desperately my pussy yearns for him too. As if he knows I may soon be well past the point of yearning, he hauls my legs around his waist, stands, and starts trudging through the mud.

"Shit!" It bursts out between my stunned gasps as soon as he slams me against the side of the cliff. At once, he braces his legs so I can descend completely over him.

Yearning is officially the old trend now.

New trend?

Desperate would be a damn good one. Critical, another good one. Or maybe more direct descriptors are a better fit here. Like soaked. Hot. Quivering. Aching. Burning.

"R-Reece!" And after all the mental prep, that's all I can utter? But can I be held to more as he makes short work of my workout jacket's zipper—thank God I changed into the gear as soon as he was choppered away this morning—and then shoves a hand inside, greedily making his way for the cups of my exercise bra? Nobody would blame me if they watched how he peels down the scoop neck so forcefully, he's just turned my boring gym wear into an erotic push-up look.

"Damn," he rumbles. My mind echoes with the same, though on the outside, all I manage are breaths the texture of static and sighs the strength of the thinning mud at our feet. The dirt he embeds with his deep boot prints while planting his feet wide, supporting my weight solely with his thighs, which frees up his other hand...

"Reece!"

To ensure he gives both my nipples those commanding pulls...

"Ahhhh!"

And then his consuming bites...

"Damn. Damn!"

But at once licking away the brief pain, transforming it into zinging pleasure. Liquid heat that swirls down into my most secret center...

"Ohhhh, shit!"

Before I'm wordless and breathless and at last able to drop my gaze—onto the iridescent blue X's he's licked into existence across my breasts.

"Oh, dear hell."

At the center of the crosses, my nipples are buttons of aroused crimson, still pulsing with need for more of his amplified dominion. The marks aren't like other scratches or abrasions he's given me before. The X's are deliberate sensual penmanship, a blatant claim.

I'm a little unnerved.

But a lot more aroused.

Though not nearly as much as he is.

I'm positive of it from the second he looks back up, raising his unblinking scrutiny from my breasts back to my face. And yes, there are still miles of dark mists in those intense gray depths, but for a second, I spot distinct flares of blue and silver too. Flashes that last long enough to reflect on the clouds of his soul...and slowly, steadily, start reminding him of himself. I watch, enraptured, as he visibly claims that knowledge. Who he really is. What he truly can be. Not just his darkness but so much of his spectacular light—the light he can only claim by embracing the fusion in his blood, powering every beat of his desire and throb of his need.

Oh, thank God for his need.

And ohhhh yes, do I watch that come back online too.

Thickening the mists in his eyes into smoke and transforming the breaths on his lips into rasps of pure seduction. "Tell me again, Velvet," he dictates in that new, sultry voice, matching the tone to how he keeps swiping the pads of his thumbs across my tingling nipples. "Tell me... exactly what you want." He bites out the final consonant while plucking harder on my swollen tips.

"Oh!" And of course, he's made it impossible to think of

anything except the new fire he's unfurled through my nerves—
and into my pussy. And unthinkable to accept those shocks
with anything but high gasps and melting desire. "Ohhhh,
God..."

What he does to me. How he knows me. Working my
flesh and fantasies like a master sculptor and his clay. Already
seeing where I need to be pressed, carved, and brought to
life. "That's not the answer." And using master's chisels like
his sure, sensual voice and his audacious, tenacious touch.
Flattening his hands to more fully massage the flesh beneath
those X's, decadent and determined about his intent. "Tell me,
Emmalina."

I open my mouth. My clutched throat isn't cooperating. I
suck down a deep breath. And then try yet again. "I...I want you
to touch me." But I'm back to practically needing a respirator,
grabbing air in desperate spurts between my gasped entreaty.
"Please. Touch me...everywhere. Yessssss."

I've been reduced to a state of surrender, plain and simple.
What other choice do I have as he kisses me along my jaw,
bringing me waves of sparkling pleasure? How do I resist the
abject awe of watching him touch me, torque me, seduce me?
And how can I do anything but gulp as he releases me, but only
because he's sinking to his knees before me—stripping away
everything north of my navel as he goes?

"Everywhere?" he echoes back, brushing my lower
abdomen with his lips while tugging at the waistline of my
workout capris. "You want me to touch absolutely everything?"

I give in to an enchanted smile on top of my raging lust. I
have to admit, it's pure entertainment to watch him struggling
to get my skintight leggings off without using a single finger
laser. His soft but frustrated grunts are adorable—and

enticing. I sort of like him a little frustrated. Okay, I like it a lot. Imbalance and flux are a pair of incredible aphrodisiacs—I should know, because the man is a master at constantly using them on me—but watching him struggle with them, and knowing it's because of me, is a turn-on that awakens my arousal in primal, deep-jungle ways.

Me Jane...want you Tarzan...

As soon as the craving growls through my head, a matching sound unfurls from his throat. His gaze widens as if he really is a wild man newly sprung from the rainforest. Has he just read my psyche that clearly, or are we simply meant to be linked like this for always?

Suddenly, his whole expression flares—stopping my heart and robbing my breath. Clearly, the same question has occurred to him too.

Just before we're both hit by the same answer.

Meant to be.

It makes no sense at all but all the sense in the world. And it reverberates in every sizzle of energy between us...every drop of truth in the charged exchange of our stares.

It's a truth he speaks perfectly to, dragging me back down into the earth with him. That resounds through his potent snarl as he slides an arm under my knees, compelling me to fall back into the cradle of his other arm. That makes me shiver and tremble and clench as he rakes his bright, intense stare across the nudity he slowly uncovers, finally getting the last of my capris free. That sends a perfect thrill through me as he simply holds my naked form for an extended, exquisite moment.

That pulls out my high, aching sigh...as he covers my bare, tremoring form with his powerfully leathered one.

It's surreal.

It's primordial.

It's dark and dirty, mortal and cold...but tender and urgent and honest and passionate.

It's paradise.

And I tell him so by grabbing his head with both hands and yanking him down until our lips mash together. Not letting him go even as our teeth knock and our breaths vanish. Molding his lips over mine so he has no choice but to lunge into me, sliding and swirling his hot, beautiful tongue with mine. Forcing the lightning collisions in his chest to collide with the wild thunder of mine, where the storm of my lust pounds and thrashes and needs...

And needs...

And needs...

He shows me his own urgency by shifting his hips over mine and shoving his knees to spread my own, making more room for his throbbing crotch against my clenching pussy. By flowing his hands along my shoulders, down the sides of my ribcage, over the flare of my hips, and then out along the most sensitive parts of my thighs, until he's swirling circles around the caps of my curled knees. Yes, because he knows even all the spots in my damn knees that make me hotter and hornier. Because he knows what to do to me...

"Everywhere." And he's doing it again—speaking the exact thought in my head before I'm done with it, and in a delicious, determined murmur he uses to tickle the inside of my left kneecap. As I shudder from that heat, he adds a silken kiss to the spot. "I want to be everywhere, baby." He reiterates the promise while giving the same languorous treatment to my right knee, not waiting for my shivers to abate before gliding

ANGEL PAYNE

his hands back the way they came, retracing my inner thighs
until he's flirting his fingertips along the edges of my spread,
quivering sex.

I gasp.

He growls.

He captures my stare with his, the glints in his grays
a perfect match for the emerging stars overhead, and then
entrances me with more of his hypnotizing touch, tracing
knowing circles along my labia before gliding inward...

To the places where I'm softest.

To the places where he opens unseen parts of me. Where
he awakens brilliant vistas in me. Where he penetrates until
I'm shaking and writhing and sighing and out of my mind with
yearning for him. Craving more and more of him...

"Everywhere." My turn to say it, though I'm shameless
about bypassing his poeticism and going right for a lusty plea.
And judging by the erotic hunger across his face, that's exactly
where the man wants me. He confirms that truth with the
probing persistence of his fingers, a force of three digits now,
and he's shifted one hand to my hipbone in order to brace me
harder and invade me by thrusting those digits deeper.

"Yes!" I arch into him, receiving all of it—and yet still
reaching for more.

"Mmmm." His insolent rumble takes over his whole
chest, taunting perfect tingles at my erect breasts. "Someone
likes me inside her."

"If that someone is me, then you're right." I shoot for a
seductive drawl, but desire turns my voice to impatience. In a
rush, I claw my hands into the base of his neck. Matching my
ferocity with a sabretooth rumble, he pulls them back down,
forming my fingers around the black zipper at the neckline of
his jacket.

"Everywhere?" The sabretooth keeps prowling his voice, still in maddening control, even as I pull down and release the steel zipper teeth from their traps. But by the time I've finished snicking the zipper free, rougher breaths conquer his lungs and his nipples are as hard as styluses.

I reach up, fascinated with their erect glory. "Yes," I whisper. "Everywhere."

He groans like a torture victim holding back way too long on a scream. And maybe, after today, that's exactly how he feels. But chunk by chunk, he's coming back to me, and if I leave this canyon walking a little funny...well, everyone has to sacrifice for the cause in some way...

"Everywhere." The renewed quicksilver in his stare shows that he hasn't ruled out that possibility either—especially as he breaches my channel with a fourth finger and starts thrusting relentlessly. As I answer him with pumping gasps and a sprinting pulse, he growls with such primeval satisfaction that nearby critters scatter, already acknowledging the force we're building, the brilliant pinnacle to which we're reaching.

Beautiful.

It's already so damn beautiful.

He's already so...

"Beautiful." I all but sob it as he rears up, his magnificent form outlined by starlight and moonglow, and rips the snaps of his leathers loose—fully freeing his cock. Without wasting another second, he lowers the pants even farther, releasing his balls too.

In all their engorged, glowing glory.

"Fuck." It's more a glug from his throat than an utterance on his lips, not surprising since he's sucking in breaths as fast and urgently as me. His chest, carved and glorious, pumps in and out from the force of them. His thighs, muscular and massive, flex and roll in time to them.

"Oh, dear hell." My declaration isn't exactly sweet and gentle either. I reach up with just as much passion, going straight for his proverbial jugular—in the form of palming his mesmerizing length. The moment I wrap my grip around him, he swells even bigger and his veins flare even brighter. "You're perfect, Reece."

To my shock, he grimaces. "You're just saying that because you have a kinky thing for Smurfs, Miss Crist."

"I'm saying that because it's true." I stroke every inch of him, glorying in the heat and energy of him. "But you really are my favorite Smurf."

The line tempts him into at least half a smile, which only makes my heart trip all over itself again. He thinks I'm joking, but I've never been more serious—though I could compose entire sonnets that wouldn't do justice to the man's sheer physical beauty, especially the magnificence of what he possesses between his thighs. Even without the electro-biology, he's a creation the angels must have been sobbing to give to humanity. I silently thank them while squeezing, kneading, and savoring the sculpted girth in my hold, unable to stop myself...needing to connect to him like this.

No heroes tonight.

Just us.

Just this.

More than ever, he just needs to let me do this for him.

"Shit." And though he does, he grits his jaw hard enough to rival the cliffs around us for rugged beauty. Its brutal strength is outlined in flashes of blue that sneak into the space between us as I continue working him from balls to crown and back again. Up and down, up and down, I massage him without shame, alternating with twists of both hands, soon chomping the inside of my lip as his tip spurts with the glowing cream that helps with heated lubrication—and my growing fascination.

"So perfect." I'm on the verge of sounding trite at this point, but it's the only word that fits—before I'm incapable of words at all.

No. Words.

It happens right after I wick a couple of the luminous blue drops off the tip of his cock and then trace them over the X centered on my left nipple. At once, my breast becomes nothing but astounding fire, searing arousal, and consuming lightning. It sharpens my nipple into a white-hot point and shoots sizzling spikes of heat throughout my whole chest.

Oh, my God.

I've never experienced anything like this.

With eager speed, I repeat the action for my right swell. I gasp and then groan. It feels even better with both breasts. So damn good...

Almost too good.

My chest now feels like an erotic power grid, circuits crisscrossing and colliding with heat and arousal, to the point that I can't feel air entering and exiting my lungs.

Am I still alive? Do I want to be?

"Em?" Reece's voice registers, though it's broken up by all the static in my senses, as if there's a crappy radio connection separating us. "Emmalina? Fuck!"

That comes through clearer. Not the words—but the panic behind them. His panic. Why?

Okay. I'm alive, then—but shifting into a strange version of the meaning. My head is swimming. My heart is hammering.

There's pressure on me—so much pressure. Who shoveled all the boulders onto me?

"Jesus God, baby. What the hell have you done?"

His growl sounds far away, registering through a mist of consciousness. I answer by lifting a weird smile. I know his question is lethally serious, but I can't give him a coherent answer. The words echo through me in my own voice but with different emphasis—what the hell have you done?—as I peer down at my chest and my hands massaging the liquid electricity all over my breasts. I moan again. The sound spins through my senses. The marks of his milk across my flesh... It's like gazing at magic come to life, and I'm covered in its hot, bright sorcery.

But how is it taking me over from the inside too?

Everywhere.

His power penetrates in places it's never been before. It scrapes at my bones. Squeezes my blood vessels. Bites at the organs that give me blood and life, patiently waiting to stab all the way inside.

That's when understanding washes in.

My breast ducts.

Which must have carried the electricity in and spread it through me that fast.

Well, hell.

But even trying to grasp that whole realization is like trying to locate the sun through smoke. Still, I look up through the heat storm, knowing it'll be there. Knowing he'll be there. My sun. My heat.

My everything.

"Emmalina!"

My killer?

Ironically, possibly...yes.

But as soon as the thought beats in, even past my wheezing lungs and thundering heart, so does its contradiction.

Definitely, imperatively, no.

Only it's damn clear, as soon as I behold the horrified lightning in his eyes, that only one of us believes that.

He's still lost to the dread of accusing, trying, and convicting himself for my murder. Because apparently, reasoning out everything that happened with Kane wasn't enough for hashing out that neurosis.

Ridiculous, senseless man.

Doesn't he see the obvious yet? That we were a tag team getting me into this mess. That we obeyed the screams of our lust and listened to the magic of our connection, not the cores of our logic.

But more critically, not recognizing that logic is the perfect way back out of this bullshit.

"Fuck!" He's bellowing again. And again. And again. The repetitions have quickened, keeping time with my strangled strains for breath, while he's completely stopped seeing the pleading in my eyes and the cries of my mind. He's picked now to turn off that crazy ability to read everything I'm thinking? Seriously? "Fuck, fuck, fuck, fuck! Emma. Oh dear fuck. Emma. Not you too." His violent movement, twisting his entire upper body, is discernible despite my fuzzed-out vision. And then how he sharply whips his face toward the stars too. "Not her too, damn it! Haven't you taken enough from me today?"

"Reece." Incredibly, perhaps only because of the fate of the stars that brought us together, I'm able to scrape my hand up to his forearm and then stab my nails in deep enough to jolt his attention. "Damn it, l-l-listen. I"—have to take a second and gulp for air—"I'm g-g-going to—"

"No!" he spits. "You're not going to die, goddamnit!"

Again through the interference of providence, I smile. Or maybe I just think I do. No matter what, something like humor floods through me. "G-Glad we're both on...the s-s-same page."

He stops. Stares hard. Damn it. No man should look this hot with dread wrenching his face and tears shimmering in his eyes. "What the hell are you—"

"I am going to die, baby...unless you sh-sh-shut up and listen. And then st-st-stop and th-th-think."

He exhales hard. Gawks at me even harder. "Think about what?"

"A-A-About how you need to h-h-help me."

He grinds so hard for air, I wonder if both his lungs have been stabbed by rogue electricity too. He rears up but only by a few inches, looking tormented about even that distance. "How?" he demands. "How, Velvet?" As his voice cracks, so does my hammering, failing heart. "Tell me what you need. Tell me! I'll pull out my own fucking heart if you can take it and use it. My lungs. My air..."

His anguish is what my fortitude needs. And my determination. "N-N-Not your heart or your lungs, baby."

"Then what?" he grates out. "How?"

My hand is still on his arm, my fingers digging in next to his wrist. Still, my teeth grit and my face twists as I focus on lowering my hold...

Directly between his thighs again.

"You...you know how."

Guided by my raw desperation to live and my utter certainty that this man is the way to that life, I work my grip along his entire length—relief drenching me as his flesh pulses and grows for me. Comes back to life for me...

"You kn-know what I need, Mr. R-R-Richards." As I grip him tighter, I look up to lock his gaze with mine. "You kn-know what elixir I can drink to be whole. You kn-know what you need t-t-to do...to be my hero now."

CHAPTER FOUR

REECE

She's got to be fucking kidding.

Or totally insane.

Or completely right?

The rebuke isn't coming from the rage in my heart or the sorrow in my soul. It's a dictate from my head, backed by the surety of my sharpest instincts. Yeah, the ones I've honed on missions throughout the last year, engaging the shitheads in the worst parts of town.

Only this time, I'm the goddamned criminal—being given a path to redemption by the one angel who should have no mercy for my soul.

Even crazier? She wants to bring me that redemption with my cock in her mouth.

Even more ludicrous? I actually see the wisdom of her plan.

I want to deck myself for even thinking it—of course you "see" that wisdom, you foul dickbrain—but even if the plan included me getting grinded from head to balls in a meat processor, I'd be just as willingly joining my fingers to hers, preparing myself for the ordeal. I'd be clenching my teeth just as tightly, fighting to ignore the strain of her skin and the struggle of her breathing, to keep myself erect. I'd be breathing just as hard and fast to keep as much of my essence inside, to give as much of myself to becoming her life force again.

To saving her life with my life...

"Lie back, Emmalina." I hate my chilled tone, and her little shiver proves she's not a fan either, but if I'm to get through this without second-guessing my every move, it's necessary. Time isn't a luxury right now. Getting inside her is.

As soon as she's flat in the dirt again, I scoot up her body until my balls graze her chin. Christ, she's so pale. How the hell am I going to do this to her? Why is she going to let me?

"Open your mouth."

Jesus fuck. Just like this.

"Wider, baby. More. Take more of me."

She's so tight. So wet. So perfect. Even more so as she expands the back of her throat to get even more of me in, until I'm hissing with a mix of torment and heat and pressure and pain. I buck my hips as my soul sobs.

And my heart prays.

Holy God, if you have never heard any of this sinner's prayers before, please hear this one. Let her live. If you have to take every drop of my life to do it, then fucking do it.

Let. Her. Live.

I'm so deep now. She's meeting the sizzling fire of my head with her eager mewls, though the rest of her body is inert and frail beneath me—an acknowledgment that brings just enough sorrow to keep me from completely coming.

"Emmalina. Fuck. We're almost there, Velvet. I...I need to pump." As if my body has a will of its own, my hips start to roll. The friction of my girth against her lips is more incredible than I want to admit. "Need to...move, okay? Need to...fuck you. So good. So good..."

Her moans gain a new pitch. I have no idea if I'm helping or hurting at this point, but as soon as she lifts one weak hand, splaying her fingers against the front of my thigh, it's all the encouragement I need. Every inch of my leg prickles and coils. My ass clenches and pushes.

Inside her mouth, I'm nothing but fire.

Inspiration.

Desperation.

And at last, explosion.

Lightning and lust. Rain and redemption. Sin and salvation. Oh fuck, how I hope—as I spill and flow and come and come and come, letting every searing drop tear through and up and out of me, every single burst taking a new prayer with it.

Fuck, fuck, fuck; please let this work; this has to work; this needs to work...

In the aftermath of the detonation, there's eerie silence.

Too much silence.

With a long groan, I pull away from Emma.

Who's joined the silence.

"Velvet?"

I slide down until I can frame her cheek with my palm.

Her still, cold cheek.

"Emmalina."

Not an entreaty anymore. A demand. A refusal to accept what I'm seeing and feeling.

What I'm not seeing and feeling.

No more of that gorgeous flush across her face. No more of the steady thrum she always brings to the air, the vibrant life she brings to my world...

"Fucking Jesus. Emma." Another command, this time

at the full force of my roar. Like that helps. Like I've done a goddamned thing to help her except lose control like the filthy mutant I am. Instead of thinking rationally and considering a plan that made even half a thought of sense—a plan a normal person would have enacted—I believed the most bizarre solution had to be the right one.

Because that's what I've become. A freak existing in a land of upside-down. Where demented bitches have control over my friends, and their final whispered words to me are a plea for their own death. Where the love of my life goes into cardiac arrest because of foreplay and then begs me for even more sex as the solution. Where I'm holding her lifeless body in the middle of a mud puddle, having fucked her to death in the mouth.

Where all of this leads to the only inevitable questions I should be asking myself.

"What the fuck have you done, Richards?" I roll back onto my haunches, pulling her close and rocking her against my chest. "What the fuck have you become?"

As fast as I've gritted them, I boot them up again on my lips—prepared to repeat them as many times as it takes for answers.

But the truth is, I already have them. Permanently stained on the walls of my soul—with the blood of my father, my friends...and now my woman.

"Ohhhhh!"

The woman who reignites all the joy, relief, and celebration in my spirit with the high, gorgeous, orgasmic scream she rips into the night.

"Ohhhhh, Reece!"

Who seizes me by my biceps, using the leverage to haul

herself off the ground, her wide turquoise eyes consuming my vision before mashing her lips on mine with ferocious, delicious need.

"Mmmmmm!"

Who sends her hot moan through my mouth and down my throat, all but making me come again from our sinuous, sizzling connection.

"Shit," she erupts when we've finally broken apart. "Shit, shit, shit!"

I'm not sure whether to growl or laugh while securing my hands beneath her, supporting her supple form in all its writhing gorgeousness. I end up doing both, unable to help myself. She's never been more hypnotizing, as if her every inhibition was left behind in the resurrection of her climax, and she's celebrating by offering her naked beauty to the moon and me. She's free and flawless and fair...

And alive.

So fucking alive.

Thank you.

My soul turns it into a litany as I continue to hold her, reveling in the erotic spell of her. At last, after she's taken at least fifty full breaths and I'm no longer dreading she'll stop, I lower my face to the crevice between her breasts, inhaling the coconut and honey ambrosia from her sweat-trickled skin, reaffirming the heartbeat that answers my fervent kiss.

"It's good, baby?" I rasp.

"Good?" She laughs. "This isn't good. This is...this is..."

"Magnificent?" I supply when it's obvious another orgasm is sneaking up on her from the inside. "A miracle?" And because I can't help myself once again, I lean in deeper, sliding my tongue into the succulent fruit at her core. At once, tangy juices drench my tongue, and I know I've found my most favorite dessert.

"Oh, God!" Her cry comes right before the vibrations through her pussy, turning into scintillating sucks on my tongue and waves of heat against my lips. She drops a hand into my hair and twists, using the hold as leverage to grind that perfect pink pulp into every corner of my mouth. It's a treat I'll savor forever. A moment I'll remember always. The night heaven returned my velvet angel to me. The night I gave thanks for that by devouring every inch of her pulsing sweet cunt.

"Fuck!" Another shudder claims her. Another flood of her hot liquid hits my mouth. I moan and swallow, taking her in as if she's life to me—because she is. "Fuck! Reece! It's...it's so much. I...I can't take any more..."

"Oh, baby." I edge my murmur with cocky chastisement. "Of course you can. And you will."

"Please." She's all breath in her throat but raw yearning in her grip, still practically tearing my hair out of my scalp. "Please. Damn it, now you really are trying to kill me!"

So much for the fun recess. Just like that, she's spiked me back to raw agony—and outrage.

I slam up and over her, replacing my lips with my fingers and hovering my glowering face over her startled one. "Bite. Your. Fucking. Tongue." I snarl it with the same vehemence as my driving thrusts into her, giving her no room to think that line will ever be a joke between us again. And while she widens those breathtaking blues with new respect, no way does it diminish their answering fire—the blazes she always brings whenever I've got her heart racing and her pussy throbbing. The infernos she knows I love, even now. Especially now.

The fuses that turn her lips into a teasing, tantalizing little smile.

"'Bite my tongue,' Mr. Richards?" she jibes back in a sultry drawl. "What, are you asking for permission or something?"

I cock my head and arch a brow. "Depends on what the answer is, Miss Crist."

Her stare drifts down to my lips. "Don't you think there's always room for another bite? Or two?"

With a savoring growl, I lower my head once again. It's not only the most direct path to that perfect bow of her mouth; it's the fastest way to show her just how thankful I am—for all of this. For all of her.

What a woman the universe has given to me.

To me.

Sometimes I still can't believe it. Other times, it feels like fate's most logical and loving wisdom. Who else but Emmalina Paisley Crist could have taken my broken soul and healed it—and saved her own damn life in the process—with the magic of her complete, crazy, near-death trust stunt? The woman has to be the bravest, boldest, most batshit bonkers person I've ever met.

But I'm pretty sure people have said that about every other miracle worker who's ever lived as well.

I just thank God—and whoever the hell else helped Him create her—that this miracle is all mine for the rest of time.

*

Several hours later, after I've carried her home from the canyon and gotten her into a shower and bed, I still can't stop staring at the woman. And yeah, unbelievably, attempting to blame it on the sorcery of the summer winds and the crystalline moonlight instead of the truth that barely tries to hide itself at the forefront of my psyche.

I've never been deeper in love with her.

And have never been more terrified of losing her.

What I did with her out in the canyon...

What I did to her...

Before I can help it, a grunt rips up the lining of my throat. By the time it hits my clenched teeth, the sound makes barely a dent on the air, but with my pillow crunched next to hers and my chest bracketing her left arm, it's enough to make her stir and fidget.

"Sssshhh." Another sound that barely brushes the air. "Sleep, my Velvet." My miracle. My love.

"Ummmph." She purses her lips and furrows her forehead but doesn't open her eyes. When the space above her eyebrows doesn't even out, I skim my mouth across that creamy plane with mist-soft care, listening to make sure I don't wake her again. There are times when the woman can sleep like the dead, but then she'll have a night like this, barely tiptoeing around the REM cycle, resulting in me getting too growly and protective of her.

Like now.

"Damn it," I mutter as soon as I lift up, seeing that my tender midnight care has been as effective as a bull sneaking through a china shop.

"Well, hi there yourself." She's already back to flinging as much sass and sardonicism as she did in the canyon. Trouble is, cocky Bunny 2.0 is just as sexy and cute as the first version.

Despite the admission, I'm unwilling to give up the cautious handling. It feels good—right—to treat her like a blown-glass treasure. My treasure. "Go back to sleep," I urge in a whisper. "You've still got a lot of hours."

She strokes a couple of soft fingertips along my jaw. Asks in just as sibilant a voice, "Did you finally get in touch with the mayor?"

I dip a fast but tight nod. "About an hour ago. Troy's holding up well, considering the circumstances."

"And the city?"

"Not so well." My lips are tight, and my head throbs with fresh tension. "Death toll's shockingly low, since so many took off early for the holiday, but the structural damage is severe. He's calling an emergency city council meeting later tomorrow—well, today—and has asked me to be there."

She hums in quiet approval. "You need to go."

"And you need to get some more sleep."

"Pssshhh. I'm fine."

"Velvet..."

"Pssshhh." She punches more fervor into it though backs up the gentle rebuke by rolling to her side and curling an elbow under her head. With her free hand, she strokes down the middle of my chest. "I was barely sleeping, and you know it."

"Says the woman barely holding back her yawn?"

"Says the superhero's girlfriend who's been dealing with the universe's most unique...hammer...knocking at her stomach?"

I narrow my eyes as she rewards herself for the humor with a soft giggle. "Says the bunny taunting the wolf when he's trying to keep the hammer in his pants?"

"Says the wench who's asking why?" Her sweet little whine penetrates where her sarcasm didn't: the core of my cock. I swallow hard, ordering the damn thing back to a reasonable status. Barely. "The bunny enjoys this wolf, remember? Besides, a wolf wielding a hammer isn't something a girl sees every day."

The little minx finishes that doozy by openly palming the hump between my legs. Before I can contain it, a moan tumbles off my lips. My sweats are as effective as rice paper for blocking the spell of her touch, especially as she strengthens her spell by looping one thigh up and over my hip. Dear fuck... this temptress. After the shit shambles of what went down in the canyon tonight, I'd have bet both my balls that she'd want nothing to do with them ever again, but here she is with her soft strokes, her clean scent, her hypnotizing warmth, and her husky breaths...roaming all of them over me until I'm clenching and shuddering beneath her kisses and touches. Until my fingertips are gently sparking and I start doing the same to her.

For long minutes, we explore each other like that. Igniting every shadow of the room with the magic of our connection. Turning the night into an electric day with the ignition of our fusion. Caressing and sighing, discovering and revealing, arousing and awakening...

Until she inserts her amazed whisper into the few inches between us. "You're so beautiful." Then seals in her truth by lifting her mouth to mine, tracing her tongue across the seam of my lips. "Never more so than now."

"Damn." My amazement isn't as eloquent as hers. Doesn't feel that way, at least. I concentrate harder, forcing more relevant words into existence. "What's...beyond beautiful?"

She frown-laughs. "Huh?"

"Because that's you, Velvet." I grunt softly. "This life of mine..." Then shake my head and restrain a bitter laugh. "Well, 'insane' is putting it all mildly. It's meant never knowing what hell or heaven the day is going to bring—and having to bank much more on the shitstorm instead of getting to ride off into the sunset." I slide a hand up to grip the back of her neck while lowering my forehead to hers. "But before you came along, Emmalina Crist, I'd forgotten what the sun even was."

A high sigh leaves her. Her whole form softens. "Reece..."

I break into her protest with a dip of my mouth. No way can I hold back any longer from claiming her with the full, passionate torrent of my mouth. Truth be known, I crave her with so much more, but this is enough for a start. More than enough, since she yields her lips with willing openness and softness, communicating how she already understands my need...with molten desire of her own.

Oh hell, yessssss.

We continue with slow, savoring rolls of our tongues... and soon, with sliding, sensual rolls of our bodies. And while my heart thunders against my ribs and my blood rushes like a flash flood, I'm actually able to pull back before my cock does the talking instead of my will—a gold star I instantly smack onto my composure report card. I'll take those goddamned stars wherever I can get them, even if she does press back in at me, so pliant and pretty and smelling like summer wind as she pleads, "Reece. Oh, baby..."

I let her feel the upturn of my smile as her whisper flicks through the corners of my mind. It blends with all the other rasps I've hoarded there over the last twelve months.

Okay, Mr. Richards.

You like that, Mr. Richards?

Ohhhh...now that I like...

And I like it when you do that too...

Oh, dear God, Reece. And that too!

I love you, Reece.

I love you so much.

There are so many more, but those are the ones I choose to stop at, drawing breath so I can repeat them to her with every force in my body and strand of my soul.

Except that my memory hasn't gotten the departure notification yet.

You're mine, Reece Richards. All mine.

And has completely jumped tracks.

How I shall enjoy this, cariño.

Into a tunnel with an echoing Spanish accent.

No. Not just any Spanish accent.

Her Spanish accent.

You are not going to escape me, Reece. Ever.

I twist and lunge up, planting elbows on my upraised knees and parking my sweaty face in my trembling hands, fighting to let the angel of my present banish the demoness of my past. Of course, it helps that Emma's already rolling back up next to me, filling her arms as fully with me from the second I reach for her, releasing a long sigh as I pull in a huge breath.

"What is it, my big bad wolf?" she asks with just the right mix of tenderness and tact.

I pull her closer and inhale even deeper, ensuring every pore of my being is drenched in her succulent summer scent, before I murmur into her hair, "Nothing, my sweet, soft bunny. Just a few ghosts."

Her quiet sigh warms the base of my neck. "Ahhh. Those." Then adds a cute bell of a laugh. "Well, maybe they need to be banished with a little distraction."

"Hmmm." I finish it with a growling nip into her shoulder. "A distraction sounds good...though I'm not quite sure how 'little' I can keep it."

The laugh becomes a saucy giggle. "You still threatening to wield that magical hammer, mister?"

"Perhaps."

"But you already have the magical Bolt Jolt necktie."

"Well, you know..." I trail my mouth down from her shoulder, setting a clear course for one of her gorgeous, puckered nipples. "We superheroes and our special toys..."

"Which means...what?" she charges. "Do I need to be set straight about the differences between magic hammers and magic neckties?"

I pause the journey of my lips long enough to let a snarl vibrate in my throat. "Fuck."

She responds with a throaty giggle. "I think that can be arranged, Mr. Richards."

I drop a hand around her ass and squeeze hard. "If I wasn't going to hell before..." That's as much as I can get out before she counters my move by tucking her head in and nipping into my neck.

"Well, if you're going..." She soothes her bite with soft, lapping licks as I slide my hand back up, burying my fingers in the white-blond silk of her hair. "I volunteer as stowaway."

I twist my grip until she lifts her head and our gazes are locked. She's so fucking stunning, bathed in moonlight and surrounded by our rumpled bed linens. Surrounded but not covered. I have a full, perfect view of her puckered berry nipples and her graceful, tapered ribcage. "You'd really do that?" I demand, shooting up a mock glower. "Hitchhike on my ride?"

"No longer just yours." She juts out her chin while spreading a hand to the center of my chest—and I try not to fixate on the proximity of her innocent pink nail polish to her dark, tight areolas. "We're in this together, mister. All of it. Partners, remember?"

I take a deep breath. It's more like a rough grate, but it does the job of keeping me alive for at least how long my answer is going to take. "Woman, I can barely remember how to breathe with you this close and sweet and soft and—"

Well, hell.

Maybe breathing's overrated. I don't miss it one fucking bit as she plunges her mouth over mine, zinging her tongue over my own with such perfect, pulsing passion, I wonder if I've dared to get naked with a live circuit box. The heat through my mouth and tongue are soon fire in my blood and nerves, turning my limbs into flares, my senses into napalm, and my cock into a ray of daybreak several hours too early.

But between her gorgeous mewls and her lunging tongue and her passionate breaths, the woman sounds very much like a morning person.

I give her half a second to refill her lungs before initiating the next kiss. And this time, I make it a kiss, twisting until she gives in and rolls beneath me, sighing as I ram my mouth hard down on her. Into her. Devouring her like a goddamned shelf of truffles, exulting in every incredible texture and flavor and cream, before pouring my ravishing roar down her welcoming throat. It's ecstasy to feel the sound drench every inch of her writhing body, until even her toes flex and knead against my thighs and ass.

When we pull apart again, we're both inhaling hard. I take advantage of the pause, reveling in the riveting sight before me, better than any fucking sunrise on earth. Her lust-swollen breasts. Her kiss-bruised lips. And her eyes—always the sorcery of her eyes—so brilliant and bold with their torrid blue flames...

"My beautiful bunny." I'm shockingly smooth about it, considering how every striation of my body practically thrums out loud for her—then louder still as she quirks half a smile before her seductive murmur of a reply.

"My magnificent Zeus." She peeks up through the thick fan of her lashes. "Is there...something I can help you with?"

"Damn." I go domineering with the tone, but the little temptress has given me no fucking choice. "You've gotten me as hard as a real hammer, woman."

"Then maybe it's time for you to pound."

"No matter what the consequences?" My tone is lethal as I grab her by the hips, intentionally holding myself away from her. "Hammers can kill, damn it. And—"

"Yours almost did exactly that," she finishes on a taut bite. "I know. I was there." With an impatient sweep, she palms the side of my face. "But we're not going to start doing this every time I need you inside me." As she claws my hairline, her lips part into an utterly erotic pout. "And Mr. Richards...I need you inside me now."

"But—"

"But what?" Her stare becomes a heated glower. "It was a glitch, Reece. And then you saved me."

"It wasn't a fucking little glitch."

"But then you saved me." She turns her grip into a command, strong and severe, before dragging me down for her equally strict kiss. But within seconds, the lock of our lips evolves into a hot, hungry meal of our mouths at each other. When our tongues are done excavating each other's throat, she reiterates in a gorgeous growl, "You saved me, baby—just like I know you always will. Just like I'll always save you." She wraps her other hand to the back of my head. "Because that's what we were put in this world to do." She roams her gaze, now the color of a twilight sky, across my whole face. "I'm fused into you, mister. Hardwired to love you, to know you, to put up with you—and yes, to save you, no matter how many more 'glitches' we have. You got that, mister?"

I huff hard while dipping my forehead against hers. Thing is, I got it from about the second she said fused to you, but the central conflict in my soul hasn't changed. If anything, with her naked glory so close, I cut right to the chase on my comeback. "I don't have anything if I don't have you."

She yanks me down again. And again, we take each other's lips in a delving, decadent mash of lust. At once, whatever reprieve my erection was granted has been rescinded, and my heartbeat calls to hers with a wild windstorm rhythm. The tattoo of hers answers right away, pulsing in time to the urgent jerks of her sweet, sweaty breasts against my chest.

"Then have me, you stubborn stick of greased lightning," she finally breaks away to pant. "And if you kill me, you can hitchhike on my ride to hell."

As I'm certain she's planned, the irreverence arrests me, dazzles me—and enflames me. But on the outside, all I give her is a slow reprobate smile.

Right before I deftly flip her over, toss her facedown into the pillows, and press my mouth to the base of her neck. I dig my teeth in while rolling my hips with wanton intent.

"Aaahhh!" Her protesting shriek is lost in the pillow as the soaked lips of her pussy surrender to my defined incursion.

"You want to play with the hounds of hell, Velvet?" I channel just enough electrons into my cock to make it come alive with intimidating heat—and deliver a jolt that already has her screaming through her first climax. "Think I've met a few of those in my time and even remember a few key moves." Urged by her perfect little clenches, I nuzzle her ear and settle in for the hot, tight ride. "I'll play nice if you will."

CHAPTER FIVE

EMMA

"Come here."

It's totally illogical yet perfectly wonderful that even after the man's rocked me through four orgasms, his soft sandpaper growl flips my stomach like a basket of butterflies—just as he upends us, deftly rolling to his back but taking me along for the ride.

Though I don't have much choice about compliance, it doesn't matter. I let out a happy gasp, all too elated to let gravity do the work of keeping us locked together. The longer we remain as one physical being, maybe the clearer he'll get the point that I'm not willing to give up the status in other forms as well.

You're mine, Reece Richards.

No matter what this existence throws at us.

You're mine.

My man. My purpose. My light. My life.

And, if the universe wills it, my death too.

"Tell me."

His whisper brings me back to the moment. "Tell you what?" I mumble, cuddling my face against his neck.

"Whatever has your mind whirring so loud, I can practically hear it."

I laugh softly. "Hmmm. Just pondering the mysteries of the universe."

"Hmmm. That all?"

"A girl has a tendency to do that after a hound's dragged her to the best damn 'hell' she's ever experienced."

"Because she's not really a girl?"

"Errrmm...excuse me?"

"Truth." He leans up, kissing the peaks of my breasts. "Really."

"Then what is she?"

"A goddess."

Small but mighty giggle. "Excuse me?"

"Oh, it's the truth." He's not messing around about the whole thing, even adding an adoring stare as he settles back down and starts combing his fingertips through the ends of my hair, staring at the strands as if they've become spun gold. "Believe me, I know about these things."

"Is that so, my Zeus?" I fix my gaze on him to prevent my eyes from sliding shut. Dear God, the man knows how to give a good finger comb-out.

"That's very so, my beauty." He keeps combing, damn near usurping my orgasms as the best thing to my senses tonight. "Because of that, heaven and hell are kind of a blurred line for her."

"Ahhhh." Though I curse myself for it, I lift a hand and curl it around his, halting his perfect ministrations. But this is important. "Blurred lines. Like the ones superheroes have to toe sometimes."

His features tighten. "Yeah. Sometimes." His mutter is just as terse, though his gaze remains the pale gray of an early winter sky. In those tender depths, I see that he gets where I'm going. That I'll never brush off where he's been, especially in the last twenty-four hours.

To his own version of hell and back.

I lean down farther, pressing my heartbeat tight along his. I want him to feel every steady beat of the blood and air in and out of my chest. To affirm him of my life exactly as I assure him of my love. They're hand-in-hand for me, and they'll never be anything different.

I love you.

I need you.

Come what may.

You'll always be mine, Reece Andrew Richards.

"What?"

His crack of a command has me jerking as sharply as him, causing us to separate whether we want to or not. But not even the leftover heat from his cream, flowing over my mound and inner thighs, deters the bewilderment from my stare. "Huh?" I stammer. "What do you mean?"

"What do you mean?" he retorts.

"I...huh?"

"What did you just say, Emmalina?"

"I—" I almost don't want to respond because I already sense how he won't like—or perhaps even believe—the answer. "I didn't say anything, baby."

Nope. He doesn't like it.

And he sure as hell doesn't believe it.

"Shit."

"Reece?"

He stabs a hand into his hair, confirming my hunch that his distracted blurt is masking a deeper concern. "Shit."

Okay, scratch concern. Bartender, make that a straight

shot of disturbed, please—with a chaser of outright confused for the man's fiancée, please.

"Reece?" I dig my fingertips into his hairline. "What's going on?"

With his hand still tangled in his dark waves, he pulls focus from his dazed glare at the ceiling to his blinking gaze at me. "N-Nothing, Bunny." He shakes his head so hard, it scratches against the pillow. "It's...nothing."

"Doesn't look like nothing." I reposition my hand, flattening it along his forehead. It's as strong and firm and warm as ever but not fever-hot. "Are you feeling okay? Maybe we should wake up Wade and Fersh and have them run some diagn—"

"I'm fine." He tilts his head back so my fingers are realigned with his bold cheekbone. "I probably just need some sleep."

"So can I help facilitate that?"

He quirks one side of his mouth. "You just did." He gathers me against him, nestling my head atop his chest. "And you still are."

I readjust a little, scooting my ear right over the strong thumping of his heart. Right away a yawn escapes me, and I start wondering who's really getting the subliminal lullaby here—but I won't push my luck on that point right now. I have bigger fish to fry with the advantage he's bounced into my court, so to speak.

"Fine. We'll sleep." I roam a hand up and down the twin ladders of his abs—each time, taking my touch more discernibly beneath his navel. "On one condition."

A taut rumble begins between his lungs. "And why don't I think it includes another stellar field trip to hell?"

"Because you'd be right."

"Should I be afraid?"

I expect him to finish that with a grumble but instead get a chuckle, making me feel a little guilty about going for the emo ballad soundtrack again. But I wouldn't be pushing that play button if this wasn't damn important. So I push back up a little, planting a hand in the middle of his chest while securing the lock of his full gaze with mine.

"The Emmalina: Handle With Care sticker stays off." I enforce the order by compressing my lips. "We're partners, damn it—and from now on, even if I can't always be on the front lines with you, we stay partners. We're going to have some bumps in the road, okay—but guess what? All couples have bumps." And because his laugh already leads me there, I invite a moment of levity into the mix too, seesawing my head with a light laugh. "Our bumps are just a little...different...than most."

And again, while I expect him to switch back to the emo rock, he quirks his lips with a sarcastic smirk and glides his hands down in a twisted bid to usurp the finger comb-out with a divine butt massage. "Says the wise and beautiful goddess with the enchanted and amazing ass?"

I sock his shoulder. "Are you trying to bribe me, Mr. Richards?"

"Depends."

"On what?"

"On if it's working."

I swallow back my blissful moan though wonder if that's really the choice of a wise goddess. Showing my hand means I get a lot more of this, albeit with the man's gloating grin in my face. But is that such a bad thing either? "Hmmm." I stall for myself as much as him. "That depends."

His long chuckle sends delicious vibrations through his whole body. Yes, even into those strong, divine fingers of his. "Ohhh, it's working," he murmurs. "Just admit it, or I'll use my x-ray eyes to tell everyone your panty color at breakfast."

I give up the shoulder bops, resorting to tweaking his nipple. "Since when were you okay with me wearing panties anywhere, Mr. Richards?" Then slither my thigh up, unable to hold back my moan any longer while gliding along the proud stalk at his center.

"Damn good point," the man softly snarls, layering his seductive sound over my aroused sigh. His jaw visibly tenses, and I run my touch along its alluring strength.

"I love you, Mr. Richards." And only because I do, I back off with the wanton thigh flirtation. The man has literally started hearing voices. He's past the point of exhaustion.

"And fuck, how I love you, Miss Crist." As he kneads my back cheeks deeper, he adds in a tender murmur, "And enjoy the fuck out of your oh-so-distinctive 'panty color.'"

I hum while dipping down to kiss his pectoral, fighting the mists of sleep threatening to snuff my consciousness. "I have trained you well, young superstud."

But in the end, I'm helpless against the onslaught of the slumber. As the fog rolls thicker over my mind, I'm aware of one last thing: the caress of his lips across my forehead followed by an equally worshipful whisper. "That you have, my velvet goddess. That you have."

REECE

Unsurprisingly, Emma has drifted easily back to sleep.

Also unsurprisingly, I haven't.

Not after what happened in my own goddamned bed.

In my own goddamned head.

Again.

I throw on a pair of nylon shorts, prowling downstairs and heading for the pool deck, intending to turn the ice beneath my skin into sweat—but I only make it as far as the ground-floor office before Faline swoops in again, even stronger now.

Reece Andrew Richards...

I try to sit. Lurch back up in such a violent rush, the rolling chair behind the desk spins away and slams the wall. Her whisper in my senses isn't such a little sigh anymore. More and more, it's as if she's standing next to me. Preparing to torture me again.

You know it's the truth.

You belong to me.

You always have and always will.

The crashing chair sends an echo through the house like a gunshot—though at the moment, if it meant expelling Faline and her goddamned sighs from my brain, I'd willingly take the brunt of a real rifle blast.

And soon, you will know that in full. And accept it with gratitude.

"Never." Yes, I'm snarling at voices that are only in my head. Yes, I'm punching at the granite stone wall that stands in for the phantoms, really seeing the wisdom of incorporating the ridge as part of the house's structure. Yes, I'm getting the horrifying correlation between this moment and the one like it from last night, when I tried taking down a whole cliff in the canyon with the same unyielding rage—at the same conniving bitch.

Only now, she hasn't just decimated one of my best friends

from the inside out.

She's tromping through my goddamned mind.

Why? How?

That same mind fires an answer at me with terrifying speed. An image, flashing through like a snippet of a nightmare—because that's what it still feels like.

The moments before Kane begged me to end him...

That electric worm he tried ramming into my ear...

The unbearable pain that made me fight back...

And what if you didn't get it all, cariño?

What if I really did get inside...just a little?

What if I am there this very moment, sliding through your synapses and wading into your blood? And what if I soon shall be swimming there? In every thought you have. In every drop you bleed...

"Never!"

But as I prepare to repeat the snarl with at least fifty more punches into the rock, there's a movement in my periphery. I whip a glare to the person attached to it, with his bleary daze, mussed hair, and barely zipped khaki shorts—though he tosses back some respect by straightening his stance and smacking a hand to the middle of his chest, which is covered by a wrinkled T-shirt centered by a grinning Naruto.

"Dude." Sawyer shakes his head. "You've either had too much coffee or need a shit ton more." He holds up a steaming coffee mug with his other hand. "Take mine if you need. Your mom brewed a pot of Peet's deliciousness."

I force myself to take a deep breath and jerk my head no. "Not going to help." I don't know why I'm so certain of that, aside from the fact that the last twenty-four hours have included one bizarre funeral, a couple of paradigm-changing orgasms, an attack on my adopted city, ending that attack by having to take my friend's life, and not a second's worth of sleep—which all leads to the last nail in my sanity coffin in the form of a Faline-themed ghost stalking my fucking mind.

And there's where my certitude comes from. Last time I checked, caffeine and coffins weren't a winning combination. I'm not going to be that guy, traumatized to the point of postmortem sympathy feels for Kane, including any credence to the bitch queen who hardwired herself into his head—and might have maneuvered him into implanting me with a similar device.

Doesn't m-m-matter anymore... It's done... All...done...

"No." Though I snarl it at the memory, Sawyer barely flinches. Clearly he still thinks I'm making a personal mission statement about the coffee—or not. Not a lot the guy doesn't know or flinch at about this crazy journey of mine so far. He knows I've already rendered my sacrifice to the Faline Garand altar in the church of the Consortium. He also knows about the two, sometimes three, torture sessions I endured each day and how that adds up to nearly four hundred hours the woman has already played Nurse Ratched with my mind while her minions played lunatic lab fun with my body.

But what he doesn't know is that I was sometimes too weak to fight it.

That at times, the pain of her in my psyche was easier to face than the agony of the changes in my blood.

But I'm not that weak anymore. Even stumbling back to the runaway rolling chair and then plunking into it, I'm five thousand kinds of ready to backhand that bitch out of my brain faster than a fly on a fucking picnic basket.

"All right." Foley extends both words with his unique

combination of casual and insightful, bypassing the two modular chairs in the room in favor of the loveseat against the wall—or at least that's what the catalogue called the thing. I haven't gone near the damn thing, which looks more like a crostini of leather supported by aluminum chopsticks, but Foley mounts the thing with the grace of a bobcat and then dangles his coffee cup from between his braced elbows. "So what will help?"

"A lobotomy?" I retort.

He takes a contemplative sip from his cup. "Things went that shitty yesterday?"

I rise again, fighting prickling heat along my skin, feeling once more like a pinball in a damn coffin. "What time is it?" I ask, though my cell is sitting on the desk.

"Little after six." Foley, being the ideal wingman he is, simply accepts the deflection. He even adds, as if knowing I need it, "In the morning."

"And you're here now...why?"

"Because Lydia is." To his credit, there's still no flinch in his tone or gaze. To his further credit, he leaves his coffee untouched as our stares lock. "Yesterday was rough on everyone. Being here for her was important."

I tilt my head and hone my gaze. "She's become that important?" As I lean against the desk, I insert, "Asking for a friend. As in my fiancée. Who's likely to grill you harder about your intentions than Laurel and Todd Crist combined."

His lips form a firm line. He still doesn't falter. Not even to take a Cool Hand Sawyer whiff of his java. "You can tell Emma I like the grill hot." And finally lifts the cup back up, indulging a huge gulp, as if knowing how thoroughly that's going to shut my maw for a long moment, before going at me again with the jabbing jade slice of his scrutiny. "We done with pissing on the charcoals now? You want to tell me what really had you ready to turn your office into a quarry?" And once more, because my brain's the real quarry and he's probably been snoring into 'Dia's chest for a few hours, he's more ready on the new uptake. "What the fuck happened on that rooftop, Richards?"

I cobble together a tight grunt. "You were there."

"Watching from the chopper," he volleys. "Which was a good thing, since Angelique kept wanting to jump out and help you."

"Help me?" I'm almost glad for the open perplexity I can display. "And she reasoned that out to you...how?"

He takes another drag on his coffee while a frown makes its way across his face. With his gaze still lowered at whatever's left in his cup, he states, "She told me she could hear your... wavelengths."

"My what?"

"Not just yours." His scowl gives way to a more typical Foley expression. His aloofness comes out when our "chats" have to veer toward off-manual curiosities like my light saber fingers and his fondness for wasabi ice cream. Right now, it's probably helpful. "Yours and Kane's."

I crunch a deep glare. "The hell?"

He smooths a hand over the air. "Well, think about it a second. Those crapsticks dicked around with her brain. In her brain. Stands to reason she'd come out of the process just as altered as you were, albeit with an incubation period for her noggin to heal from the trauma and relearn its new electrical pathways. With her, it's more of a cerebral thing, based in biofeedback and the static force of emotions on the air."

I shove back to my feet. "And you're saying that these

new—what, powers?—just magically manifested yesterday during my showdown with Kane?"

"Not powers," Foley counters. "At least not to her. For fuck's sake"—he glances out the door, as if worried Angie might fly out in a rage any second from the guest-room wing—"don't say powers around her."

"Why not?" As if I'm that fond of the term.

"Her longing to be one of the 'miracle mutants' was how Faline got her claws into Angie to begin with. It's the downfall that led her to the Consortium's dark side."

"Those fuckers have a light side?"

"You know what I mean," he rebuts, swinging his posture back around. "Though apparently, she's been dealing with this shit, as well as how to hide it better, for a few weeks now." He throws both hands up. "But you didn't hear that part from me."

"A few weeks." That nearly falls out of me as a question too—though as I say the words, the answer already starts to fill itself in. "Which was another reason she played hide-and-seek with the remote check-ins." And favoring the hide part.

"And the fact that she was attempting to salvage Kane's sorry ass."

I can't help but let a morose silence go by. "A lot of good the effort did her," I mumble. "Or any of us."

Another heavy pause, this time of Foley's choosing. In the second before I get uncomfortably curious about it, the guy speaks up again. "You had to do what you had to do, man."

And suddenly, uncomfortable is the tip of the fucking iceberg of what I feel. "What...I..."

"It's all right." Foley clunks his empty mug on a platform built into the loveseat and rolls easily to his feet at the same time I stumble back, feeling freakishly cold. "Seriously, buddy.

He wanted to go. He was begging you for it. Angie sensed that too. She was torn apart by it, but she got it—especially after I told her I'd be doing the same thing in Kane's place."

From the new stiffness in his posture to the steady empathy on his face, I see that every word he speaks is real and heartfelt. That doesn't stop me from wheeling away, lacing my hands at the back of my head as I spit out, "That fucking so?" As rage and remorse sweep in, I squeeze the heels of my hands in, praying I have the power to push every thought out of my skull. "You'd be fucking begging me to zap your neck in half like a toothpick?"

"Or jam a pistol up my mouth and pull the trigger," Foley answers quietly. "Or stab a dagger through my heart or wrap a noose around my neck." His tone is so absolute, I almost wonder if he's pausing just to scroll through his phone for extra morbid images. "Whatever it took to take me out before facing a lifetime of being Faline Garand's dancing monkey."

I lean forward until my forehead knocks against the plate-glass window behind the desk. "You don't fucking say."

Despite the heat already permeating the glass, a shiver invades my body as well as my voice. Foley doesn't miss either. "And what the hell are you saying?"

I drop my hands, only to lift one back up and sprawl my fingers against the window. Behind me, Foley is thankfully still. Around us, the air is equally so. Still, I don't allow myself any easy breaths. The ghost could return any second.

But maybe, if I just say something first...

Especially to a friend who gets it more than most. The only person on the globe who literally might be hiding more violent secrets than me...

"Richards?" he prompts again. It's not a mandate, but

he's not going to just walk out of here for a refill on his coffee because I've chosen to clam up.

So it's time to haul in a long breath and find my fucking voice again.

"Foley." All right, it's a start. Not a great one, but he'll have to deal. "You really do know what it's like to be a dancing monkey for someone, don't you?"

At last he does move, coming around to occupy the same spot on the desk I vacated. "It was more like being a pinned moth, but yeah."

"Better." I snort. "Pinned moth. Yeah. That's it." I twist my fingers into a tight fist and then turn my whole hand, perfectly positioned to take out the entire window if I have to. "So...did you...do you...ever think about the monster who put the pins in?" A morning wind kicks up across the ridge. I watch it move through the bright wildflowers and grasses, ordering myself to absorb the inherent peace of the swaying plants. "I mean, still?" I stammer. "Not on purpose or anything."

"Like in nightmares?" Foley probes. "Well, fuck yeah. You can't help what your subconscious drums up."

"Or even...not in nightmares."

He grunts softly. "Not if I can help it." Then shifts a little, his T-shirt and khakis rustling as if he's crossing his arms. "But sometimes, something will bring up...memories. Visceral shit, mostly. A smell or a sound." A new rustle, giving away his shrug this time. "Still can't listen to Van Morrison for that very reason."

"Van Morrison?" I pivot enough to shoot him a quizzical look. "You have to avoid Van Morrison?"

"Didn't say it was easy, man."

"No shit."

We're quiet again, though I turn to look out the window once more—and nearly hope he'll drop the subject and just get back to offering me coffee. The sun's nearly all the way up, and the bitch-ghost in my head seems to have vanished along with the night. Thank fuck.

Are you ready for more fun, papi? I certainly am...

And that's what I get for allowing myself to breathe normally again.

"Shit!"

And as deeply as I stash the hiss beneath my lower registers, Foley's back on both feet again. Looming in my peripheral again. Intense and unyielding and one hundred percent his undeterred PI self again. In short, he's yanked out every trait I keep him on the payroll for. I'm just not sure how epic the proverbial shoe feels on the other goddamned foot.

"All right, man." He comes closer but seems to know what's too close, stopping short of that boundary before turning and leaning back against the support beam that bisects the window. "Ice breaker time is over. Time for the real work."

He pauses again, as if really waiting for me to pick up on that riff. I don't move. I don't allow myself even the luxury of half a breath. If I don't allow the universe to know I'm here, then Faline won't either.

"Richards."

Goddamnit.

"Reece."

I'm cold again. So cold. With gritted effort, I hold myself back from visibly shivering. It feels like coming down off one of my wilder weekends, only worse. Much worse. Maybe I'm just getting sick. Is this all some strange fever dream? I haven't been sick since escaping the hive, an item added to the small plus column of Consortium torture aftereffects. Who needs penicillin and Nyquil when a guy's got megawatt sterilization in his blood, right?

But if it's not the flu, then it's got to be...

Not the worm.

Not that fucking worm.

That stupid. Fucking. Worm.

For some strange reason, the words are suddenly comical.

The mighty lightning bolt. Taken down by a...worm.

I laugh. Hard. The action unlocks my restraint—and more chills. They rack me as I flip around and slide down the window, hugging myself.

"Richards." The alarm in Foley's exclamation tells me more. Great. I really look as craptastic as I feel. "What the fuck is going on?"

I roll my head back and forth in a show of haphazard denial. It's another move borrowed from my party king days, which makes me laugh again. I can't believe I remember how to do this. I can't believe I'm still admitting there really is an art to this.

And I really can't believe how loud the voice is, returning to my head in all its crooning, cruel glory.

That's it. You're learning. Just let me in, cariño. It's so much easier when you don't fight.

"Christ," I bite out, barely keeping my teeth from chattering. "A f-f-fucking worm. A fucking w-w-worm."

Foley double-takes. "What the hell?"

"It's th-th-the only ex-explanation. Th-The worm."

"Explanation for what?"

"F-F-For her. T-T-Talking to me." I jack my head back, straining for even a little of the sunlight stretching across the hills. Needing the heat to blast me. To banish her.

"Her?" Foley crouches closer. Grabs my shoulder. "Her who?"

I slam my eyes closed. Gulp hard. Realize that I've got to say it. Comprehend, with some stabbing part of my psyche, that I have to tell someone. That I have to say it out loud before I can't say anything anymore.

"Faline."

"Faline?"

"She's...she's inside my head." And though my teeth are chattering like humping chipmunks and even my toe hairs have icicles, I hear the pitch of desperation in my voice. Jesus, is this really happening? "I can hear her, as if she's parked her bony ass on top of my brain. Like she's here." I manage to curl a hand up and around, twisting the sleeve of his shirt with my fingertips. "But like she wants even more. As if...as...if..."

"What?" Foley's growl fills the space left by my stammering fade. The dwindle of my voice...because of the explosion in my awareness.

Oh, holy fuck.

Not an explosion.

A revelation.

"As if she's getting ready to control me like she controlled Kane."

No stuttering this time. Funny how a guy forgets to be cold when he's terrified out of his goddamned mind. And if the stupefaction seared across Foley's face is any accurate gauge, I'm not steering at all toward melodrama.

Fuck.

Fuck.

Fuck.

Which, surprise surprise, are the exact three words that

seethe out of Foley—

As another cold front broadsides me.

And knocks me all the way over to the floor.

"Fuck!" It's a yell from Foley now before he's got me rolled to my back with his face consuming my vision. "Reece. Buddy. You have to stay with me."

I want to laugh again. I think I do. Well, hell. I got a Reece and a buddy at the same time. Must be my lucky day. Or my unluckiest. Why do I feel like laying strong odds on the latter?

"Dude. Can you hear me? Reece, you bastard. You've got to stay with me!"

"Yeah." I try to nod, but the motion's more like my post-bender weekend loll. "I'm...I'm here. St-Stop yelling."

"When?" he charges without his normal one-liner of preface. Just right into the nitty-gritty. Makes me want to shoot out a quip of my own, something involving his lack of conversational lube, but the guy's brain is clearly firing on more cylinders than mine. On the other hand, he doesn't have a bitch supreme filling up his mental plate, complete with a side of fuck-you-up salsa. "When did this start happening, man? How long has she been there?"

I swivel my head to the side. Focus my gaze randomly. There's a bush abloom in purple flowers outside sheltering a little family of wild rabbits. Bunnies. My favorite. I almost blurt that out but remember something at the last minute. Foley needs an answer. The information is important. "Last night," I finally get out. "Yeah. Last night. Right after I got back from...from..."

"From saving the fucking city." Foley's growl is fucking scary now. Yeah, even to me. "And having to put down your friend because he—" The growl is upended by a fierce choke.

"Holy shit." Then an even harsher snarl. "Having to put down your friend!"

From the middle of my mental and physical glacier, I groan as if his thumping hand to my chest is a dump of boiling water instead. That succeeds in getting me to open my eyes at least, since I throw the force of any remaining strength into my hard glare up at the man.

Which becomes self-inflicted torture, from the second Emma's face swoops into my focus too. Her irises are the color—and size—of storm-tossed oceans. Her lips are seized with shock. Her throat is a column of solid strain.

"Reece? Dear God. Reece?"

"Velvet..."

"Uh-uh." Foley clamps a hand around the underside of my jaw, jerking my focus back his way. "Soliloquies later, lightning boy. I need facts. Concentrate, goddamnit." His gaze is filled with the same holy-shit-this-is-bad sprawl as Em's, but I don't have the strength to point that out. Every force in my blood and will of my body is converged on fighting off the ice that keeps creeping and the winter witch that's bringing it. "Now you've got to focus, dude." Foley rises up, thumping the middle of my chest with even more force. "And remember for me—"

"Remember what?" Emma inserts herself into the small space between the window and me. She's stretched with most of her weight on one curled knee, with the opposite leg extended along the outside of mine. "Holy shit. Reece? Why does he look like this? Why is he so cold? What the hell is—"

"Emma." The interjection doesn't belong to Foley. Not unless he's turned into a female with a smoky French accent. "Please, you must let Foley—"

"Do what?" She shirks Angie's hand away from her

shoulder but doesn't rip her gaze from my face. "Do what? And why? Sawyer? Wh-What's happened?"

As if she hasn't spoken, Sawyer balls his hand and thumps the middle of my chest. "Richards, I need to know what went down between you and Kane on the roof."

"Are you joking?" Emma lashes. "He looks and feels like a damn iceberg, and you want him to recount all that now?"

Again, Sawyer hardly flinches, but mutters, "Good point." Directly to me, he says, "Just the last of it, man." He pushes in, eclipsing even Emma from my view, and turns his words into a matching order. "You need to tell me, word for word, exactly what the fuck Kane did and said to you, dude."

I swallow deep in my throat while diving my mind back through memories I swore I'd never touch again. But if Faline gets any further into my gray matter, I won't even have a will to control that touch. So Nightmare Lane, here I come. "I told him I was s-s-sorry. Then he s-s-said...he was sorry too. No. Wait. The worm came first. Or did it come after?"

"Huh? But—"

As soon as Emma goes quiet at Foley's halting hand, Foley rasps to me, "What worm, dude? And did you ask him exactly why he was sorry?"

I push some energy into my head. Whether the nod is discernible, I don't care. I can't care. I'm without the physical capability. My lungs are ice caverns. My heart pumps arctic rivers. My thoughts are practically crystals of cold fusion. "He...he said...didn't matter. He said...it was already done."

"It...what?" Emma rasps.

But all Foley spits back is, "Fuck."

Angelique releases a dire sigh and whispers, "Mon dieu."

I let my hand drop from Foley's shirt, across my woman's

trembling, bent knee. Then funnel as much fortitude through my system as I can, digging my mental claws in to hold on to the parts that are still all me, to take in that perfect face wearing nothing but my heart's adoration across my face.

But there's no time to add the thousand sonnets, three thousand songs, and ten thousand novels' worth of words that'd be necessary to even start expressing my love. There's not time for even a handful of words. Not with the more exigent ones that need to be issued.

"Foley," I say, though without deterring my stare from Emma for a second. "You...you know what to do, right? If this all really goes to crap..."

"Goes to crap?" She speed rockets a glare between Foley and me that tempts me to close my eyes again. The fuel in her rockets is thick aqua tears, and they're fissuring every inch of my heart. But I don't look away, because in the pain, I find a miraculous kernel of truth. If Faline really pulls this crazy stunt off—has somehow managed to use Kane to plant phantom code into my DNA—then she'll have conquered my mind and my will, but never my heart.

And never the soul that belongs solely, completely to Emmalina Paisley Crist.

"I asked a damn question," my gorgeous goddess reiterates. "If what goes to crap? And what the hell is it that you'll 'know what to do,' Foley?"

He gives me a succinct nod, totally ignoring the fact that she's used his last name instead of first for about the third time since they met. "I got you, buddy," he assures. "Don't worry."

Emma lets out a war cry worthy of the Wakanda veldt. "If someone doesn't freaking tell me what the hell is—" But she sobs herself to a stop as soon as I grip her knee even tighter with an equally strained sound. "Baby." She leans over, stroking the side of my face. "Please. You're...you're scaring me."

"I'm sorry, Bunny."

"Don't be sorry. Just talk to me."

My protesting wheeze doesn't help—but I'm unable to help it. The electrons in my veins are slowing and freezing, slaves to another program now. To another power. "I'm so fucking sorry, Emmalina."

"But why?" She shoves Foley's hand away and replaces it with her own, circling the space over my heart as if the mixture of her frantic touch and her raining tears will be enough to bring me back online. And God help me, how I long for the same thing—with every fiber of the heart that still beats for her, worships her, needs her. With every shred of the soul that will never stop loving her, longing for her, being grateful for how she's rescued it.

How, because of her love, it'll be able to hold on to a tiny piece of heaven, despite the hell for which the rest of me is headed.

"I love you, Velvet." A massive shudder takes over me. "I do, okay? Always, okay? Until the end of time."

Until the end of my time.

"Nooooo!"

Emma's scream echoes through the freezing darkness behind my descending eyelids...

As the bitch inside my mind lets out a long, victorious hiss.

Oh, yessssss.

FUSE

PART 12

CHAPTER ONE

EMMA

"Wake up. Please, *please*, wake up!"

No matter how many times I whisper it, the man I love is cold as ice and still as death where he lies on a steel medical bed, covered in nothing but a hundred medical leads and one small loincloth.

And me.

I lean over farther, press my cheek to the indent between his unnaturally chilled pecs, and listen for the slow, faint thrum from within. With gritted teeth, I shove everything else in the room out of my awareness. The bleeping machines, ticking monitors, plain gray walls, rubbing alcohol smell—none of it is as important as the organ pumping the lifeblood into his body. Not that it's a difficult feat. Despite this mini hospital and the attached command center being located just across the driveway from the broad steps of the home we've built together, I've always tried to deny their very existence—but now, my existence is centered on everything that's right here. As his heart thumps, so does mine. Every lift of my chest waits for the rise and fall of the broad plane of his beneath my hand. I stretch my aching spirit into the darkness he's fallen into, fighting to make him see my light. *Our* light. The connection, like a pair of colliding comets, that only we know. That only we share.

"I'm here, you beautiful man." *You magnificent hero.* My hero.

I press a fervent kiss to his sternum. "You know me, Reece. And I know you can still feel me. Damn it, I *know* you can. Lightning needs the earth." My breath hitches. My senses sting. "And damn it, the earth needs her lightning."

Despite the savage battle I've waged against myself, the tears escape. Drip between my fingers. Drive deeper stings behind my eyes. Blur my blinking vision.

"Come back to me, baby. *Please*...come back." It's a rasp from my lips to his skin. "I...I can't lose you like this. Not like this, damn it!"

As my gut-deep sobs splash into the salty puddle I've created in his chest, I realize irony is intent on making me her bitch today. Emmalina Crist, the girl who swore she'd never be so weak as to "need" a man, has become the idiot blubbering all over her fallen hero.

Because I'm not that girl anymore.

Because I'm a woman fully changed.

Because I've learned about the transformation of true love.

Because I've realized that in needing and loving, the real lessons of strength and courage are found.

Because even if that weren't the case, no way in hell am I'm stopping *any* of this shit—until one thing alone occurs: this man opens his eyes and looks at me with the full strength of his soul again.

"Reece." His name becomes my pleading mantra, the only bond I still seem to have to him since he collapsed on the home-office floor three hours ago.

Collapsed.

I shake my head in sharp disbelief...but also to confront another piercing truth. If his proper name is my mantra for everything I love about his masculinity and humanity, his public name has come to have meaning as well. In twelve months of living with Bolt the superhero, I've watched the man cripple bad guys in three different cities, in a thousand different ways, brandishing his power at eighty electrical settings. I've also been the focus of that force in ways no other woman has dreamed of, let alone experienced. I've even seen that strength ripped away from him by a custom EMP wielded by his own father.

But never did I think I'd witness what I did three hours ago. The man willingly giving up. Telling me he was sorry. Right before surrendering to darkness.

What kind of darkness?

What the hell *has happened to him?*

Like fate tossing salt into my wound, everyone reenters the room. But I can't let my exhaustion and fury get in the way of my compassion. They're just as tired and mad as me, but they're all determined to help. So despite every pore of my skin aching from the effort, I push up and face the semicircle of friends who now comprise Team Bolt. Wade, his dark-ginger brows hunched over his deep-set eyes. Fershan, with his black hair disheveled and his fingernails bitten to their beds. Sawyer, just as tumbled, looking ready to go out and raid a Caribbean village in his brigantine. And then Lydia, saved for last because she's worried more than all of the guys combined—though my walking planner notebook of a big sister does *not* do worry well. That just means I can't look at her for very long.

I will not lose my shit again.

I will not lose my shit again.

For the time being, *that* needs to be my new theme song. Just to get me to where it's even possible to form some cohesive thoughts and understandable words.

"A virus." I'm stunned the syllables actually sound the way I want them to. Composed but furious. Grasping the concept but still refusing to believe it. Still thinking some director beyond the walls is going to yell "cut!" before telling everyone to go take a break while the scene is reset. Still hoping Reece will rise up with a laugh while a cute babe in hot pants flits in, cooing and brandishing makeup brushes while I decide which of her lip piercings to rip out first.

Because even hot-pants girl is a better reality than the one the guys are still pushing on me.

"A virus." Repeating it doesn't help the issue. "You're really telling me that Faline remote-controlled Kane into shoving some kind of electric *virus* into him? Something that's letting that bitch prowl through *his* bloodstream now too?"

Yeah. Definitely the opposite.

After exchanging a brief nod with Wade, Fershan rolls his shoulders back—geek shorthand for girding his loins—and steps forward. "It is the closest we have to a theory, based on Angelique's testimony of what happened at the Source. Based on Sawyer's recap of Reece's final words—"

I brake his analysis with my tight glare and sharp seethe. "Does anyone see a dead man lying here?" I bite out. "*Not* his final words, damn it!"

For a long—too long—moment, the only sounds in the room are those god-awful machines with their heartless beeps. Finally, Lydia is everyone's savior with her quiet but firm statement. "Em is right. We can't give up. There's got to be a way to reverse, isolate, or block what Faline's done to Reece.

How much of his blood could that shit really have gotten into anyway?"

"How fast can *any* supervirus spread in a guy with supercharged blood?" While Wade's mutter is nearly imperceptible, it's not silent. The damning glare my sister throws at him might as well be an answering scream. I direct a grateful stare at her for it...and the strength I desperately reap from it.

At once, Sawyer grits out, "Draw more blood, you guys. Then get your asses in there and run as many tests as you have to until we know what the fuck we're dealing with here."

By *there*, he means the attached lab, filled with every state-of-the-art blood-analysis machine available on today's market, plus a few that aren't. Team Bolt has not wanted for every advance in the hematological realm since the lab and command center were fully functional, and they damn well have plenty of baseline readings of Reece's blood from the last month, so they should be able to run some comparative readings and find at least a sketchy path to whatever's turning his bloodstream into a platelet omelet.

Though maybe it's *not* a *whatever*.

Maybe it's a *whoever*.

I order myself not to go there, even as the lab door opens and Alex Trestle appears in the portal, wearing a determined scowl. His lanky frame is already dressed in a poly lab coat, and a pair of latex gloves dangles from one of his strong hands. The team's master of disguises also has the chops to be a nerves-of-steel scientist if he chooses, and I've never been more grateful for his multiple talents than right now.

"Ready for another fun round of weird science, kids?" he asks, sliding a hand into one of the gloves with a loud *smack*.

Wade grunts while leaning over Reece's arm, brandishing a needle with a blood sample tube attached. "Depends on what you're calling 'science' today, class dork."

Oddly, everyone gives in to fast smiles. The nickname, which Wade has been using since we got back from Paris and Alex started helping out in the lab, is the reminder we all need of the "good old days"—aka three days ago, when life wasn't exactly carefree but was a *lot* closer to the description than now. When all we were worried about was a group of insane scientists coming after us before we had any intel that would help us go after *them*. Before we learned Kane Alighieri never went to Tibet to mourn his dead husband but tried to go after the insane bastards himself. Before he ended up shackled in their lab instead, at the mercy of those lunatics—though as we also learned, *at their mercy* had very little to do with mercy itself.

Especially when, just a few weeks later, Kane showed back up in downtown Los Angeles...and razed half the city in a mindless rampage.

Purposeful emphasis here? *Mindless.*

Faline Garand had gotten her hands on his self-will.

No. Had gotten her *claws* on it. Then *into* it.

And now has tried the same with Reece.

We're *not* going to let that happen—no matter what we have to do. And right now, every damn option is on the table.

Except killing him.

Nope, nope, nope. The "killing him" shit is absolutely not an option.

As if the man has read my damn thoughts from the midst of his bizarre blackness, he flinches to the point of rattling the bed. I look up in alarm before realizing it's just an involuntary reaction to the needle prick as Wade locates a vein and starts to collect the new blood sample. I drop my hand and wrap it around Reece's freezing fingers, unable to identify why I'm reacting as if Wade's slicing a whole knife down the middle of Reece's arm. What's wrong with me? I know Reece has *consciously* succumbed to this procedure a hundred times in the last month. But on all those other occasions, his blood has been *red*—not iridescent blue.

Electric blood should *not* be happening for him right now...

But it is.

Oh holy shit, it *is*.

An anomaly that really isn't a trick of my imagination, if the deeper grooves between Wade's brows mean anything. The icicles in my vitals lengthen as soon as he raises the vial, twisting his lips as if preparing to embellish the scowl with one of his classic profanities, which I find myself yearning for desperately instead of what he *does* spit.

"We have to simmer this stew at once, kids." Alex flings open the door to the lab. "Kitchen's open."

"Outstanding." The word is the only heartening aspect about Wade's vibe as he leads the exodus from the room, which allows me the solitude to focus on taking one deep breath after another as the room is consumed by a strange stillness.

Yes, *stillness*. Not a single bleep, tick, ring, or ding...

"What the he— *Oh!*"

And suddenly, I'm swept off my feet with a rush of invisible but instantly recognizable energy.

"Oh, my... *Reece?*"

He knocks me back, lifts me up, and then brings me down right on top of him—where he digs a ferocious grip into my thighs and spreads me to straddle him. At once, he rocks my shocked core up and down his surging crotch as he raises up to claim my gasping mouth, stabbing his tongue up and then in, focusing on dominating me with fierce, almost violent, desperation.

His charge is invasive and startling but passionate and hot, inciting a war between my mind and my libido. What's going on? On the other hand, do I want to know? He's back. He's awake. Oh dear *God*, is he awake. But how? And why? And most importantly, as who? On the outside, every inch of him is still my muscled superhero warrior, but there's something different about how he's maneuvering that form. His actions are so furious and fevered, I'm at once hesitant *and* urgent to return his passion.

As soon as I hold back, he stalls too. I take it as a good sign, though he adds a growl that's different than any sound he's ever given me before. He seems like a beast that's been deeply wounded but is fighting to keep the whining evidence away from the air. Battling to hide his pain...

From *me*?

"Baby." I press the word against his lips while he gets back to working my *other* set of lips. His cock, freed from its shroud, swells and jerks against my center, which is only covered by the flimsy cotton sleep shorts I hastily threw on hours ago. "*Reece.* It's all right. It's *all right* now, my love. I'm here. *I'm here.*"

He snarls again but finishes with a wolfish whimper this time. "Need...more. Need you, Velvet. *Need you.*"

"I'm right here. I'm not going anywhere."

He growls again. Thrusts his hips harder. "Mmmph. Not enough."

"Reece..." Again, I'm not sure whether to protest or

encourage him. I'm so damn wet. The tang of my arousal mingles with the metallic scent of his. Both our essences thicken as he keeps sliding me up and down his erection, slickening his flesh with the soaked crotch of my shorts. But what would giving in to this animal attraction really be? Our sexual chemistry is directly tied into the force of our spiritual and mental connection. With a good chunk of those cylinders not firing for him, would this be just a bestial fuck and nothing more?

The question alone is an open invitation for a dervish of dread into my gut...followed by a slam of confusion through my brain. Why my stress? The two of us aren't strangers to wild monkey sex. We *like* wild monkey sex. Less than twenty-four hours ago, we were going at each other in the mud in the canyon, resulting in some of the most amazing orgasms of my life and the light show every canyon critter is likely still chittering about today.

But what the hell is wrong now?

The answer hits too easily. And too painfully.

Spiritually, there's nothing there. No answer from his heart when mine calls out to it. No charge of love beneath his touch. And as I meet his gaze directly, the experience is like looking at lightning—in black and white photo form.

"More." If Reece notices the same thing, he sure as hell isn't getting deterred about it. "These. Off. *Now.*" He dips a hand to shove aside the thin cotton that separates his hard flesh from my soaked tissues. "No," he murmurs swiftly. "Fuck it. Just need to be—*yessss*. Oh, Christ. Oh, yes!"

I layer my high gasp atop his lusty grate as he surges up to breach me. At once, he's filling my sex and conquering my body. And though I'm physically ready, the incursion is abrupt and fierce, his cock stretching my walls, his savagery stealing my breath. My astonishment makes me clench for a few seconds, squeezing his length until he rocks his head back and hisses through his teeth. "God*damn*."

"Unnnnhhh." My moan is as dark and just as conflicted as his. This is so right but so wrong. *Something's missing. What the hell is missing?*

"Emma." He focuses on the glistening juncture of our bodies. Where he's pushing up as I'm slamming down, seeking more friction. Needing him...

To do what?

"Reece!" I gaze down, marveling at the beauty of his locked teeth against his burnished skin. He's concentrating so hard.

Trying to do what?

"Reece...please!"

And that's when the answer hits.

It's not what he's trying to do.

It's what he's trying *not* to do.

What I usually start to feel by now, pinging against the walls of my womb with transformative energy. The electrons of his essence. The lightning of his life force.

But right now, the come he's deliberately holding back. By every excruciating drop.

What the hell?

The mystery's too thick for me to even pretend at being his Sherlock. I tell him exactly that by jerking his face up with both hands.

"Oh, my God."

His gaze is a full spectrum again, blasting me with so many intense shades. The hurricane grays of his irises. The cobalt lightning rods erupting out of them, delivered to the edges of his eyes on strands of blinding silver, where they collide with strands of crimson rage. The kind of anger he only reserves for one person alone—only she's not here right now.

Or is she?

Oh, shit, shit, shit, shit, shit.

I plummet my hands to his chest. Push vehemently up from him.

"Oh, *shit!*"

I'm impaled deeper on him, though for the first time since we've been lovers, he grimaces in tangible pain about the fact. "Emma." The whimper has taken over *all* of his tone now, but in place of his beautiful baritone, his agony delivers *him* to me again. The clear connection of our spirits. The bright ignition of our souls. The dazzling bond of every fuse between us, slamming the air like headlights blaring in a moonless night. It's so overwhelming, my eyes sting and my throat convulses.

Just before he grits his teeth and bites out, "Get off me, baby. Right now."

My eyes sting worse. I blink hard. "Excuse the hell out of—"

"God*damn*it, Emma!" he cuts in. "There's no time. I can't block her totally out for much longer."

"*Shit.*" The reiteration comes with a new deluge of tears. I swing my head in wide but useless back-and-forths. "No. No. *No!*"

"*Emmalina.*" Though he's back to channeling his inner wolf, the effort clearly costs him in resilience. "We don't have time, baby. *Listen* to me." When I pull back a little, he looks like I've given him water in the desert...and I hate it. My body has been hardwired by the universe to mesh with his, but his grip on my thighs conveys a defined message. He's holding back. "Damn it, Velvet. Can't you see? This is what she wants me to do. Why she chose now, when you and I were alone, to wake me back up."

He could have told me Faline decided to blow up the rest of LA and gutted me less. Everything he's said is a perfect string back to what Wade and Fershan have already posited... and though I confront that reality in the torment of his eyes, I state it aloud anyway. "Because Kane *did* put something into you." As soon as the harsh angles of his face confirm that, I fight the yearning to bury my fist in one of the bedside monitors. "Something awful," I rasp. "Her...her evil. Oh, *God*. It *is* a damn virus...and she woke you up, commanding you to fuck me...so you'd give me the electric flu as well."

The grim validation on his face becomes the horrific motivation for me to slide all the way free from him. The second we're apart, his cock springs up like an ignited flare, blue veins straining at the flesh, stretching him to the point that the shaft visibly jerks, his lips part on a rough groan, and thick drops of his stunning, glowing essence gush out of the slit at his erect tip.

"Holy...shit." I facepalm myself, wishing I could toss off the motion as melodrama...but this situation is really that eye-poppingly insane. "H-How could you...*did* you...hold back?" His stunning cock is still dripping with those heavy, glistening drops—none of which are inside me.

"With me, all the code gives her is control," he utters back through clenched teeth. "But if it gets inside *you*—"

"I'm dead." I state it because I have to. Because I have no choice but to accept it. We were ready to screw each other like a couple of *Grand Theft Auto* horndogs, but Reece fought off

Faline's sadistic control *and* his raging libido, not spilling even one cell of himself inside me.

Unbelievable.

This man, identified for so many years because of the prowess of his penis, just saved my life because of his *abstinence.*

"Well, damn." I pull in a shaky breath. Let it out on a wobbly sigh. "You *do* love me." To depths that astound and move me as never before.

"Yeah, little Bunny." His gaze glitters with matching intensity. "I do." While he skates his touch up my arm, his tone descends into a concentrated growl. "And you love me too."

"Yeah, you big ox." I declare it through lingering tears. "I really do."

"Good." He curls his fingertips around the back of my elbow. "That's...really good."

My heartbeat clutches...and not in a mushy I'm-sixteen-again way. "Why?" I draw it out with open suspicion, *not* encouraged when he sets his mouth into a determined line.

"Because I'm going to ask you to prove it."

"How?"

"No," he amends. "I'm going to order you to."

"*How?*"

He raises his hold and grips my upper arm now. "I can't fight her off much longer, Emma. And when she gets back into my head, she *can't* have access to my free will." He pauses as if knowing I need a second to process that. To envision what would happen to this place, and possibly all of us, if Faline Garand were able to control Reece like her personal drone. "She can't get even one crack of access to my consciousness," he finally utters. "Do you understand?"

I lift my head, giving him an unobstructed view of the

pulse pounding at the base of my throat. "I'm... I'm not sure."

He nods toward a glass-fronted case on top of a nearby counter. "In there. Rear right side. You'll find some vials of Pentobarbital. I'll walk you through how to use them."

"Annnnnd we're throwing a flag on this play, stud." Somehow I get it out past my lurching stomach. "You... You want me to do *what*?"

"Emma. *Baby*." He twists his fingers around the ball of my shoulder now. "If there were time to let you peruse YouTube on this, I would, but—"

"Don't need the video. I get it." Except that the closest experience I've had to this was jabbing a classmate in high school with an epi pen after she rolled onto a bee in PE. She was fine; I nearly passed out. And more recently, having to hold Reece's hand, while he was *unconscious*, while Wade drew his blood...

Wade.

Oh, thank God. *Wade.*

"Just let me... I'll get Wade or Fersh—"

"No time," Reece snarls before falling all the way back down, as if I've thrown over one of the machines onto his chest. Only I'm nowhere near him now. I'm watching, helpless and wide-eyed, though he no longer sees me. With his body going stiff and his pupils disappearing into his eyelids, he's got a great start for an impressive horror movie scene—except that this is all hideously real. He's actually subjecting himself to some strange seizure in the name of fighting off Faline's mental invasion—and all I can do is sit here and think about bees.

"Shit!"

But not anymore.

"Shit, shit, shit, shit!"

I bound off the table and sprint toward the medications cabinet. The second I haul it open, there's a seismic rattle behind me. Reece is jerking from head to toe now, going for the ideal punk-rock-video audition.

Shit, shit, shit, shit!

"Hang on, baby." It's intelligible past my tears, but I'm not so lucky with my vision. Everything looks like a bad soap opera flashback, watery and confused, as I try reading the tiny labels on the vials inside the cabinet. "Hang on! I'm getting it, okay? I'm...I'm getting—"

"What the hell?" Suddenly, thank *God*, Wade bursts back in. "Emma? What the hell is going on?"

"Did he wake up?" Fershan enters right behind, rushing toward the bed as Reece goes into worse convulsions. "His readings jumped and then dipped, and now they are all over the place..."

"She woke him up." I refuse to give Faline any more verbal credit than that. "And then he fought her back, but—"

"He is weakening." Fershan dips an efficient nod. Though I've seen the exact same motion from him so many times before, it's accompanied by a layer of badass that earns a new river of my respect. I only wish it weren't because of these circumstances, especially when his lips compress as he looks over Reece's spasming form. "He is weakening *fast*," he stresses. "So we must save him even faster."

Badass or not, I step into the gap with shoulders squared. "But Reece told me—"

"I am fairly certain of what he told you." Fersh pivots like a captain on the bridge of his own battleship but tempers the vibe with enough of the aligned-chakras Fersh that I'm double-taking again. Not that he's even noticing. "Grab the

Pentobarbital," he charges to Wade. "*Stat.*"

The guys work fast, Fershan slamming an air mask over Reece's face as Wade sets up to push the coma-inducing medicine into Reece's IV tube. But while they're moving like a well-oiled triage team straight out of Grey Sloan Memorial, I stand here with my proverbial girl dick in one hand though manage to throw a hand towel across Reece's crotch. The larger loincloth has gone missing, so I'm thanking God his erection has finally waned.

But so have all his violent jerks.

And the tension in his muscles.

And the energy of his presence.

Waned. But not gone.

I clutch his hand and hold it tight. Tighter.

When Wade looks up again, it's to jog his head toward the juncture of our hands. "Good," he barks, ginger curls falling into his eyes. "That's really good, Emma. You keep doing exactly that, okay?"

I compress my lips, hoping it helps to rein back the tears. "Uh...okay."

"He is right." Fershan ticks his head in a matching nod of firm purpose. "You have the most important job right now, Emma," he murmurs. "Before the darkness takes him completely, remind him of the light he must return for."

"The light we'll bring him back to." Wade circles and faces me in full. His posture is full of purpose, and his gaze gleams with a strength it's never had before. "And damn it, Em, we *will* bring him back."

"*Without* the wicked witch and her ding dongs."

Even when Wade scrubs a hand along his jaw and mutters, "Dude, no more Judy Garland bingeing for you," I can't summon even a smile. Even thinking of Faline without her damn "ding dongs" isn't pulling down the fuzzy feels for me right now.

Not as Reece's hand goes as lax as a rag doll's in my grip.

Not as his body goes so still and his breaths turn so shallow, I splay a hand across his chest, desperately feeling for his heartbeat.

Not as the last tiny ember of our connection fades from my spirit...leaving me in a vast darkness of my own.

A night in which I'm locked and will continue to be trapped. Until we figure out a way to break Reece out of Faline's wavelength that won't involve giving him a lobotomy or keeping him in a coma for weeks—or even months.

But right now, this is all we can do.

To keep him locked away from Faline, he has to stay locked away from us as well.

"But not forever."

I whisper to Reece—and to myself—the acute vow of my heart. The organ is already threatening to explode out of my chest, just for the chance to burrow into his and stay nestled there forever. Those desperate beats take up the slack for the sparse thumps of his. I flatten my hand across his sternum, grateful for every soft tap I get in return. Cherishing every sign of life his body will give me despite the shroud of midnight in which we've trapped it.

"Hang on, my bold, brave Zeus. We'll figure this out, and you'll be back to slinging lightning at the world in no time. I *promise* you, okay?" I pause and wait, but for what, I don't know. His stillness should reassure me, but it doesn't. There's just...nothing for me to hold on to. Not a single rasp. Not the barest sigh. Not even a hint of his smoke and cinnamon in my nostrils.

Which only leaves one last window.

Faith.

The blindest, hardest, most desperate version of the stuff.

He's still in there. He's still listening. You know he is. You know *it.*

Now, you have to believe *it.*

"I do." I declare it on a thread of breath, pouring all my strength into the clasp of my fingers around his. "I do believe, baby. In you. In the you that's still inside me. *I believe.*"

"Baby girl." It's not exactly the response I was yearning for, but Lydia's murmur is still a welcome addition to the air. She doesn't add to it until she's done spreading out the blanket she's brought, the velour throw from our bed upstairs, helping me cover Reece from the waist down. "You look like the walking dead, sweetie."

"Thanks," I deadpan. "Though technically, wouldn't that be the standing dead?"

"Doesn't matter." She cups my shoulders from behind. "You need rest, and you need it now."

"Then bring me one of the rockers from the living room."

"I mean *sleep* rest. As in, laying your head on a pillow, in a bed."

"Then bring a bed in here."

"I've brought *myself* in here." She flashes her phone into my line of vision. "And I know where to get you if anything beeps or buzzes strangely. Now go. Please. At least for an hour or two."

"Not happening, 'Dia."

"Fine," she says breezily. "Then I guess I'll have to use this *other* handy speed-dial button. Sawyer's always *so* ready to help me out whenever I jingle..."

I spin and reach for her phone—but as the wench has made clear, I really am past the point of exhaustion. All too easily, she swings away, flashing a catty smirk along with the landing page displaying Sawyer's picture and number.

"You're such a bitch."

"Why yes, darling. Yes, I am."

With a seething sneer, I pivot toward the door that leads to the driveway. "I'm setting my alarm for *one hour* from now."

She jerks a golden eyebrow. "Make it two and you can have my extra-frosting cupcake." In response to the questioning quirk of mine, she clarifies. "Apparently Joany stress-bakes."

I school my features against exposing too much of my open drool. Beyond the sandwich I forced down sometime yesterday afternoon, I haven't had anything to eat in the last twenty-four hours. "Ninety minutes." I attempt to bargain.

"That starts when your head hits the pillow," 'Dia counters.

"And I still get the whole cupcake?"

"*After* you wake up."

I roll my eyes, realizing she's probably already sampled the frosting in globby spoonfuls by now, though calling her out will do nothing for this negotiation. Finally, I capitulate. "Fine."

My sister grins. "Sweet." Then wiggles the tips of her fingers. "Rest well."

"*Resting* is part of the bargain, sister. But I didn't promise anything else."

She raises both hands as if I've drawn a pistol on her. "Fair enough."

CHAPTER TWO

EMMA

The second I reenter the house and turn toward the stairs up to the master bedroom, I can't push my foot past the bottom step. I can't think about going back to the bedroom—*our* bedroom—as if this is just another stressful day in the adventures of Bolt and his lady and taking a nap will prepare me for facing the rest of it better. It's too great a pretense to ask, no matter how deeply my exhaustion is embedded into my bones.

Prowling through the house likely won't count as a worthier effort, but after issuing a silent apology to Lydia and saying a wistful goodbye to the cupcake on the kitchen counter with its flawless frosting rose, I'm off for my first lap of my stress-induced journey.

I make fast work of carousing through the kitchen, the dining room, and the den. I stop halfway down the glass-lined hall that leads to the gym and the downstairs office.

Where just a few hours ago, I'd found Sawyer crouched over a fallen, depleted Reece.

Where I'd dropped to his side too and watched in helpless dread as Faline ripped his mind away from me. As she's just tried to do again, bringing on a hundred times that agony.

Because she's that much closer to succeeding?

No. *No.*

228

I wrap my arms around my middle so the resolve has to stay locked inside, despite the chaos of my heartbeat, the tumult of my nerves, and the churn of my belly. But there's no wiggle room on this. I *will* drive everyone on this team to the point of no return if I have to—starting with the girl reflected back at me from the window, with her exhaustion-hollowed eyes—until we find a way to snatch back Faline's new play toy.

The bitch has picked the *wrong* freaking shiny this time.

I drop my hands and straighten my shoulders as the resolve fortifies me, all but trumpeting through me—until that victory parade is roadblocked by another voice from inside.

Oh, yeah? Says you and what army, honey?

Because in the end, without the "Bolt" part, "Team Bolt" is just three tech geeks and a couple of girls from Newport Beach, though there's a chance the surf god and Deneuve's double might decide to stick around if Joany keeps plying them with cupcakes. But even killer cupcakes will only take us so far. While each of us understands a different part of Reece's drive, none of us has the entire scope of it the way he does. As close as *I* am to the man, I have to accept that there'll still be lots of nights on the figurative prairie porch, wringing my hands and staring out at dirt and twigs. Though at least now, that last part is literal.

"Emmalina?" The quiet query hits the air like a whip, making me behave the same way. I snap around though order myself to chill out when confronting a familiar pair of catlike eyes, perfectly made up in shades of blue and gray, perfectly matching her mottled skull. "Are you all right?"

I chuff softly, not sure how to answer. *Well played, fate.* I've mentally parked myself on the porch, only to get an offer of companionship by Angelique La Salle, whom I watched

Reece walk away with the first time I was here, nearly a day ago. Practically a lifetime ago...

In that pivotal moment, I'd been so viciously tempted to give the woman some very choice words and an oh-so-eloquent finger flip. I fight the same provocation now, only the conflict stings a lot worse and burns a lot deeper.

But damn it, Angelique's stare is brimming with true sincerity. She even attempts a little smile. What if fate wants me to see some kind of lesson here, despite its timing needing some serious help?

So I turn a little, leaning against the dark-wood wall comprising the other side of the hall, and mutter, "No. Not really."

Angelique steps a little closer but doesn't push for a therapy session dump. It's pretty nice—a rare quality, actually. Sometimes, though rarely, I've been capable of it myself. Being given the double-X chromosome somehow includes the universe's bonus download of the talking-about-it-will-help chip. But sometimes, instant words *don't* help. Sometimes it's nice to have a friend who's willing to wait through the silence until they do.

"Reece wants to go Japanese Zen garden out here." I nod toward the atrium on the other side of the windows. "Bonsai trees, meditation sand, one of those rocking bamboo fountains..." I look over as Angie hums with understanding. "But I've been arguing for something more tropical. Lush bushes and palms, maybe even some Tiki gods..." I'm on the brink of laughing about how I'd even threatened pink flamingoes to Reece, but the sentiment succumbs fast to a watery wince. "Seemed like such a good idea to put in an atrium when my mom first suggested it. But now..." I shake my head. "It's one of the few things the two of us can't agree on." I push off the wall and swallow hard, battling the urge to drive my whole fist through the glass. "I'd let him have it all now, Angelique. The sand and the bonsai and the fountain and even some damn koi fish, if only..."

As my rasped ramblings are swallowed by my tight choke, Angie steps over and pulls me close. "I know." She rubs my back in comforting circles, and I'm positive that she really does know—but not just because she can fill in the rest of that phrase due to losing the love of her own life. She knows because she *knows*. Her empathy is tangible on the air, flitting at the edge of my senses like a rare butterfly. I can see it and marvel at it, but I can't catch it—nor am I certain that I want to. "I *know*, Emmalina," she repeats, and I know I won't get a better opportunity to at least make the butterfly hold still for a few seconds, so I do.

"You do, don't you?" I angle myself around with a meaningful dip of my head. She needs to see that I'm not only serious but curious. "Just like you were able to discern all the unspoken stuff when Reece first collapsed. Like you were able to *see* things and just *know* them..."

And since I realize I sound like a huge loon, I let myself trail off...only to see that Angie's expression has taken on a reassuring smile. "I cannot *see* anything, *mon ami*," she states. "It is more like..."

"What?" I consciously make the word as open and accepting as it can be. She responds with a look of sincere gratitude before continuing with quiet care.

"I *hear* them first. After that is when the feelings come. The...energies on the air that tell me the rest of the story..." And suddenly, her confidence gives way to nervous fidgeting.

"Please; never mind me. This must sound like *insanité—*"

"*Angie.*" I'm the one grabbing her shoulders now. "I'm engaged to a man who can put on a laser light show using his fingers and knock bad guys on their asses from twenty feet away." A smile tempts my lips, and I let it take over. "I tossed out sanity a long time ago and haven't missed it."

The woman actually giggles, though all too quickly is back to her typical serene smile. "Well, that makes two of us."

"Especially lately?" I prompt.

"*Oui.*" She sobers a little more. "Especially lately."

"Which means what?" I don't ramp the energy all the way to a dominatrix interrogation but make it clear my query isn't casual thing either. Judging from the woman's averted gaze and dropped shoulders, she's hiding a bigger truth and might even want me to drag it out of her—whatever *it* is—but I'm going to borrow from the woman's own wisdom and purposely keep my mouth shut during a patient wait for her to go on when she's ready.

"It simply means that I am learning to...readjust...to a few new things in my life. That is all, Emma."

It's tough—translation: impossible—to accept that as her full explanation. She's already skittered her gaze to the floor too many times. Has feigned way too much interest in following the path of a hummingbird that's visiting the atrium in search of nonexistent flowers.

In return, I lean a sideways stance along the wall, though make it clear that my casual pose is just for show. "A few new things like what?" I don't lower my gaze from her profile, still as perfect as a Bisson painting even without her flowing wig as a finisher. "Like what you're capable of doing now? Or... hearing? Or whatev—" I halt, robbed of the words by my lungs' stunned seizures. "Holy crap." I gasp. Then again. "Holy *crap*." And then hope that forcing my lips around the next word will be worth it. "Faline?" I blurt. "Are you really *hearing* Faline?" When the woman gives away her reaction by flickering barely *any* reaction, I rush on, "How? When? Where?" My breath locks up even harder. "She...she isn't anywhere near *here*, is she?"

"No!" Angie is all over issuing that right away, slowing my pulse rate at least a little, before pressing a hand over the center of her chest in an obvious gesture to settle hers too. "If she gets within ten miles of this place, I am certain I would know it."

Okay, so that returns my heartrate right back to where it was. "Are you saying there's a possibility of that?"

The hummingbird has zoomed away—though even if it hadn't, I'm sure the woman's regard would be honed back in on me. Not that it's helpful. Her face is blank. *Too* blank.

"I began picking up on her frequency while we were watching Reece and Kane's confrontation on that rooftop." A few emerald glints appear in her gaze as she shakes her head, betraying her perplexity about the declaration. "And *oui*; I definitely *knew* it was her." As she closes her eyes, her forehead crinkles. "Such focused fury but joined with cold disdain. So very cold..."

"Like Reece was," I supply. "Just before—" And redistribute my weight back to both feet, as if *that's* going to bash back the memories from invading again. "Right before he was...gone," I mutter. "That was how I knew..." A hard swallow. A slow head shake. "He's *never* cold. But suddenly it was as if he were forced into a freezer."

Angie emits a soft hum. "That makes sense. *She* used to never be cold either."

"Who?" I don't hide my glower. "You mean the ice queen on high?" And why the hell is she suddenly affording Faline even half a tone of friendliness?

"I mean Faline Nicole Garand, the girl I knew back in Catholic high school."

"*You* went to Catholic school?" Bugged eyes don't feel like enough of a reaction, but they'll have to do. "With *her*?"

"Only for the final two years," she explains. "She transferred in from Spain, where she mostly grew up after her parents divorced. That is why you hear her native language as mostly Spanish."

"Were you friends?"

She purses her lips. "Not especially." Then seesaws her head as a stand-in move for a gawky shrug. "I was shy, skinny, awkward. Faline was certainly *not*."

Under different circumstances, I'd laugh. Though the woman does the Catherine Deneuve airs better than anyone I know, it's clear she's learned them recently. The vulnerability beneath her finesse makes the high school stories easy to believe—but stranger to vocalize my next point. "And yet, several years later, you readily signed on for recruitment duty with her and the Consortium."

"I did." Her willingness to admit it, so openly and humbly, is both satisfying and strange to observe. "But I was penniless and gullible, and by that time, Faline had learned how to work both to her advantage, dazzling me with tales of what the Consortium was doing to elevate 'chosen' members of the human race."

"And you wanted to be one of the chosen ones."

"*Oui.*" She pushes off the wall and starts a slow pace along the glass, gazing out at the summer sunshine as if every ray holds a shadowed memory—because it likely does. "For once in my life, I wanted to be one of the beautiful ones. But by the time I realized how huge a trap Faline had set, it was too late. At first, I was bound by financial obligations to the Consortium. They not only resolved my debts but paid for a life of luxury I had never known—as long as I repaid their investment with interest, of course. Once those debts were paid, I'd begun falling in love with Dario and would never think of leaving him in that place by himself." Her shoulders jolt up, and she rocks her head back as if the reflected sunlight has become stabs of lightning. "Perhaps...they knew that somehow. Even back then..."

"I wouldn't put it past Faline." I sniff. "She might have known and then simply waited for the best moment to use it against you."

She turns back, lifting one hand against the glass wall with enough pressure to form defined prints. "I would not put it past her, either."

The snarl beneath her voice has me regarding the woman with distinctly new eyes. "You really do hate her as much as we all do."

The woman doesn't move a muscle. "*Oui.*"

"And you've hated her for a long damn time now. Even on that night when you and I first met...when you came into the Brocade and deliberately baited me about having been out with Reece earlier that night..."

Still not a single flinch. Until she finally confesses, "That week...I was not in my right mind. Faline promised me half the world if I helped her get Reece back. She was desperate and dangled the brightest rewards to gain my cooperation." She blinks a few times. "And I just wanted to be done with all the dirty missions..."

As she tilts her head, seemingly to soothe her guilt, curiosity drives me to copy the action. "I don't get it, though. That woman's obsession with Reece..." I squirm from just having to voice it aloud for the first time, admitting that I'm hoping Angie will echo my puzzlement. I want to think Faline's fixation is just a weird Svengalian thing, or perhaps an issue of pride because he escaped in the first place. But deep down, I sense it's not. I sense it's more. And damn it, that's exactly what every terse line across her face confirms as well.

"Well." Angie pulls her arms around herself, rubbing opposite shoulders. "It is most definitely an obsession." She tips her head back the other way. "As I clearly learned when I failed the mission."

As I fill in the inevitable, and awful, conclusion to that, it's hard to keep looking at her—but with matching certainty, I know that Angie isn't dredging this all up to throw it back in my face. It's written across *her* face when she circles her regard back to me, her gaze glittering and her chest pumping.

"I have performed so many hideous tasks for that woman, Emma—and I am deeply sorry for all of them," she grits out. "But right now, I am resolved to make *her* sorry for them too." She drops her arms—with her hands already fisted. "More importantly, I am going to make her pay for them."

Though I'm tempted to stumble backward, as if her declaration should make me reel, I'm not sure why. "Errrmm... excuse the freak out of me?" I face her fully, planting my feet wide with my arms at my sides. Fleetingly, I imagine Reece taking in my ready-for-anything superhero pose and then chuckling beneath his breath while ordering my clothes off with his eyes. *Arrogant bastard. Beautiful soulmate. Live for my light, Reece. Hang on for me. Please hang on...*

Angie indulges half a smile at my astonishment but only gives herself that one moment before going on. "I think I know where she is, Emma."

And I reel. *Oh, God...I knew it.* "And it *is* a little closer than Barcelona?"

"*Absolutement.*" She squares her shoulders beneath her trendy pink blouse, wearing the frothy fabric as if it's become battle leather. "Yesterday, as Reece and Kane were fighting, I heard her as loud as one of those helicopters circling the city." Her confidence becomes a discernible vibe on the air. "It was *her*, Emmalina. I *know* it."

"How?" I shake my head. "I mean, I'm not doubting that you heard *something*, but—"

"It sounded like a cat in heat crossed with a chainsaw."

So much for the last drops of my skepticism. "Okay, so maybe it was her."

"She was loud this time." She fortifies her stance even more, banishing the last of the tears from her gaze. "And strong." The tears vanish from her gaze, becoming the brilliant greens of Mademoiselle La Salle, world class femme fatale. "She was close, Emma—if I must be honest, closer than I wanted to admit at first." The rest of her classic features align with the new sobriety in her stare. "But in this game, with these bastards, denial can bring disaster."

I should probably borrow a good chunk of the woman's gravity, but I'm too damn excited for the emo rock channel right now. I go straight for the stunned-but-excited gawk before charging, "Where? Can you home in the Angie Antenna to a more specific location than all of downtown?" Which is, according to the news updates scrolling on the muted TV I passed in the living room, still just a few red tags shy of a war zone—though to get my hands on Faline Garand, I'm more than ready for the risk.

Which is why I allow myself half a breath of relief as soon as Angie scoops her chin a little higher and gives in to half a grin. "I believe I can be very specific."

"Okay..." I extend the second syllable, all but turning it into a full question.

Luckily, Angie doesn't waste any more time on being coy. "Rancho Palos Verdes," she declares.

"RPV." I rock back on one foot while fully contemplating the answer. "Where the Consortium used to own a mansion..."

"In my name," she fills in quickly. "Though it was, according to them, sold off a long time ago."

"But you don't know that for certain?" I press. "And how is that even possible?" Something about her somber reaction cranks the severity of mine. "If the deed was in your name, you had to sign the sale papers. They couldn't have just... forged..." But I stammer to a halt from the second she jumps her eyebrows. "Oh, shit. They certainly could have."

Though she hitches a casual shrug, the serious layer of her demeanor persists—to the point that I give in to a bugged stare while she takes a second before disclosing, "They waited for a while to tell me about the sale to my face." Another casual-not-casual shrug. "It was the moment before they informed me about having killed Dario, as well. It was all very well calculated, I am sure. Their aim was clear, after all. To prove, at the best moment possible, that they could do whatever they wanted with my existence and get away with it."

As I release a long breath, I let my shoulders sag by an inch. "No wonder you want to kill that woman."

Her lips are back to their tense line. "Now more than ever."

"And you need my help to do it."

"Now more than ever."

"And you're that certain I will?"

She quirks one corner of the scowl. "I am certain you would kill *me* if I did not ask."

I feel myself returning the look, despite how I fight not to. Damn it, I shouldn't be admitting that she's right—but she is, and overwhelmingly so. She hasn't just asked for a risk-taking favor. She's given me an enormous gift. The sooner I admit it, the sooner I can deal with the thrill rushing my blood—on top of the guilt clutching my heart. This isn't the sanest of plans—if Reece were close to conscious, he'd be hauling out the handcuffs from under the mattress for every reason but the fun ones—but holy shit, how many of *his* adventures broke the mold on crazy, electric blood or not? Nobody willingly wants to face street criminals, speeding cars, jet turbines, cartel armies, city-destroying hulks, and an induced coma, only to be rewarded for it all with their father's betrayal and their brother's death.

Who's ever going to be the hero for *him*? And *when*?

My pulse speeds faster as my heart and soul scream with the answer.

It's going to be me. And it's going to be now.

The moment's been handed down by fate. Though it's had to get here because he's lying in a coma, fighting for his sanity, I refuse to ignore the opportunity. The chance to take down the monstress at the center of so many of his nightmares. To send Faline to the hell she deserves and being there to tell her the trip is courtesy of Reece Richards's woman. Who will always, *always* be there to put down scum like her on his behalf.

With that purpose straightening my stance, I meet Angie's

gaze with determination of my own. "Guess we don't need to review how boldly I just signed on that dotted line," I state. "But what happens if we get to that mansion and it really *has* been sold to someone else? Or she's simply not there?"

She's nodding practically before I'm done asking. "There is a way we can check. I am just not quite certain how possible..."

"Well, you've got to lay it on me first, lady." I issue it while moving past her and leading the way back out into the kitchen. If we're going to storm the evil witch's castle, we're going to need protein bars and water bottles. Last time I checked, neither of us was a real superhero. "You'd be amazed what a hotel front desk staff has to define as the realm of 'possible.'"

Angelique braces a hand to the front of the refrigerator much like she just did to the atrium's window. After an equally fortifying inhalation, she states, "The Consortium installed an elaborate backup security camera system in the mansion. It was completely undetectable to anyone in the house who did not know about it because all of the controls were virtual. The lenses were state-of-the-art, disguised as things like vent screws and switch-plate covers..."

"So they're probably still in there and functioning?" I prompt.

"*Oui.*"

"You'd have to find a way to get back in and remotely access them."

"If you mean completely hacking the system, since I have likely been removed from the users list by now, then *oui.*"

"Hmmm." Though what I really mean is *ugh*. Because unless either of our names have been changed to Neo and we've been plugged into a giant intelligence-sharing device called the Matrix, I doubt either of us will suddenly become an expert security network hacker just because we stick our finger in the port and wish for it.

"Guess my timing on retrieving a team snack couldn't have been better."

Angie and I whip around together, nearly bonking heads, to face the source of that startling interjection—a face with a shit-eating grin we should know all too well by now but doesn't fail to smack us both with visible surprise. Perhaps it's because we both don't want to admit what we already know: the truth that's plastered plainly across Wade's self-sure face.

Mr. Tavish has overheard every word we've said.

"So." And he doesn't hesitate to clarify it to us, even in the space of one audacious syllable. "Sounds like you ladies are in need of a tech wizard."

I rush out a breath, returning his frank assessment. "We might be." And I'm unwilling to commit to more than that yet...

"In order to track down the bitch who's responsible for our squad's misery."

...because of exactly that.

"Wade." I slide a hand atop the counter, guided by some strange sense that the CEO pose will lend me the same air, even in my rumpled sleep shorts and tank top. "Look, I totally value your loyalty—"

"And you clearly need my help."

Angelique scoots forward, dipping her head to pierce a pointed stare at me. "*Yes*." She squints as if I really *have* turned into a stuffy CEO. "We *clearly* need his help."

I shoot back a narrowed glower at her. "And in return, he's going to demand we take him along to the mansion."

She gives me a fresh shrug. The girl is damn fond of doling them out today, along with their matching whiplash moments—gee, like this one. "And just *how* do we have an issue with that?"

"Says the person in the room who *is* thinking?" Wade quips.

"And one of the people in *this* room who won't be missed right away in *that* room?" I jerk my head the direction of the lab. "If Angie or I don't show up for a few hours, everyone will think we've gone down for naps." I spin back to face Wade. "But unless you can convince them all that you're going to *Arizona* for a snack run…"

He tenses his jaw beneath his ginger stubble—for about two seconds. "*Pfffttt.*" Then proves there must have been an Amazon Prime deal on shrugs I somehow missed. "I'll think of something. One of us is always breaking away to brainstorm. When I do, I play *Shadow of Mordor*, and they refuse to join me."

"And they *will* actually believe you would play that for several hours?" Angelique winces. "When you have *Breath of the Wild* and *Persona 5* sitting nearby?"

Wade blink-blinks at her. Then strips off his *Nerf This* T-shirt, balls it in his hands, and drops to the floor at her feet, wiping the toes of her ankle boots with it. "I've reached nirvana—and *you* are the goddess at its center."

"Wade!" The shock beneath my exclamation is eased a little by the matching look on Angie's face—until the guy rises, tempting us to succumb to full coronaries. "*Wade!*"

He jogs a perplexed glance between us. "What?"

"You…you have *abs.*"

"And biceps," Angelique stammers. "And *triceps.* And"— her jaw drops as Wade pivots, giving us both an eyeful of how well his jeans fit him in certain areas better than others—"oh, *merde.*"

The guy ticks up one side of his mouth, looking for all the world like the July dude for the *Geeks with Guns* calendar. "Hey, exercise is good for brain cells."

"Sure. *Brain* cells." Angie murmurs, letting her head lope over to eyeball my friend's ass like the shameless Frenchwoman she is. I'd give the moment a full giggle if my mental capacity wasn't so focused on more vital things.

Accessing the mansion's security cameras.

Confirming the Consortium—more specifically, their psychotic bitch of a leader—are still playing house inside that place.

And as soon as we've done that...

The field trip to RPV is *on*.

We're so close. *She's* so close.

And we're just a few minutes away from being able to do something about it.

No point in even attempting to hide my anticipation about this convergence—a fact I expect Wade to take instant and full advantage of.

"So it's settled? We're a tag team on this one?"

Yyyyep. He's right on time.

Angelique responds by assessing him again—completely north of the waistline this time. "Like the Three Musketeers then, *oui*?"

Wade is fast with his huff-smirk. "Or the Powerpuff Girls."

"Oh, my God," I mutter.

"The who?" Angie queries.

Wade winks my way. "I'll even let you be Bubbles."

"The *what*?" Angie demands.

"*You* can be Bubbles." I glower at Wade while turning and making my way back down the hall toward the office. "Provided you get us into that security cam system and we confirm that Faline is still orchestrating her fuckery from that place."

"Give me ten minutes," he ripostes from two steps behind me.

"You have five."

I use the three hundred seconds well: to race up to the bedroom, strip out of my pajamas faster than a pop starlet in a costume change, and then hurry into the custom black battle camos Alex designed and ordered three months ago, when Wade and Fersh suggested I have a set ready for an occasion just like this. As soon as that's done, I punch a button to reveal our hidden bedroom safe and reach in for the sleek silver Glock that Reece bought me for Valentine's Day. Right now, it means more to me than the diamond tennis bracelet that followed it.

All right, so realistically speaking, the weapon likely isn't going to get me far when confronting Faline Garand's goons—but once it's in my palm, I'm emboldened a little more. My spirit grips my resolve the same way I wrap my palm around the pistol's handle. And weirdly, I don't feel one speck of guilt about it.

I know, without a doubt, that if fate brings me face-to-face with Faline Garand today, I won't hesitate to blow hers right off her hideous neck.

CHAPTER THREE

"Do you like it?"

Her eyes are fucking breathtaking in the glow from the candles and twinkle lights surrounding us in the gazebo table at the Inn of the Seventh Ray. "I love it, Mr. Richards."

I snap the clasp of the tennis bracelet around her wrist. It sparkles in the special lighting too—but still isn't as stunning as those twin pools of turquoise. She damn near makes me forget I have a tongue in my mouth, let alone how to use it to lay a passionate kiss meant to zap her down to her toes.

Why am I remembering this? Right *now*?

Is this a memory?

It feels so real. It feels so real and perfect and joyous, that if it isn't, I'm sure whatever I've escaped isn't worth returning to. Not yet. Not right now.

"It's so stunning, baby." She shakes her head, her forehead furrowing. "But..."

I frown. "But what?"

"It's so much. It's too much."

"Emmalina Paisley." The growl is at once a rebuke.

"Reece Andrew!" she retorts.

"It's Valentine's Day." I snatch up her hand and press fervent kisses to her knuckles. "It's Valentine's Day. Our first

Valentine's Day." Then, because I can't help myself, I lean in and press my lips to hers again. Savoring the feel. Relishing all her tastes. She's salty, like our caviar appetizer, but sweet as the white wine we've been sipping. Her sigh sounds like heaven, and her tongue feels like nirvana.

But as thoroughly as I'd like to ravish her like this all night long, there are still words I've got to say. Important ones. "Our first...of what needs to be many. So, so many."

She lifts her free hand to my face and scrapes the tips through my stubble, while the mists of fucking Avalon itself join the magic in her eyes. I'm not referring to the teeny island town twenty-six miles away on Catalina island, either. "It will be, my love. It will be."

But when the bracelet catches the light again, she's back to peering at it like she expects it to turn into real mist any second. And I had to go and evoke a book about Arthurian legend.

"Are you sure you like it, Bunny?"

"Oh, my God." She laughs and kisses me again. "Baby, it's incredible."

I nip my lips at the corners of her delectable bow of a mouth. "And so are you."

"I just thought that the Glock was my present. You told me that it was for Valentine's Day—"

"I lied." A fresh smirk, infused with every insolent cell in my body. "I said that because you wouldn't have accepted it otherwise."

Rosy circles invade the high cheeks beneath her teasing glower. "You're probably right."

"Tell you what. Let's say the bracelet's for you but the gun is for me, okay?" I give her a needed moment for contemplation and take an appreciative sip of my wine. "I'm going to rest a lot *better knowing that if I'm ever not around, you have the means to protect yourself."*

She scoffs. "Like you're ever not going to be around?"

I deliberately focus my stare on my wine. "You know what we're dealing with here, Velvet," I level, wishing like hell we could be talking about how sweet her cleavage looks in that red dress or how thoroughly I long to drag her out into the lush woods around this place, slam her up against a tree, and take her in complete caveman style. Instead, I have to continue with, "That bitch thought nothing of throwing you and Lydia into a net, with the full intent of feeding you into a jet turbine while I watched. She wants to earn that Consortium achievement patch for retrieving Alpha Two, no matter how many girlfriends she has to murder."

"And if the girlfriend is ready to murder her first..."

"Not an achievement patch you should be aiming for."

"Not unless she fucks with you first."

I set down my wine. Meet her gaze directly again. "Let me prioritize that part, okay?"

She twists her fingers through mine. "You're my priority."

I send a gentle smile. "I know that."

"So just for the record, if she fucks with you, she fucks with me. I'll design a new achievement patch and stitch it right onto her Pixie Stick backside before unloading a full clip into it." She tilts her head, but the move is as unwavering as every word that just spilled from her. "What?" she finally blurts, challenging what must be the rise of bewilderment in my gaze.

No. Not bewilderment.

Utter astonishment.

The woman is fucking serious. Down to the last syllable.

I clear my mind for the dilemma we really need to address.

The query that intensifies as she leans in, giving me some serious side breast viewing pleasure.

"I'm just wondering... How am I going to survive the remaining three courses of this meal if you get any sexier than you are in this moment?"

She runs the tip of her tongue across the seam of her lips. "Who says I'm hungry for the rest of this meal?"

With that, I am damn sure I'm the guy in the restaurant with the hugest boner.

And the heart closest to exploding.

And the soul flying closest to every star in the sky.

And the body that now moves past the controls of my mind, rising and yanking her up with me. Making our excuses to the waiter—something about wanting to stretch our legs between courses—before I haul her into the darkness, sweep her off her high-heeled feet, and don't let her down until I find that perfect tree. The one I'm going to smash her against as I do nasty and lustful things to her body...starting with sliding my hand beneath her dress and then shoving aside the center panel of her panties before lunging up and in with one finger. Then two. Then three...

"Reece!" Her gasp is gorgeous. She repeats it in time to the compressions of her walls around my fingers, as all ten of her digits dig into my shoulders despite the slick fabric of my dress shirt. I twist my hand, adding to the friction on her delectable pussy. There's a fresh tang on the air, smelling wholly of the aroused nectar she's coating all over my fingers. "Reece. Yes! Deeper. Harder. Reece...Reece..."

"Reece. Reece!"

"Hell. Maybe we should give him a few minutes to reacclimate, Foley."

"We don't have *one* minute, let alone a *few*, Trestle. Just in case you've forgotten?"

"I'm just saying—"

"If it's not a suggestion for waking this bastard up, I don't *care* about what you're 'just saying.'"

"All right. You want a real suggestion?" An impatient huff. An answering one, more resigned. "Stop smacking his face."

"And what? Play some Zen sleep cycles so his chakras are in the proper order for optimal biorhythms?"

Yet another huff, though a wary one this time. I've exited enough of my mental fog to recognize the sound when Foley makes it. God knows, working full-time for me the last ten months has given him full opportunity to refine the sound. It's the exhalation he reserves for the times he's double-checking his grip on reality right before agreeing to do something that wasn't included in his "Essential Private Eye Duties" manual. Knowing him, that damn manual really exists too.

"Mmmppph." It sounds much better in my brain, but it's a start. "Mawww...mooo...fuhhh..." But on the bright side, hearing my voice chorusing through my head with the vocal grace of a porg is the perfect incentive for unsticking my tongue. "Wh-What's...going on?"

"Oh, thank fuck." The spew is from Foley, positioned off to my right, while Alex's distinct chuckle comes from somewhere near my feet. I'd open my eyes to confirm all that, but the light penetrating my eyelids is already a ruthless glare, sending the porgs still left in my brain into more screams.

"Ah! Progress!" The new voice in the room, accompanied by the plastic rustle of a poly lab coat and a disposition brighter than a Bollywood score, would be distinguishable even if I were still in the damn coma.

In the coma...

I'm able to rear back, almost viewing myself lying here, and recognize the perception for what it is. For the first time since waking up, my consciousness connects to the comprehension. I've been...gone...for a while. But for how long? And why?

The answers are so vital, I'm <u>willing to sacrifice</u> my comfort, sketchy as it is. But the second I crack open my eyes, comfort is definitely a foreign concept. Maybe that's a good thing. With my heartrate jacked from the light blast, my brain also goes on warp speed. At once, it remembers the last time I felt all this at once.

I was on my back and staring up at the ceiling of the downstairs office. Foley was gawking down at me, looking a lot like he does now, messy and intense and wearing a scowl infused with that metaphysical shit he likes borrowing from his favorite Muse tracks. But Alex and Fersh weren't the ones with him. It'd been Angelique and Emma. Angelique with her new radio wave powers and Emma simply with *all* the power. Ruling me. Sustaining me. Guiding me.

Saving me.

Literally.

Giving me the will to go on, even as the ice invaded my blood. Even as the chill took over my system, blowing in with its inexorable control. Numbing me to the point that the only choice for survival was surrender.

And so I had.

Or so I'd thought.

Until her voice followed me right into the dark. Her soul invaded the shadows of Faline's grip and wouldn't let go. Her will made it possible for me to go beyond that blackness, into a deeper night where I was safe...

And that takes care of the why. But crashes my consciousness with all the other "pertinent" issues here.

"Progress." I repeat Fershan's word in a dazed mutter. Seems a damn good place to start. "And how, exactly, have we gotten to that hashtag?" I address it to all three of them in a sweep of my gaze before pinching the bridge of my nose in an effort to cut the thundering pain behind my eyes.

Foley clears his throat, and I'm relieved to hear the confidence beneath it. "It's still Saturday. Time is twenty-fifteen, give or take a few seconds," he starts in. "We induced you into the coma about four and a half hours ago, with Emma's permission. Do you remember any of that?"

"Emma." I repeat the part of that worth the effort, though after a few long seconds, attempt to expand on the answer. "I—no. Nothing, really. I only get...pieces."

Begging Em to push the Pentobarbital in my IV. Doing that after I'd literally nearly fucked her to death. Doing *that* after being hauled back to consciousness as Faline's horrified puppet, my every move guided by the witch's bioelectric strings on my limbs. And her haughty purr in my head...

"Well, that's probably a good thing." Foley breaks me free from the downward spiral of the memories. "Though even pieces of shit are still shit."

"I'd say you could say *that* again, but don't you fucking dare." I'm glad for the excuse of getting to trade some smartass with him. The guy looks like someone dragged *him* to Faline's mental ice castle and back.

"Got it, man. Loud and clear." He rubs the back of his neck while darting a quick glance at me—"quick" being subjective. What's the proper velocity for a look filled with three novels' worth of hidden meanings but not leaving a sole lasting impression? "We've got to move on to other subjects anyway," he states. "*Right* away."

I tap the button that raises the table beneath my head and shoulders. "Sounds like I need to be upright." Even if my ass is stuck to a steel slab, the guy who treats flying bullets and pursuing goons with the same ease as a choppy onshore flow is now grimacing like he got handed a full-on hurricane watch.

"Yeah." Foley rocks his head back over his massaging hand. "Maybe. Sure."

I narrow my stare. Ping it between him, Alex, and Fersh, unable to ignore how Foley's unease has seeped into their demeanors too.

"For the love of fuck." I throw up a hand in exasperation. "You assholes actually going to draw straws about who gets to give the update to the sap in the bed here? Because it's a huge damn relief I haven't woken up as Faline's dick-on-demand, but I don't have the strength or patience to even thumb wrestle anyone for that intel right now."

When their stares continue to be the finest combination of hesitation and observation I've ever seen, I plunge on without any mercy. "You *still* just going to play the coy game? Going to make me guess at how long I have left? Does this all at least get better as I get closer? Will I start seeing psychedelic candy corn in synchronized swimming routines? The Rock singing 'Let it Go' in drag while keeping time with himself on a ten-pound pickle tub?"

Alex finally tosses me a bone. "We're sorry, man." He spreads his hands like a diplomat. "You were tossed into a psychological wormhole for half a day, and now we're giving you our fucking triumvirate of tension."

"Because we have good reason to be tense?" Fershan mumbles.

"Shut. Up," Foley spits.

"What the hell?" I laser him with a glare.

"One step at a time." Foley includes everyone in the reproof, even me, before nodding back at Alex. "Go ahead, Trestle." When Alex replies with a questioning brow, he states, "Tag team. You're part one."

"There are *parts*?" I don't hold back on the new flare of my eyes. "And now that we're talking the team, where's Wade?"

Foley dips his head, working way too hard to maintain the neutrality across his face. "Like I said, man, one step at a time."

"But how many steps are we talking?" I snap. "You did say I was only out for four hours, yeah?" How much of a shit show could've gone down in that time?

My apprehension is nudged as Foley whisks back by a step, deferring to Alex while cocking a sardonic brow. "After you, boy wonder."

Alex gives back as good as he gets with the sardonic expression. Trestle, our king of disguises on the outside and prince of tech expertise on the inside, has chosen to channel George Patton's grit with Edward Cullen's pathos—which is either pure weirdness or complete genius. I'm too exhausted to attempt a final call on the matter now.

Without further ado, he starts in. "In a nutshell, there's good news and weird news."

I lean forward. The action drops the blanket around my waist down to my hips, but I don't give a shit. What Alex says is a lot more important than what he sees right now. "*Weird* news?"

"Because it's not necessarily bad news." Fershan steps forward, looking like a flight attendant having to tell the passengers the plane has "a wee bit of engine trouble."

I sit up higher. Drop the blanket lower. And care even less.

"What the hell does *that* mean?"

"It's a slight blip, and we're fixing it." Alex is right on time as the "sensible" flight attendant.

"A slight blip." I swing my legs over the side of the bed. Then, fighting dizziness and nausea, force myself to fully sit up. "You want to explain why every instinct in my gut is calling bullshit on that?" And continues to do so, no matter how fiercely my brain bellows that I've just spent half a day in a psychological no-man's land and it might be prudent to cut my "instincts" a huge break?

Which will happen. Just as soon as I get a straight answer, with an honest gaze, from even one of these fuckers.

"Okay, okay." Alex spreads his hands wider, as if smoothing bed wrinkles off the air. "We're putting carts in front of horses, and the animals aren't even saddled yet." More calming wrinkle-smoothing as the guy turns to fully face me—and at *last* grows the *cajones* to level his gaze with mine.

I drop my brows even lower. "*What?*" My trepidation doesn't budge by a single degree.

Until I'm cognizant enough to ask myself the same damn question.

And realize that my brain already has the answer.

Because of what it's *not* full of.

Because of *who* it's not full of.

"Holy fuck." I release one hand from its punishing grip on the edge of the table and wham it against my temple. "Holy, glorious, fuck of all fucks." I add a gleeful cackle that could make me the next worthy contender for the Joker. "Where'd the bitch go? Wait. Scratch that. I don't want to know. She's gone, and I'm close to French kissing every one of you beautiful bastards for it."

"Easy, Romeo." Foley joins Alex in flattening the invisible bedspread. "We're not sure Radio Faline is totally off the air yet."

"We had to MacGyver a fix faster than we expected." Getting to shout-out for one of his favorite heroes has detached Fersh from the awkward flight attendant thing—though his assertion reintroduces *me* to the well of troubled confusion.

"Why?" I prompt. "What was your *original* expectation?"

"He means we had to go in cold with an untested solution," Alex inserts. "Going on the theory that Faline is really using radio waves to patch into your head, hopping onto whatever code Kane managed to cram into you, we figured that those waves would be interrupted if we could ionize your blood."

Unlike a lot of conversations I have had with these guys, I actually follow what they're saying. So far. "So you thought blasting me with a concentrated version of sun radiation would cause the radio frequencies to defract from the positive ions and free electrons—and then silence them."

"Right on the money!" Fersh pushes up a thumb as if there's a gold star on the end and he wants to smack it to my forehead.

"So how'd you make that happen?" I ask, genuinely interested despite the bizarreness that we're discussing my fucking brain cells here. Back at Columbia, I'd picked a radio station conglomerate to study for an Investment Strategies midterm paper. It was one of a few times I'd actually been engaged by a college project. I'd learned an understanding of radio waves and how solar radiation and sun spots affect their strength. I also learned that most of those effects were temporary and that ions and electrons eventually equalize and recombine, allowing radio waves back through.

Leading back to the caution Foley's already tossed out.

"We rewired the lines from all the photovoltaic cells in this place." Alex darts a smirk toward the ceiling as emphasis. There are enough panels across this complex to give full power to a dozen Inglewood bungalows, three Simi Valley McMansions, and a couple of Santa Ynez ostrich farms. "Funneled them down here, where we switched out your IV lines for electric-safe PVC conduits, then shot the charge directly into you."

As he relays the story, Fershan jams his hands into his lab coat pockets and fiddles with his favorite stress marbles. Even Foley gives in to a smirk. I don't blame either of them.

"And you really just went for it," I reply. "Balls to the wall? No test punch?" After confirming that much via their collective silence, I mutter, "That's simultaneously cool and horrifying." They saved me—but just as easily could've killed me.

"We had no time!" Fersh's outburst seems to be borrowing another MacGyver meme—obscure as hell if that's the case—but mixing it with genuine objection.

"Fersh is right," Foley states. "There really wasn't any time." But as soon as I jump my brows and cock my head, demanding an explanation without having to *demand* it, he swings his stare back toward Alex. "And here's where the master of tact gets to take it away again."

"Dickwad," Alex flings.

"For fuck's sake. Just go for it," Foley rumbles.

"What *he* said." My rumble tackles the thunder cloud he won't touch. Not that it's necessary. Alex has known Foley longer, which means he also can tell when Foley's simply being moody as opposed to don't-fuck-with-me-I'm-on-a-mission grim. Right now, it's blatantly the latter.

Alex yanks his shoulders back, clearly determined to

support his explanation with an all-business posture. "We rushed because we knew you'd want to be woken up as soon as possible."

"Why?" Though at once, my mind has plummeted to the same realm as my voice. Into the pit of caution—followed at once by the valley of apprehension.

And then right away into a swamp of fear.

It's irrational at first, and I know that. Just because Emma's not *right* here doesn't mean she's not *here* here. Which sounds, even in my head, like I've lingered too long at the Crazytown oxygen bar. But the recognition, coupled with Alex's spidery tension and Foley's vulture gloom, has me anxious to get moving. *Now.*

I grit my teeth and shove off the table as fast as possible but pay for it as soon as the room spins and my senses lurch. Still, I force my feet to stumble forward and push through the fallen blanket to make my way into the lab.

Where is she?

Where is she?

My balance reels harder. My gut clenches tighter.

As I realize she isn't the only one missing here.

As I fight to write that off as coincidence—though my gut already seems to know it's not.

"Wade," I blurt, because vocalizing *his* absence is easier. "And Angie." I purposely stop there, forcing a wry tone past the bizarre ball of dread growing in my gut. "Where'd those crazy kids run off to?"

Please tell me they're just grabbing snacks.

And please tell me Emmalina's with them.

Please, goddamnit, tell me they're all in the kitchen inhaling bowls of Ben and Jerry's Bolt Jolt Brittle Sundae...

"Reece." Foley's already moved on from his grim mission voice—though the new tone comes as *no* fucking reassurance. This demeanor was likely perfected when an advocate for calm was needed despite every detail of the situation dictating otherwise.

Like now. When key details of the situation *are* missing.

"Where is she?" My gut has turned into the goddamned ice cream churn now, only the flavor is "Salted Caramel Craptastic." I pretend I'm standing in bespoke Prada instead of my wobbly birthday suit and that Foley's in cahoots with Emma on pranking me with a twisted game of hide-and-seek. "Come on, asshole. Give it up for the guy who signs your paychecks. Where's she hiding her cute little ass this time?" Which only betrays how thinly stretched my neurons still are. Because no way in hell do I want Foley, or *anyone*, sparing half a brain cell on envisioning my woman's ass.

Which, thank fuck, the guy gets right away—evidenced in his slight grimace at my innuendo. But when he hardly flinches, even to offer me some kind of reasonable explanation, the churn in my belly is replaced by worse—mechanics I've never experienced from my system before. Gears of dread that spiral so fast, the revolutions are blinding whirs. Those spins getting so hot, they ignite rocket boosters. Those fires getting so intense, every part of my logic is a blur of dangerous heat. *Houston, we have lift-off.*

But no sign of Emmalina Crist.

Ground control doesn't look filled with great news on that front.

"She's...not here, man."

I wait a beat. Another. Accept my sweats from Alex and then jam my legs into them without wavering my gaze from

Foley. Once the pants are on, I mutter, "Okay." And edge as close to making it a question as I can. That's all he's going to get, since anything I'd add would squander time that's now precious. Seconds he could be filling me in on what's going on.

Finally I violate my own mandate and growl, "For Christ's sake, Foley. Spit it the fuck out. She wasn't taken, right?"

I almost retract the fucking question mark, let alone the words themselves. If that had been the case, I'd have woken up to a much different world. Who am I kidding? I wouldn't have woken up at all. As loyal as all these guys are to me, they'd each slice off their left testicle and eat it for Emma. They'd have left me in that Pentobarbital haze for weeks more if it meant saving her. And Foley? He'd be stomping around here like a fucking starship captain on crack, ordering everyone to move at warp speed for the sake of finding her, including everyone he knows in the FBI, his spec ops buddies, and *their* special "resources." The dude is maintaining the moody glower, making him look like a blond version of the sulking Beast without his Beauty. Thank fuck we didn't build any real turrets into this place.

Wait.

A beast. Without his beauty.

I snap up, posture going rigid. Wheel around, double-checking both rooms again. "Lydia," I pronounce. "Where is *she*? Maybe she dragged Em off on a walk...to distract her..."

"Except that the last time I saw her, I'd ordered her to go get some sleep while I watched over you in her place?" says the woman now entering through the door from the driveway, her red-tinted curls blown askew—with a matching tinge at the edges of her eyes. The redness isn't from crying, though. It's from deeper stress. A darker fear. "Wade and Angelique are gone too."

And just like that, this shit has gotten shittier. "I noticed," I growl, performing a fast evaluation of the Crist sister who *is* standing in front of me. It's one thing when Foley gets dramatic and dystopian with us. It's another when Lydia sports a red-rimmed gaze, tightly wound stance, and distinctly wobbly voice—without a single bit of Lydia sarcasm to lighten the impression.

Damn it.

Ground control, we've got a tiny hitch.

No fucking wonder they woke me up early.

But somehow—I really don't *know* how—I fight every flame of the panic and rage. Refuse to punch either of those fucking buttons. It's like fighting a forest fire with a blowtorch, but I have no choice. Now more than ever, I've got to keep this holocaust contained. To conserve the energy of the ions as much as possible. Every collision and spark to my system means less ionization and a greater possibility that the team's grueling work will be for nothing. I'll return to being the dead brick on their table again—or worse.

Because if Faline finds a way back into my blood again...

With that injunction in mind, I face Lydia again. Fold my arms over my chest, deciding to just go for the obvious. "I take it you *did* look in our bedroom?"

She nods. "Even out on the sun deck."

It doesn't surprise me that she knows about Emma's little "happy spot" for escaping the world, and normally I'd be happy about the sisters' special closeness, except for the way Lydia's wearing every shred of her stress now. Something's wrong, and the woman knows it. On top of that, I'm unable to feel Em at all for myself. Reaching out to her feels like trying to hear a whisper at a rock concert. There's a fuck ton of extra noise in my senses right now, and organizing it into manageable files is going to take some time.

Time I don't have.

Where's a cosmic MacGyver when I fucking need one?

A question that 'Dia's obviously asked for herself, as she swallows hard and lifts her dark, watery gaze back to me. "We've covered the rest of the house and grounds too—but they're not here."

Through sheer force of will, I summon strength to my legs and some balance to my head and use both to stumble outside to the driveway, where Foley is already waiting with a clenched expression and a stiff stance. "We've done the motor pool inventory," he declares. "Angie's rental is gone."

Ground control, we'll need to upgrade that hitch to a full shit storm, please...

I breathe hard, fighting a total nosedive into moroseness while leading the way into the house.

Once we're in the foyer, I'm slammed by air that doesn't feel right at all. Doesn't smell right or even sound right either. Not without Emmalina here. Suddenly, the house has simply become a building. A structure. Walls and steps and furniture and a roof. Not my home.

Not *our* home.

Still, I suck all that shit back up and smack my hands together with a defined *whomp*—a sound loud enough to drown the cacophony in my senses so I can turn and grab one of my tablets from the foyer hutch. Swiftly, I swipe to the app that'll show me where Emma's phone is located—only I'm still waiting for it to load when Lydia grabs me by the wrist, already shaking her head. "I already tried. She left it here."

I stare as if her head has fallen off. Clench my teeth as

my bloodstream's electrons eat away at their solar infusion. "What the *hell*?"

'Dia chews into her bottom lip. She's picked up the habit from Emma and emulates her little sister to the point that I rub against the ache in my chest. "Reece," she rasps. "The serve's *not* lining up with the box here."

"*Bingo*." Foley's exclamation goes with that like an orgasm in church, though his victorious grin only widens as Lydia and I toss over a pair of gapes. He holds his phone aloft as if toasting with the communion wine. "Emma left her phone behind, but Angelique didn't."

"Thank God." Lydia rushes over, grabbing his device while popping on tiptoes to buss the bottom of his jaw. "You're brilliant."

I swear to God, Foley puffs up just like that kid on *Stranger Things* after locking lips with Eleven at the Snow Ball, though he recovers rapidly enough to mumble, "Not brilliant enough to have thought of it before now—though it says the signal's been parked at that spot for several hours now."

"*There?* In Rancho Palos Verdes?" Lydia responds. "But what the heck *is* that place?"

"Fuck." Foley and I spew it together. But even with his fraternity, I fight to use the acid in my gut to dissolve my horror instead of my reason. For talking myself *out* of remembering that RPV contains a lot of other structures in it than just the one the Consortium once used as their stateside recruitment facility. And that maybe Angelique has a damn good reason for traipsing off there without telling anyone here.

With Wade and Emmalina in tow.

After she demonstrated, very vividly, that there's more going on under her skull than a marbled light show.

Synapses that Faline has claimed now too? And now controls? And calls to her bidding the same way she remote-controlled Kane?

"Fuck." I all but punch the echo onto the air. Foley leans in to look after Lydia spreads her thumb and forefinger across the screen to zoom in.

Don't leap to conclusions. It could just be a fluke. Cart before the horse only makes a mess, especially if the horse just got out of a four-hour coma.

I grit back the damn tizzy, even while watching Foley and Lydia staring at the screen, the separate gold shades of their hair mingling as they lean in. I'm doing damn well until Lydia mutters, "What the hell is that? Church? Shopping plaza?" She jumps an astounded stare to Foley's profile and then back to the screen. "That can't be a *house*, can it?"

I already know what Foley's going to say before he snarls our favorite four-letter word again. I know it because the instincts I couldn't link to Emma just a minute ago are now going off like fucking fireworks, compelling my mind to face the truth before I yank the phone from Lydia. Before I blink back the furious fog from the edges of my gaze, knowing I've taken tizzy to advanced ionization but I'm unable to fight the fucker. Before I swipe the map back down in order to orient the pin to the surrounding areas.

And sure enough, there's Christmas Tree Cove to the north, Golden Cove to the south, and the exclusive strip of oceanfront mansions along one of Southern California's most prime coastal bluffs. When I switch the view to a satellite overhead, I see the Consortium's estate, with its sloped Mediterranean roof and an electric security fence along the perimeter. The designer pool is still in the backyard, with deck chairs as pristine as the last time I laid eyes on the place. The damn things have likely never been used.

Because the place is still being used as a Consortium recruiting station?

"Holy. *Fuck.*" One good repetition deserves another, right? Except when a guy has to focus on ionization containment and the words burst from a gut that's grinding and roaring, powered by rockets with bile as their fuel.

In the haze in my periphery, there's mindful movement. "Richards." I've suddenly never been more thankful for Foley and his ability to play Spec Ops Buddha when I need him the most. "Talk to me, man."

His posture is more tense than usual, as if he's dropped into mental starting blocks and is simply waiting for me to fire the race gun. I hate thinking about how accurate that comparison might be.

"The fuckers never left the place," I finally grate. "They just pretended to close it all up. Covered the furniture and kept the lawn up, probably so the HOA wouldn't hound them, and have continued using it with someone else's name on the deed."

"Guy's name is Roman Engrid." The information comes courtesy of Alex, who's tapping efficiently on another smart pad. "He's the middle son of the Engrid Seafood dynasty."

Foley licks his lips. "I love their cod bites."

Fershan, the team's adamant vegetarian, mumbles, "I shall tick your word for it."

Foley cocks his head. "You can *take* my word too, if you want."

"No." Fersh waves a hand. "You can keep it."

Ignoring them both, Alex goes on. "Engrid was a small local outfit in Norway, until Roman had aspirations of taking the brand global. He did so by signing on with Meta Seafood Packaging..."

"A known Scorpio cartel conglomerate," Foley finishes for him, frowning.

"Fuck," I spit again. "Fuck, fuck, fuck!" My fingertips crackle with blue and gold sparks, which intensify as I yank open the storage closet under the stairs. Inside are at least three sets of mission leathers. I waste no time dropping my sweats and switching them out for the thickest black fighting pants I own.

With one-two-three efficiency, Foley's got his hoodie shucked without releasing his expectant stare on me. "So we *are* riding the same wavelength here, yeah?" he prompts, pulling out the leathers I had customized for him.

"Depends." I knife one arm and then the other into my jacket. "What's on *your* wavelength?"

"The fact that Angie looked a little strange during our drive back here yesterday, especially when we hit the area near RPV," he asserts. "Maybe she was zoning out because the mental woo-woo stick was connecting to *that* pin"—he jogs a nod back at the phone as I return it to Lydia's grip—"and that the feeling got worse as soon as Faline tried to hook up the link to *you*..."

"And now Angie's coerced Wade and Em to go back there with her."

"Probably selling them tickets for the 'Retribution on Faline' bandwagon."

As Foley zips his jacket to his neck, his jaw turns into a blade of tension. "Which may or may not be the truth."

"Does it really fucking matter?"

He dips a terse nod. "Damn good point."

Why doesn't that make anything feel better?

As a matter of fact, why does it only rev the rocket blasts in my gut, melting everything from my waist down, including the ice cubes of my knees? Why did I think I could even get out the damn door before yearning to plummet to those knees and vomit from the most violent craving to kill I've ever known? And why is it now stacked on top of the most dreading fear I've ever endured?

But why do I remain on my feet, picking up my pace out the front door and making my way to the Range Rover with wider, faster strides? Why do I hike myself into the passenger's seat, knowing that if Foley drives, I can think more clearly about what has to happen once we get to that bitch's mansion? And why do I already start narrowing down the list of possibilities, despite how that tops off the bile fuel tanks in my gut?

My bold, brave, selfless, dauntless woman actually thinks the *princess* can save the *prince* now by slaying the fucking dragon.

But killing the dragon isn't the solution to the quest. There's only one way to do that, and I've figured out that secret already.

Winning this quest means *becoming* the dragon.

CHAPTER FOUR

E M M A

Why don't the movies ever go over *this* part of secret missions?

Or the fact that it has to be endured with a nonstop loop of French profanities in the background?

Or the fact that answering nature's it-won't-wait call is a *hell* of a lot harder to finish on a time limit than picking a lock, cracking a safe, or stealing through a garden under full moonlight?

The fact that we haven't done any of those things yet, even after sneaking inside a mansion that should have its own zip code, isn't the point.

Or maybe it's exactly the point—because I'm sure that if the *Sneaky Spy Shit* instruction manual really existed, all that *other* stuff would obviously be included, complete with pretty chapter headings, detailed line drawings, and even a few step-by-step instructions.

What they *wouldn't* include is what Angie, Wade, and I have figured out minus the manual. Thanks to our friendly neighborhood tech hunk, who hacked the city's database and downloaded the mansion's blueprints during the drive down from the ridge, we easily found the laundry room. After that, Angie became the mission's stud operative. Her ability to size up a person at first glance, as well as her knowledge of the secret dressing room behind the laundry racks, got our camos successfully stowed and our new personas in place: executive housekeepers for Angelique and me and sous chef's whites for Wade. I even lent some confidence-building tips, courtesy of too many PR courses to count, helping us act like said "official" staffers in walking past two sets of security guards just to find one damn bathroom.

Relatively speaking.

If this palace inside a palace is really a bathroom, then I'm the goddess Aphrodite and all this luxury shouldn't be making my eyes pop out of my head. But I continue to bulge my gaze at the pool-sized tub, multi-head shower, and toilet stall in which two thoroughbred stallions could easily fit—which, of course, makes it impossible to even *think* once I've plunked down for the "business" I've insisted on getting in here for.

Holy shit, shit, shit.

"*Mon dieu.* Any chance of hurrying things along, darling? *S'il vous plait?*"

I toss a glower at Angelique through the mullioned glass partition. "Make you a deal," I growl back. "I'll attempt to get this done *tout suite*, and you let go of the pee whisperer duties, okay?"

"Hmmph." She stops and stamps now. Even through the textured glass, I watch her long blond waves fall back into perfect place. "You would prefer I trade places with Wade? I am sure he would like to get out of pretending he is still on his way to the kitchen."

"Are you freaking kidding?"

She has to be freaking kidding. But when there's no answer from the other side of the wall, I wonder if she's gone and utilized her mighty French girl balls to make good on the threat. And *that* yikes me out even more than having to take care of business in this marble sepulcher of a bathroom.

But this bathroom, and the concept of Wade's presence in it, shouldn't even be making my list of qualms about what we decided to come here to do. Qualms that began the second Wade hacked into the mansion's security system, rebooted this place's gazillion super-secret cameras, and showed the feeds to Angie and me. Qualms that were amplified when I saw Faline through those cold lenses. Not because of the doubts about killing her—because there have never been any doubts, nor are there now—but because I *don't* have those misgivings. Not a single damn one. A revelation, of course, that *does* cause me doubts.

Ugh.

I never considered killing another person prior to a few hours ago. Is it possible to be so certain that I'm ready to do this...now? Shouldn't I be on some kind of spirit quest, debating about this? Taking a figurative, if not literal, hike into the woods to talk to the Big Spirit in the Sky about this?

Remarkably—or again, maybe not—all those quandaries are resolved when I return to a single word.

Faline.

Since talking with Angie back at the ridge, I know the enemy better than ever. She's a years-in-the-making psychopath. A damaged creature, genuinely convinced that she's been ordained by the universe to mess with the lives—and deaths—of others. Her thinking's as whacked as images in carnival mirrors, but those mirrors have become her reality. She's dived fully into the glass, creating her own demented court and kingdom from all the broken shards.

And dragging her bleeding army through the carnage behind her.

It's time for Queen Faline to fall.

Before she turns my man into her casualty.

A purpose I'm able to reclaim in full as Angie's heavy sigh fills the bathroom. *Oh, thank God.* I've been granted a pass on the Wade retrieval threat, and taking care of business is finally easy.

"Let's get out of here," I mutter once I've smoothed my "borrowed" uniform back into place—only to be hauled back by the woman now grabbing my elbow and spewing a string of disgruntled French. But just when I think she's about to give me a lecture about letting nerves drive me to chug a whole liter of water between the ridge and here, she jerks up her head. Then swings around a stare with anxiety that visibly matches my pre-mission water-chugging levels. "Angie? What the—"

But then I hear it too. No. Not "it." *Her.* The queen of the crazies herself, heels clunking louder and louder in the long, tiled hallway.

"*Merde!*" Angie rasps, instantly *whump*ing the air with the force of her stress. Her energy bears a similar jolt to Reece's, but instead of flashing lightning, hers is like the *whoosh* of a comet. Brilliant and blinding, leaving only faint trails behind, until once more flashing the atmosphere.

The cycle keeps up as she whips out her phone and taps in a two-digit text. Before she hits Send, I know what the message means. It's the emergencies-only code she's preestablished with Wade.

I definitely think this qualifies as an emergency.

Faline's bootsteps come with an accompaniment now. She's rattling off orders to her minions. I can't make out anything specific, soon realizing it's because she's speaking fluid Spanish. Every few seconds, there's a soft, "*Sí, maestra,*" in a quiet male tone, interjected between her orders.

"Holy *shit*," I blurt.

"Holy fuck." The response nearly overlaps me. But just when I think I've really lost it and am hearing voices, Wade's rough bark becomes tangible on the air—as the man himself breaks into the bathroom. Literally, he's broken in. Angie and I didn't notice the door on the other side of the vanity, since there's no knob on this side and the seam is totally plastered over. But thank God—again—for those blueprints, allowing him to kick through the rubble he's created, one hand extended, already shouting, "Come on! This hall dumps back out into the other one. We can circle around and take her and her goons by surprise!"

By the time he's done, his yell has become a full roar. By necessity.

Because of the alarms that start wailing throughout the entire building. But not just any peals. These are the we're-all-going-to-die kind, straight out of duck-and-cover reels from the last century. I honestly suspect we're going to burst out of the secret passage and find ourselves face-to-face with aliens, terrorists, or biologically restored dinosaurs.

What awaits us is worse.

Or better, depending how we choose to perceive it.

Because technically, finding Faline Garand *is* exactly why we came here.

Just maybe not looking so dewy and fabulous, even while jogging up on the heels of the henchmen who have summoned her to our exit point. And especially not being so damn prepared, despite having swapped out her sleek catsuit for a dark-red sheath she probably poured herself into, joined with black suede hip boots that take the term "statement shoe" to a new stratosphere. But at the moment, it's not her boots I'm fixated on. It's the gleaming daggers in her hands that catch the light as she twirls them with practiced ease.

Crap, crap, crap.

I hold myself back from saying it, no matter how hard the words gurgle and push at the base of my throat. Could have something to do with the moisture causing me problems elsewhere: whopping beads of perspiration, dripping past my eyebrows and collecting on my lashes, start fuzzing out my vision. I compel myself to take the valuable seconds and attempt to shake the fog free, but everything's still a blur even as I haul my Glock out of my uniform's other pocket. But my periphery is still fully functional, and it gives me the welcome notification of Wade brandishing a similar pistol, along with a Bowie that makes Faline's knives look like fast food plasticware. I send up a fast prayer that Angelique has taken precaution to come equally prepared.

Only to realize, in the next moment, that she would have been wasting the time and effort.

Two more goons rush onto the scene, obediently bracketing Angie with nothing but a commanding jerk of Faline's head. Before they're fully in place, Angie's eyes pop wide, her predictive psychic hearing going to work...

Giving her the heads-up that her handlers are going to clamp bright-red glow ropes around her ankles and wrists.

Glow ropes?

Only...they're not.

These shackles are worse. A terrifying whole bunch of worse.

At once, as Wade and I watch with widening gapes, Angelique's energy changes. While it's still clear her vital organs and mental functions are intact, those glaring shackles have immobilized every muscle up and down her arms and legs.

"Holy. Shit," Wade grits out—a shock I share but feel as paralyzed as Angie about expressing. If I repeat those words, I have to face the reality that's brought them. That just like that, Faline has used our own damn tactic against us and hijacked the surprise party *we* were bringing for *her*.

My pulse triples, beating what is left of my nerves to a pulp. I whip a glance Wade's way, taking in his pumping chest, flexing fists, and throbbing veins in the sides of his neck. *Ohhhh, shit.* The bitch has flipped the tables on us, but my friend looks ready to take a try at flipping them back.

Damn it, Wade. Don't do anything crazy. Don't do anything crazy!

And I've given myself permission to say that...why? Because I hadn't made one of the craziest calls of my life when I decided to break in here and do this? Because I'm *not* standing here in front of Reece's hugest nemesis, still telling myself not to feel like a geek in a maid's costume while she's approaching with the serenity of a practiced geisha? Because I'm not still struggling in vain against the invisible strands around my arms and legs, frantically thinking—violently *praying*—the bonds will somehow give way just because we're the good guys?

That's the movies, you dumb shit.

The good guys only get to win in the movies.

But they get to move *in the movies too.*

"You bitch!" Wade seethes.

"*Salope.*" Angie's version, while rasped like a title of a poem, carries ten times the insulting intent. But if the witch notices or cares about either version, she doesn't show it by one iota.

"Well, well, well. Angelique, my old friend." Faline pivots to slide the back of a finger down the side of Angie's face, though her steady scrutiny doesn't falter from Wade and me. "You certainly took your time, darling. I expected you hours ago, *amiga*. And you really did not have to bring apology gifts... though I am most grateful for the kind gesture."

Shit.

By *gifts*, the woman isn't referring to a couple of potted plants or some scented candles. Though at the moment, I wish I felt more like a pillar candle than a fern in a pot, the roots of my balance hopelessly knotted while just a breeze would knock me over.

In contrast to my stupefied silence, Angie breaks into hissing French profanity. But Faline is much more interested in Wade and me, appraising us from head to toe. My heart thunders faster, wondering what will happen once she's done.

And dreading the unnatural stillness she takes on when she is.

And flinching when she finally does move, flicking just the tip of one twiggy finger.

And watching, unable to hide my incredulity, as that tiny move rips the golden waves off Angelique's head and sends them flying down the corridor. With another finger tick, Angie is driven to her knees, the lattice of electricity across her skull transforming into furious purple pulses. She drops her head. Hunches her shoulders. Curls her fingers in, scrabbling so hard at the floor that her nails audibly screech. Everything about her form screams in humiliation and mortification.

"Ahhh, well, look at that," the bitch purrs. "You are not the only 'special' one in the room anymore, *amiga*." Then rocks back on one heel, hands hitching to her hips. "But what was it that Sister Anais always said to us? Ah, yes. *Everyone* is special in God's eyes."

Wade bares his teeth. Raises his gun. "Yeah? Well, guess what? The dude down in hell also saves special places for people. I think yours is already engraved and waiting, baby."

Faline lifts a smooth smile. She still looks like she's tolerating a fly, only now it's as if the insect has done a backflip and awaits her approval. "And *you* are going to be the one to show me the way?" she drawls. "Is that it?"

As she's getting coy with Wade, a tormented whimper falls out of Angelique—spurring me to stomp forward and align the Glock with the center of the woman's smirking face. "If he doesn't, I will."

But why are we even standing here *talking* about this? The time for action was practically a minute ago, when this bony harpy and her threadbare soul first appeared in front of us. I came here to rid this world—and the mind and will of the man I love—from her. And here she is, right before me, in all her elegant insolence, wearing the color of all the blood she's spilled and ruined for so many—and I've become an indecisive mess.

But why? How?

Just shoot her.

Just. Shoot. Her.

I resecure the gun in my grip and focus on all its steely might and potent power in my palm...but am helpless to move beyond that. My hands are sweaty and slick. My arms start trembling. My aim wavers. If the Glock's barrel were a paintbrush, I'd be creating a shallow infinity symbol on the air with the thing.

What the hell is wrong with me?

Wait.

Maybe that's not the right question.

What the hell is she doing to me?

Oh, God. Is *that* it?

Why are my heart and spirit—and yes, now even my head—a crashing chaos of remembrance stuffed full of all the hideous acts I can recount the woman being directly or indirectly responsible over the last year but am unable to squeeze just one finger to claim payback for them? Why can't I exact the vengeance the whole team has dreamed of getting for Mitch and Kane, for Tyce, and yes, even for Dario? Most crucially, the requital for Reece. For the body she ravaged for six months and the soul she scarred forever.

For the mind she's ruthlessly fighting to control.

For the will she will *not* be allowed to steal.

I vow it.

But somehow, I'm not able to act on it.

And with a skittish glance, I realize Wade is waging the same struggle with his weapons. He's held back by the same bizarre, invisible bondage that I am.

Damn it.

He's wobbling his pistol barrel worse than me. His Bowie topples from his grip, clattering to the floor. One of Faline's goons sweeps a foot over, kicking the knife hard enough so that it only stops when jabbing into the baseboard.

What is going on?

I stare at my arms, still stiff and flexed in front of me. But they're *not* a part of me. My system's been cleaved in two. My body has rebelled against the demands of my heart.

No. That's not right, either. My body is ready and able to cooperate here—but it's not being allowed to. My bones and muscles and synapses have been denied access to their free will.

"Holy. *Fuck*." Wade's hoarse cry brings a flood of comfort but a jolt of anxiety. The good news is, I'm not going totally crazy. The bad news is, I'm not going totally crazy. There *is* a metaphysical spider web across the entire room, and the three of us are stuck in it, gawking at the treacherous arachnid who created it.

"You sick bitch." Wade's seethe brings more of my psychic conflict. On one hand, every note of his fury mirrors my own—but the second he spits it, I yearn to give him a good head smack. Whatever's going on with Faline—however the hell she's making all this happen, whether it's Consortium technological trickery or her own DNA upgrade—now is *not* the time to be *goading* the unstable witch. And yet Wade torques his lips, fires up his glare, and stabs on. "You think we're going to dissolve and slink into submission just because you can Jedi-fuck the air?"

But Wade's the one answering his own charge—with a strange sound from deep in his windpipe. All right, not a sound. A gurgle. Because he's *choking*. Because with just one lift of her hand, Faline's shutting him up by *strangling* him.

"Hmmm. Now look at that," the bitch drawls as my friend gasps and gags for air. "And I thought you were the go-to boy of Team Bolt."

I've never been more thrilled to welcome a surge of rage to my blood before. I let the floodgates slam wide, every drop rushing and blasting, the inferno consuming me faster than a smoldering log tossed into a drought-ravaged ravine. Growing me. Empowering me. Incinerating every last speck of fear in me—until I clench the Glock harder than I can imagine. I point it steady and true now, tracking the barrel with the back of the bitch's head as she leans over Angelique, her ink-thick waterfall of hair brushing over Angie's mottled dome and downturned cheek.

"Stop it!" My snarl lays on top of Angie's taut sobs and Wade's heartbreaking chokes. Sounding and feeling just as useless as both. "Let them go, damn it, or I'll..."

"What?" Faline croons it while tracing one of Angelique's electric trails with a shiny red fingernail. "Tell me, little rabbit." She deliberately taunts out that last word, slanting a preening glance over her shoulder. "I really *do* want to know."

I curl my finger tighter against the trigger.

Tighter.

One instant. One snick. She'll be gone. Angelique will be free. Wade will be free.

Reece will be free.

But I can't squeeze any more. No matter how hard I clench my muscles or how thoroughly I focus my resolve, my finger's frozen where it is. If I let go of the gun at this very moment, I wouldn't be surprised if the whole thing simply hung from my immovable digit.

"Oh, my God."

But my rasp isn't quiet enough. The bitch has heard me and unfurls a smooth laugh to match her satiny rise—and then the slick curl of her hand, right before the adroit snap of her fingers.

Spearing pain into everything from my ribs down.

No. It's more than a spear. It's a gash of agony and then a twist of evisceration, followed by an infusion of ice so dire, the torture feels more like a burn than a freeze. Yet when I lower my head, hating yet needing to behold the damage, there's not one rip in my dress or drop of blood marring my middle. With my free hand, I grab the area over my navel. Everything is intact to my touch, though the movement brings worse torment. It feels like I've just grabbed my intestines and yanked them out of my body.

"Well." Faline sweeps around and then cocks out a hip, appraising me as if she's eyeing a horse for auction. "Aren't you so special too, *chiquita*? But of course, we already know that, do we not?"

She steps over to jerk on my chin, pivoting my head from side to side and smiling softly while taking in my wobbling jaw and tear-streaked face. "Pain is quite an alluring look for you, I think. Hmmm." Her dark gaze narrows. "I should have considered that angle before—though in New York, I hardly had the resources that are available here. And *sí*, I must also admit, back then, I never thought that you would last."

I blink hard. Pledge not to reveal that the new pain she delivers is so intense, I'm now seeing two of her—though there's a damn good chance she's already figuring it out. "Th-That I would l-l-last...h-h-how?"

"Oh, come now." Her smile returns, borne on a pair of saucy clucks. "We selected Reece for the program for very special reasons, you know. His virility made him infamous. Even when he escaped, we considered that aspect of his *enhancement* an interesting experiment. What kind of impact would his seed bear when sown among a variety of females?" Her cluck deepens into a sound of assessment. "We anticipated most would not survive, of course—but science comes at a price, you know."

"No," I spit. "I don't know."

"Well, obviously." When she punctuates herself with

a long velvet laugh, only to see I'm not sharing the joke, she explicates, "What we did not anticipate, darling, was *you*."

Deep frown. "Me? How?"

"You and your...stamina, Emmalina." She rakes me from head to toe with a stare that has me sympathizing with a pinned butterfly. "Do you not see? You are still here, *chiquita*. Not only still alive, after clearly letting the man fuck you repeatedly and with such force and passion. After all this time..."

Her gaze gains a weird gleam, tempting me to let out a full scream—though I already feel as if I'm being strangled by barbed wire. But even if I really were, she wouldn't get the satisfaction from me. I swear it to myself, even when she releases her hold on Angie and Wade and motions for a couple of her henchmen to drag them away. As they go, she calls out, "*Muchos gracias* for the gift, my Angelique. Oh, yes, yes." Her voice returns to its assessing murmur as she impales me with a more clinical air. "This is going to be such *fun*, little rabbit!"

"Go...fuck yourself," I spit past teeth that taste like chalk, from a throat as dry as that chalk dust.

"Thank you, darling. Perhaps later, if no better offers come along. But right now, I am having so much fun fucking with *you*."

And nausea was just what my gut needed right now.

Everything hurts. It hurts so much.

The only consolation I cling to in the middle of this madness is that Reece is still lost to the darkness of his coma and doesn't have any consciousness to attach to any thoughts of me. No shred of our electric connection. No sixth sense to reach out to me or comprehend any part of this surreal sadism the woman is inflicting on me...

How?

How the *hell* is she really altering my will, controlling my actions?

At last she releases my chin with a sharp push and then backs off by a few elegant steps. "Do you know, little rabbit pellet, how pathetically easy it is to dither with you?" She rocks her head back. Releases an airy scoff while waving a hand with equally frothy laxity. "I do not even need a remote control for most of your kind. What do you basic humans find so fascinating about each other?"

I battle to think around the pain, attempting to get in as much air while keeping my glower fixed on the damn harpy. "And yet...I share Reece Richards's bed...every night."

The incensed glare she returns to my stammer isn't surprising. *Who's the predictable one now, Faline the Magnificent?* I hang on to the gloat while watching more turbulence enter her eyes, and then there's an incensed flare of her nostrils. If she can read the snark across my mind, I certainly haven't helped my cause—but something tells me I could have been meditating about a Bob Ross painting framed in 3-D puppies and earned myself the same vitriol from the bitch.

So why not let it all fly now?

But by the time I unstick my pasty tongue from the back of my chalk-tastic teeth and think of a moment alluding to the night Reece and I spent on the Seine reenacting the Kama Sutra for about five hours, I've regained consciousness in another room. Hardly comprehending what landed me here— for a second or two. But then it starts to return in petrifying, torturing flashes.

Another flick of Faline's wrist.

The henchmen lunging over, resembling flying monkeys

in their speed and impact.

Their disconnected murmurs in my ears—*sí, our queen*—before Faline gives them more quiet orders and they're grabbing me. Restraining me. Carrying me.

A hall. Another.

Around a curve. Through a locked door that buzzes and startles me—but not as much as new hands on me that belong to a trio of females in medical scrubs and face masks. I'm free again—but not. I'm unable to move *anything* now, even my mouth to protest how they efficiently strip me naked and then carry me again, laboratory Oompa-Loompa style, and roll me onto a steel table.

A steel table.

Where I am now.

Where I try to scream now.

And I do.

As loud as I can. As long as I can. An hour? Two? Three? What's time in a world of nothing but white walls, steel equipment, and blaring lights? What are sounds if I'm the only one left to hear them?

What's going on? What's going on? What's going on?

I trade the scream for a grateful sob when there's suddenly another voice in the room. When there's a shift on the air, probably belonging to the voice. I don't even try to swivel my head, already having discovered that the Oompa Loompas secured me from the neck up in a steel collar contraption, rendering it impossible to shift anything other than my eyes.

A woman, also in scrubs and a mask—but with nearly black eyes I'll never forget and will always be able to identify—steps into my view.

Her.

It's *her*.

And I cry harder—because it doesn't matter.

Because the white, endless solitude was worse.

Because even the hatred I have for her is like a miracle. A reminder that I'm still here. I'm still me. I'm still existing.

Oh, God.

I flinch, shocked to hear the words tumble intelligibly out of me. But I jolt even harder, filled with twice as much dread, as she dips closer to me, her black gaze spreading like ravens' wings, annihilating everything I see.

"Ahhhh, no, *chiquita*. Just me." She strokes her knuckles over my cheek. "How are you feeling?"

Fuck you.

If she picks up the thought from my head this time, she doesn't show it. "The pain is better, *sí*?" she murmurs. "Almost gone?"

"Yes."

Though I force civility into it, Faline pulls down her mask to give me a full view of her pinched scowl. "The proper address is, 'Yes, my queen.'"

I tighten my glare. "Now you can really go fuck yourself." And at once am rewarded with the pain of fifty drills in my belly, churning my internal organs until I'm amazed the bright-white lights aren't shattering from my screams. "Yes, my queen!" I shriek. "*Yes, my queen!*"

Faline waves a finger.

The torment instantly halts.

"So much better." She puts her mask back into place and then gently pats the side of my face. "I do regret this crash course in obedience training, little pellet," she murmurs, rising up. "It was considerably more fun to break in your fiancé, such as it was. Men can be so...stimulating...when they're pushed to the limit, over and over and over again." She's no longer visible to me, but my skin prickles as I gauge her presence around me by the calm taps of her shoes. "But alas, we have such a limited amount of time and so much work to get done."

Yes.

Shivering.

But not terrified.

What's the next stage of fear beyond that? The phase where a query has to be stuttered out, no matter how hideous the answer is surely going to be?

"Wh-What k-k-kind of w-w-work?"

The bitch makes me wait for it. Through a bunch of awful minutes, filled with yet more of her tapping those heels, she twists knobs and adjusts a bunch of other equipment— including, I now discern, the tubing connected to at least three IV lines secured to both my arms.

"Upgrading you, of course, *chiquita*. Expanding you. Empowering you. *Improving* your pathetic existence."

I shiver harder.

So hard, my shudders become a wild, jerking fight of their own.

Until I can't shiver anymore. Because everything in my body is fire.

No.

Not fire.

Heat.

Scorching me. Razing me. Taking over me.

Every shade of blue and then every spectrum of silver.

Then every level of pain.

Until I know. *I know.*

I'll never be the same again.

If I survive this hell at all.

REECE

"It's quiet."

Though Alex issues the observation in an equally subdued tone, his voice is loud, clear, and completely understandable through the radio comm in my ear—probably because what he's saying is true.

Freakishly true.

"Yeah," Foley returns, his hands tense on the Range Rover's steering wheel as we roll past the Lunada Pointe mansion for the third time. "Too fucking quiet."

I turn my head toward the mansion, which is just as sprawling as the others on this exclusive strip of oceanfront real estate, with its lush landscaping and Italianate architectural lines. But it's almost nine o'clock, and the rest of the homes have at least exterior lights on by now. The mansion in front of us is a collection of darkness and shadows, despite the fact that the air around it pulses with the energy one can only experience from another human being. That's not my magical Bolt-ometer talking, either. That's common sense, honed after tracking more than my fair share of bad guys in too many "quiet" Los Angeles alleys—and it's confirmed by Foley's driving too. He feels it too. He *knows* it too.

"You picking up anything on the infrared, Trestle?"

"Nada," Alex answers. "Not even a goddamned lizard in the bushes."

His reply contains a dial-back on the stealthy and a boost on the fury. He and Fershan closed in on my level of freaked—but not surprised—upon realizing their teammate had insta-volunteered for mission duty with Emmalina and Angie and then pushed themselves into overdrive so Foley and I could have as many high-tech gadgets as possible once we rolled. Watching their frenzy was racking but reassuring. Nothing conveys stress faster or more wildly than a tech team scramble, but the fact that it *was* a scramble had been the right encouragement at the right moment. I'm not the only one who's ready to put everything on the line to bring the three of them home.

"Roger that," I mutter back over the comm. "Not a creature is stirring, not even a lizard."

"Under normal circumstances, that might even be a good thing."

Brief snort. "Should I be the first to point out the obvious here?"

Fersh is our resident optimist, not usually the one growling.

"Fuck." It tumbles out of Foley with so much grit, I glance over and expect him to be foaming at the mouth.

"You guys have to go in." The decree belongs to Lydia, her scythe of a tone clarifying that the dictate isn't open for discussion. Fine by me. There's no time for a debate right now. Not a goddamned second to waste in pursuing our singular goal.

Finding Emma.

Then kissing the oxygen out of every cell in her body.

Christ in heaven. Why did I fall in love with a woman who even thinks it's okay to do shit like this, anyway? Who, after the first time I told her my secret identity was Bolt, tackled me, kissed me, and then called me the most beautiful thing she'd ever seen? Who hasn't once whined that my "extracurricular fun" is training ninja murder techniques with Foley or reading a hundred pages of blood sample analyses?

Who, after just one year of becoming the completion of my life and the center of my soul, has been assaulted, uprooted, kidnapped, deceived, horrified, scrutinized, and paparazzied— on top of being bombarded with sights, concepts, and an alternate reality that no woman should ever be forced to believe, let alone accept as her life?

All right, so maybe it's hardly a wonder that she's sneaked off with Angelique and Wade. Further, that she thoroughly believes it's possible to save me from Faline armed with a simple Glock and a few motivational mantras.

Impetuous, impervious Tinkerbell.

Stupid, intrepid Bunny.

Noble, unshakable woman.

The sole person I can't live without.

"Damn it," I rasp after we've parked the Rover down the block and start toward the mansion, sticking to the shadows of the miniature rainforests that double as front lawns around here. *Goddamnit, Emmalina, if you've gone and gotten yourself into a shitstorm of trouble...or worse...*

I refuse to think about the *worse*.

But I do.

And because of it, endure a flood of neurotoxins called *panic*, which suddenly stops me in place.

Thank fuck for Foley. "Yo." Who gets it already and doubles back with a look of tight concern. "You all right, AC/DC?"

And succeeds in shaking me back to the moment with his latest contribution to the team's nicknames pond. Raw bewilderment will do that to a guy, and I concede to a slam of the stuff while contemplating the reference to a band I never imagined as Foley's jam. With every fiber of my heart, I plead to heaven that after Em and Angie got here, they found nothing and dropped Angie's phone on their way to an impromptu stroll on the beach. That they stopped somewhere for drinks and lost track of the time. That Roman Engrid just wants to use this place for giant cod bite parties.

Now that my brain's filled with scenarios only bleach will erase, I refocus on Foley. "I'm fine. I'm *fine*." I nod toward the house. "I just need to know *she* is too."

Foley returns the nod as we crouch behind a giant elephant ear plant, eyeballing the mansion more fully from our vantage point. "She's got a sharp head on her shoulders, Richards."

"Not saying she doesn't," I retort.

"Then what's with the bee in your lovely bonnet?"

I toss a stiff side-eye. Copy his huff, only with a lot more emphasis on the irritation, while fighting mental images of Emma inside the house, tied up and gagged and—

Enough.

"She just doesn't know everything Faline is capable of."

"The fuck she doesn't." Foley's comeback is immediate. At the same time, he frees his SIG from his body holster, steadying his grip with one hand around his carrying wrist. "She just loves your sorry ass more than she hates and fears that bitch." A fast glance, just to prove he's as serious as a sommelier calling out cheese pairings. "You really don't get that yet, do you?"

"Of course I do."

The guy grunts. "Great." Then elbows me in the gut. "So let's get this show on the road before you trip over your nose, Pinocchio."

"Fuck you," I mumble, with Alex and Fersh's snickers as my backdrop.

"Sorry, broheim," Lydia cuts in. "That's my job, remember?"

"And on *that* piece of TMI..." Sawyer snorts. "That's going to earn a certain brat a visit from my spanking hand."

I copy his elbow jab. "And *that* piece of TMI, *none* of us should have heard..."

He snort-laughs before leading the way out of the bushes and onto the mansion's property line. We stick to the shadows along the far perimeter until spotting the power breaker box that Alex located on the satellite overview of the place. Not that his task was easy, since the thing is shrouded by an eight-foot-high Bird of Paradise, but the guy didn't quit enhancing shots even after we took off in the Rover, and he finally found this intel when we were ten minutes out from the house.

It's our critical key to moving faster now.

After buzzing the flowers down with some effortless lightning blades, I have to zap a little more effort into slicing the padlock from the breaker box itself. But a few seconds after that, Foley has the backyard lights and security system completely shut off.

And then, we brace.

Through twenty seconds.

Thirty.

Forty.

At just over fifty, we're rewarded for the patience—"reward" being relative, since it's in the form of at least fifteen of Faline's minions who scurry like chickens in the path of a hurricane, clearly attempting to troubleshoot the security system breakdown before their mistress on high takes over to do it. Because with Faline, "troubleshooting" usually carries a much different meaning.

"Uh-oh." Foley's comment is no more than a snarky vibration on the air, though even if he'd gone full volume, nobody would've noticed. It's pandemonium inside the house, for which we have a full ringside seat thanks to the towering glass windows along the ocean side of the structure. "Looks like Mom won't be letting the kids have dessert tonight, dear."

It's ripe for a good follow-up, but my sarcasm is eliminated as soon as my logic kicks in. "But where *is* Mom?" I lean out from behind the pool equipment hutch now providing our cover, though I'm hardly sure we need it. For a bunch of chickens facing a Cat Five rager, the goons are weirdly oblivious about anything outside the mansion's physical boundaries. Almost as if they don't *see* what's outside...

"Damn good point," Foley mutters, joining my scrutiny of the scene.

"Could she just not be here?"

Fershan's huff comes over the line. "But would the worker bees get that frantic without the queen in the hive?"

"Damn *great* point," Foley answers.

"Agreed," I add.

A new grunt from Alex roughens the line. There's a sound of the comm piece being muffled but not thoroughly enough to drown out Trestle's spitting passion for the F-word. "Uhhhh... Alex?" Fersh ventures. "You okay? You need me to come up to the lab or some—"

"Trestle?" Foley's already dropped his demand to a growl. "Talk to us, man."

Suddenly, as soon as memory hits me in a rush, I blurt, "The infrared." And then double-palm my torso and thighs before explaining to Foley, "The detectors aren't just in the Rover anymore. The guys wired a bunch of them into the battle leathers a few weeks ago."

Foley eyes my leathers with an approving nod. "*Sweet.*"

But we celebrate only a second longer, since the line is roughened to static by an explosive snarl from Alex. "Jesus Clark Kent Christ with a Kryponite dildo," he finally spits out.

"Trestle?" Foley sputters.

"What the hell?" I demand, rising all the way. There's not a single double-take from any of the goons inside, so I stalk all the way out into the open. The backhoe scoop of gravel in Alex's voice has buried any remaining cell of calm in my body. All that's left are the nerves that blaze in trepidation and the senses straining to see or hear anything unusual.

Who the fuck am I kidding?

Is there *anything* "usual" about any of this?

"Okay...shit...there are more than a few lizards stirring inside there," Alex rushes on. "They—they must've had steel blocker walls across the front of the house. Fuck, I'm sorry."

"Don't be sorry," I snap. "Just be on the game now. *Damn it*, Trestle," I dictate when his end of the line is too silent for too many seconds. "If you don't talk to me, I'm just going in." And am even more driven, along with savagely grateful, when Foley quickens his stride to match my stalk across the pool deck.

"Uh...yeah," Alex finally stammers. "That's a damn good idea."

"*What* is?" Foley retorts.

"Going in," Alex returns. "Like, *now.*"

I break into a jog. Okay, maybe a full run. "What the hell does that—"

"Just do it." The brutal punch of Trestle's ordinance

makes me instantly wish for the stammering again. "Once you're in, cut a hard right through the sun room. Then down the hall after that."

We're not running hard, but Foley's breaths are heavy huffs on the line. "Then what?"

"Just keep going." Another harsh breath, but definitely Alex's this time. "Just...fucking...*please* keep going."

Before he's even done choking it out, we're using the Bolt battering ram to enter the sun room—aka, me *whomp*ing the window with a directed pulse, sending the whole pane of glass to the ground—before continuing to head right. A few seconds later, our sprint begins down a long, tiled corridor with ornate sconces along the walls out of some damn vampire movie.

As we run down the passage, members of the Faline happy squad seem to materialize out of the walls. They're really only bursting out from doorways, though the fuck-all with my imagination is the same, sending my mind into surreal gamer mode. The eerie light from the sconces adds to the effect, the dimness accenting the unblinking gold glow in all their eyes, making me feel like Van Helsing without his cool weaponry— or any of the adversaries sprouting fangs. Like that matters.

I take each of them out with the same ruthless instinct, either spearing their chests or slicing their throats with the lightning firing through my senses and shooting out my fingers. I barely think about the actions, adapting each for optimal destruction. And yes, goddamnit, that's all this is right now. Later, I'll need to confront the fact that they're humans—or that maybe they once were—but right now, with Alex's hoarse pleas echoing in my head, all I can think about is getting down this fucking hall.

Getting to Emmalina.

Because she *is* here. I know it now. Every lash of my breath, pierce of my pulse, and agony of my muscles confirms it. Stabs it. Torments me with it.

Until they don't.

Until I reach the massive steel door at the end of the hall and tear it off its hinges with a massive roar.

Until I yell even louder, as her misery hits me like a full gale.

Until I struggle to comprehend the scene before me.

Standing stock still, stupefied and ashamed. Thinking if I stay this way, the horror will vanish. My gut will give my imagination back to my mind and clarify what I'm really supposed to be seeing. That I'm not really supposed to be digging a hand at my head, singeing my scalp as I drive my fingers through my hair, yearning to burn them through my skull. I want to gouge out my brains and hurl them against the wall.

Because I'm not supposed to be seeing this.

Because this isn't real.

Because this is just another nightmare, only worse.

Because unlike the thousand other times I've relived it, when memory has attacked me in the midst of exhaustion or sleep, *I'm* not the one on that steel table, naked and shackled and terrified.

No.

"Jesus God." Foley spews it on behalf of us both. My holocaust of a throat has turned my voice to ash. My spirit is a thunderstorm of horror, raining lava through every tendon, bone, muscle, and nerve in my body.

I want to fucking die.

But I can't.

I can't.

If I die, there's no hope for Emma. There's no way out for her. And yes, she still *has* a way out. Somehow, I'm able to take a mental triage on her, even from here. Her skin is still the color of pale cream. There's no discernible energy sparking from her extremities. While the machines Faline has her wired to are advanced versions of the torture devices they used on me, I recognize the humanity in her bit-gagged whimpers. The bitch hasn't stripped everything from her yet.

Yet.

"*Darling!* What a lovely surprise!" Faline attempts to croon it, but the soprano to which her voice jumps, instead of its worldly alto, is blatant. Clearly she hasn't anticipated our arrival at all, meaning the solar flare infusion is holding steady in my bloodstream. Thank fuck, because right now, I feel completely bloodless.

"Jesus...God." Foley's repetition, while still a sandpaper snarl, is dunked in a deeper vat of shock this time. The impression makes me look over to where my friend's stance is racked by tiny, violent lurches. He seems to want to step forward but is being held back by a thousand filaments of invisible wire.

"Hmmm," Faline hums then. "Close, *cariño*, but not quite. I am definitely the upgrade." As she finishes by swooping a couple of fingers toward him, missing only a wand to seal her Slytherin membership, I suddenly realize—it's *her*. Whatever strange electric spider's web has taken over the air and trapped Foley in place, it's being controlled by her.

And "upgrade" or not, I take advantage of the seconds in which she preens for Foley to pulse myself to Emma's side. But as her scream splits the air, I leap back with my hands in the air, heart thundering at my ribs. If I ever hear that agonized sound erupt from my Emma again, I won't just tear my brains out of my head. I'll rip my skull off my shoulders.

This is killing me.

But even worse, I know exactly what it's doing to Emmalina.

Every excruciating notch of pain throughout her body. Every terrible plea for it to stop in her mind.

Matched by every tormented muscle in my body, holding back from spinning and strangling the bitch who stomps back over with furious hisses. But I can't kill her. Not yet. The shackles on Emma are controlled by codes that are likely known and controlled by Faline alone. *Ding dong, the witch has to live on.*

"Attempt to touch her again, or override the codes on those restraints, and I will not hesitate to redline the voltage."

Though I know she can already see my hands, I hitch them a little higher. The bitch means every word. I've never seen her redline someone on the table before, but I've heard the word whispered as she performed the punishment—and eventually, the horrendous death—on others. Expendable others. Which may or may not be how she perceives Emma now...

Why *is* she doing this to Emma?

Revenge is the first option to surface, though I rule it out just as fast. Why would she go to the trouble if she assumed I was still in the induced coma and wouldn't know about all this? Recruitment is next on the list, but once again I have to wonder why. It would make more sense for Faline to kill Emma instead of attempt to turn her. Why draft a soldier so patently hostile to the cause?

That leaves...what?

Research?

Or simple sadism?

Which, I'm nauseated to admit, would both fit. And yes, both right here and now. Putting Emma through an accelerated transformation—which all the dials and settings in front of me indicate—would neatly check both those boxes for Faline.

Boxes I've got to *un*check. And then erase.

"You don't want her anyway." Though it's brutal and guttural, I turn it into an undisputable order—hitting the woman, nearly literally, below the belt. Because as thoroughly as Faline Garand knows all of my triggers and motivations, *I* know *hers*. I'm sickened by even admitting the knowledge now, especially after shutting it down so many times since taking my first step away from the Source, during that moonless midnight, so long ago.

But not long enough.

Or perhaps, in some demented depth of my psyche, I've purposely never let go of it due to realizing all of this. Recognizing that Faline would never set it free. That she'd remember every one of those days I was chained down for her, forced to forge that link with her faceless voice. I'd needed her for survival—and, in the months to come, I came to the twisted acceptance that she needed me too. I provided some strange connection for her...some unattainable goal, maybe. Back to her humanity? Or maybe the opposite direction, toward reaching for a higher purpose? Seeking her immortality through me?

And do any of those clarifications even matter?

She has the tool to get back to them again.

Me.

Standing before her, saying exactly this.

"We both know what you want, Faline."

But it's not Faline's voice that fills the awful silence that falls then. It's the high, tearful whimper of the woman on the table. The destiny of my existence. The center of my heart. The pulse in my blood. The *more* in my world.

The reason Faline isn't on the floor right now, her throat ripped open by lightning and her heart yanked from her chest and fried into the black stone it really is. I could still try it, but I really do know the bitch that well. Her death by my hand would mean more than the shackle codes dying with her. As soon as she breathed her last, there'd be a dozen hits called on Emma's life. I know better. The shitty thing is, Faline also knows I know better.

But I still hold the ace here.

Even if she doesn't see it for herself.

Which she clearly doesn't, judging by the slither in her step and the gleam in her eyes, as she moves to cover the last couple of steps between us. Or even as I back up by equal steps but twice the distance, giving off the exact vibe I intend. As she follows me, tracing her bottom lip with one crimson nail, she starts gloating in her perceived triumph. But I'm the real winner of round one, having diverted her away from Emma's bedside—though my girl, seeing only Faline making cat-in-heat moves on me, has no way of knowing that. Her heartsick mewl impacts every inch of Faline's body like a rush of pure cocaine.

"Oh, do go on, *papi*," she stage whispers at me, purposefully leaning over as if I'm hanging on her every word. The thing is, I am. Waiting. Watching. Evaluating. Gauging when to speak. When to strike. "Tell me exactly what I want."

I swallow down a fuck ton of bile. Picture a steel vise

ramming up my spine, fortifying my posture. Staying that way, no matter how wrenching the anguish in Emma's next groan or how heavily her grief weighs the air. I run the risk of even glancing at her now. Hearing her, smelling her, and *feeling* her are enough. Goddamnit, more than enough.

But I'm setting up the strike...

"Me."

Somehow, I declare it exactly like my inner titan dictated it. No matter how deeply this starts to hurt. Holy *fuck*, does it hurt. Not in the blood cells that hold their charge or the muscles that keep their strength. In the other way. The worse way. In every cavern of my soul and all the tunnels of truth that connect them. In the ice that's taking over the energy that once lived in them. The truth and energy and life of being with Emma.

Emma, lying there in such misery, helplessness, and God only knows what kind of physical fragility now.

Because of me.

Oh, holy *fuck*, how this hurts.

"You want *me*, Faline."

I steel my jaw, closing off all sounds but one. The searing beats of my heart, echoing through my chest, my mind, my will. The will that's still holding—and now is clearly starting to bother her. She wants the secret about the signal-blocking miracle we pulled off, but that's not going to be enough to sway her to this deal. The only thing that changes a bully's mind is to punch right back, and I'm prepared to do exactly that—with a blow beneath the belt if I have to.

The woman twists her dark-red lips, clearly getting at least that message from my widened stance and hardened glare. But to make this shit crystal clear, I state once more,

"You want me." And then through gritted teeth, "So let's talk about the terms under which you'll get me."

As Faline contemplates that, I refocus on my heartbeat again. In every thud, I imagine the vibrant thumps of Emma's too. I can hear her breathing. Envision her living. Know she's alive and filling the world with her light and her love.

And in so many ways, continuing to infuse mine with the same.

It's the only way, Velvet.

Forgive me...forgive me.

This is the only way...

The ink goes darker in Faline's tight gaze. "And what terms would those be, *cariño*?"

I loosen the fists at my sides but reset the clench of my jaw. The moves share the same purpose. If need be, I'm ready to prove how serious I am. "Let them go. Emmalina, Angelique, and Wade. Set them free, and you get me."

She quirks her lips again—this time to set up her derisive laugh. Just fine by me. I'm setting up my shot too. If it comes down to that.

"Now why would I do a thing like *that*, darling?" She crosses her arms, forearm atop forearm, like a lioness reveling over prey. "A queen doesn't just give back the spoils of war, especially when the treasures are an insurance policy to ensure her consort's good behavior."

I notch my jaw up by another degree. "Guess it depends on what you value most about the consort."

And because I already know the answer to that—and before she can see that I do—I strike. Swiftly. Ruthlessly. Accurately.

Directly to my crotch.

With a bolt so swift and strict, her appalled shriek doesn't detonate until my leathers are smoking and a gash of my charred skin shows through them.

The shock impacts the bitch better than I'd hoped, compacting her focus and fizzling her electric web off the air. Foley, who's never ripped his brain cells off the same track as mine, already knows exactly what to do with his three seconds of freedom—and before Faline's goons can react, he's at Emma's side, examining the shackles just in case they can be hacked. I indulge a split second of gratitude that it's Foley at her side right now, knowing he's looking at my woman and seeing only a hostage in pain, needing to be freed, and not the glorious naked curves of the woman I love. If that weren't the case, appreciation or not, I may have to consider lopping *his* dick off, right after mine.

But first things first.

Without ripping my glare from Faline, I take advantage of her distraction from all the goons too. They're all just a step into pouncing toward Foley before I shoot up my free hand, pulsing them across the room until they slam against the far wall like a pile of human banana peels. By the time all that figurative dust settles, some tables have definitely been flipped—but more importantly, some doors have been opened. Several of my key suspicions are confirmed. They're sure as fuck not comfortable to confront but are the gory truth all the same.

Which may or may not be great news for the appendage to which I've drawn the bitch's terrified focus.

"Next time, I won't go for the top of my thigh." I drill my glare into her while gritting out every word. "And I *guarantee* I'll start with my balls, *darling*."

Her jaw falls open. She snaps it shut with an audible clash of teeth, only to part her lips again on a vicious seethe. "You. Will. Do. No. Such. Thing."

I direct a new tine in, slicing so close to that sensitive sack that my thighs flinch from raw reflex. "Screw with Emma again, in any way, and both of them are gone." It's fate's sick joke that I can't enjoy every second of her dawning dread, but none of my fantasies included a potential castration as part of the plan. "You'll stand and watch as your consort becomes your eunuch."

"No!" She unleashes it on a fully bared snarl before trying to come at me again, fingers flicking wildly, only to learn I can toss her onto her ass with half the effort I used on her banana men—with twice the satisfied smirk. Seems the woman's "superpower"—or whatever the hell she's using to create her electronic web—has a limited battery life. Interesting. *Very* interesting...

"Oh, yes." I extend each word longer than I have to. If anything about this standoff is going to be enjoyable, then damn it, I'll seize the moment now. "I'll spill every drop of what you're after the most here, Faline. And don't think I don't know exactly what it is—exactly what you *ordered* me to do when you woke me up the first time."

And just like that, the moment of fun is over. I pace forward as it's replaced by memories, my mind blasted with horror from those moments I was certain I couldn't hold myself back, and I was about to literally fuck Emma to death. *Again.*

"You wanted to start hardwiring me to be a sperm machine for you. For the fucking Consortium."

I'm stunned the statement *doesn't* stun me more, even when its matter-of-fact inflection collides with the astonishment across Faline's. But as she finishes rising, I'm certain she's more flustered by her sudden power drain than my accusation, which is fine by me. It all feeds more into my mounting ultimatum—and my only goal.

Getting Emmalina the hell out of here.

"You need my DNA because there's nothing else like it. Nothing you've been able to find in three hundred and twenty-two other alphas, at least." *Bull's-eye.* I've hit the sweet red dot at the middle of the circle, verified by the blaze that takes over the centers of her eyes before she stretches back to full lioness pose. "That's why the Consortium's burned through so many, isn't it?" I charge. "You're all looking to repeat what you did with me"—*what you did* to *me*—"and you haven't been able to, even with all the same protocols in place."

By the time I finish, I'm literally winging it—though the wind beneath my mental feathers is everything I'm getting from Faline as I go on and on. No. What I'm *not* getting—which would usually be her scoffing chuckle, disparaging smirk, or both.

Meaning I haven't just hit the bull's-eye.

I've conquered the whole goddamned target.

What that *doesn't* mean is that I can cue up the Bee Gees and kick into my white-suited victory strut. Faline has backup procedures in place—evidenced by the ten fresh guards who storm in, four of whom are on drag-in-the-prisoners duty. As soon as they're ten paces in, Emma erupts in another high-pitched keen, shattering my heart beyond the cracks it's gotten from viewing the damage to Wade and Angie. While their little "vacation" at the Spa de Consortium hasn't included all the "amenities" of Emma's, it's clear they've still been "pampered" with some of the minions' finest treatments. Wade's shirtless torso is a roadmap of blue and purple bruises, while Angelique's naked skull has lost all its vibrance, matching the blank of her gaze.

The henchmen jerk both of them to the front of the pack, clearly causing them each more agony—until Faline jerks up a hand and spits an order in Spanish. At once, they let Wade and Angie fall to the floor, and they crumple next to each other with terrible groans. The only sound that knives worse than their torment is the slice of Emma's new cry, more grieving than before. I'm no longer able to prevent the tortured coils of my fists, but it's the only way to hold back on running to her and giving away the advantage I've won.

The edge that's going to get her out of here.

"Let them go!" I lunge toward Faline while exploding with it. Big mistake. I'm rushed by the majority of the fresh guards, while two stay behind to wrench Wade and Angie back to their feet. A third covers Foley, who grimaces as Emma screams and writhes under a fresh blast of pain courtesy of our hostess from hell. "Let them go, damn you, or I *will* chop this fucker loose like Ahab chopping fishing line!"

As everyone in the room stops, a scream shatters the air. At first, I wonder if it's mine and I really have gone ahead and sliced my cock free. After just another second, I realize it's because Emma isn't having to issue it from around her gag anymore. Somehow, Wade's stumbled over as Foley helps her sit up. Her shackles have been sprung open. Physically, she's free.

And...I'm down.

Weak in the knees—literally—from the *kaboom* of relief. My walls burned down by a thousand flaming arrows of gratitude.

Knowing this is the beginning of my end and completely not caring.

All that matters is her.

All that's still real now is her.

"So..." Faline's drawl still isn't back to its purring edge, but she's much closer now than two minutes ago. Like tapping on a two-bladed dagger, she knows her little "gift" has tipped the balance on all of this back to center, though she's not about to let it rock any further. I can feel the energy humming from her again, and I watch her strange web take fresh form on the air. Even if Wade, Angelique, and Emma were in prime condition to race out of here with Foley, she—and the countless minions she's likely still got patrolling around in parts unknown of the mansion—will be rendering that retreat close to impossible. I know it—and she sure as *hell* knows it. "Exactly what kind of an exchange are you proposing, *cariño*?"

"Reece!" The shriek, beautiful even in its anguish, tears up the air before I can get half a breath up my throat. "Noooooo!" But the sobs that buttress it hardly seem of this world, gashing at my senses until I'm nothing but dark resignation and visceral grief.

Maybe that's the best way.

Because this is the only way.

I need to know they'll get out of here safely.

I need to know *she'll* be safe.

So I lift my head and accept those shadows again. Stare down the witch who'll bring the entity who isn't me again. And maybe that's for the best. Maybe it'll be easier this way, thinking of Reece Andrew Richards as another entity altogether...that creature being led back to his cage after daring to think he could live peacefully in the wild for a while. Presuming he had the right to grasp something like freedom. *Stupid beast. Free rein isn't for an animal like you. It never will be again. Get used to it right now.*

"You know damn well what I'm proposing, Faline." I suck in a harsh breath. Then another, feeling just as much broken glass crammed down my throat. "Me for them." I gore her with my glare and every bolt of command I can summon into it. "As long as they get out of here safely, I'll remand myself to you again."

The bitch takes a careful step closer. Eyes me with even deeper deliberation. "Just like that?" she charges.

I tick a tight nod. "Just like that."

Her lips do a weird little dance. She looks ready to laugh at me or spit on me but instead rocks her head back with more intense scrutiny. "You love her that much?"

I square my shoulders. Firm my jaw. "I love her that much."

My declaration seems to flip a switch inside her. She's no longer quiet and contemplative but sure and decisive, bringing on the words that are the gut punch I've prayed for—but a punch nonetheless.

"Then we have a deal, darling."

And here come's fate's newest practical joke. Because suddenly, even though I've just entered the world's shittiest prison again, I'm flying completely free. Into miles of cyan summer skies in a goddess's gorgeous eyes—only they're sparkling with a thousand liquid stars too. In the expanse above them, there are deep hills of sorrow. In the lips below them, a twist of despair reigns.

But I can't think about the despair.

I need to pour my mind and heart into soaking up

Emmalina's love. Into savoring my last seconds of freedom. Into reveling in the warmth and light of her kiss, no matter how violently she lunges at me, wrapping herself around me, desperately repeating one word against me. "No. No. *No. No!*"

I fold her against me, gashing a glare at Faline to dare her to stop me, and then bend myself around and over, trying to press as much of her scent and softness and love directly into me. Every fucking second. Every damn moment. Every breath and sob and sigh and memory I can possibly soak up, taking her inside as deeply as I can.

"You can't, you big ox. You won't. You *can't*. You *won't!*"

At least it's not no—though I refrain from wasting time on the sarcasm. Humor isn't going to make this easier. *Fuck*; nothing's going to make this easier.

"Baby," I finally utter, brushing my lips through the silk of her hair. "I have to."

"No. *No.*" Her face is a shimmer of solid tears. Her voice is a crack of heartbroken grief. I don't soothe any of it away, pretty damn certain mine is exactly the same. "No, no, no, no!"

I consume her cheeks with my palms, yanking her face up for another press of my lips. "I love you."

"I hate you." She wraps herself around me with shuddering force. Beats her fists against my back, right then left then right then left, a relentless mortar fire of misery. "I hate you, Reece Richards, and I *don't* forgive you for this!"

I gulp hard as my torso continues to be a war zone and my heart ignites with unending adoration.

This. Here. Now. Her pure fire. Her searing spirit. The stark beauty of so much love, she's brave enough to hate me with it as well. Strong enough to sob out her fury against my chest, baring the center of her soul as boldly as her pale, shaking body. Naked in every form...exposed until she's fully stripped *me*. Fuck. *Fuck*. How have I come to deserve her? *Why* does the world call me its hero when it's so damn clear from where my true strength surges...from *whom* it surges?

This. Here. Now.

She overwhelms me. Overcomes me. Tears me apart. Caves me in. She's my star, my sun, my moon, my sky. The lightning of my existence. The *more* of my world.

The *more* she'll always give me, no matter what lies ahead. No matter how much pain I'll endure, experiments I'll survive, or solitude I'll bear. Because of her, I'll never really be alone anymore.

She needs to know that. I need to tell her. I need to *show* her. And I try, so damn desperately, pulling her close and tight until our lips are meshed again. And she sighs into my mouth. And I groan into hers. And I take her. And taste her. And breathe her in, colliding our tongues in need and our lips in love, until an impatient boot stamp breaks the air, forcing us apart. Faline is quickly becoming an unhappy camper. Like I fucking care. But I *have* to care.

I keep Emma clasped close for several more long seconds, one hand at her chin and the other at her nape, cherishing the last tangible tangle of our breaths. Into that precious space, I order her in a rasp, "Don't you *dare* forgive me, woman. Not ever."

She grabs the back of my head. Impales me with the aqua iridescence of her gaze, replete with all the meaning of what I've just said. Of what I've just pleaded, in the form of that fervent command. "Never," she whispers. "For as long as I live."

"Good." I gulp hard, so fucking hard, but the effort is useless. Tears burn the corners of my eyes, caught by her fingertips as she drags her hands around to my jaw. The second she curls her nails in, I swear there are pin-sized jolts of bright-blue light, but I reject the impression as a residual effect of her flared gaze. "Good," I repeat, focusing fully on her again—and the soul I fight to see past the thick sheen coating her eyes. "Because I'll never stop not forgiving you, either."

She drops her head in a small nod, trying to use the motion to pull away. The words, standing proxy for the three others we've said so many times to each other but don't dare say now, are the closest thing we're going to get to an easy goodbye.

Which becomes pure hell anyway.

As soon as four of Faline's goons surround me and jerk me away.

As soon as four more march around and pull Emma back too.

As soon as I'm put into new shackles and led past another steel door.

Which Faline shuts behind us, completely slicing Emma's sobs from the air.

Leaving only the terrified thuds of my heartbeat mingled with the low hum from the bitch's lips.

"Oh, *now* we are going to have some fun, *cariño.*"

I reply, without a single octave above a murmur, "Fuck you."

I brace myself for the crack of her hand across my face or worse, but I'm not sure what to do with her extended chuckle. Not until she embellishes it with a matching murmur—full of sultry intent. "Now that *is* the spirit, Alpha Two." She does raise a palm now, but it's to stroke my cheek with a caress that brings a flood of bile up my throat. As she digs her nails into my hairline, she uses her other hand to motion at the henchmen who are still securing me. "Strip him," she states. "And then secure him to the *special* table."

CHAPTER FIVE

EMMA

"Come on, baby girl. Just one more step."

My sister's careful voice snaps me back to reality for an awful moment. My senses sharpen, reminding me that only a few minutes and not years have passed since Sawyer parked the Rover and Lydia rushed out of the house to retrieve me.

What's the difference?

Minutes, years. They're the same now. My existence is porridge, sludge without color or distinction.

Without him.

"Reece."

I huddle in on myself as my whisper spills out, clinging to that remnant of him as long as time will let me. At the same moment, I look up to one of the mullioned windows that frame our front archway. Embedded throughout the glass are splotches of brilliant color: petals from the bouquet of yellow and orange bush poppies he'd plucked for me on the first incredible night we came up here, after he'd slipped an eye-popping tanzanite ring on my finger and uttered the words that had officially made me the happiest woman on the planet.

Accept it as a symbol of everything you are to me...of all the more you are to me...

I lift my hand, tracing one of the petals, as every detail of that night fills my mind. The caress of the canyon breeze on my face. The smell of those poppies on the air. The stunning silver magic in his eyes as I'd laughed out my reply.

Just shut up and put that damn bowling ball on my finger...

And then, once we'd gotten back to the car, how he'd matched the electricity of his eyes with the mastery of his body. How he'd claimed my desire as perfectly as he'd just asked for my hand.

How he'd shown me that life would always, *always* be more with him in it.

My fingers flatten against the glass as the others pass by. Vaguely, I recognize Joany helping Angelique with the trek, while Chase helps Wade with his limping journey. I'm back in the present but still fighting to reconcile it with the past. I'm gazing at my left hand, right? So where's the ring? *Where's the ring?*

But that's when the past *really* collides with the present.

Reminding me.

Accusing me.

It's my fault.

I'd left the gem here so as to not lose it during my grand gallivant to the castle to kill the queen. So noble; a heroine's quest. I was going to free my man from the evil witch. *I* was going to be the savior this time. I was going to make everything all right and show Reece I could do more than wring my hands, tell him to be careful, and take up extra space in the mission team van.

"But I did nothing." I sough it from a dry and aching throat despite how my heart is suddenly a whole ocean that crashes the dam of my composure.

No. You did everything.

All the important stuff—just like the grown-up superheroes.

Sneaking into the evil castle? Check.

Scamming the brainless guards? Check.

Holding a gun to the bitch-on-high? Check.

Getting trapped in said bitch's energy web and then winding up in her mad scientist electricity chamber, tortured to pain I never knew a human could survive? Check, check, *and* check.

But knowing my sacrifice, in the end, ended up with Faline in the grave and my man sane and safe?

My hand makes a long squeak on the glass as I skid it back down to my level. Then curl it into my lap...and drench it with my tears.

"Fool." My rasping rage grows with every scalding tear, every racking sob. "You're a fucking *fool*, and now you've made damn sure to carve the point in stone!"

My words only seem to recall more of his. All the times he kissed me, held me, reassured me...

I only want you, baby.

I only need you, my sweet Bunny.

You're my life, my beautiful Velvet.

You're my more*, my Emmalina.*

And every time, I hadn't truly believed him. Hadn't really known...

That I really was.

But as the truth slams me now, I'm racked with emptiness, drained by remorse, sapped by despair. I have no damn idea how Lydia and Foley got me to move again, let alone stand and walk—if that's what this aching shuffle is. How can I take another step? Or even think about *breathing* inside this place without him? Every thread of my soul is unraveled. Every light in my world has been snuffed.

Wait.

I jolt my head a little higher.

The lights.

Is it just me? Or...

"Why aren't the lights on?" I spin in a tight circle, picking up on even more in the air. More accurately, on even *less*. The touchable silence throughout the house isn't solely due to Reece's absence, as I'd first thought when we arrived minutes-that-felt-like-years ago. This is a sizable difference. A noticeable stillness. I dart a questioning glance at 'Dia. "Why isn't *anything* on?"

Before she can answer, Alex seems to appear out of the air that still feels like Cream of Wheat. Though I know that's not the case, it's still a fight to restrain my shock at suddenly seeing him there—and soon, my anger at his walking-on-eggshells mien. Being treated like a breakable collectible is what made me flee the china shop of Orange County to begin with.

But wouldn't I be doing the same if I were any of them? Even I'm not sure whether I'm Teflon or Wedgewood right now. Though my heart and soul are more fissured than the San Andreas Fault, I'm shocked at how physically *wired* I am. Just the memory of what happened on that table in the mansion, for even a few hours, has me gasping for breath from the battle to erase it. The burning. The destruction. The pressure. *The pain...*

But the hyperventilation doesn't exhaust me. There's just more air where that came from, along with heat that sharpens me and pressure that pushes me. Elevates every single one of my physical senses...

Wow. I mean...seriously...*wow*.

As Alex shifts forward, I can hear the scrape of dust beneath his shoes. As he looks up, I can practically count the pores in his skin. As he speaks, even in a strained grate, it's like someone's turned the foyer into an amplification chamber.

"Hey. Welcome home." He jabs his hands into his front pockets, and I hear the scrape of his fingertips against the change inside one of them. There's only lint in the other one. I know it because I hear that too. "Sorry that the Welcome Wagon had to be so gloomy." I also discern every note of regret he's masking with the light tone. "We worked so fast to rewire everything for the zap to Reece, we somehow took the backup generator offline too. We're working as fast as we can to untangle everyth—"

"Whoa." I mean it as a dictate, not an exclamation. "Hold on." Then snap my hands to my waist, recognizing every confrontational vibe I'm giving off but can't seem—or want—to temper. "The *zap* to Reece? Why? You had to rewire everything of *what*?"

Whoa, the silent sequel version. Fidgeting is a fascinating look for Alex, who usually covers discomfort by diving into his theatrical side. But right now, he looks struck by Reece-level lightning as I wait for an answer.

Which I get from the *new* arrival to the foyer instead. "The solar panels," Fershan explains. "We concluded that diverting power directly off them, we could inject Reece with an effect similar to atmospheric ionization..."

"Only directly in his blood." Alex has finally forgotten to be awestruck—a good thing, because I'm so fascinated by what they've just said, I feel a huge smile forming as Fershan takes over again.

"Thereby disrupting any radio signals that would be trying to get through to certain electrical viruses." As he finishes, the guy practically lights up the house with the resplendence of his grin. Still, I can feel him holding back on his pride and joy, deferring more tiptoeing diplomacy to me, which only makes me spin into the same frustrating mix of ire and compassion.

With a determined breath, I take a conscious stab at the latter. Even try to inch up my lips a little before saying, "Wow. Team Bolt sure leveled up, didn't they?"

They snort and then chuckle together.

"So *that's* what we did?" Alex murmurs.

"Leveled up," Fersh snorts back. "Yeah. That's us. The level-uppers."

They join in a fit of laughter, giving me a long moment to observe them in full. I can see I played that one right when observing the extra twinkle in Alex's eyes and the proud blush even on Fersh's copper skin.

But I can also *see* all that. *Plainly.*

As if an invisible artist is standing there with a chisel for Wade's cheeks and a dripping paintbrush for Fersh's. And now, I can *hear* the rush of air in and out of both their lungs, betraying the extra happiness I gave them with the sarcastic but meaningful compliment.

Whoa, yet again.

What the hell is going on with me?

I ask myself the question as I turn my focus inward for a long second. The sensation is like the first day of catching a cold, when I wonder if a cold is all it'll be. I examine each symptom, one by one, in better detail—and start to notice the little things my grief has clouded from me until now. The extra sizzle in all my nerve endings. The light-gold halo that appears whenever I look at anything that gives off electrical energy. Yes, even humans. *Especially* humans. That was probably an extra reason why the power outage was so jarring to me.

No.

Not the power *outage*.

The power *redirection*.

The power...that's all still here. Just all in another room.

In the lab.

Where they gave Reece back his power. And his ability to be shielded from Faline's influence so he could come find me. Only to offer himself back over to her because there was nothing I could do to help him. No matter what I'd done or how hard I'd tried, I'd still turned into his anchor instead of his wings. The chink in his gauntlets, fully exploited by the bitch with the Hos-R-Us lifetime membership.

"*Wait.*"

I practically shout it out, making the guys dagger their laughter to a stop and snap their attention to me with sharper conviction. Lydia and Foley turn with nearly the same speed.

"Oh, my God."

But now, my voice is just a rasp. A sound laced with conflict. *A lot* of conflict. This is the exact mission map I followed before. The same thinking that shut off my logic for the consequences, my consideration for the team, and any sense about how things would turn out if things went wrong and I ended up on Faline's table, wired to her psychotic whims. Worse, what would happen if Reece came and found me that way and then lost every rational thought in his own damn head about getting me out of there.

"What is it, baby girl?" Lydia moves back in and gently scoops a hand into mine.

"Oh." It's almost an afterthought, sluiced away on the rush of my breath as understanding continues to rush my brain. "Oh...my *God*."

And in the middle of that same ferocious flood, I'm suddenly thankful for every second of Faline's electrified hell.

Because what she did to me is the reason I can stand here, about to ask them to do the same thing.

"Don't fix the power." I lower my hands all the way down, tempted to punch them into fists at the ends of my A-framed arms. I'm ready for this skirmish.

I think.

No. I *know*.

Nothing else is an option.

I do this—take the crazy, massive risk of this—or accept a life without Reece in it.

Not. An. Option.

And so, it's *this* option.

"Don't do *what*?" Fershan rocks his head back, giving away his incredulity.

I turn and brace my stance again, reconfirming my determination. "You heard me. Leave everything as it is. Plugged into the solar inverters."

"*Merde*." Angie's reentrance, with her mouth agog and her eyes wide, is well timed but still useless as a deterrent. "You... you do not seriously think..." she sputters, "that after just a few hours on Faline's table..."

"I don't think," I snap. "I *know*."

She huffs. "Emma, it is not such a simple process as—"

I raise a firm finger. "I know, okay?" And reinforce the point with a direct lock of our gazes, reminding her how much I really *do* know. Like her, I've been locked down on Faline's fun slab. Had that special firsthand view of all the technology and intricacy that goes into altering a human being's bloodstream. Personally known the horrifying race of my pulse and hammering of my heart. "I know all about it, Angelique—just like I know that it took her weeks or months to transform most of the others, including Reece." I straighten my spine while sucking in as big a breath as I can. This time, both moves are strictly for me. I need the fortification to state the rest of my case. "But you weren't there today, when she was with *me*."

Though Alex's scrutiny tightens the most, it's Fershan who screws his composure back together first. "What did she do...with you, Emmalina?"

Alex pushes his lips into a harder line. "What did she do *to* you?"

I make sure they watch me pull in a deep, determined breath. I need to make sure they're clear about what they're getting into, despite the fact that I'm not really giving them a choice about it. I just need to know they'll still be the guys who won't let the lights go out on me at any part of this—no matter how high I scream or how thoroughly I beg them to relieve the torment.

They have to love me enough to *not* love me right now.

I won't ever stop not forgiving you, Velvet...

One more deep breath before I continue my explanation. "Faline kept talking about 'crash coursing' me," I tell them. "And I noticed she had to keep confirming overrides on the machinery's limits. Nearly all of my settings were pegged way over what the outputs on those things were set for." I allow two seconds' worth of a wince across my face. "If the pain was any indication, she was definitely trying to crash *something*."

"*Mon dieu*," Angie utters.

"So what does that mean?" Alex shifts forward, the corner of his left eye crimping, his open tell of curiosity. "What exactly are you asking us to do that has this one '*mon dieu*'ing on my shoulder?" He uses his right eye to flash a sardonic wink back at Angie.

Fershan puts *both* eyes into his reaction, popping them wide in a look that's either total shock or complete horror. Or maybe—probably—a crazy mash-up of the two. "You think we can channel the power into *you*—and use it to finish whatever the hell Faline started."

"Holy shit." Alex's twinge of mirth has vanished—his stare, swung from Angie onto me. "Is that possible, Emma? Did Faline get *that* much started?"

I tilt my head, focusing on the rim of gold around his light-chestnut hair. "Depends on what you mean by 'started.' Does that lead to the part where everything looks like the gold fairy swung by and sneezed?"

"*Quelle?*" Angie's curiosity is a thick current in her query.

I jog a glance back at her before explaining, "Exactly what I'm saying it is." Then return my stare back to the rest of them, still blinking fast as if *that's* going to change the view. "All of you have these...halos now. You look like a season finale of *Touched by an Angel*. Or maybe *Supernatural*, depending on which season."

"My word," Fershan blurts.

"Holy fuck," Alex chokes.

"No...*no*." The exclamation defeating them both is a wrenching sob on the air. Even before Lydia falls into Sawyer's comforting embrace, I know I haven't exactly won over my sister's vote for my plan.

Not that I'm letting her have one either.

"Honey." I step over and rub her back. "I'm so, so sorry." I issue it from the depths of my heart. "But right now, this is the only plan we've got." I demand it from the steeled grit of my will.

The resolve that's going to get me through hell for a second time.

Because we have to at least try.

For Reece.

For the part of me that can't live without him.

The part that includes everything except my toenails.

Wait. Wrong. My toenails need him too.

So it's decided. This *will* happen—if I want to gain the team a fighting chance of stealing Reece back from Faline at all. I have no illusions that any of this is going to be neat or easy, especially with what I've just resolved myself to go through again—but my determination rises by matching degrees, pulsing brighter and bolder through my system before flowing over every speck of my vision. The golden outlines continue for me, many of them like dazzling amber crystals—though once again, living things are the most vivid. Because of that, I focus extra hard on Alex and Fersh. They return the scrutiny right away, and in the reflections of their irises, I see why. My mirror image now looks like some crazy new photo filter, its title likely called something like "Lycan Eyes" or "Wild Golden Girl."

If adding the flare to my eyes had only been as easy as pushing a button.

"So...will you guys do it?" I secure a hand around each of their forearms, hoping they see beyond the new weirdness in my gaze, to the supplication and yearning of the woman underneath. "I need this, okay?" I rasp. "I need more than just a fighting chance to get him back. I need to have the advantage

ANGEL PAYNE

over that witch, and we all know it."

The desperate, guilty, beyond grieving woman underneath.

Who has no idea what kind of woman she'll even be after all this is done.

Recognizable? Identifiable? Knowable?

I don't care.

I don't care.

The words become my mantra, blaring in my head and my heart in time to the terrified throb in my veins, as I follow Alex and Fershan out the front door and back to the lab—their version of a definitive reply to my entreaty.

I don't care.

Pushing away all thoughts of the agony to come as I get up on the lab table and then let Lydia shackle me down.

I don't care.

The words now stand in for others, throughout my spirit and soul, as my body shifts into a mode beyond my control. From head to toe, I shiver from unseen ice. I stutter through uneven breaths. I clench and unclench my trembling hands as my eyes drag open and closed, open and closed, open and closed...

Before the blast of pure sun scalds my blood.

And a silent scream of anguish tears past my open lips.

And my heart shrieks with the words from the only part of me I'll fight to keep. With everything I am. With everything I ever will be.

I love you, Reece Richards.

I love you.

I love you.

And I will fight for you—with every damn weapon within my reach.

Even if I have to become one of them.

R E E C E

Consciousness returns like the parts of a Picasso painting. Cubes of reality and dreams try to piece together in my mind but don't really look or sound right, forming a whole that isn't whole. A me that's not quite me.

Come back to me, Reece.

Remember the light...

But it's quiet. Too fucking quiet.

Would the worker bees get that frantic without the queen...

The queen.

I gash into the painting with a vicious snarl.

Only to realize I can't.

Not past the rubber bit rammed between my teeth. But even as my rage turns into drool and I recognize the cubes as aching memories, I fight—only to realize I can't. My arms are locked down, and heavy gloves cover both my hands. My snarl becomes an agonized moan as soon as I comprehend that my legs are buckled down with the same diligence, a lead-enforced strap every few inches, like I'm some circus stuntman on a spinning wheel, waiting for knives to be thrown at me.

And I suddenly remember. All of it. Where I really am. How I got here.

Welcome to the freak show.

The table is a leather-lined slab in a makeshift lab, outfitted with lips of electrodes at either end to fully absorb the brunt of my power should I even dare to try to exercise it. As if I have the strength to. Those nodes are damn good at draining my strength as well as restricting it. This circus's ringmaster has thought of everything. Could I have expected anything less, considering what she did to get me here?

Speak of the devil in neoprene.

Faline struts back into her center ring, having traded out her skintight red number for one of her favorite catsuits. Her pace is neither hurried nor languid, and she clacks her high heels against the concrete floor with a steady mix of the two. Not that it matters. Relaxed or rushed, the woman's bringing the exact same agony.

The agony...like this.

"*Unnnhhh!*"

I bite hard into the bit, vowing she won't get a full scream out of me, as my bloodstream is shot up with a thousand silver bullets of electricity. A thousand points of pain. Liquid energy jolts me, searing and sizzling, burning and brutal, virulent and vile. As my system fights the invasion, I jerk against every lock on my body, and their sickening clanks are swiftly absorbed by the soundproofed walls. Though I weave straining groans between the metallic bursts, it's the only sound she'll fucking get from me.

I breathe through my nose like an overheated bull. Puff out furious air, coating the bit with more of my saliva, while ordering myself past terror and back into full alertness. Passing out right now wouldn't be pretty. Faline won't go for something as urbane as Picasso as her alarm clock. She's more fond of methods that decimate a man's mind on their way to gouging out his soul. *Too bad, so sad, bitch.* No matter how strongly I'm compelled to gaze at the edge of the abyss that could be my perfect, numb surrender, she's not getting anything but my body for the show this time. The rest of me is spoken for now. *For always.*

The witch leans over, injecting an intent stare into me, already seeming to extract that declaration out of my brain—and answering it with a slow extension of her crimson smile. Not that her fresh epiphany is going to change any of her tactics about all this.

The procedures, along with the equipment, that have definitely changed since the last time I was locked to a table for her.

That I'm sure I'm about to be reacquainted with. In extreme detail.

"Comfy, *cariño*?" She leans over even more, pressing her neoprene-clad curves against my prone and shuddering body. I form new teeth prints into the bit as she kisses my neck—and wraps her hand around my exposed cock.

And all the power she's just pumped into my body becomes a massive power surge to my core.

At once, because I can't help it, precome jets from my tip. I can't see it, but I can feel it, hot and scalding, especially as Faline mewls in approval.

"Ohhh, you magnificent man. That is perfect. *Perfect.*" She spreads the shit down the length of my shaft, working my erection with expert technique. While she strokes, she goes on in a conversational tone. "You know, Alpha Two, there were so many times when I thought what heaven it would be to simply be your lover. To offer you freedom from the hive for the chance to be the glamour girl on Reece Richards's arm. We would have been beautiful together, you know. One of the world's most stunning couples. And every night, you could bury this big, beautiful, electric cock in my tight, juicy cunt, and..."

She stops for a second, frowning hard. Well, if she thinks talking about fucking *her* is going to keep me stiff, she's more delusional than I thought.

"Well, I am sorry it has to be this way, *papi*—but now that I am nearly a goddess in my own right"—she flicks out a pinky, giving me another jolt without touching the control board—"and you've openly admitted your insipid attachment to that blond peasant, the idea of getting messy with *emotions* over you has gotten—how do you say?—pedestrian."

She rewards herself for that with a little bark of a laugh, like a kid comprehending "hot dog" as an expression as well as a food. She tilts her head, suddenly inspecting me like a Pink's nacho chili special. I pray the woman doesn't have a thing for nacho chili. If she puts her mouth on me to do this, I'll lose the contents of my stomach like *I've* binged on those fuckers.

Luckily, she doesn't stretch out the torture of her scrutiny for long. Or the wait for her next thorough stroke up my shaft, making it clear she's not here to "service" me beyond what's brutally necessary.

"Shall we get on with things, then?" A ruthless rub of my balls and another pump up my prick. "Because the sooner you give me your liquid gold, the sooner they will be able to put it inside me," she rasps, once more licking up the column of my neck. "And the sooner I will be the *mother* of a god."

A seething grunt stands in for my roar of protest, but it fades as fast as it erupted. While knowing I've figured out *what* she and the Consortium want the most from me, I've held back on theorizing *why*. Is their purpose for my jizz truly that obvious? Does their army of so-called geniuses clearly not know the truth yet? That I'll never be a viable father for *anyone's* child? If my stuff hasn't taken hold inside a normal, fertile female like Emmalina, then—

Emmalina.

She comes to me now, her light my perfect beacon in this hell. Keeping me sane as Faline starts milking me like a stud horse. Keeps me remembering that, even if this is my life from now on, be it hours or days or months that the Almighty chooses to keep my sorry ass alive, there *was* a time when my existence meant something. That there was one chance I didn't throw away. The one massive good I really got right.

The whisper that won't stop in my heart.

Emmalina.

The presence that seems to fill the room—yes, *this* room— and yes, even now.

Emmalina.

The light of her, so blinding and beautiful, that it makes the air hum and pulse and shiver. Yes, even louder than Faline's anticipating hiss. Even louder than my thundering blood. The brilliance that shines brighter with every step she seems to stride closer...like there's a full halo around the top of her hair, and feathers of gold light flaring from her fingertips, and damn beams from the dawn itself shining out of her eyes...

So bright.

So damn bright.

Fuck. *Fuck.*

Has it really happened, then? Did Faline really do it? Have I already given her what she wanted and she's killed me so quickly that I didn't even feel it? Or maybe getting murdered was a walk in the metaphysical park compared to being tortured Consortium style, and fate decided to give me a bye on all the pain parts.

But it sure as hell feels like I'm still breathing—hard and heavily. My chest still pumps like the ocean in a tide pool, and my heart hammers like huge waves against those rocks. Is this just the way of things? How one passes from one dimension to the next? If so, it's a shit ton easier than everyone says it is.

But if that's really the case, am I in heaven or hell?

Because while Emmalina is truly here, so is Faline. Dear *fuck*, so is Faline. She's not moaning or sighing anymore. She's screaming—or at least trying to. I really don't care. I don't notice anything beyond Emma's splendor. Her light is like a living creature come to life inside her, refusing to be contained in the confines of her lush, perfect curves. And holy *God*, what curves. I'd swear on my balls—still intact, thank fuck—that her breasts have gotten fuller, her hips have gotten lusher, and even her hair has grown longer, fanning from her head with the glowing glory of white-gold wings.

Wings.

Yes.

Jesus God, maybe she really *is* an angel. But from which side? And do I care, when she's this magnificent a sight? Will I even notice if I'm floating on clouds or walking through fire, especially if that fire is hers?

Holy shit. *That fire.* It's as if the cosmos peeled off a strip of the sun and then poured it inside her, turning her gaze into a pair of endless skies and her exultant smile into star-bright resplendence. If she walked in here naked, I'm damn sure I'd be blind and burned to a skeleton by now...but I can't imagine any better experience for my final memories. As it is, I'm positive *this* view will be embedded in my soul forever. My badass Bunny in head-to-toe leather, undaunted purpose in her steps and unfettered vengeance in her eyes, all but exploding the air itself just by entering the room.

"Fuck. Me."

Croaking the words this close to Faline, even in her

seething state of distraction, probably isn't the wisest choice of my limited lung power, but I'm not being given much of a choice. I need the words, from my own lips, as a barometer of reality. *If* this is still reality. And if it isn't, then what the hell has just happened? Is still happening?

"Fuck. Me." Still sounds real. A good thing, yes? No? "What...the hell...have you done, Emmalina?"

Though the vibrations of the words are agony in my throat, the pain sparks my brain back to life. Synapses I'd ordered into dormancy zap back online, plugging what I'm seeing—and now sensing and smelling, as her presence jolts my pores and her sea-and-sunshine scent floods my nostrils—into what I know.

That she's real.

That she's here.

And that she's—

"Holy. *Shit!*"

Like a rhino on Ritalin, the comprehension finally, fully, slams me. She's back. And different.

Really. Fucking. Different.

After a visit back to the ridge. Where she's had access to all that equipment in the lab...

The power that the guys rigged from the solar panels, to zap *me* again...

"Holy *fuck*, Emmalina Paisley. What the hell did you—"

"Shut. Up." Faline underlines it with a punch to my ribs, making speaking impossible—though only sharpening my curiosity. Why is the harpy trying to *hide* next to me? If I weren't still fighting for air, thanks to my pummeled ribs, I'd laugh. *Faline Garand* is taking cover next to the prisoner she's got in at least twenty locked shackles?

"Ding dong!"

ANGEL PAYNE

The shout, a mix of confidence and radiance, *does* induce me to laugh. Though I pay the price for it with a stab of pain through my middle, she's well worth it.

She sounds like the sun itself.

"Well, hello there, ma'am. I'm in the neighborhood, collecting charitable donations for hell. They're especially in need of skank bitches in bad latex. So happy to see I've found exactly what those poor souls need."

The sun who's arrived with a hell of a lot more attitude than when she left.

After a gritted growl, Faline straightens to her full height. With the new angle to my view, I can see every bony cord in her neck, leading up to the combative jut of her jaw. If the woman were wearing anything but her shiny black body condom, I'd mistake her for a cross-dresser about to get the fail-whale medal for attempting to channel Morticia Addams.

"Well. Congratulations, Miss Crist. You thought to surprise me earlier and failed—but now it seems the depths of your stupidity have truly succeeded at the quest."

My heartrate triples as Emma advances by a couple of calm steps. Jesus, if that's really her...and she's really facing off against Faline...

"I don't give a shit if you're entertained or not, Faline. Or about your assessment of my IQ, for that matter." Another two steps, in which her self-sure strut is augmented by a battle-ready flick of her hands. "I don't care because you don't matter. Because you can try to hold me back right now—and maybe you can—but that won't stop me from getting right back up, no matter how hard it is or deeply it hurts, and coming at you with every molecule of air left in my lungs and every drop of strength left in my limbs."

In response to Faline's scoff, Emma merely shakes her head. "Because in the end, I'll still have what you desire most—yet can never understand enough to have."

For the very first time, she fully looks over to me. Then straight *into* me.

"I have true love. *Real* love. Complete fusion with another, beyond labels and legacies and who-saved-who." For the first time, her hear-me-roar countenance gives way to another look. A face full of the Emmalina from before. The tender longing of the woman who owns my heart and now captivates my soul all over again. "Not just the love of my life," she rasps. "The love of my existence."

Once more, I give up on even trying to breathe. Or comprehend. Or figure any of this the hell out.

Even as Faline breaks apart the air with her slow, mocking smacks of applause. "What an adorable little oration," she spits. "The 'love of your existence,' *si*?" She shakes out her reddened fingers and jerks them upward, abandoning Morticia for a true witch resonance this time. With palms turned in and fingers slashing upward, she bursts with a gloating shout before charging, "Then you will certainly not have any issue about dying for him, hmmm?"

With that, she twists and lifts her hands again, and I almost expect a black cauldron to explode out of the floor to suck Emma down into its glowing morass.

What *does* happen is no less jarring.

The bitch's electric web is back, only now it sizzles across the air over and around us, an electric force field reinforced with strands of bright-red light. If every inch of those strands weren't sparking like electrical wires in the rain, I'd call them pretty—but when they start splitting on themselves in order to slither horizontally through the air, it's past time for poetry. Each of those buzzing snakes hisses and crackles with the obvious potential for killing someone at first touch.

And three of them are headed toward Emma now.

Then four.

Then five.

"Fuck!" I shout. "No!" And wrestle like a madman against my bonds, shaking the entire table. And finally, *finally*, have managed enough residual power to notch a tear in the shackle on my right ankle. To ram it hard enough over and over to loosen the damn thing. And then to do the same on the binding around my calf. Then my knee, and my lower thigh, and my upper thigh.

Not fast enough.

She'll be dead before I can...

But she's sure as fuck not dead.

With balletic sweeps of her arms, my avenging angel fries every damn one of those crimson snakes—literally, she's cooked them off the air like drips of butter in an atmospheric pan. Once that's handled, she spins and burns half of the spider webs lining the room too—not a development Faline takes with diva dignity. Her shriek is like a Gorgon with bubonic plague, medieval fury mixed with a leaf blower that just sucked up a ground squirrel, as she lunges forward with hands outstretched. The sickening sound worsens as her fingers slam into another strand of Emma's heat, and the eight tips of her longest digits are burned to nubs like candles stabbed into the sun. Which, when it comes to my girl's power, is a damn appropriate comparison.

Christ.

My girl's power.

I seriously just thought that.

For a second, I can't even focus on escaping more of my bonds. Confusion and bewilderment mix with awe and elation, centering on one actuality that can't be ignored any more than the blinding, resounding, resplendent star my woman has become.

The freak she's turned herself into...for me.

And is now fighting as an army of one to *save* me.

Not acceptable.

"Goddamnit," I snarl.

Not. Acceptable.

But I don't waste the time or the oxygen to vocalize it. Every cell in my blood is ordered to the warfront of my body, blasting back into my limbs and muscles until I burst with a roar, straining and pushing—and popping every shackle on my arms free at once.

My yell has barely been noticed. Faline, barely taking breaks for air between charges at Emma, has clearly turned up the game on her volume to offset the epic fail on her offensive. Where she's plunging and squawking like a deluded sailor, Emma is still a poised ballerina of light and lucidity—though swapping the tutu for the tightest, hottest leather. Every move she makes is the epitome of flawless brevity, corresponding to at least four or five from Faline. Not that the bitch stops long enough to notice. Not that Faline is even thinking straight anymore.

Funny what happens when the queen doesn't get her way.

Amazing what happens when a guy gets to watch the train wreck of a follow-up meltdown.

To feel my eyes pop open as wide as my sockets will allow them—as I vow to commit the sight before me to my fondest memories for life. Perhaps beyond that.

Because it's not every day a guy gets a chance to see a sadistic witch taken down and laid out. Then locked that way, flat on a concrete floor, as her skin starts resembling a wince-worthy sunburn-spray ad.

Courtesy of a thousand ribbons of white-gold sun.

That are emanating from his fiancée's palms.

Nope. A guy usually doesn't get to watch as the bitch spits and hisses and spews with every filthy word ever conceived. Nor does he usually get to witness the edges of her catsuit start to shrivel beneath those concentrated rays, threatening to burst into tiny flames any second—as he hopes they really do.

But he especially doesn't get to behold every shred of *his* woman's fiery beauty, her eyes filled with blue flames and her skin shimmering like crushed gold, as she whips toward him and commands in the most wicked-sexy voice the ages ever gave a warrior, "Baby, I can't do this for much longer. *Please*, get your ass out into the car!"

Yeah. I really will remember this for a thousand damn years.

But I'm also going to remember the clenched distress in her voice—and the sudden realization that I can't do a fucking thing to help her get past it except oblige with her dictate the best way I can.

So I do.

Grunting hard as I slide off the table, barely keeping my balance.

Growling at my legs through clenched teeth as I stumble toward the door—"Move, move, *move*!"—and then out into the hall, where a half-dozen more henchmen are sprawled across the floor, alive but unconscious. Next to each of them is a melted mangle of black steel. As I take agonizing hops over the assholes, I try not to gawk but quickly accept that impossibility. My fiancée has just turned a bunch of high-powered rifles into oversized licorice twists.

"Good and *Plenty*," I mutter, my careening brain dropping imaginary white and pink coating on top of the decimated weapons. I get two seconds to indulge the vision before being snapped back to the purpose by a pained moan underneath me—to which I respond with a vicious spit when it's accompanied by a desperate hand around my ankle. "Shit! *Asswad!*"

The minion turns a half-burnt grimace up at me. "We... will find you again," he snarls from between his charred teeth. "*She*...will find you...again. She...she...is...everywh—"

A boot on the dick's neck cuts him off from spewing anything more. Not mine. Number one, I don't have a cock sock to my name at the moment, let alone boots. Number two, the eerie surety in the guy's voice has tugged at a visceral part of my being. A part I abhor acknowledging. The part that, for as long as I fucking live, will never completely go away.

The part permanently haunted by Faline Garand.

"Time for night-night again, boo-boo bear."

The part easily shoved away and out of my psyche as soon as Foley puts an end to the guy's consciousness with a swift smack of his rifle butt. He's barely done with the task before snapping his regard back up to me.

"And now it's time to get *your* sorry ass out the damn— *eeowww*." He whips the back of his free hand over his eyes. "I didn't literally mean *ass*."

I fling a glower. "Sorry about your delicate sensibilities, precious. Didn't have time to muck around for my leathers while Emma and Faline were—" I seize to a stop before we clear the next archway in the hall, doubling over as horror lances me with physical pain. "Holy fuck. Holy Christ. What the hell am I doing?"

Foley jerks a hand into my armpit, yanking me back up with agonizing intensity. His features are a daunting match to the mood, confirming he's been on this E-ticket ride a bunch of times before. "You're doing the best thing for the situation right now, gimp-orina. Getting the hell out of the way."

"Emma—"

"Yeah. Exactly. Getting the hell out of *her* way."

As if he's shot all the syllables at me from a nail gun, I sag. And even look down, expecting to find a couple dozen steel heads turned into sippy straws for my bloodstream. Though I come up empty, I growl at Foley, "This feels disgusting." Against the demand of every bone in my body. Every calling of my instinct. Every need in my soul. *Must fucking protect her. Must fucking save her. Must keep her away from that horrific, heartless bitch...*

"I know, man." Foley's low rumble conveys that he really does—though it's less than a drop of comfort for my spirit. And as I let the guy help me hobble all the way out to the Rover, I pledge a solemn vow to myself. And to Emma.

This is the first *and* last time she'll ever have to do this. To shoulder the burden of conquering our enemies for the sake of saving my sorry, naked ass.

I'm going to remember.

All of it.

All the fear and the pain and the desperation and the helplessness.

And yeah, I'm even going to remember the dire, consuming

relief of this moment too—as she finally joins me in the Rover's back seat, tumbling into the car headfirst as Foley guns the engine, peeling the tires in the peaceful Palos Verdes night. Every blue-hair in every other estate on this block has likely scribbled the car's license and reported us to the police by now, but I don't give a flying fuck. If I'm never welcomed back in this neighborhood again, it'll be too soon. I only want to get to our ridge again. Everything I need is there.

Correction.

Everything I need is finally, *finally*, back in my arms again.

My sweet Bunny.

My perfect Velvet.

My astounding angel.

And now, truly, the magnificent *more* of my world.

What an adventure *this* is going to be.

I can't fucking wait.

CHAPTER SIX

EMMA

The drive up the canyon back to the ridge has never been more incredible or magical.

The air, blowing in through the open windows because Reece insists on it, is redolent with sage and lavender and night jasmine. A little bit of ocean damp mingles with the canyon's lingering warmth, even at this late hour. As the earth spins and officially kicks over the time from one day to the next, there are distant spurts in the sky. Despite the hell that LA has endured over the last few days, Angelenos across the land insist on giving the Consortium a giant fuck-you by celebrating our nation's independence as they'd originally planned.

It's perfect. So perfect.

Freedom.

It's the ideal designation for the new road Reece and I are now looking toward. As I gaze up at him, with my head against his shoulder and my hand against his blanket-covered chest, I see that truth gleaming in the gorgeous silver lights in his eyes and in the golden outline around his tousled hair. The halo is so much thicker around him than anyone else—an anomaly I first attributed to the stampede of my adrenaline after securing Faline to the floor by melting the ends of some zip ties around her wrists and ankles.

But even as I'd left her that way—after our brief but meaningful "girl talk"—and was safe in Reece's embrace, I almost shouted at Sawyer to stop the Rover so I could go back and end things differently at the mansion. End *her* differently.

Another misnomer, since I chickened the hell out and haven't "ended" her at all.

So *freedom* isn't really the most perfect tag.

But maybe *freedom for now* will be okay?

I don't freaking know. And can't come to any kind of peace about that. And because of *that*, can't seem to settle comfortably, no matter how magnificent the night or ideal the occasion.

Damn it.

"Hey." Reece's gravelly prompt, along with a gentle slide of his thumb across my cheek, are the ideal incentives for focusing back up to his devastating stare. "What is it?" he urges, drawing my attention to his full, strong mouth. The color's returned to both his lips, as well as the masculine burnish to his cheeks, though his jawline still seems more rugged than usual, and his thick hair clings to sweat from our ordeal.

But now more than ever, he takes my breath away. So much so, I'm having trouble summoning an honest answer. Maybe *any* kind of an answer. I mean, is he for real? The man's been through another round of that bitch's hell, and yet here he is, beseeching me to go ahead and boo-hoo with *my* issues?

Beautiful, unbelievable man.

Devoted, daring hero.

But does he still want to be my partner too?

Does he still respect me, after every irrational decision I made today? Does he perceive me the same way at all? And do I have any right to even ask him that, just an hour after he staggered off Faline's magical mystery lab table of horrors?

"Emmalina..." He goes for a reproving edge now, and I slice him short with a resigned sigh as Sawyer slows the Rover in front of the house. The second we stop, 'Dia's already got the front door flung open and is all but flying out to greet us, followed in short order by Trixie, Joany, Chase, and Angelique. From the lab's side of the driveway, Alex and Fershan escort an exhausted but grinning Wade, still blatantly basking in his moment of being the hero returned from battle.

But even as we're immersed in warmth and embraces and concern, the ox next to me remains...well, an ox. He's reading my thoughts better than ever, damn it. Revision. He's probably always been this annoyingly clairvoyant; I'm just really aware of the talent now.

Astoundingly aware...

"Hey! Gang!" His shout booms into the night, sending birds out of the trees and nocturnal animals scurrying away but definitely gaining everyone's undivided attention. After giving them all a grateful nod, though still shrouded in just a blanket, he declares in a more reasonable tone, "Look. We're damn thankful for every single one of you"—and flicks a meaningful gaze toward Wade, Fersh, and Alex—"especially those who poured so much of their talent and courage into helping both of us today." While winging his dazzling smile around to everyone else, he loops an arm around my neck. "But right now, Em and I need a second to break this all down for ourselves."

As soon as he hits the middle of that sentence, I duck my head. I'm probably not the only one who heard his stress on "all," but I'm damn sure I'm alone in understanding what it really covers.

The *more* for which it's come to truly stand for.

"Oh, my sweet boy." Trixie takes the lead on responding for the entire group. With tears turning her seafoam eyes to peridot, she approaches with both hands outstretched, cupping her son's face with tight adoration. "You two take all the time you need. You've earned it."

Reece closes his eyes for a long second, rubbing his free hand atop hers. "Thanks, Mom. I love you."

"Not as much as I lo— *Reece Andrew?*"

Her flustered demand halts him as he's scooping up my hand and heading toward the footpath leading to the lookout point beneath the peak of our memorial hill. "What?" He jogs his head back over a shoulder.

"Wh-What are you doing?"

"Taking time with Emma?" His dark brows hunch. "Like you just told me I should?"

"Not in the middle of the wilderness! In nothing but a blanket! Reece? *Reece?*"

I want to giggle but don't give in until we're well out of range of the house lights—their power now fully restored by Alex and Fersh, thank goodness—and into the silver and gray depths where night shadows are mingling with the moonlight. As we climb the path, Chase's soothing voice drifts out on the wind. "Mom, it's July. And he *is* his own personal space heater. And if something decides to bite him on the ass, it's his own damn fault."

Reece joins me in the laughter now, though tacks on a grunt before muttering, "Can't help it if I have a bitable ass, can I?"

"Mmmm." I fit myself to his side, reaching beneath the blanket to cop a generous feel. *Damn.* The man does possess a *very* nice ass. "Seems delectable to me." So fine. So firm. So—

"Do *not* tempt me, woman." He grabs my hand and then threads my fingers with his. "*Yet.*" He qualifies it with a wink—earning him my sultry pout.

"All right, all right," I concede. "You win, Mr. Richards."

"I usually do, Miss Crist."

"Bet you're glad *that* hasn't changed now."

He doesn't respond for a long beat. But with low sagacity, he finally murmurs, "Aha."

"Oh, dear." I release the mutter as he plunks down in a small patch of wild clover. A tall sage bush flanks the area on one side while an olive tree stretches overhead from the other. "Why am I already dreading the subtext of *that*?"

"No subtext, Bunny." He somehow spreads the blanket to make room for me and opens the flap to beckon me in next to him. "That's exactly what it means."

"Which is what?"

I make the requisition with a quiet but watchful gaze. Somehow, this feels like the most important conversation of our relationship—and there have been a lot of important ones over the last twelve months. The night he first revealed himself to me as Bolt. The day we conceived Richards Reaches Out together. The new understandings after New York. Our fight, and then unforgettable night of making up, in Paris. The hours after he went globally public about the Consortium.

All such significant moments...

All of which I'd gone into—and come out of—as a normal woman. Okay, so "normal" means something different in this man's world, though enlightening him about *that* is like telling a fireman he's got a bit of ash on his shoulder.

"Hmmm. Forget I asked that." I pull back by a few inches,

realizing we probably both need the room—but especially me as I regroup thoughts. Oddly, the blackness of the view before us is a help. Far away, I can hear the crash of the sea upon the shore. Closer in, it's the *shoosh* of the wind through the grasses and its haunting echo back through the canyon. All around me, signs and proof of life and power, though I can't see them. It's the same with the force now churning inside me. It's invisible right now, but I already see it.

I already *know* it.

Part of me now. Defining me.

But how does it change *us*?

Ding, ding, ding. And there, kids, is the million-dollar question of the night.

The dilemma I already feel him reading in me. Thank God *some* things haven't changed.

"So what *are* you asking, Emmalina?"

A deep breath. Another. And then a study of the dark beyond, borrowing from its vastness for strength. Because even though this vista is black, I still know there's a ridge beneath us. A foundation, even in the unknown.

"Everything's different now," I finally utter.

"Is it?"

I shoulder-bump him. "You know what I mean." But then scoop my head over, tucking myself against that carved, broad plateau of muscle. "So I guess I'm just wondering..."

"What?" Though Reece's voice is rough, his demeanor is gentle. I have no way of telling him how grateful I am, besides the equally tender grasp I form around his raised knee. I don't dare try anything more. With glaring clarity, I now understand what he goes through after intense missions. The aftereffect of burning through so much energy in such a short amount of time... It's like when the sugar kicks in after drinking too much wine, the mellow buzz replaced by a tired but sizzling restlessness. It's hard to stay still. It's *really* hard to mind my manners. I get double points for doing so, since I'm pressed against my sculpted, sinewy, and completely naked fiancé.

But we have to talk this out. And it has to be now.

After another fortifying inhalation, I lick my lips, lift my head, and state, "I guess I'm wondering how you feel about that."

And there it is. Bald and exposed and truthful and scary.

Especially because his answer isn't immediate.

Which means he must either love or hate the question—a perception I can't get an accurate reading on, even with my fab new "Emma ESP."

So I stammer on, attempting to compensate for my wild nervousness. "Okay, so I—I guess I mean that—well, that *I'm* different now, so it would stand to reason that *we'll* be too, so if you're freaked out and need some time to think about it or whatever, then I underst—"

The man razes my words—and damn near all my senses— down to their scorched, charred foundations with his fierce grip to my face and his brutal possession of my lips. I don't even get out an answering sigh because he steals it from me, breaching me with a ruthless sweep of his tongue, which possesses me with commanding force.

Dear *God*. I thought I'd experienced every passionate kiss in the man's arsenal. Right now, it feels like I've never kissed him—or anyone else. My senses are like virgin grass beneath a forest fire, seared to the roots and then exposed for punishment by all the elements. It hurts, but I've never felt more alive. It's hot, but I've never wanted more blisters.

Sound finally tumbles from me in the form of a protesting moan when he pulls away and we can both suck down some air. He answers my dissent with a maddening, mesmerizing smile. His perfect white teeth glow against the gloom, an ideal accompaniment for the silver sparks in his eyes.

"My beautiful Velvet," he murmurs, a soft chide in his voice. "Of course I'm freaked out."

"Oh." I stutter it out in three separate parts. "Um. Okay..."

"But why is that a bad thing?" He twists to face me fully, going nearly crisscross with his legs. Only with sheer force of will do I keep my stare from dropping into the gap between his timber-log thighs. My climbing libido will *not* be able to handle the sight of the perfect treasure there...

"Well, it wasn't like you had any warning about this." I'm bemused by how defined I now am, thirty seconds after bumbling through my sentences. "And I know it probably wasn't the best-thought-out plan, but when I got back here, all that filled my mind were images of them dragging you away into Faline's torture chamber..."

So much for clarity and composure. Tears take over my voice, and not delicate little princess ones either.

"Ssshhh," Reece consoles, spreading his hand to the back of my neck and kneading me steadily there. "It's all right, baby. I get it. I know."

"I felt so helpless," I grate. "After *my* shitty call had landed you back in your worst nightmare..."

"A nightmare *you* had to endure too," he counters. "Apparently twice—and willingly volunteering yourself for the repeat ride too."

I swallow hard. "Just as you did." And I don't hide the subtle accusation in my voice.

"Yeah." He presses harder on my neck, pulling me closer to feather his full lips across my forehead. "Just as I did—and as I would all over again, given the same set of circumstances courtesy of that deranged witch."

I slide my eyes shut, savoring the feeling of having him so close and big and near, before steeling myself for being the one that's likely about to blow it to shreds. "Reece?"

"Hmmm?"

"I...I didn't kill her." I dot that stunner with a soft wince, hoping it sufficiently relays everything I can't add out loud. *I couldn't. I have no idea why. She doesn't deserve to live. I would've been doing the entire world a favor. But—*

"I know."

"You do?" I blurt it at his throat, since he still hasn't stopped his caressing kisses across my eyebrows.

"From the second you got into the Rover, yes." He drops his head so our gazes are completely aligned. "Despite the fact that you were still glowing like my avenging angel, there was still too much of *you* left." A thoughtful intensity takes over his face. "Taking someone else's life... There's part of a person that gets lost along with that," he utters. "A part I'm not sure ever comes back." As a few blue and gold fireworks burst over the ocean, turning the faraway haze in his eyes to similar shades, he adds with quiet ferocity, "So, in a lot of ways, I'm damn glad you didn't do it. What?" he cuts in on himself, addressing *my* bewilderment. "Aren't you?"

With slow deliberation, I raise my fingertips to the edge of his jaw. His skin is electric vibrancy beneath the spikes of his stubble, and I lift a small smile as his energy resonates inside me...deeper and more significantly than ever before. "You... thought I looked like an angel?"

At once, I'm aware of the renewed sprint of his pulse, the harder concentration of his senses, the spiked sorcery of his allure. While the man has always hypnotized me, this is a new spell completely. A new elevation of attraction. As the awareness hits me, I'm also awakened to how everything inside me answers him. The magic in my spirit. The devotion of my soul.

And oh, holy hell...the heat in my body.

None of them are separate from each other anymore, even by the smallest fraction. Each feeds my undeniable connection to him. My perfect fusion to him.

Liquid silver thickens in the depths of Reece's gaze, seeming to inundate his whole face before turning into poetry on his lips. "My angel," he whispers, stroking the pad of a thumb across my cheek. "And so much more." He pushes in, leaning forward until he rolls me all the way to my back, stretched out in all his flawless nudity next to me. "Every day with you has been a heaven in itself, Emmalina Crist. But now..."

He interrupts himself with a harsh growl as his words flow into me, surging light and energy through me...literally. A stunned gasp escapes me, blending with his eruption, as the space between us is suddenly suffused with molten, golden light.

Light that's coming from me. From *all* of me, as we discover together when Reece reaches and jerks down the zipper of my leather jacket. I'm braless underneath, since the rush to rescue him didn't exactly include time for a leisurely riffle through my lingerie drawer. That means the full beam of my torso is exposed to the night.

And I do mean *beam*.

"Holy...*shit*," I rasp, taking in how every pore of my skin is like one of those dorky tap lights, only without a dimmer option. "I'm a damn glowworm." Oh, yeah. There's only one setting to this desk lamp, and it's holy-shit-turn-that-thing-off bright.

Only that's not the exclamation that spills out of my man, who leans over me looking like a jubilant, resplendent god. In the radiance from my skin, every bold angle of his face is defined. The fog in his eyes gives in to a billion strands of expressive lightning.

"You're fucking stunning." He pushes feverishly at both sides of my jacket. "Take it off. *Now*. I need to see all of you."

As I sit up, obliging just because he sounds so much like a kid on Christmas morning, he's already twisting at the button on my pants. Regrettably, the fit there is much tighter, and even the two of us working in passionate tandem don't shuck them very quickly.

"Screw it," he finally snarls, pushing me once more down to my back. The second I'm there, he snaps his fingers. At once, those graceful tips ignite into bright-blue sparks. "Hold still."

An order easier given than obeyed. *Much* easier. As his blue bolts shred apart my pants, the residual lightning dances along my bare skin, and it's all I can do to not squirm in delight as my nerve endings pop wide, empowered and enkindled. "Damn!" I exclaim. "Oh, *damn!*"

Reece declares the same thing at the same time—making me jerk my sights back up. "Oh, holy shit," I blurt, taking in the pumps of his chest and the wide part of his lips. "You *are* freaked out."

"Bet your sweet, amazing ass I am." He hurls aside what's left of my pants before lunging back over me. "And dear fucking God, I never want to be *un*freaked again."

"Reece..." But I'm already stammering into silence, questioning if I'll ever be able to form coherent words again. With electrical storms taking over his gaze and his entire hands joining his fingers for the blue light show, *he's* as much a celestial miracle he's just called *me*. My rugged resplendent angel strips every breath from my lungs, thought from my mind, and sense from my head. All that's left is raw, blinding belief—in everything I never thought possible. In a love I never thought conceivable.

"I need to be freaked out...from the inside." It's not anywhere near a request, as the man proves by ramming his thighs between mine and spreading his knees, opening my throbbing core for the trajectory of his magnificent cock. If I had any doubt about the archangel thing before, the sight of the man's sex would abolish the dispute. *Thank you, God, for the gift of this man's penis.* With its swollen, gorgeous girth enhanced by all those thrumming blue veins and crowned with that weeping purple head, the sight is my heaven on earth.

His heaven...sliding closer and closer toward the shining heart of my dripping core...

Until he noticeably pauses, curling a hand in to stroke along the side of my face. "You ready, Velvet Angel?"

I turn my face and kiss his palm. "Are *you* ready, Electric Angel?"

I expect a wolfish smirk. What I get is a stunningly grave stare, communicating things he definitely doesn't want to talk about. Not right now, at least. *Especially* not now. "I need this, Emma."

I reach up, grabbing him by the hair and pulling his face close. "Then take it, my perfect beast."

"I need *you*, Emmalina Paisley."

"You have me forever, Reece Andrew."

But he still doesn't enter me. Instead, he dips in and kisses me. Not hard but with a lunging, lingering thoroughness that tells me so much. *Gives* me so much. The adoration of his libido, despite how I truly look like a damn glowworm now. The acceptance of his soul, despite how I went and became a different being before he could say or do anything about it. The offering of his spirit, to help me—and perhaps even himself—understand every new and crazy change inside me now. And yes, the commitment of his mind, despite how absolutely everything is going to change for us now.

Absolutely everything.

But absolutely nothing.

As he slides into me at last, spurring us to lust-drenched shouts and undeniable ecstasy, that surety rings through my being like the most perfect bells of our heaven. Not that this journey is always going to be fireworks, summer stars, and epic angel sex—but if we're headed for the grandest, wildest freak-out of our insane, incredible journey yet, I can't think of a better way to take the first curve than this.

Ignited together, spirit and soul, as we've always been. Loving each other, heart and mind, as we always will.

But now, with something more.

We're fused together, in light and purpose, as we've never been before. A storm the world has yet to know. A force the stars have yet to make room for. A power the planet has yet to experience.

A ride I can only imagine taking with one man in all the cosmos. Reece Andrew Richards.

My Bolt. My love. My *more*.

And now, the partner in the greatest adventure of my

existence.

I'm ready.

Let's ride the lightning, superhero.

Continue the Bolt Saga with

Surge

Coming Soon!

ALSO BY ANGEL PAYNE

The Bolt Saga:
Bolt
Ignite
Pulse
Fuse
Surge (Coming Soon)
Light (Coming Soon)

Honor Bound:
Saved
Cuffed
Seduced
Wild
Wet
Hot
Masked
Mastered
Conquered
Ruled

Secrets of Stone Series:
No Prince Charming
No More Masquerade
No Perfect Princess
No Magic Moment
No Lucky Number
No Simple Sacrifice
No Broken Bond
No White Knight
No Longer Lost
No Curtain Call

Cimarron Series:
Into His Dark
Into His Command
Into Her Fantasies

Temptation Court:
Naughty Little Gift
Pretty Perfect Toy
Bold Beautiful Love

Suited for Sin:
Sing
Sigh
Submit

**For a full list of Angel's other titles,
visit her at AngelPayne.com**

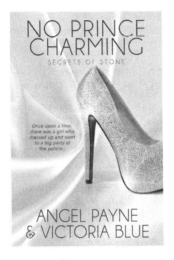

EXCERPT FROM
NO PRINCE CHARMING
BOOK ONE IN THE SECRETS OF STONE SERIES

PROLOGUE

C l a i r e

April...

Oh my God.

The words sprinted through my head, over and over, as I prodded at my lips in assurance I wasn't dreaming. Or hopping dimensions. Or remembering the last half hour in a *really* crazy way. Or had hours passed, instead? I didn't know anymore. Time was suddenly contorted.

Oh. My. God.

What the hell had just happened?

Forget my lips. My whole mouth felt like I'd just had dental work done, tingling in all the places his lips had touched moments ago—which had been everywhere.

My mind raced, trying to match the erratic beat of my heart. "Christ," I whispered. My voice shook like a damn teenager's, so I repeated myself. Because *that* helped, right?

Wrong. So wrong.

It was all because of that man. That dictatorial, demanding...

Nerve-numbing, bone-melting...

Man.

Who really knew how to deliver a kiss.

Hell. That kiss.

Okay, by this age, I'd been kissed before. I'd been *everything* before. But after what we'd just done, I'd be awake for long hours tonight. *Long* hours. Shaking with need... Shivering with fear.

I pressed the Call button for the elevator with trembling fingers. Turning back to face the door I'd just emerged from, I reconsidered pushing the buzzer next to it instead. The black lacquer panel around the button was still smudged by the angry fingerprints I'd left when arriving here not more than thirty minutes ago—answering his damn summons.

Yeah. He'd summoned me. And, like a breathless backstage groupie, I'd dropped everything and come. Why? He was my hemlock. He could be nothing else.

I was even more pissed now. At him. At me. At the thoughts that wouldn't leave me alone now, all in answer to one tormenting question.

If Killian Stone kissed like that, what could he do to the rest of my body?

No. That kind of thinking was dangerous. The tiny hairs on the back of my neck stood up as if the air conditioner just kicked on at full power.

It had been a while since I'd been with a man. At least like...that.

Okay, it had been a long while.

For the last three years, career had come before all else.

After the disaster I simply called the Nick Years, Dad had fought hard to help rebuild my spirit, including the doors he'd finagled open for me. Wasting those opportunities in favor of relationships wasn't an option. My focus had paid off, leading to a coveted position at Asher and Associates PR, where I'd quickly advanced to the elite field team for Andrea Asher herself. The six of us, including Andrea and her daughter, Margaux, were called corporate America's PR dream team. We were brought in when the blemishes were too big and horrid for in-house specialists, hired on a project-by-project basis for our thoroughness and objectivity. That also meant the assignments were intense, ruthless, and very temporary.

The gig at Stone Global was exactly such a job. And things were going well. Better than well. People were cooperating. The press was moving on to new prey. The job was actually ahead of schedule, and thank God for that. Soon, I'd be back in my rightful place at the home office in San Diego and what had just happened in Killian Stone's penthouse would remain no more than a blip in my memory. A very secret blip.

I shook my head in defiance. What was wrong with having lived a little? At twenty-six, I was due for at least one heart-stopping kiss with a man who looked like dark sin, was built like a navy SEAL, and kissed like a fantasy. *Sweet God, what a fantasy.*

"You didn't do anything wrong," I muttered. "You didn't break any rules...technically. He consented. And you sure as *hell* consented. So you're—"

Having an argument with yourself in the middle of a hallway in the Lincoln Park 2550 building, waiting on the world's slowest damn elevator.

I leaned on the Call button again.

While *still* trying to talk myself out of pouncing on Killian's buzzer too. Or perhaps back into it. If I could concoct an excuse to ring his doorbell before the elevator arrived...

No. This is dangerous, remember? He's *dangerous. You know all the sordid reasons why, his* and *yours.*

Maybe I could just say I accidentally left my purse inside.

And that'll fly...how? One glance down at my oversize Michael Kors clutch had me cursing the fashion-trend gods, along with their penchant for large handbags.

I leaned against the wall, closing my eyes and hoping for a lightbulb. I was bombarded with Killian's smell instead. Armani Code. The cologne was still strong in my head, its rich bergamot and lemon mingling with the spice of his shampoo and the Scotch on his breath, like he'd scent-marked me through the intimacy of our skin...

My fingers roamed to my cheek, tracing the abrasion where he'd rubbed me with his stubble. My head fell back at the impact of the recollection.

In an instant, my mind conjured an image of him again, standing in front of me. Commanding. Looming. Hot...and hard. I felt his breath on my face again as he yanked me close. The press of his wool pants against my legs. The metallic scrape of his cufflinks on the wood of his desk as he shoved everything away to make room for our bodies. Then the wild throb of my heart as he tangled his hands in my hair, lifted my face toward his, and...

Yes.

The memory was so vivid, so good. I used the flat of my palm on my face now, thinking I could save the magic if I covered it. Protecting it from the outside world. Our perfect, shared moment in the middle of all this chaos.

Whoa.

"Get a grip." I dropped my hand along with the furious whisper. It was one kiss. Incredible, yes, but I guaranteed *he* wasn't still thinking about it like this. Behind that majestic door, Killian Stone moved again in his world, already focused on the next of his hundred priorities, none of them bearing my name. And he expected me to get back to mine, cushioning his company from that big, bad outside world I'd just been brooding over. *You've been hired to help clean up the Stone family's mess, not add to it.*

The elevator finally dinged.

At the same time, Killian's condo door opened behind me.

I locked a smile on my face, trying to look like I had been patiently waiting for the elevator the entire time.

"Miss Montgomery?"

Not Killian. I didn't know whether to curse or laugh.

"Yes?" I managed a Girl Scout-sweet reply.

A kind face was waiting when I turned around. The man wore such a warm expression I was tempted to call him Fred. *Not* Alfred. Just Fred. The man was too handsome for a full Alfred.

Fred handed me a small ivory envelope and then stepped over into the elevator. He held the doors open while I got into the car with him. We rode in silence down to the lobby. I squirmed while Fred smiled as if it were Saturday in the park. Did he know what his boss had just done with me?

I winced toward the wall. Technically, Killian was *my* boss right now too.

Mr. Stone. Mr. Stone. Mr. Stone.

He can never be "Killian" again.

The sooner you remember that, the better.

I was dying to open that little envelope but carefully slipped it into my queen-size clutch for when I was alone again in the cab on my way back to the hotel.

"I'll call the car round for you." Like his employer, Fred made it obvious the subject wasn't up for debate, so I forced a smile and followed him across the gleaming lobby to the building's front awning. In less than a minute, the black town car with the Stone Global logo on its doors appeared. I climbed in, all the while yearning for the anonymity of a city cab instead.

Chicago was a great city, but the traffic was insane, even as evening officially blended into nighttime. Nevertheless, Killian's building was swiftly swallowed by the lush trees of the neighborhood. I was on my way back to the hotel. Back to real life—and all the dangers that waited if anyone on the team ever learned where I'd just been.

For just a few more seconds, I yearned to remember the fantasy instead. Perhaps the treasure in my purse would help.

I pulled it out, running reverent fingers over it again. Nothing was written on the outside. Killian—Mr. Stone—had simply expected it would be delivered straight to me.

The elegant handwriting inside, dedicated to just one sentence, dried out my throat upon impact.

I must see you again.

ACKNOWLEDGMENTS

Readers, if you're still here, riding the lightning love as we enter into double digits on this ride: *thank you*! Emma and Reece's world would not be possible without you believing in all of this craziness and wanting to follow this story into double digits! I'm more grateful than you can ever know, and I'm thrilled you are loving the Bolt Saga.

To the pop-culture, comics, and romance-blogging communities, the way you have embraced Bolt with open minds and open hearts has been so humbling, honoring, and, to be utterly mushy, heart-moving. Getting to collide the two genres I love best has been a dream come true. Thank you so much for all of the kind words and acceptance for the saga. It all means more than you will ever know.

As always, and with a perpetually full heart, thank you to Meredith Wild, Jon McInerney, and David Grishman at Waterhouse Press, for being the first to believe so thoroughly in the "bigger idea" of the Bolt Saga. Your support continues to mean the world!

I cannot express enough thanks to the Waterhouse Press editing team, especially the amazing Jeanne De Vita and editing god on high Scott Saunders, who guided this part of the Bolt plot to its ultimate epicness (yeah, that's still a word—no, just believe me). This chunk was heart-wrenching and soul-ripping to write, and I know the editing process couldn't have been easy—but we did it! I cannot thank you two enough. You are the rockets beneath this star ship, and I simply cannot thank you enough for continuing to be my ultimate guides on this journey.

A project this huge is simply not possible without a support team beyond compare. In this case, that starts with the logistics and promo crew at Waterhouse Press: Kurt, Haley, Robyn, Amber, Yvonne, Jennifer, and Jesse—you all work so tirelessly to make the behind-the-scenes go so perfectly. I also need to thank, from bottom of my soul, the incredible Martha Frantz, virtual assistant extraordinaire, for being my sanity, sounding board, and organizational guru on so many days. I can't do any of it without you!

Writers are strange and fascinating creatures. Choosing to be our friend can often feel like tossing your sanity into the drink—but believe me, there's never a day we don't appreciate the shoulder to bawl on, the hand to hold, and the people in our lives who don't think we're one brain cell shy of crazy when we talk about all our fictional friends like they're sitting right next to us on the way to the drycleaners and insist we order that extra order of fries at In-N-Out—because, you know, In-N-Out fries, people. These rare and special people in my life are beyond compare. Thank you, Victoria Blue, Meredith Wild, Cheryl Stern, Chelle Bliss, Lauren Rowe, and Tia Louise. You ladies are more sunshine in my life than I deserve, and I'm so grateful.

A special and incredible piece of gratitude to all the amazing people, gods *and* goddesses, who comprise the Payne Passion fandom. I hope you'll always know how much I love and appreciate your notes, feedback, and support, no matter which platform you're reaching out on. Honestly, it means more than I usually tell you—and I'm beyond thankful.

A geek girl's immense gratitude to all the other geeks out there who have stepped outside your comfort zone to give this one a try. Whether you're a "romancinista" (yeah, that's a word too) or a spectacular superhero nut, thank you for being here and honoring the theme of Bolt: let your special lightning strike, and love it in yourself and others. Superpowers don't happen unless they're honored—so honor all of yours, no matter what they are, each and every day!

ABOUT ANGEL PAYNE

USA Today bestselling romance author Angel Payne loves to focus on high-heat romance starring memorable alpha men and the women who love them. She has numerous book series to her credit, including the popular Honor Bound series, the Secrets of Stone series (with Victoria Blue), the Cimarron series, the Temptation Court series, the Suited for Sin series, and the Lords of Sin historicals, as well as several standalone titles.

Angel is a native Southern Californian, leading to her love of being in the outdoors, where she often reads and writes. She still lives in Southern California with her soul-mate husband and beautiful daughter, to whom she is a proud cosplay/culture con mom. Her passions also include whisky tasting, shoe shopping, and travel.

Visit her at AngelPayne.com